USA TODAY bestselling author **Janice Maynard** loved books and writing even as a child. After multiple rejections, she finally sold her first manuscript! Since then, she has written fifty-plus books and novellas. Janice lives in Tennessee with her husband, Charles. They love hiking, travelling and family time.

You can connect with Janice at www.janicemaynard.com, www.Twitter.com/janicemaynard, www.Facebook.com/janicemaynardreaderpage, www.Facebook.com/janicesmaynard and www.Instagram.com/therealjanicemaynard

Sheri WhiteFeather is an award-winning bestselling author. She lives in Southern California and enjoys shopping in vintage stores and visiting art galleries and museums. She is known for incorporating Native American elements into her books and has two grown children who are tribally enrolled members of the Muscogee Creek Nation. Visit her website at www.sheriwhitefeather.com

D1331895

UPSTAIRS DOWNSTAIRS TEMPTATION

JANICE MAYNARD

HOT NASHVILLE NIGHTS

SHERI WHITEFEATHER

MILLS & BOON

First Published in Great Britain 2020
by Mills & Boon, an imprint of HarperCollinsPublishers,
1 London Bridge Street, London, SE1 9GF

Upstairs Downstairs Temptation © 2020 Janice Maynard
Hot Nashville Nights © 2020 Sheree Henry-WhiteFeather

ISBN: 978-0-263-27926-9

0620

Printed and bound in Spain
by CPI, Barcelona

UPSTAIRS DOWNSTAIRS TEMPTATION

JANICE MAYNARD

For Ainsley.

You're smart and creative,
and you always make me laugh!
I love you bunches...

One

Farrell Stone didn't like asking for help. Rarely would he do so when it came to business, and even less in his personal life. He went his own way. Handled his own affairs. Kept his own counsel.

Unfortunately, his administrative assistant, Katie, was a pro at butting in...which was why he now found himself in the midst of this odd interview with Katie's protégée.

The woman who sat quietly across the desk from him was thin and not too tall. Barely five-three, perhaps. Her thick, shiny hair, the color of rich chocolate, was cut short in choppy layers that emphasized her pointed chin.

Huge, long-lashed eyes seemed too big for her face. The expression in her wary feminine gaze was equal parts fearful and hopeful. Hazel irises sparkled with flecks of gold and green.

Though she was not traditionally beautiful, there was something compelling about her. Farrell was drawn to her soft femininity and her almost palpable aura of vulnerability. She was exactly the kind of woman he found sexually appealing. The fact that he felt a flutter of physical response alarmed him.

He had trained himself to ignore sexual need. Now was not the time to break that habit.

Though she was originally from here in Maine, Ivy Danby had spent most of the last two decades in South Carolina. The résumé in Farrell's hand was so slim as to be nonexistent. Graduated high school. Worked a handful of jobs. Married. Then nothing. Although the fact that the woman held a sleeping baby in her arms pointed to a few details that might have been omitted.

He dropped the single sheet of paper and drummed his fingers on his desk. "I appreciate you coming in for an interview, Ms. Danby, but—"

She leaned forward urgently, taking him by surprise. Halting his polite brush-off. "Whatever you need me to do, I can learn," she said. She stared at him, unblinking. As if sheer determination could manipulate him.

He liked her confidence, but with every minute that passed, he became more sure that he didn't need the complication of being attracted to an employee.

The woman's voice was husky and slow as honey in winter. *Whatever you need me to do...* It was only Farrell's surprisingly naughty libido that added the sexual subtext.

It irked him that he wasn't entirely ready for this conversation. But opportunity had come knocking, as they say. He sighed. "I haven't advertised for this position. You understand that, right?"

Ivy nodded. "I do. But your administrative assistant, Katie, apparently knows something is coming available. And she also knows I need a job. I'm currently sharing an apartment with her sister."

Farrell rubbed the center of his forehead with two fingers, trying to stave off a headache. "My admin is now my sister-in-law. She and my brother Quin were married three months ago."

The woman lifted an eyebrow. "And she still comes to work every day?"

The question struck Farrell as odd. "I think Quin assumed she might quit. But Katie is very much her own person. She likes running the R & D department. I honestly don't know what I would do without her."

Ivy Danby nodded. "I've only met her once, and it was a wonderful conversation. She's an amazing person."

"That she is." Farrell hesitated. "Here's the thing, Ivy. The job is in the middle of nowhere in northern Maine."

She blinked. "Oh."

Farrell was an engineer. An inventor. Traditionally, he had worked from his state-of-the-art lab here in this building in Portland...on this floor. In the past twenty-four months, though, he had seen his best and newest ideas pop up in the marketplace before he had a chance to get them there.

Though it was possible he was paranoid, the prospect of corporate espionage was something he couldn't rule out.

"My brothers and I each own homes on the northern coast," he said. "I've recently built a small lab and a guesthouse on my property. As soon as possible, I'm going to move my work up there."

"Do you mind me asking why?"

"Aspects of my designs are highly confidential. I've decided I need to be more vigilant in protecting my research. Not only that, but I like being on my own, and I work best in solitude."

"Then why does Katie think you need to hire someone?"

He grimaced and ran his hands through his hair. "I'm single-minded when I'm in the midst of a project. I've been known to work for thirty-six hours straight if I'm in the zone. I need someone to run my house and prepare meals. Particularly a person who can be discreet and trustworthy."

An odd expression flashed through her eyes. Something dark. Something that surprised him.

"I can keep my mouth shut, Mr. Stone. I can keep secrets."

Finally, he asked the question he'd been putting off. "Why would you want a job like this, Ivy? We have internet and TV up north, but nothing else. Not even a convenience store nearby."

Was it his imagination, or did she clutch the baby more tightly? For the first time, she revealed agitation. Anxiety.

"I have to be honest with you," she said.

That sexy voice affected him in ways he couldn't explain. "Please do."

Her bottom lip trembled the slightest bit. Her eyes sheened with moisture. "I'm desperate, Mr. Stone. My husband died a few months ago. He left me nothing. No life insurance. Nothing. The house was sold, and the money went elsewhere. My parents are gone. I have no other family. I need a job where I can have Dolly with me."

"Dolly?"

Ivy stroked her baby's head. "Dorothy Alice Danby. That's a mouthful, so Dolly for short." Ivy paused. Stared at him with an intensity that took him off guard. "I know you don't remember me from our childhood. We were at the same elementary school. But everybody in Portland knows your family—your father, your brothers, Zachary and Quinten. Stone River Outdoors provides hundreds of good jobs. I'm only asking for a chance. I'm a hard worker. And the baby still takes two long naps every day. I also have an infant carrier, so she can stay on my back while I'm cooking or cleaning. If you hire me, I swear you won't regret it."

Ruefully, Farrell realized he was regretting it already.

His life needed fewer complications, not more. As far as he could tell, Ivy Danby with her artless sex appeal and her tiny daughter was a whole huge bundle of complications.

With an inward sigh, he admitted defeat. "You make a compelling argument. But for the record, I do remember you, Ivy. We were both in Mrs. Hansard's third-grade class together. You had pigtails. Your desk was in the row beside mine two seats back. I gave you a valentine that year. One I made myself."

Her eyes widened, and her cheeks flushed. "Oh," she said. "You do remember."

"Give me twenty-four hours to think about it. I'll call you tomorrow and let you know what I've decided."

He saw on her face that she wanted an answer right now. Wanted it badly, in fact. But she swallowed the protest on her lips and managed a wobbly smile. "I understand. Thank you for the interview."

As soon as his guest departed, Farrell stabbed a button on his intercom and barked an order. Moments later, Katie Duncan Stone appeared in his doorway. The blue-eyed blonde was both beautiful and competent. She was also stubborn and dogged about helping people, whether they deserved it or not.

Farrell folded his arms across his chest and glared. "Really, Katie? A new mom with a baby?"

"Don't be so sexist, Farrell Stone." She took the comfy seat at his desk that Ivy had recently vacated. "New moms can work."

"If they have access to childcare. My house is in the woods on a cliff above the ocean." He ground his teeth, haunted by the memory of entreaty in Ivy's hazel-eyed gaze, but even more disturbed by how very much he wanted to say yes to this idea.

Katie visibly dismissed his protest. "A hundred years

ago, regular women didn't have childcare. But they worked their asses off. It can be done."

"Why are you pushing this so hard?" His brother Quin had warned him about Katie's penchant for rescuing humans and the occasional animal, too. She had a huge heart.

"I met Ivy when I dropped by my sister's apartment over on Kimball Street the other day. In conversation, we realized that you and Ivy were in school together."

"*Elementary* school," Farrell said with a sigh. "That's hardly a character reference."

His new sister-in-law was not to be deterred. "Ivy moved in with nothing, Farrell. No furniture. No belongings. She had two suitcases, a port-a-crib and a diaper bag. Nothing else. Don't you think that's kind of strange?"

"Maybe, maybe not."

"She's hurting. And alone. Surely you, of all people, can sympathize. Losing a spouse changes your whole world."

Farrell took the hit stoically. Only Katie would have the guts to bring up his past. It had been seven years since Sasha died. Even his own brothers didn't go there. "Dirty pool," he muttered.

Katie stood and kissed him on the cheek. "You and I are family now. I get to meddle. But in this instance, I'm begging you, Farrell. Ivy Danby needs a fresh start. She needs a home and security. She needs exactly what you have to offer. Please give her a chance."

Ten days after the uncomfortable interview at Stone River Outdoors headquarters in Portland, Ivy found herself in an expensive luxury sedan being driven north by Katie Stone, herself.

Ivy had been shocked when the big boss contacted her. In a terse, four-minute conversation, Farrell Stone had offered her the job and a salary that made her eyes bug out. Katie called soon afterward to outline the specifics. As Farrell's admin, Katie knew what would be required of Ivy. She also knew that Ivy had no car, no furniture and no money.

Katie had a solution for every problem. She insisted she needed to check on her husband's house, now hers also, and thus it would be no trouble at all to take Ivy and Dolly to their new home.

The trip had been pleasant so far. Dolly babbled and played in the back. When she became fussy, Katie found a rest area and pulled off so Ivy could prepare a bottle for the baby, get Dolly out of her car seat and feed her comfortably.

They rolled down the windows and enjoyed the pleasant breeze. Katie's gaze was wistful. "I want to have kids," she said softly. "I don't know if my husband is ready, though."

Ivy cradled Dolly's cheek. "You haven't been married long. There's plenty of time."

"I know," Katie said. "But that biological clock you hear about is ticking loudly." She flicked at a mosquito that tried to enter the car. "How did you know you wanted kids?"

Ivy stiffened, keeping her eyes locked on her daughter. "I didn't," she said. "It just happened."

"Ah, well, I guess you were one of the lucky ones."

"I suppose." Ivy's throat was tight. She let the silence build, knowing she had to keep it together. Crying over the past at this stage in the game might cost her this precious job. "She's had enough," she said, gently loosening the baby's lock on the nipple. Dolly's mouth and tiny tongue still made little sucking motions, but her head lolled back. "We can get on the road."

Katie grinned. "Ah, to be that young and innocent again."

While Ivy tucked Dolly back into her car seat, Katie visited the restroom and then Ivy took her turn. Soon, they were driving north again. For so long, Ivy had kept her emotions in lockdown mode. But today, of all days, she had reason to smile. She was headed to a job and a place to live and a salary that would support her tiny family. On this warm autumn day with the sunshine beaming down and the skies a brilliant blue, a tiny sprout of hope unfurled.

Birches, oaks and maples put on a fantastic display of color. Vibrant reds and orangey golds…deep yellows and every shade of brown. Mother Nature had outdone herself this season.

Maybe by next year Ivy would have the opportunity and the financial means to explore this area with her daughter. The prospect seemed like a really wonderful fantasy.

She shook herself inwardly. Grief had stolen her hopes and dreams, but that was in the past. She was rebuilding her life, reinventing who she was. Nothing was beyond her reach if she believed in Ivy Danby.

The fact that Farrell Stone was the author of her good fortune gave her pause. She liked him. A lot. He was honorable and handsome and sexy in a gruff, understated kind of way.

She honestly thought her life experiences had erased her ability to feel like a woman. But when she sat across the desk from Farrell, she found herself wanting more than a job. Maybe a smile. A shared laugh.

She would have to be very careful not to make a fool of herself.

Ivy had plenty to think about as Katie concentrated on the traffic. In Bangor, they merged south and east onto the narrower 1A toward Bar Harbor. At Ellsworth, just before the crowded tourist playground that included Acadia National Park, they turned onto a less traveled road for the last leg to Stone River.

Here, nobody but locals traversed the winding rural highway. Nothing much to see but acres of forest and fields and peaceful ponds and lakes. The pastoral scenery soothed some of Ivy's apprehensions.

Katie glanced at the clock on the dash. "Not much longer now. Can you tell we're near the ocean?"

"Actually, yes. Living in Charleston for so long taught me the smell and feel of the air at the coast. It's not as warm or humid here, but I remember the northern sea from my childhood."

"It's just beyond those trees. In the other direction, north and west of us, is the Moosehorn National Wildlife Refuge. And of course, north and east, if you keep going, is the Canadian border."

Ivy had never been this far up in Maine, but in Farrell's office she had seen aerial photographs of three spectacular homes on rocky promontories overlooking the sea, each one bearing the stamp of its owner.

Almost two centuries before, a Stone ancestor had acquired an enormous tract of pristine wilderness. He named the small river meandering through his property after himself. Subsequent generations sold off the bulk of the land, but the current Stone brothers still owned several hundred square miles. They liked their privacy. The company that had made them all wildly wealthy was born in this forested paradise.

The isolation and seclusion weren't daunting to Ivy at all. They represented safety and security. A chance to finally be herself.

When Katie turned off onto the road that accessed Stone family property, she entered a code at the gate and kept right on going. A perfectly paved road meandered for the next seven miles.

Dolly was beginning to stir when they reached Farrell's house. On the way, they had passed turnoffs leading to homes Zachary and Quin had built. "I'll show you our place another day," Katie said. "I know you probably want to get settled in. Shall we go to the big house first and see Farrell, or head straight for the cabin?"

"Cabin, please."

As they wound around the side of Farrell's magnificent house, Ivy craned her neck to get a better view. The place was huge, easily six thousand square feet. Maybe more. It had a traditional New England look to it with lots of blue clapboard and white trim, and even a widow's walk at the very top. Windows everywhere offered views of the ocean.

Behind Farrell's home, deeper into the woods, sat a charming dollhouse of a cabin, constructed of rough-hewn logs. It was perfect in every way, and when Ivy stepped out of the car and inhaled, the scent of freshly cut wood assailed her nose.

"This is it," Katie said, looking over the top of the car at Ivy. "Do you think you and Dolly will be comfortable here?"

Ivy wanted to laugh incredulously. The setting was sheer wonder. "Who wouldn't be?" she said calmly. "It looks perfect."

The inside was even better than the outside. The cabin was small, barely eight hundred square feet. Two neat bedrooms with a shared bath between. A compact kitchen with the latest appliances. And a comfy living room with a couch, two matching armchairs and a real wood-burning fireplace.

Someone—Farrell, maybe—had stacked a neat pile of firewood near the hearth. A wooden crate filled with kindling and a mason jar of matches flanked the opposite side.

Ivy felt tears burn her eyelids. She held them back by sheer force of will. Katie wouldn't understand, and Ivy didn't have it in her to explain. Not now. Not today. Maybe not ever.

"Who got the baby bed for us? Was it you?" Ivy asked.

Katie shook her head. "No. That was Farrell's idea. He thought you could leave the port-a-crib at his place, so you'd be able to nap Dolly in either location. That's an engineer for you. Always studying and planning."

"It was very thoughtful." Actually, the magnitude of the gesture spoke volumes about the kind of man Farrell Stone was. Ivy was overwhelmed and trying not to show it.

Dolly began to fuss, so Ivy opened the back door of Katie's car. "Don't cry, sweet girl. I know it's time to get out." The novelty of the great outdoors soothed the baby's grievances immediately.

Katie laughed. "Look at her face. I think she likes it here."

It was true. The baby's head swiveled from side to side, taking it all in. She stuck her fist in her mouth and sucked it contentedly.

Ivy took a deep breath, searching for composure, gathering herself. "I don't want to keep you too long," she said. "You've already done so much. If it's okay with you, let's go on to the other house so your brother-in-law can show me around and tell me his routine."

Two

Farrell was nervous. The emotion was such an anomaly, he examined it to see if it was actually hunger or fatigue in disguise.

Nope. He was nervous.

Perhaps it was because he was upending his entire working life. Maybe he was afraid the new digs wouldn't be as conducive to creativity as his old lab in Portland.

Or maybe he was still anxious about the possibility of espionage. Was that it? Was he worried about losing another design?

He was a man of measured thoughts and actions. Neither as reckless as his younger brother nor as carefree as his middle brother. Farrell was the oldest. The responsible one.

After examining and discarding all the possible sources of his unease, he came to the only remaining conclusion.

He was nervous about having Ivy Danby move in with him.

Ah, hell. She wasn't moving in with him. He paced the

length of the living room, gazing out the huge windows, trying to draw comfort from the ever-changing ocean.

Ivy Danby was going to prepare his meals and clean his house. She and her daughter would *not* be guests beneath his roof. They had another roof. Their own roof.

One that belongs to you, said his annoying inner voice.

Farrell had spotted Katie's car in the driveway almost half an hour ago. Clearly, she was showing Ivy the cabin and helping her settle in. They would be here soon.

When the doorbell finally rang, he ran his hands through his hair and opened the door, hoping he didn't look as rattled as he felt. "Hello, Katie," he said. "And Ivy. Come in."

Dolly stared at him as if he had sprouted a second head. What did Farrell know about kids anyway? Zip. Nada.

So he focused on the two adult women. "Was the trip okay?"

Katie waved a breezy hand. "Piece of cake. They finished that construction on I-95, so we made great time."

"Good. Good."

She eyed him strangely. "I have the last two boxes of your files in my trunk. I think that's everything you need."

During the past four days, his two brothers and Katie had helped him pack up his lab. There had been confusion in the Portland office. No one but his immediate family knew why he was making this change. He still wondered if it was necessary, but time would tell.

Katie took charge of the awkward moment. "Why don't I play with this cute little munchkin while you two talk?"

When she walked out of the room, Ivy stared at Farrell with those big eyes. He cleared his throat. "I suppose we could start in the kitchen."

Ivy nodded soberly. "Of course."

He showed her the fridge and the pantry and how the cupboards were organized. All things an intelligent grown woman could have figured out on her own. Then he shrugged. "I'm not hard to please. I set the coffee maker the night before, so you don't have to worry about that. I usually work from six a.m. to eight and then take a break for breakfast. I like everything except oatmeal. No oatmeal, please."

For the first time, a little smile tilted Ivy's lips. "Oatmeal is good for your heart," she said.

He scowled. "My heart is fine. No oatmeal."

She saluted him. "No oatmeal. Got it, Mr. Stone."

"You'll have to call me Farrell."

It was her turn to frown. "Why?"

Her stubbornness frustrated him. "Because it's only going to be the two of us up here, and we knew each other years ago, damn it."

Ivy eyed him with disapproval. "There are *three* of us," she reminded him, her voice tart. "And I don't want you cursing around my impressionable daughter. If that's a problem, you can fire me now."

He gaped at her, his normally placid temper igniting. "Seriously? Damn, woman, you're uptight."

"That's number two," she said primly.

In all honesty, he hadn't realized that he had cursed at her a second time. He felt his face get hot. "I will be careful around your daughter."

Ivy gnawed her lip. "Are you a volatile man, Farrell?"

"Volatile?" His jaw dropped again. Never in his life had he been described as volatile. Stubborn, maybe. Too focused when he was working. Emotionally closed off. But never volatile.

Farrell swallowed his frustration and moderated his voice. "I promise you, Ivy, most people think of me as easygoing. I do get lost in my projects at times. It's possible I might forget you're here. But ours will be an even-keeled working relationship. I swear it." *As long as I pretend she's not the most fascinating woman I've met in years.* "I'll go talk to my sister-in-law and let you familiarize yourself with the kitchen."

He found Katie on the front porch showing Dolly the squirrels in the yard. When she spotted Farrell, she smiled. "We're staying in the shade. I doubt Miss Dolly has on sunscreen."

Farrell lowered his voice. "So what's Ivy's deal, Katie? How long ago did her husband die? Did he see his kid born? What happened?"

Katie sobered. "Her private life isn't any of our business, Farrell. The truth is, she won't be gossiping about *your* work. She's in a difficult place, and you're giving her a chance to start over. Delanna said it sounded like Ivy had come from a bad situation, though details were vague. As shell-shocked as Ivy was, she didn't have a lot to say."

"How is your sister these days? Isn't she pissed that you snatched up her roommate and spirited her away?"

"A little. She'll get over it. There'll be another roommate. Now that she ditched her loser boyfriend, Delanna is doing great. She doesn't even ask to borrow money anymore. I'm proud of her." Katie smoothed the baby's hair and kissed the top of her head. She held out her arms. "Do you want to hold her? She's a sweetie pie, aren't you, love?"

Farrell took the baby automatically, only to find that she weighed a lot less than he'd expected. Her little body was warm and pudgy, her skin soft and scented with good baby smells. His heart flopped in his chest. He'd never agonized over not being a father. It wasn't meant to be. But for a fleeting second, he felt a moment's pity for the poor bastard who had died without getting to see his daughter grow up.

He rubbed the baby's back absently. The autumn breeze was cool, but not cold. The day was perfect. "Thank you, Katie," he said, giving his sister-in-law a grateful smile.

She stretched her arms over her head, staring out at the

panorama of colorful fall foliage and brilliant blue ocean. "For what?"

"For bringing Ivy to me and helping her get settled, but mostly for making Quin happy."

Katie's small smile was happy, too, and maybe a bit smug. "Did he tell you we're going skiing in December? Nothing major. Just a few runs at Aspen. So he can find his mojo again. And plenty of nights by the fire with hot buttered rum and—"

Farrell held up a hand in alarm. "I don't want to hear about your sexual escapades with my brother."

"How do you know that's what I was going to say?" She grinned.

Farrell chuckled. "You know, Katie, I'm actually looking forward to working in this unorthodox arrangement. A brand-new lab… I may come up with a few brilliant designs."

"I hope you do," Katie said. "Stone River Outdoors needs a boost. These last few years have been hard."

"Yes. They have." He handed the child back to Katie.

His sister-in-law gave him a wry look as if she knew exactly how unwilling he was to bond with the baby. "What did you do with Ivy?"

"She's getting her bearings in the kitchen. I'm sure she'll come find us shortly."

Ivy opened the huge built-in wall refrigerator and stared. Someone had stocked it well. She wondered how far afield she would have to go to replenish perishables, but then she spotted a delivery-service notepad on a corner of the beautiful gray-and-silver-quartz countertop. Apparently, Farrell could get deliveries whenever he liked.

This kitchen was a dream. Ivy was a good cook. She'd had plenty of time to practice over the years with a demanding spouse. Preparing meals here would be no hardship. Farrell's house was like something off one of those HGTV shows. The "after" version on steroids. She knew the Stone family was wealthy, but this was something else again.

More to the point, this was Farrell's *second* home. He owned a large condo in Portland that was probably even swankier than this. She couldn't imagine having that kind of money.

For Ivy's part, she only wanted enough to care for her daughter and keep a roof over their heads. As long as Farrell Stone needed to work in a secret lab deep in the forest, she was determined to make herself indispensable to him.

The kitchen door swung open. The object of her thoughts strode in looking like the alpha male he was. Masculine. In charge. Gorgeous. On his heels was Katie.

Farrell smiled. "Everything okay?"

"More than okay," Ivy said. "This kitchen is amazing." She took Dolly from Katie. "But what about cleaning? How often do you want me to give the whole house a once-over?"

"I can answer that," Katie said. "Men are clueless about these things. Farrell entertains fairly often, at least once a month. Primarily business functions. The top two floors have four bedrooms each, all with their own small en suites. I'm sure you'll want to do a bit of touch-up if there's an event on the calendar. Other than that, you shouldn't have to bother with upstairs until the guests depart."

Farrell frowned. "I can call in a cleaning service after we have a big house party. That shouldn't fall to Ivy. We agreed on meal preparation and *light* housekeeping."

Ivy bristled. "I can handle it."

"No." Farrell's brows drew together in a frown. "That's my decision. Not yours."

She opened her mouth to protest, but he stared her down. "Fine," she muttered. "Waste your money if you want to."

Farrell was an imposing male. His size and visible strength might have unnerved her if she hadn't been so aware of him in a shivery, fascinated way. Besides, he seemed to downplay the fact that he could probably bench-press three hundred pounds.

He topped six feet by several inches. Katie, standing near him, was tall for a woman. Five-eight, maybe. Beside Farrell, she looked positively petite.

Farrell's hair was an intriguing mix. Dark brown like Ivy's, but his was streaked with caramel and gold, a color many women would pay high dollar to achieve. He wore it long enough to be casual, but short enough to fit in with his role as one of the bosses.

His eyes were an odd shade of green, and like his hair—streaked with gold. They were eyes that held a wealth of life knowledge. He seemed a serious man. Grounded. Not prone to whimsy.

That was fine with Ivy. She didn't want any surprises.

Katie glanced at her watch. "I've gotta run," she said. "Have to be back in Portland by six."

The two women hugged. Katie kissed Dolly's forehead. Ivy felt a stab of panic that her benefactor was leaving. "Thank you for all your help, Katie. I appreciate it more than you know."

"Not a problem. I love it up here. Quin and I may head this way sometime soon. I'll see you then."

Farrell left the kitchen to follow his sister-in-law out to her car…like a good host. Or maybe he was simply unloading the boxes of files Katie had mentioned. Ivy lingered behind, pondering the dinner options. This first meal might be tricky. Learning to work in someone else's kitchen was always a challenge. Everyone organized cabinets and drawers differently. She opened the pantry again, and then peeked in the freezer.

Moments later, Farrell returned, his hair tousled from

the breeze. "Why don't you and Dolly spend the rest of the afternoon getting to know your new home? I'll throw something together for dinner tonight."

Ivy's eyes widened. It was her turn to stand her ground. "No," she said. "No, Farrell. You hired me to do a job. I appreciate your hospitable nature, but I'll be the one cooking. Is six okay?"

He folded his arms across his chest, his expression telegraphing his displeasure. "I sense that you and I may have the occasional run-in. Do you agree?"

"I don't need your charity. I want to work for my living."

"And yet your résumé had not a single scrap of job experience listed in the previous ten years. Would you care to explain?"

She sucked in a sharp breath, not expecting him to go on the attack. Her jaw trembled despite her best efforts to steady it. "No," she said quietly. "I wouldn't." She gnawed her lip, trying not to slide into despair. *Fight, Ivy. Fight for yourself and Dolly.* "Have you changed your mind about me?" she asked, her throat dry and tight.

His gaze was puzzled. Concerned. Frustrated. "The job is yours," he said bluntly. "I don't go back on my word. But I also expect my employees to follow my direction."

"Don't you mean your *orders*?" she snapped, horrified the moment the words left her mouth. She closed her eyes briefly and grimaced. "I'm sorry. I know I'm not making the best first impression." She hesitated, for the first time feeling the tsunami of exhaustion that always follows substantive change. "I appreciate your consideration. Dolly will be wanting a nap, and I could use one, too. Please let me know when to return for dinner."

Farrell leaned over the sink and watched his newest employee make her way to the cabin that stood twenty-five yards from the house. *His* new working quarters were housed in a similar structure, just beyond the cabin and to the right.

He had a few hours' grace before he needed to start dinner. But for some reason, he was too unsettled to head out to the lab. It was a perfect spot. The building included a nice office in addition to the lab itself. Today, though, he was off his game. Perhaps it would take time to adjust.

Instead, he went to the porch and carried in the two boxes Katie had brought up from Portland. After dropping them one at a time onto the island in the kitchen, he began to extract files and separate them into the appropriate piles. As he worked, he wondered for the hundredth time how someone had accessed his research and designs.

Was it a cybercrime? Or something as simple as breaking into the building and photographing pieces of paper? Farrell usually did his initial sketches on yellow legal pads. When he was happy with the general idea, he moved everything to an actual design program. He changed his password frequently. Zachary was the only person who knew those passwords, and he memorized them rather than writing them down.

As far as Farrell could tell, Stone River Outdoors was taking normal, prudent precautions in protecting their proprietary intellectual property. Yet somehow, Farrell's last two innovative products had surfaced on the market before he was finished perfecting them. The impostors were substandard. And poorly reviewed online.

But that didn't help the fact that Farrell had labored for months with nothing to show for it. Later, perhaps, in a year or so, he could push his own version of the designs to market. But they wouldn't have the excitement and freshness of a completely new launch.

Carefully, he loaded organized piles back into the boxes. Tomorrow, he would carry them to the lab. In the meantime, he needed to come to terms with Ivy being in his life. Her loss was a painful reminder of his own.

Could he see her day in and day out and not continually think about Sasha? He'd told himself that he was done grieving.

But the heart had its own timetable.

Three

Dolly went to sleep in her new bed as if she had been napping there her whole life. Ivy was desperately glad the baby was so adaptable. Her daughter's short existence had been turbulent at best. Would a tiny child internalize and remember those experiences at a deep level?

Was her psyche permanently damaged?

Was Ivy's?

She shoved aside the dark thoughts. It was a mental exercise she had perfected. Instead of thinking about the past, she took the baby monitor into the second bedroom and set it on the dresser.

Suddenly, she couldn't resist the tempting bed. Exhaustion—mental and physical—was a constant cloak she wore now. Everyone knew that caring for an infant was demanding work. But many new mothers had help. Husbands. Other family members. And not all new mothers dealt with guilt and regret.

Ivy took off her jeans and light cotton sweater and

climbed between the covers. She had never slept on any-thing so soft. The perfect mattress, high-thread-count sheets and heavy, luxurious down-filled comforter were the stuff of dreams.

The Stone family was accustomed to only the best. This "cabin" Farrell had built in the woods was more like a min-iature palace. Luxury was imprinted on every item that he, or someone, had selected.

Handmade furniture. Expensive woods. One-of-a-kind paintings on the walls. The cabin might be thematically rus-tic, but in reality, everything about this little home-away-from-home was exquisite and delightful.

Ivy closed her eyes, thinking about Farrell Stone…

When she awoke an hour and a half later, her heart raced with sudden panic. Dolly. She stumbled to her feet and then sagged against the bed when she saw the image on the monitor. Dolly had clearly just roused from her nap. She was happily playing with her toes and cooing softly. The sweet baby sounds had awakened her mother.

Ivy exhaled slowly, her heart rate slowing to a manage-able pace. Everything was okay. She and her baby were safe. It was going to take some time to believe that. She dressed rapidly and prepared a bottle before Dolly went into full temper-tantrum mode. Apparently, the empty-stomach phenomenon was one her daughter embraced.

Sure enough, as Ivy opened the door to the other bed-room, Dolly let out a wail. Ivy scooped her up and smiled. "Don't be such a diva, my love. Mommy is here to feed you." She settled into the gorgeous rocking chair and tucked Dolly against her breast. It was far too soon for the baby to hold her own bottle, but little hands reached out anyway.

Ivy would never get tired of the way Dolly looked up at her with that earnest, wide-eyed expression. "I love you, my sweet girl," she whispered softly. "I think we're going to be happy here." Though financial security and a cozy place to live were the main reasons she could give her daughter that assurance, a little voice inside Ivy's head said that getting reacquainted with the handsome, all-grown-up Farrell would be a bonus.

At a quarter before six, Ivy checked the contents of the diaper bag and then surveyed her own appearance one last time. She hadn't changed clothes. Same faded jeans. Same pink cotton sweater. Farrell had been dressed casually when she met him. He didn't strike her as the kind of man who dressed for dinner when he was in residence at his secluded retreat.

As she gazed in the mirror, she cataloged the evidence of her ordeal. She was too thin. That was something she could work on now that she was settled. Her once shoulder-length waves now barely reached her chin. But that was a good change. Without all the heavy hair, she felt freer. And it was certainly an easier style to care for with an infant demanding her attention.

After finger combing her straight, wispy bangs, and smoothing her lips with cherry-tinted gloss, she gathered up her daughter and the diaper bag and headed toward the big house. It occurred to her that on rainy or snowy days, this trek might be problematic with a baby in tow. She would cross that bridge later.

The stroll was an easy one.

Farrell hadn't given her keys, but the door was unlocked. Presumably, he lived too far in the boonies to worry about anyone stealing his ideas here.

She entered via a tidy mudroom filled with boots, coats and fishing gear and proceeded down the hall past a laundry room, a small guest room and then on to the kitchen. It wasn't hard to find. She had only to follow her nose. The smells wafting down the hall were amazing. She realized suddenly that she was starving. She and Katie had stopped for a fast-food lunch en route, but that was hours ago.

Farrell looked up when she entered. "Hey, there you are. I was about to come check on you two ladies."

"We're here. We're good. The naps helped." Farrell's broad, uncomplicated smile made Ivy's heart kick in her chest. It had been so long since she had felt anything as pleasurable as sexual arousal, the momentary jolt of attraction shocked her.

It was normal, she told herself, trying not to overreact. Farrell Stone was a gorgeous, appealing man. When he returned his gaze to the thick slices of bread he was smearing with butter, she studied him.

She'd been right not to change clothes. He was still wearing jeans, too. His moss green pullover stretched to accommodate broad shoulders. His sleeves were rolled up. Tanned, long-fingered hands were large and capable, working smoothly.

"It's almost ready," he said, popping the tray of bread in the oven. He paused and grimaced. "I ordered a high chair this afternoon. It will be here tomorrow. I apologize for not thinking of it sooner. In my defense, I'm seldom around babies."

Ivy shook her head. "You didn't have to do that. High chairs are expensive. But I'll pay you back out of my first check."

His cool stare chastised her silently. "No," he said. "You won't. Whatever items you and Dolly need while you're here are simply the cost of doing business. Like a printer or a computer. It's my job to make sure you're comfortable. I've taken you away from civilization. The least I can do is make your stay here as pleasant as possible."

After that, there wasn't much to say. Ivy entertained Dolly. She would have offered to help, but the table in the breakfast nook was already set.

Soon, they were sitting down to steaming plates of angel-hair pasta smothered in meat sauce. The freshly grated Parmesan cheese was a nice touch. And the perfectly browned garlic bread.

Ivy juggled Dolly on one knee and took a bite. "I'm impressed," she said. "This is delicious."

"Don't be." He chuckled. "Mrs. Peterson made the sauce and left it in the fridge. All I did was heat it and throw some pasta in boiling water. Any doofus can do that."

"Mrs. Peterson?"

"Quin's housekeeper. She offered to stock my kitchen and the cabin when she heard I would be working here. In fact, if you ever have any questions, and I'm buried in work, she said for you to feel free to call her."

For a few minutes, they ate without speaking, but the silence made Ivy nervous. "Tell me about your brothers," she said. "I think they're younger than you… Am I remembering that right?"

Farrell stood and topped off their wineglasses with a zinfandel that was smooth and deceptively mild. "Yes. We were stair-steps. Two years apart. You and I are the same age, of course. Then Zachary, then Quin."

"And Quin is the Olympian?"

Farrell nodded. "He was a world-class skier until the accident that claimed our father's life."

"I did know about the wreck. I subscribe to the Portland newspaper online—you know, just to keep up with my old friends. I saw the article and your father's obituary."

"Quin was in the car also. His leg was crushed. He's had multiple surgeries and rehab. He can walk normally now, but competitive skiing is not an option anymore."

"That's awful. He must have been devastated."

"You could say that. We all have moments that change our lives. Fortunately for Quin, Katie came along and helped him pick up the pieces. My baby brother is a new man. A better man, really. Skiing consumed him. He's more balanced now. More at peace with the world."

"And Zachary?"

"Zachary plays the field. I doubt any woman will ever tame him."

Ivy wanted to ask about Farrell's dead wife. She knew he was a widower…nothing more. But if she skated into personal territory with *him*, she would open herself up to questions about her own past. That was not an option, so she ate her spaghetti and kept her curiosity to herself.

Even so, her new boss probed gently. "I know you moved away from Portland a long time ago. What took your family to South Carolina?"

She breathed an inward sigh of relief. This, she could handle. "My dad was a lobster fisherman. But he had aunts and uncles down south. Through one of those connections, he got offered a job as a charter boat captain—taking tourists out for half-day and full-day fishing expeditions. Mom was ready to leave the cold winters, so we packed up and moved. I was twelve, and I wasn't a fan of leaving my friends behind. But it turned out okay."

Ivy could tell he was poised for more questions, so she changed the subject awkwardly. "Will you be coming to the house for your meals, or shall I bring them out to you at the lab? I don't mind. I know you said you can be single-minded when you're working."

He shook his head. "That's far too much trouble. Why don't we compromise? I have a mini fridge in my new office. If you'll make me a sandwich for lunch every morning, I'll take it with me. Then I'll make a point of being back here for dinner at six thirty. Does that work for you?"

Ivy debated rapidly. She normally put Dolly to bed at seven. But she could always nap her a little later and keep her awake until eight. That should be enough time to get the kitchen cleaned up. Especially if she tidied things as she went along. Farrell Stone was being very generous and amenable. She would do her best to fit his schedule and not the other way around.

"Of course," she said. "And please let me know if I prepare foods that are not your favorites. I want you to be satisfied."

He blinked and stood up suddenly.

When she realized how her words had sounded, she was mortified. Though her face must have been bright red, she pretended nothing was wrong for the fifteen minutes it took Farrell to get a carton of ice cream out of the freezer and dish up dessert.

By the time he sat down again, the moment had passed. She hoped.

She ate her ice cream quickly. "Thank you for dinner. If you don't mind, Dolly and I will have an early night. I'll have your breakfast ready at eight tomorrow morning unless you text me otherwise."

Farrell stared at her, his expression impassive. "Relax, Ivy. This isn't a factory job where you'll be punching a clock."

"I know that. But you're paying for a service." Again, unwittingly, she had cast her comment with an ambiguous word choice. She pushed her chair back from the table, feeling jittery and unsure of herself. "Do you mind if we go on back to the cabin?"

"Of course not. Rest well. I never lock the doors here at the house unless I'm gone. We're perfectly safe. But I'll give you a set of keys for the cabin just in case. It's always hard to sleep in a strange place at first. Having everything secured before you go to bed will make you feel better, I'm sure."

He set the two empty ice-cream bowls in the sink and reached in a drawer. "Here," he said. "These are yours."

Ivy took the keys, gripped them in her palm, felt the

sharp press of metal and recognized that she had crossed an enormous hurdle. The past was the past. She wouldn't let herself be defined by what had happened to her.

Holding her small daughter, who was all she had left in the world, she smiled up at Farrell Stone, trying not to get emotional. At least not until she could fall apart in private.

"Thank you," she said huskily, her throat tight.

He cocked his head, his emerald-and-amber gaze assessing her. Making assumptions. Trying to dissect her reticence. "You're very welcome, Ivy."

She stood her ground a moment longer, to prove to herself that she could, and then she fled with a muttered goodbye.

Down the hall. Out the door. Into the crisp chill of a New England autumn night. Dolly was sleepy by now. She burrowed into her mother's shoulder, not even protesting the cool air after the warmth of Farrell's kitchen.

Ivy paused in the clearing and looked up at the sky. No moon. In fact, she'd had to pick her way carefully from the house to make sure she stayed on the path. The stars dotted the sky by the billions. Impossibly beautiful. Remote, though. Making Ivy feel small.

She yearned for peace. For happiness. Her dreams were nothing out of the ordinary. Over her life, she had learned valuable lessons. About herself. About the world.

At last, when her skin was chilled, she moved on into the trees and opened the cabin door, then locked it behind her. Though it was childish, perhaps, she checked every room and closet, making sure she and Dolly were alone.

Some people thought the bogeyman was a fictional character. Ivy knew differently.

It had been too long a day to worry about bathing Dolly. Instead, Ivy undressed her and put her in one-piece pajamas and an overnight diaper. Then she fixed a bottle and walked through to the bedroom that would serve as a nursery.

The baby-bed sheet was covered in a tiny circus-animal print. In the drawers she found more bedding and all sorts of infant paraphernalia, including a medium-sized, glossy purple shopping bag on its side. The raffia handles were tied with silver ribbon.

Ivy bent and slid out the gift one-handed. Dolly was getting grumpy, but Ivy wanted to see what was in the fancy sack. Tied to the handle was a note—*I don't have any kids of my own yet, so please let me spoil precious Dolly. Your friend, Katie.*

"Oh, dear," Ivy said aloud, even though Dolly wouldn't understand the words. "What has she done?"

When the contents of the lovely shopping bag were spread out on the bed, Ivy didn't know whether to laugh or cry. No one had hosted a baby shower for her. There had been no work friends to drop by with gifts and food when Dolly was born. The contrast between then and now was stark. Katie's thoughtful generosity was overwhelming.

Katie had bought Dolly a dozen outfits, half in the size Dolly wore now and half that were the next larger size. The baby clothes were high-end and adorable. Though there were a few pink things, Katie had chosen teal and bright yellow and other vivid colors. Even a miniature designer cardigan that was completely impractical but too cute not to wear.

Ivy took a deep breath. This largesse felt like charity. She hated it when people felt sorry for her. Yet Katie knew none of the specifics of Ivy's life. She merely knew that Dolly was a baby who would grow out of clothes quickly and would need new outfits to wear.

Not only that, but Katie was married to one of the wildly wealthy Stone brothers. This purchase would have been no more than a blip on Katie's platinum credit card.

Before Ivy could overthink it, she picked up her cell

phone and pecked out a note, still with one hand. I found the clothes! You are too kind. Dolly and I thank you so much...

By this time, Dolly was no longer willing to wait for her meal any longer. Ivy settled into the rocker. One of Ivy's favorite moments at the end of the day was watching Dolly's beautiful eyelashes settle on her plump, downy cheeks.

The pediatrician recommended putting the baby to bed awake and letting her soothe herself to sleep. But Ivy couldn't give up these precious minutes.

When she climbed into bed later and turned out the lights, the room filled with unfamiliar shadows. The house settled for the night with creaks and muted pops.

Nothing sinister. Only new surroundings.

As she drifted between waking and sleeping, one image filled her imagination. Farrell Stone. A man she had known literally since childhood. But those words were deceptive. Who knew what kind of human he had become in the intervening years? She remembered a quiet boy. A good student.

Already, those hazy memories were being replaced with new data. Her boss was a full-grown man. Large. Strong. Impressive.

He made her heart beat faster.

God help her...

Four

Farrell dreamed about Sasha. About wandering the hospital halls, unable to find her room. And the doctor who confronted him with sad eyes and said, "She's gone."

He came awake with a start, his heart pounding, his stomach clenched. *Hell.* He thought he was long past this crap. Seven years was plenty of time to grieve, wasn't it?

He rubbed his hands over his face. The alarm would go off in fifteen minutes. Might as well face the day.

The two cups of coffee he swallowed—hot and strong—jump-started his brain. The third serving, in a larger insulated carafe, went with him to the lab. Overhead, birdsong and the sound of the wind in the trees soothed his unease. He walked slowly, feeling his limbs stretch and loosen.

He had to admit, even though he had always been happy working in Portland, this new arrangement had much to commend it. After his father died, he and his brothers had been forced to go from part-time employees to full-time owners in Stone River Outdoors. Little opportunity to stop and smell the roses, or in Farrell's case, the scent of evergreens.

Their father had been a harsh man, but generally fair. He had raised his sons on his own after his wife's death. When the three boys were in their twenties, he hadn't blinked or protested when they wandered the globe sowing their wild oats.

Of course, Farrell had sown fewer oats than the other two. He had married his beloved Sasha young. Been widowed young. After that, he'd been happy to pour most of his energy into research and development for SRO. The company his great-grandfather founded had grown beyond anyone's wildest imagination.

Now Quin was running things, and Zachary had the brains to keep their finances in order. Which left Farrell free to create.

He hadn't realized until this move how much of a routine he had for getting started on his work. Sharpen a few pencils. Straighten his desk. Stare into space, summon the memory of where he had left off.

Now the setting was different. The office layout not the same. But in the end, his methodical approach served him well. In half an hour, he was deep into his latest project.

The next time he surfaced, he glanced at his watch and groaned. Nearly eleven. He'd asked Ivy to have his breakfast ready at eight. She was probably either frustrated or pissed, or both.

He knew he was a hard person to live with. But he didn't want to starve. Or eat peanut butter 24/7. He would assure her he'd do better. Respect her time and effort.

When he rushed into the kitchen, Ivy and Dolly were seated at the island. Ivy wore a simple white cotton button-up top and the same jeans. He knew they were the same, because he'd memorized the rip at one knee.

Ivy had found a set of colorful miniature bowls in his

cabinets. The kind of small containers that were good for dipping sauces or individual servings of queso. Dolly had a blue one in her left hand and a green one in her right. The rest were scattered in front of her.

"I'm so sorry," Farrell said. "I promise I'll be on time tomorrow. Maybe set an alarm."

Ivy's expression was noncommittal. "It's your house and your food. You have a right to eat whenever it's good for you."

Something about her careful speech bothered him. "I didn't mean to inconvenience you."

An odd *something* flashed through her eyes. "My job is to have your meal ready when you want it. I've been scrambling eggs every half hour, so they would be warm. The bacon has held up okay." She stood with the baby. "I'll do eggs one more time."

He walked over to the trash can, lifted the lid and stared at the contents. Good God. He turned around to find his new employee watching him warily. He cocked his head. "Weren't you afraid I'd be mad about the wasted food?" He said it jokingly.

Ivy went white. Her mouth opened and closed. "I'm sorry," she muttered. "I'll order more eggs. You can take it out of my check."

She had backed away from him until she was at the farthest point of the kitchen. For one stunned moment, he felt as if he was in a play and didn't know his lines. He'd been hungry before. Starving, actually. But now his appetite fled. "We need to talk," he said slowly. "What kind of man do you think I am?"

She shrugged half-heartedly, clutching the baby as a shield. "I don't know you at all," she said.

He sighed. "I'm the kind of man who won't shout at you if I'm late and the eggs are cold. Are we clear on that?"

A bit of color returned to her face, though her body language still telegraphed her distress. "Okay," she said slowly. "You won't shout. Got it." She paused. "So do I scramble the eggs or not?"

Somewhere, somebody must be laughing at Farrell. He wanted to say *Forget about the damn breakfast*, but he was afraid to upset her. Ivy Danby was fragile. Not in spirit. Not in determination. But she had survived *something*. The hints he was beginning to pick up ate at him.

Should he probe for the truth, or leave her alone to heal on her own?

While he debated how to handle the situation, Ivy cocked her head. "Eggs, Farrell?"

He shrugged and scraped his hands through his hair. "No. I'll grab a sandwich and eat an early lunch." He hesitated. "I may not have been completely honest. I won't shout at you about eggs, but I do sometimes get frustrated. If I *were* to yell, it wouldn't be because I'm upset with you."

This time she stared at him so intently he felt the back of his neck prickle. That steady female gaze got under his skin. Was she always so serious, so focused?

"Do you mean that you have a temper?" she asked.

In another situation, it might have seemed an innocuous question. But to Ivy, it wasn't. He knew that in his gut.

"Doesn't everyone from time to time?" he said lightly, trying to defuse the fraught conversation with humor.

She gnawed her lower lip, a lip that was soft and pink but bore no makeup, not even lip gloss. "No. Not me," she said. "But most people do, I guess."

"There are different kinds of temper," he said gently. "Some people let off steam by being loud. But they don't mean anything by it. They aren't evil or dangerous."

She jerked when he said the word *dangerous*. He saw the slight physical reaction. And he also saw the way she tried to cover up her response.

Too late, Ivy.

"I understand," she said.

Those two words were the biggest lie she had told him. He would have to handle her with care. He was good at caring for people. Sasha told him once it was his love language. But only for her, his wife. Not for any other woman. Sasha had been strong and independent until cancer beat her down.

He cleared his throat. "Why don't you take a look around the house? Make yourself at home. Nothing is off-limits. I'll throw a sandwich together and get back to the lab."

For the first time, a hint of humor blossomed on Ivy's heart-shaped face. With the short haircut and the big eyes, she looked far younger than he knew her to be. She shook her head slowly. "If I let *you* fix the sandwich, that will be *three* meals I haven't fed you. Hold Dolly. I'll make the sandwich."

Before he could protest, the baby was in his arms, smelling sweetly of lotion and some indefinable infant smell. "How old is she?" he asked abruptly. He could hazard a guess, but suddenly, he wanted to know for sure. Ivy and her little daughter were a puzzle that obsessed him at the moment.

That wary expression came back. Ivy turned to rummage in the fridge, her voice muffled as she took out a package of roast beef and another of Swiss cheese. "Seven months."

He stroked the baby's chubby arm. "So her father got to know her before he passed?"

Ivy straightened and whirled around. "Don't," she said sharply. "Don't do that."

"Do what?"

"Don't try to analyze me, or my life, or Dolly. I'm here to do a job. Nothing more. You and I aren't friends, Farrell."

He chuckled, feeling better suddenly. "So you *do* have a temper, Ivy. Right? It's not a crime."

Her face was the picture of astonishment. Was she really so lacking in self-awareness? Or had she battened down her natural responses for so long that she had forgotten what it felt like to experience true emotions, whether positive or negative?

"I'm sorry I pried," he said. "I'll take Miss Dolly out to the front porch to look at the ocean while you handle things in here."

Ivy fretted as she prepared Farrell's lunch. How could she have been so rude to him? He was paying her a ridiculous amount of money to do a relatively modest amount of work. She should be catering to his every whim, not snapping at him.

But maybe her days of tiptoeing around men were over. She was a grown woman with her own ideas, her own way of doing things. The novelty of that freedom was not something she took for granted.

She added fresh tomato slices and a crisp leaf of lettuce to the thick sandwich and slapped the second piece of bread on top. Since she hadn't actually *cooked* for the man yet, she'd better make sure this lunch was a work of art. After washing an apple and tucking it into one of the brown paper sacks she had found in the cabinet, she added napkins, packaged condiments and the cellophane-wrapped sandwich on top.

Farrell could choose his own drink. The fridge was stocked with bottled sodas, tea and plenty of water. She didn't know his preference.

When the lunch was ready and the kitchen restored to its pristine condition, she made her way through the house to the front door. Pausing by a window, she observed Farrell Stone interacting with her daughter.

He was talking to Dolly, pointing toward the ocean. Though Ivy couldn't hear the exact words, she watched his body language. The infant was secure in his left arm. Her little face was tipped up to his, her smile happy. Contented. The expression on her daughter's face filled Ivy with relief.

Supposedly dogs and babies were good judges of character. If that was true, Farrell Stone was passing the test with ease. Ivy wasn't so easily won over, though. She had learned the hard way that people could present a facade to the world that was entirely false.

Even now, she cringed inwardly as she recalled how easily she had been deceived. Her many missteps and mistakes would haunt her for the rest of her life. More than anything, she wanted to protect Dolly from being as vulnerable as Ivy had been.

Farrell laughed suddenly and kissed the baby on the top of her head. That unscripted bit of affection caught Ivy off guard and twisted her heart. He was so good with Dolly, so natural. Was he really the man he seemed?

With his back to her, she was able to watch him unobserved. Broad shoulders, a powerful torso. The navy Henley shirt he wore revealed bone and muscle. Farrell Stone was intensely masculine. She shivered, caught in something she didn't want to name.

Sexual desire was like an endangered species. She recognized it. Was even drawn to it. But a smart woman would keep her distance.

Farrell must have sensed he was being watched. He turned toward the window, waved and beckoned her to come outdoors. Reluctantly, she joined him. The day was warmer now, much warmer than when she and Dolly had walked over from the cabin.

"Your lunch is ready," she said quietly. Dolly made no move to reach for her mother. Apparently, she was fascinated with her new friend. Dolly's whole world had centered around her mother up until now. It would be good for her to broaden her circle of relationships with adults.

Farrell nodded. "Thanks," he said, keeping his gaze focused on the sea. As they watched, a trio of sailboats danced across the waves on the open water, their sails pure white against the glistening azure water.

"Do you sail?" Ivy asked.

He shot her a sideways glance. "I do. Why? Are you interested in trying it? I'm happy to give you lessons."

She sighed, ignoring his offer. "I'm very sorry I said we weren't friends. That wasn't nice at all."

His smile was a flash of white teeth that sent her stomach into free fall. "I believe in second chances, Ivy Danby. Why don't you and I start over? My name is Farrell, and I'm very happy you're here with me in the Maine woods."

"You are?" She looked up at him, frowning slightly. "That day in your office I got the impression you were hiring me under duress."

His cheeks reddened as if her question had embarrassed him. But that was impossible. Men like Farrell Stone possessed unshakable confidence.

He shrugged. "It's true I prefer to be alone when I work. I'm sorry if I made you feel unwelcome."

She chuckled, almost stunned to feel the jolt of amusement. "I'm not a guest, Farrell. And you haven't made me feel unwelcome. Not at all. You gave me a fabulous place to live, and you bought my daughter a baby bed. I'm in your debt."

"Absolutely not." His frown was dark. "We're even partners in this arrangement, Ivy. Your contributions to this setup are important. I want you to understand that."

"You mean it, don't you?" Staring at him, she searched his brilliant green eyes, the amber bits catching the sun. Could she take him at face value? Did she dare?

"Of course I do," he said. "I have my failings, but I like to think I'm a man of my word."

They were standing so close she could see a tiny spot

on the underside of his chin where he had nicked himself shaving. Did he normally shave here in his admittedly luxurious getaway home, or had he done it because Ivy and Dolly were with him?

She held out her right hand. "Starting over is a good idea," she said. "Let's shake on it." That last bit was a mistake. Did she really want to touch the man? Her subconscious said *yes*.

When Farrell took her hand in his much larger one, she sucked in a tiny breath, hoping he hadn't noticed. His grip was firm and warm, telegraphing their mutual accord, but other things, as well.

Ivy was assailed with a dozen feelings she couldn't separate. Relief that he hadn't been irreparably offended by her snit earlier. Amazement that something as simple as a handshake could turn her knees wobbly.

Was Farrell Stone affecting her so deeply because he had been kind to her daughter? Or was Ivy, herself, desperate to believe that good men still existed? Surely she wasn't so pathetically needy.

The handshake was over far too soon. Farrell let go first. His gaze was inscrutable now, his jaw tight. He handed her the baby. "I need to get back to work," he said gruffly.

"Of course." She swallowed her hurt that he was so eager to rush away. He had come here to make progress on his designs for new Stone River products. Naturally he wanted to focus in his lab.

Ivy was still dealing with the touch of his hand against hers. A touch that felt incredibly good. But she didn't trust her own judgment.

She couldn't. She shouldn't.

More amazing was the fact that she hadn't flinched when their hands came together. His tangible strength hadn't frightened her. Maybe she was making progress.

Five

Farrell was accustomed—when necessary—to concentrating in the midst of distractions. In fact, his ability to shut out peripheral commotion and disturbances was part of what made him good at his job. Creating—inventing—required quiet time and open *space*.

He had plenty of both here in northern Maine. The silence helped him think. The natural beauty of the landscape refreshed his soul.

By all accounts, he should be able to zero in on his goals better than he ever had before. His new digs were an innovator's dream. Now that he was away from the Portland office, he no longer had to worry about some mysterious person stealing his ideas. He was far off the beaten path, and the locals could spot an intruder a mile away.

Yet he found himself far too often staring out the window into the woods, his thoughts scattering in all directions. One of those compass points always landed on Ivy.

She'd been here almost three weeks now. They had fallen

into a routine of sorts. As he promised her that very first morning, he had made a point of being on time for breakfast. His meal was always waiting on him when he loped from the lab to the house at eight sharp.

Ivy was a good cook. Excellent, in fact. In his kitchen, with the sun streaming through the windows and the scent of bacon in the air, she always claimed to have eaten earlier when the baby woke up. So Farrell consumed his eggs or his pancakes alone. He checked email on his phone, scrolled through a few *New York Times* articles. Wondered about Ivy.

Dinner took an opposite tack. He had insisted, somewhat doggedly, that Ivy eat her evening meal with him. The high chair he ordered had arrived. The three of them—man, woman and baby—were cozy in the breakfast nook.

Once, when Ivy tried to serve him dinner in the formal dining room with a single place setting of china and silver, he rolled his eyes and carried everything back to the kitchen. After the second night, she gave up.

Never again had he asked about her late husband. He and Ivy had brokered an unspoken accord. He avoided personal questions, and she kept him fed. It was working for now.

What really disturbed him most was the conviction that he was obligated to dig out the truth about her past and help her.

He didn't want to. That reluctance, by all accounts, made him a selfish son of a bitch. When Sasha died, he promised himself never again to get so wrapped up in another woman. The pain of losing his high school sweetheart had turned him into a shell of a man.

Eventually, his world had started spinning again. Sasha's ordeal faded into memory. Time healed all wounds, or so he had been told. Almost imperceptibly, he began to live again. And his life had turned out to be pretty good in many ways.

But intimacy? No, thanks. When sexual hunger drove him beyond what he could handle, he occasionally traveled. Found a woman who was as much of a loner as he was. The two of them enjoyed something strictly physical. It wasn't ideal, but it was all he wanted.

Ivy scared him, because he was attracted to her. She was so very *real*. He wanted to take care of her, and he wanted to *have* her. In his bed.

If he delved into her life, her past, he would get too involved. He might step over the line. Not only for boss/employee, but for his own personal boundaries.

He didn't have the emotional bandwidth to give a woman what she needed.

Or maybe that wasn't true. Maybe he simply didn't ever want to be so vulnerable. He knew what it felt like to lose someone important. He couldn't go through that pain again.

Ivy liked her job. She and Dolly were adjusting well to the new environment. It had taken a couple of days to feel comfortable in Farrell's fabulous kitchen, but even that was easier by the end of the first week.

One Friday morning, she was surprised when Katie showed up out of the blue right after breakfast. She and Farrell put their heads together for an hour about R & D department issues. Then Katie sought out Ivy at the cabin.

The attractive, sexy blonde made Ivy feel inadequate in all sorts of ways. Not on purpose, of course. But Katie was gorgeous. And confident. And blissfully happy as a newlywed. She was also running things back in Portland while Farrell worked here in the middle of nowhere.

When Katie begged to play with the baby, Ivy got Dolly up from her nap and changed her. As Ivy returned to the living room, Katie grinned. "Is it possible she's grown since the last time I saw her?"

"Maybe," Ivy said. "She's healthy and happy here."

Katie cocked her head. "And you?"

Ivy flushed. "Yes. Things are going well."

"Farrell says you cook like a dream."

"I'm glad he thinks so."

"Do the two of you get along?"

"We had a few spats the first couple of days. But we understand each other now."

"Good." Katie gave her a pointed stare. "I need to talk to you about something. But you have to promise not to freak out."

"That's not a reassuring way to start a conversation." Ivy's stomach flipped and flopped. "Is it Farrell? Has he changed his mind? And he's too chicken to tell me himself?"

The last eight words came tumbling out indignantly.

Katie gaped, then laughed. "Farrell Stone is the bravest man I know...after my husband. And no. He hasn't changed his mind. But you know how I mentioned that Farrell entertains often?"

"Yes."

"Well, next weekend is a big event. Farrell and I have been trying to pull it together. But we didn't know until yesterday that it was going to work out. Stone River Outdoors is hoping to partner with a few overseas entities to extend our global reach."

"I see." Ivy told herself not to overreact.

Katie continued. "We have some heavy hitters flying in for a 'summit' here at Farrell's house. A watchmaker from Switzerland. A well-known safari company from Namibia. A couple of ecotour operators from the British Virgin Islands. Plus, a husband and wife who organize walking tours in Tuscany. Farrell, Zachary and Quin are hoping to convince them all to use Stone River products, and in turn, we'll advertise for each of our partners."

"So lots of cooking."

Katie looked guilty. "Not exactly. We're bringing in a professional chef for the weekend. Farrell wants *you* to act as his hostess. My sister has agreed to come with me and babysit Dolly. Here at the cabin, of course. So you won't have to worry about her."

Ivy shook her head, her fists clenching. "Delanna? Oh, no," she said. "That won't work."

"I'll be here the whole time," Katie said. "Except at night. Quin and I will sleep at our place."

"And Zachary? Does he have a significant other? Somebody better suited than me to take over here?"

"Zachary is the quintessential bachelor. He goes where the wind blows him. Although to be fair," she said quickly, "he really *has* curtailed his traveling since Mr. Stone died. Zachary is the financial genius at headquarters. He keeps us in the black. He'll be staying up here, too, but in his own house."

"When you talked to me about this job back in Portland, I thought you meant the occasional dinner party," Ivy muttered. "I'm not who you need. Besides, I don't have the right clothes."

Katie juggled Dolly in one arm and reached into an expensive leather tote. "We're going to take care of that right now." She pulled out a sheaf of catalogs. "I've made a list of everything you'll want. Farrell is paying, of course. If you don't like the colors and styles I've picked, feel free to say so. I've folded down the appropriate pages. We'll do overnight shipping. If there are things that don't fit, that will give us time to do exchanges."

When Katie handed over the catalogs, Ivy looked at them in a daze. Farrell hadn't been kidding about his efficient admin. Katie was a military general, planning…executing. There were dressy pants and tops. Couture negligees. A trio of cocktail dresses. Casual hiking clothes.

Ivy shook her head. "I can't," she said. Her nose burned

and her eyes stung. This was a world she knew nothing about.

Katie read her distress. Her smile was kind. "You can do this, Ivy."

"But I'm not like you." Ivy indicated the glossy catalogs. "I've never worn anything so nice."

The other woman smiled wryly. "You may not know this, but my life before I married Quin was far more blue-collar than black-tie. I *worked* with the Farrell men, but that was as far as it went. Now I'm one of the family. It's been sink or swim. I've had to keep up with their lifestyle, but it's really not as bad as it sounds, Ivy. It's kind of nice being pampered."

Ivy changed course. "I don't even really know your sister."

"You moved in with her."

"For three nights. That's all. She advertised for a roommate."

"She already loves Dolly. And though my sister can be flaky at times, she's great with kids. Plus, as I mentioned, you'll be close by the entire time. Nothing to worry about."

"Why can't you be the hostess?"

Katie's smile was smug. "Because Farrell wants *you*. I'm a newlywed. My husband and I will go home every evening. You'll be on hand to juggle any overnight emergencies."

"Overnight?" Ivy's eyes widened.

For the first time, Katie looked guilty. "Did I forget to mention that? Farrell wants you to stay in one of the guest rooms."

"Why didn't he ask me himself?" Ivy demanded. "This doesn't sound like him at all."

"Well, you'd be wrong, then. He says you're smart and capable, and he thinks you'll be the perfect person to make his guests comfortable."

After that, things snowballed out of Ivy's control. It

made sense that Katie was organizing the entire weekend. After all, she had been Farrell's administrative assistant for a long time. What didn't make sense was expecting *Ivy* to jump into a high-octane situation and pretend she moved in these circles.

Over lunch, Farrell added his two cents' worth. "Thank you, Ivy," he said. "Katie tells me she went over all the particulars with you. We'll have barely a week to get ready, but Katie and Quin will fly up Thursday morning to help with final details. Zachary will be in charge of hiring limos to collect our guests at the Portland airport on Friday and shepherd them up here."

Ivy looked from her boss to the woman who had been instrumental in getting Ivy this well-paid job. Both of them appeared oddly certain that Ivy could handle this extraordinary upcoming event. Both of them had believed in her when she was desperate and had no clue how she was going to support herself and her child.

Already, she was in their debt. What could she say other than yes?

"I'll help however I can," she said. "With one caveat."

Farrell raised an eyebrow. "And that would be?"

"I'll be the one to put Dolly to bed at night. It doesn't take long. I don't want her thinking I've abandoned her."

Katie nodded. "Of course. Besides, Quin and I will still be here that early in the evening. So no worries."

Farrell was already second-guessing himself. It was true that he needed a hostess for the weekend. But Katie had served that role in the past and would have done so again if he'd asked. Somehow, though, he believed Ivy would add an important element to the upcoming event. She was practical and adaptable. And she would tell him honestly if aspects of the summit weren't working.

Right now, she looked uneasy. Katie had thrown a lot

of stuff at her, and there would be more to come. Was Farrell pushing her too far?

Before he could answer that question, Ivy stood and began clearing the table. Katie stood, as well. "I can handle cleanup," Katie said. "Ivy, the chicken salad was amazing. Farrell, you go back to work. Ivy, you put Dolly down for her nap. I've got this."

When Ivy disappeared with Dolly in her arms, Farrell shook his head slowly. "Was she open to the hostess idea?"

Katie grimaced. "Not really. I had to sell it hard. But I think you're right. She'll be an asset this weekend. And even though she had reservations about being so visible, she'll enjoy it. I hope."

After lunch, when Katie had gone down the road to her and Quin's house, Farrell went back to the lab and tried to work with little success. He wasn't worried about the summit weekend. The prospect of a new venture was exciting. But Ivy was a conundrum that stuck with him.

This past week, he'd found himself watching her when he thought she wouldn't notice. The gentle swell of her breasts. The way her hips filled out a pair of jeans. The glimmer of mischief in her eyes when she laughed.

With a mutter of disgust, he dropped his pencil and stood. All he'd managed to accomplish in the last half hour was a series of amateur doodles. He might as well take a break and satisfy his curiosity at the same time.

When he knocked on the front door of the cabin, he took a moment to appreciate how it had turned out. He had envisioned it as an addition to the three large houses he and his brothers had built here in northern Maine.

The cabin was smaller. And cozy. Maybe one day, Quin and Katie's kids would come stay in the cabin between semesters in college. Or even honeymoon here. It was a great hideaway.

He knocked a second time, and the door abruptly opened. Ivy was visibly shocked. "Farrell. Did you need me?"

Suddenly, he questioned his judgment. Ivy's face was flushed. One cheek sported a visible blanket crease. "Ah, hell," he said. "You were napping. I'm sorry. Never mind."

He turned on his heel, but Ivy's soft, unintentionally sexy voice stopped him. "You can come in, Farrell. I needed to get up anyway."

"Is the baby awake?"

"No. She'll sleep for another forty-five minutes at least."

He should have walked away. But he didn't. "I don't want to interrupt," he said gruffly, feeling the tops of his ears get hot. There was no reason in the world for him to be here. But still, he stayed.

Ivy opened the door wider and stepped back. "You're fine. Come on in."

Together, they took the few steps to the living room. Ivy curled up in an armchair upholstered in moss green velvet. Farrell sat on the green-and-gold-plaid sofa. "Shall I start a fire?" he asked. The day was cold and dreary.

"That would be nice."

She was eyeing him with suspicion, and no wonder. He was acting weird. Even he could see that.

Conscious of her gaze on his back, he squatted beside the fireplace and put together the kindling and larger logs. With some kerosene-soaked pine cones and newspaper and a couple of matches, he soon had a creditable blaze going.

"There you go," he said, standing and brushing a bit of soot off his pants. "Is this the first one you've had?"

Ivy nodded, wrinkling her nose. "I tried twice, but apparently, pyromania is not one of my gifts."

"It takes practice," he said, sitting back down with a sigh. There were worse ways to spend a fall afternoon.

"Shouldn't you be inventing stuff?"

He chuckled. "Yes. I'm blocked at the moment. It happens."

"Am I allowed to ask what you're working on?"

"Of course. It's a motion-activated emergency signal. Sometimes in an avalanche or a climbing accident, the person involved can't use their cell phone. Maybe it's lost. Maybe the signal is poor."

"Maybe they can't reach it, or they're too badly injured to call for help?"

"Exactly. The device I'm trying to create would be triggered when there is an abrupt change in altitude. That signal could be picked up by any number of rescue frequencies."

"Impressive."

He shrugged. "It might be, if I ever get it done."

Ivy picked at a loose thread on the sofa arm. "Why did you ask me to be your hostess this weekend?"

He hadn't seen that one coming. "Well, uh…"

She pinned him with a sharp gaze. "The truth, please."

Six

Ivy couldn't believe she'd had the courage to ask the question, but she badly wanted to know.

Farrell's expression was hard to read. He shot her a glance and then stood to poke the fire. When it blazed up to his satisfaction, he leaned an arm on the mantel and faced her. "You could say my motives were multilayered."

It was difficult to stay focused when he was such a beautiful man to look at. Despite the cerebral nature of his work, it was clear he spent a great deal of time outdoors. The honey streaks in his brown hair were natural. His skin was tanned to a golden color, and his sinewy muscles were that of an experienced athlete.

She had studied up on the Stone brothers. Google was a wonderful thing. Quin, Katie's husband, had missed a gold medal for skiing by a fraction of a second. She'd seen photos of a laughing Zachary camel racing in Morocco. And as for Farrell, well, he seemed to have been everywhere and done everything. Maybe grief had made it too hard to stay in Maine, or maybe he simply liked the challenge of climbing mountains and flying over glaciers.

"Multilayered," she muttered. "That's not an answer."

"Fine," he said, sounding grumpy. "I thought it would be fun for you."

"Wait, what?" As the words penetrated her fog, she frowned. "Since when do I need to have fun?"

"*Everybody* needs to have fun, Ivy. And I've been told that new moms sometimes struggle, because they get over-whelmed with the demands of a baby, and they begin to miss adult interactions."

"I don't want you *handling* me," Ivy said defensively. "I'm perfectly capable of looking after myself."

His green eyes sparked with irritation. "Of course you are. But I also thought you might be an asset this week-end, because you aren't part of Stone River Outdoors. I was hoping you could give us a new perspective. We want to do more of these co-op weekends. You can comment on things that Zachary and Quin and Katie and I might not see, because we're too close to the subject matter. I'd like to hear what you think when it's all over."

Shame was not a good feeling. "Oh," she said stiffly. "Well, that's different. I'm sure I'll enjoy it."

Her prim assurance made him grin. "No, you're not. But you're also probably a little bit curious. So you agreed."

"I agreed because you're my boss."

His face went blank. "I see." He stood abruptly and headed for the door. "Then forget about it. Katie will han-dle what needs to be done. I'm sorry to intrude."

Now she had really done it. "Wait," she cried. She ran after him and caught him at the door. When she put her hand on his forearm, all the air left her lungs. Until Far-rell entered her life, she hadn't touched a man who wasn't her husband in over a decade. From what she remembered of the opposite sex, those long-ago college boys hadn't felt like this.

Farrell's arm was muscled, warm, strong enough to rescue a woman if she needed rescuing. "I'm sorry," she said urgently, making herself step back. "You're right. I *was* curious, and even though I'm scared, I'm honored that you offered me this opportunity."

"I don't want your gratitude," he snapped. He ran a hand over his face and leaned back against the door. "I don't understand you, Ivy, but I'm trying. I'm not the enemy here."

"No," she said. "You're not."

"Do you want to talk about it?" His green-eyed gaze, clear and steady, told her he had pieced together at least some of her truth. On his face, she saw compassion. Kindness. Wariness.

She wanted to... She desperately wanted to tell him everything that had happened to her. But she was so ashamed. "No," she said. "Not today. Maybe never. But it's kind of you to ask."

"I'll tell you about Sasha," he said abruptly. "If you ever want to know. Not a quid pro quo. My tragedy is further in the past than yours. I don't expect you to bare your soul to me."

Tragedy wasn't the right word, but she couldn't explain. "Now," she said quietly. "Tell me about Sasha now. If you have time."

Some of the tension in his shoulders relaxed. "I don't talk about her often. But you're someone who would understand."

"Then sit down," Ivy said. "I'll behave."

He touched her cheek with a single fingertip, barely a brushstroke, the flutter of a butterfly wing. "Don't make promises you can't keep."

They had reached some kind of milestone, Ivy realized. She had let down her guard, and Farrell, without her noticing, had slipped into her heart and made a place for himself.

"So how did you meet?" she asked, when they resumed their seats. The fire burned merrily. The room was warm. She saw the giant inhalation and exhalation that lifted his chest and let it fall.

Perhaps to him, the tragedy didn't seem so long ago after all.

"High school," Farrell said simply. "Once we realized it was more than puppy love, we knew it was forever. But my father intervened. Sasha's background wasn't as privileged as mine. He sent me to school on the West Coast, and he manipulated Sasha's emotions."

"What did you do?"

"We waited for each other," he said simply. "I graduated. We were both twenty-one by then. There was nothing more for my father to destroy. Eventually, she won him over. We had three wonderful years. I look back sometimes and ask myself if they were really as good as I remember."

"But they were."

He nodded slowly, his gaze focused on something far away. "They were incredible. Right up until the day she was diagnosed with a rare, aggressive form of breast cancer. She made it eleven months and died holding my hand."

"I'm so sorry, Farrell." The idea that he had found such a beautiful love and lost it broke her heart.

He shook his head as if to remove the threads that bound him to the past. "You understand what it's like. I don't know if your husband's death was unexpected or if, like me, you had time to say goodbye. Either way, death sucks. That door slams shut, and no matter how much you try to pry it open, the person on the other side is gone."

Ivy found herself in a quandary. She could let his assumptions ride. But he was being so wonderfully decent and open and amazingly kind, her lies by omission choked her.

"I do understand. In a way. But my experience was not like yours."

He grimaced. "Death never is…"

"You lost the great love of your life."

"Yes. I did."

She stared down at her lap, unable to face him. "I didn't," she whispered. "I'm not grieving like you have all these years."

Farrell tried to conceal his shock. What was she saying? Talking about Sasha had not been as painful as he'd expected. Particularly with someone who had been through a similar experience. Since Ivy was recently widowed, he'd wanted to encourage her to open up about her loss. Apparently, he was way off base. Now he was speechless.

Though as he sifted through what he knew of Ivy, hadn't he guessed there might have been something amiss?

He cleared his throat. "I see."

"No," she said. "You don't. And I can't explain. But I'm so glad you had someone like Sasha in your life. No matter what happens down the road, no one can take that away from you."

"I would never betray your confidence," he said slowly. "It's not healthy to keep things bottled up inside."

Her smile was gently mocking. "Psychology 101?"

He thought about it for a moment. "No. Actually, personal experience. I had to see a counselor after Sasha died. I couldn't deal with the emotions. I'd been brought up to believe that men don't whine and they sure as hell don't cry. But I was on the verge of a breakdown, I think. It was Zachary who finally made me go. I owe him a lot. He and Quin, both."

Suddenly, Dolly's plaintive cries came through on the monitor. Farrell lurched to his feet, wildly relieved to have an escape route. What in the hell had he started? "She's awake," he said. "I should get back to the lab. I'll let myself out."

For the remainder of the afternoon, he worked on his project with half of his brain. But the gray matter that was unoccupied kept poking at the Ivy situation.

She isn't grieving? He knew a bit about denial. All the stages of grief, in fact, were familiar to him. He'd experienced every one of them in varying degrees.

Was Ivy still in shock? Was that it? She'd said in her interview that her husband had died *a few months ago.* That could mean three or six or nine. When Farrell had asked if the baby's dad had time to know his daughter, Ivy had shut down that conversation quickly.

Fortunately, Katie and Quin were coming over for dinner tonight. If not, Farrell would have been hard-pressed to know what to say to Ivy when he saw her again.

As it was, the evening unfolded naturally. Ivy prepared an incredible meal of beef Stroganoff, spinach salad and homemade bread. Dolly played happily with metal spoons in her high chair while the adults chatted.

Quin seemed particularly taken with the baby. "She's really sweet and smart," he said.

Ivy laughed. "And now you're my new best friend. Praising a woman's child is a sure way to win points."

"But it's true," Quin protested. "Has she started walking yet?"

"No. It's not quite time. Possibly in eight or ten weeks. Or later—who knows? I've heard everything from eight months to fifteen months."

Katie helped Ivy dish up the apple pie and ice cream for dessert. "Quin was always ahead of the curve physically. Or so I've heard."

Farrell snorted. "Did he tell you that? I'd take my baby brother's boasts with a grain of salt. He once broke his wrist falling out of bed. Quin wasn't exactly a child prodigy when it came to athletics."

While Quin and Katie squabbled good-naturedly about his childhood exploits, Farrell glanced over at Ivy and caught her watching the other two with a smile on her face.

He was stunned. Why had he ever thought she was not conventionally beautiful? Her face lit up with humor and amusement. The smile altered her serious expression, gave life and energy to her delicate features.

The unexpected transformation left him breathless. He was drawn to her...to Ivy, this complex woman with the prickly exterior. Telling her about Sasha had fulfilled a need he didn't know he had. Other people always wanted to "make it better." Ivy simply listened.

As Katie and Quin continued their pretend argument, Ivy joined in, her sharp wit and dry remarks egging them on. Farrell understood suddenly that he was seeing the real woman behind the careful mask.

That very first day in his Portland office, he'd met a fragile female beaten down by life. A person who had hit bottom. A new mother, lost and afraid.

Katie must have seen it, too, and Katie being Katie, she had decided Ivy needed to be Farrell's new hire. Not for Farrell's sake, but for Ivy's.

Who or what had turned Ivy Danby from the glowing, confident girl he suspected she once had been into a frightened shadow of herself?

He had a suspicion or two. Both of which made him sick to his stomach. But before he jumped to any conclusions, he would have to get Ivy to trust him. She was growing more comfortable day by day. There was time.

But what was he going to do about the other? The reluctant attraction? He suspected it went both ways, but he couldn't be sure. And even if he *was* sure, Ivy was too vulnerable right now.

Eventually, the others noticed that he wasn't joining in the fun.

Quin gestured theatrically. "Jeez, even my own brother isn't jumping in to defend me. Tell her, Farrell. Tell Ivy how good I was at everything in junior high and high school."

"Well," Farrell drawled. "There was that D+ you made in chemistry. And the C- in calculus. Is that what you mean?"

Ivy and Katie giggled when Quin glared. "Sports," he said between clenched teeth. "Tell her how good I was at sports."

"Oh." Farrell smiled at Ivy. "My brother was good at sports."

The smile she gave him was utterly sweet and uncomplicated. It packed a powerful punch. "So I've heard," she said.

Perhaps kindly, she changed the subject. "What about Zachary?" she asked. "The two of you are the first and the last. How does Zachary fit into your family dynamics?"

There was a split second of silence while Quin looked at Farrell and vice versa. Quin rubbed his chin, grinning. "Zachary is what one might call a ladies' man."

Katie shook her head. "Oh, please. Don't be ridiculous. Zachary is wonderful, Ivy," she said. "Don't let them lead you astray. Zachary is a perfect gentleman. It's true that he dates a lot, but that's not a crime."

Quin stood up to pour more wine. "The phrase *girl in every port* comes to mind."

Ivy accepted the refill with a smile. "And will he have a lady friend in tow when he arrives?"

"Not this time," Katie said. "Next weekend is going to be an important business function. Most of my brother-in-law's girlfriends can't even spell *business*."

Farrell chuckled. "Now who's being catty?"

Katie looked guilty. "I shouldn't have said that. You'll like him, Ivy. He's a sweetheart."

Quin nodded. "Who knows—maybe he'll take a shine to Ivy. It would do him good to meet a woman of substance."

Farrell tensed. Incredibly, jealousy curled in his gut. "Ivy is recently widowed. This conversation is in poor taste."

The room fell silent. Ivy was visibly mortified. She glared at him. "They were just having a bit of fun." She turned to the other two. "I enjoyed dinner. If you'll excuse me, I need to take Dolly to the cabin and get her ready for bed."

Katie protested. "Oh, don't go yet. Can't you put her down in the port-a-crib? And carry her to the cabin later? I'll help."

Ivy hesitated.

Quin gave her a hangdog expression. "Sorry, Miss Ivy. I won't do it again, I swear."

Farrell had reached his limit in a lot of ways. "I'm sure Ivy is tired. It's been a long day." Only after the words left his mouth did he realize how he sounded. As if he was glad to be rid of her.

Ivy's face turned red. Katie shot him a bewildered glance. She patted Ivy's arm. "I'll come with you to the cabin for some girl talk. You don't mind, do you?" She scooped Dolly out of her high chair. "Besides, I can't get enough of this sweetie pie."

When the women walked out of the house, Quin stared at Farrell. "What the hell is wrong with you, man?"

Farrell rubbed his temples where a headache was beginning to pound. "I don't know. Nothing, really. Let's forget about it."

"You acted like a jackass. Embarrassed Ivy on the one hand, and then practically shoved her out of the house. That kind of wacko behavior is bad for employee retention, you know."

"Enough, Quin," he snapped. "Just because you're nauseatingly happy doesn't mean the rest of us are."

His brother's eyes widened, then filled with sympathy. "Damn, Farrell. It's been so long since you were interested in a woman, I didn't see the signs. That's it. Am I right? You've got the hots for sweet little Ivy Danby, and it's making you crazy." Quin shook his head slowly. "As someone who only recently was on the precipice of romantic disaster myself, I feel your pain."

"I'm not interested in Ivy Danby," Farrell protested. But the words lacked heat.

Quin sobered. "Maybe you shouldn't go there, bro. You, of all people, know how long it takes to deal with grief. The timing is off. You'll only hurt yourself. Or maybe her."

"Do you think I don't know that?" Farrell muttered.

"I've never known you to do something rash. You're our rock-steady big brother. I can't handle a ripple in the force."

Farrell grinned weakly. "You are so full of it. I guess that must be what regular sex does for a guy."

Quin leaned his chair back on two legs and laced his hands across his flat belly. "Marriage is the best institution in the world. I can't believe I waited so long to try it."

Seven

Ivy was humiliated and hurt by Farrell's behavior during the impromptu Friday night dinner party. She couldn't decide if she was happy or sad that Katie and Quin headed back to Portland Saturday morning.

Their presence meant that Ivy didn't have to speak directly to Farrell. But with them gone, it was easier to simply avoid her boss.

When he had talked to her about Sasha, she felt a moment of *something*. A simple connection born of shared experiences? But if there had been a fleeting second of kinship, it was gone.

Perhaps he regretted being so honest with Ivy. Men didn't usually spill their guts with ease. He had said there was no expectation of reciprocity, but deep down she suspected that wasn't true.

Farrell was curious about Ivy. About her past.

She liked him. A lot. But not enough to dredge up the worst of her secrets. Farrell's tale about a man and a woman who were high school sweethearts—and then one of them died—was a tender, innocent story of loss.

Ivy couldn't begin to compete.

For the remainder of the weekend and the days that followed, she worked hard getting Farrell's house in order. It wasn't a huge chore. Everything had been pretty much shipshape when she arrived. But there was always the occasional dust bunny to corral and rugs to be vacuumed.

She had his breakfast waiting every morning. His lunch prepared. And a decent dinner in the evenings. What she did *not* do was eat with him anymore. She offered up excuses, and he accepted them at face value.

Whenever he returned to the main house, his handsome face was sculpted in planes and angles. No emerald-eyed smiles. No teasing remarks. They had somehow ended up on opposite sides of an enormous chasm.

Dolly, thank goodness, was happy almost all the time. She was such an easy baby. Ivy knew how lucky she was. This job would be much more difficult with a cranky infant to juggle.

As promised by Katie, several boxes landed on Farrell's doorstep, all of them addressed to Ivy. During naptime for the next few days, Ivy tried on her new wardrobe.

Katie might have grown up in a modest household, but her instincts for fashion were spot-on. As much as Ivy had dreaded this Pygmalion-like makeover, it turned out to be not so bad. None of her new clothes made her feel self-conscious. In fact, they boosted her self-esteem considerably.

It had been years since she'd had anything new to wear. Now the pile of dresses and pants and shoes and jewelry—and even underwear—on the guest bed made her dizzy with anticipation.

Despite their current differences, she wanted to make Farrell proud. He had invested a great deal of time and money in this upcoming house party. She would do her part.

Tuesday morning, Ivy received a text from Katie. The chef was bringing everything with her, but she had asked if there were several large platters available. Ivy promised to check.

As was her custom now, Ivy put Dolly down around ten in the port-a-crib in Farrell's beautiful study. The walls were lined with floor-to-ceiling bookshelves. Several of the paintings looked wildly expensive, though Ivy was no art critic. She closed the heavy velvet drapes and turned on a tiny fan that would provide enough white noise for Dolly to sleep peacefully.

With the baby monitor in hand, Ivy tiptoed out of the room and closed the door. She remembered seeing serving pieces in one of the cabinets. Once she located them, she would text Katie what was available.

Farrell's home had ten-foot ceilings, which made the kitchen beautiful and roomy. But it also meant that the highest of the cabinet shelves were far above Ivy's reach. As a "vertically challenged" adult, she had spent her life on her tiptoes or asking for help.

But Farrell was tucked away in the lab, and she didn't want to bother him, certainly not after what had happened Friday. They had barely exchanged a dozen words in the interim. He was gruff and monotone. She was equally withdrawn. They had achieved an uneasy détente.

In the pantry, she found a small two-step stool. It wasn't much, but it might work. She moved around the room, examining each cabinet. Finally, she found what she had remembered spotting on an earlier scouting mission.

Stacked one on top of each other were three stoneware platters, clearly handmade. The graduated sizes would probably work for whatever the chef had in mind. The free-form swirls of gray and navy and green were elegant and well suited to the ambience in Farrell's beautiful home.

Ivy could only touch the edge of the bottom tray. And pottery was notoriously heavy. The last thing she needed was to break them.

With her hands on her hips, she debated her options. A return to the pantry produced no answers until she spotted an old phone book on a bottom shelf. She made a mental note to recycle it, but in the meantime, the thick paper publication might be just the thing.

Carefully, she adjusted the stool. Then she rested the phone book in the exact center. Holding on to two cabinet handles to steady herself, she stepped up onto her new perch. Bingo. Now she could get her hands on the top piece of pottery. If she slid it off the pile carefully, she could step down, set it aside and go back for the other two.

Farrell was restless. And his coffee had run dry. The project was going well despite the turmoil in his gut. He'd managed to separate the two portions of his life for a few hours, but now the prospect that he might run into Ivy drew him back to the main house.

When he entered quietly and rounded the corner into the kitchen, his chest squeezed. Tiny, five-foot-three Ivy Danby was perched precariously on what looked like a damn phone book, about to break her neck.

He roared at her, his heart in his throat. "What in the hell are you doing? Are you crazy?" He lunged across the room at her, desperate to break her fall. And she was surely going to fall. The heavy platter above her head already teetered.

When he jumped in front of her and reached for the stoneware, Ivy flinched backward and threw her hands in front of her face.

He was so shocked, he barely caught her before she lost

her balance. If he had left well enough alone, she might have managed her balancing act, but it was too late. The platter eluded both of them and shattered on the floor.

Farrell felt a piece hit his ankle, but he was more worried about Ivy. She was glassy-eyed with shock. And she avoided his gaze.

Without speaking another word, he scooped up the monitor and carried Ivy across the hall into his bedroom. It was the closest place that had a sofa. The master suite was huge and included a seating area. He set her down and crouched in front of her. "Ivy," he said, the next words stuck in his throat. He was still trying to process them. "Did you think I was going to hit you?"

She was pale as milk, big-eyed, tragic. "Yes," she whispered.

If she had struck him, the shock would have been less. He sat back on his ass, horrified. Aghast. Suddenly, so many things made sense.

His mouth was dry. His brain spun in a million directions.

Those hazel eyes filled with tears. Eventually, drops spilled over and ran down her cheeks. The fact that Ivy's distress was completely silent made it worse somehow.

Though he was afraid of upsetting her further, he couldn't bear to see her like this. Carefully, he stood and joined her on the sofa, putting his arm around her shoulders and trying to convey his compassion and concern.

If she had evaded his touch or seemed uncomfortable in any way, he would have released her immediately. But Ivy turned into his embrace and buried her face against his shoulder. The quiet tears turned into sobs that shook her small frame.

One of her hands gripped his shirt as if she were trying to latch on to something in the midst of a storm. Her fingers clenched the cloth right over his heart.

He held her loosely, his throat painful with emotions he didn't try to analyze. It was clear to him now how very badly he wanted her. Her feminine curves made him ache. The sexual hunger was something he couldn't control. But he didn't have to let her know. And he sure as hell didn't have to let himself get sucked into this relationship that was bound to tear him apart.

It already was, though he had tried to keep his distance.

Eventually, the tears ran out. He suspected they had been building for a very long time. He suddenly realized that he was stroking her hair. That had to stop.

Ivy exhaled on a shuddering breath. "I'm sorry," she muttered. When she tried to stand up, he released her immediately. "I should check on the baby," she said.

Farrell pointed to the tiny screen on the monitor. "She hasn't stirred. Talk to me, Ivy. Or if not me, someone. Katie, maybe?"

Ivy wiped the tears from her face with her hands and then wrapped her arms around her waist. She chewed her bottom lip. "It's not exactly what you think."

"So your husband didn't physically abuse you?" He heard the angry indignation in his voice. Ivy did also.

When she spoke again, there was almost no emotion on her face. "This is a long story," she warned.

Farrell realized in that instant that he had a choice. He could make an excuse and go back to the lab. Ivy would let him leave without protest. Maybe she might even be glad. The two of them would continue in a guarded employer/employee relationship.

His other option was to try helping her. And thus open himself up to a deeper relationship. One that on his side, at least, had the potential to develop into something more.

He had run from intimacy for seven years. His life was on an even keel now. No devastating lows. But no exhilarating highs either.

Did he really want to let Ivy into his heart? She had already carved out a tiny niche in his life. Could he handle anything more?

He cleared his throat. "I'm listening, Ivy. And I'm not going anywhere."

For a moment, tears threatened again. He watched as she blinked them back. Twisted her hands. Composed herself.

"Richard was ten years older than me," she said quietly. "A professor at my college. In the business department. I didn't have any classes with him, but we had met a time or two. When my parents were killed in a boating accident during the final semester of my senior year, it was Richard who kept tabs on my assignments and made sure I graduated."

"Why would he do that?"

She shrugged. "I thought at the time he was simply a nice person. I was drowning in grief. As an only child, I was utterly bereft. Richard made himself indispensable."

"And then what happened?"

"I've had some counseling in recent years," she said. "And read some books on the subject. I understand now that he used my vulnerability to groom me. It was all very gradual and unremarkable. I didn't even realize that he was carefully separating me from the few relatives who could have provided a link to my parents. It was the same with my classmates. If I thought about it, I concluded that my girlfriends and I had all drifted apart after graduation. Soon, Richard was the only constant in my world."

"He was a predator," Farrell said flatly, trying to keep his anger under control. Ivy didn't need that from him.

Her bottom lip trembled, but she didn't agree or disagree with him. "There were dinners and long conversations in his office," she said. "One day he kissed me. Four months after graduation, we were married."

"And then he started hitting you?" Farrell was incensed

on her behalf, but Ivy actually smiled. It was a heartbreaking smile, but it was a smile. "Richard's thing was control. He was obsessive about everything in his environment. Forget arguing about which way the toilet paper should unroll from the dispenser. Richard wanted the cabinets and the refrigerator organized daily. He expected me to accommodate his every whim. And I did," she said simply. "Because he had done so much for me."

"When did you first know something was wrong?"

"Two years after my parents died, their loss finally became manageable. It was like coming out of a fog for me. People say that grief is different for everyone, and that's true. When I started thinking about the future, I realized I was healing. I knew it was time to get a job."

"What was your major?"

"Early childhood education. I filled out applications and began interviewing with principals for positions in the fall. I didn't tell Richard, because I wanted to surprise him."

"Did you get hired?"

"I had callbacks for some follow-up interviews, but before that could happen, Richard found out. He was furious. Not simply irritated that I had initiated this step without consulting him, but completely berserk with rage. At first, I was confused. But when I had the temerity to defend myself, he backhanded me so hard I slammed into the wall."

"My God, Ivy." Farrell didn't know what to say. He felt ill.

"It only happened that one time. He apologized instantly. But he insisted that our family life would run more smoothly if I stayed at home. He said he made plenty of money for the two of us to live comfortably."

"As a college professor?"

"He had a second job. In fact, he traveled often for two and three days at a time. I wondered how his class load worked with his schedule, but I didn't ask. I learned early on that he didn't like explaining himself."

Farrell frowned. "So you didn't teach?"

"No. I convinced myself that I was overreacting. Of *course* he was hurt that I would hunt for a job without telling him. And I knew that some men were supermacho and liked supporting their wives. It wasn't the life I had planned for myself, but I told myself that all couples compromise."

"Only Richard wasn't compromising," Farrell said, wishing the guy was alive so he could beat the hell out of him.

Ivy sat suddenly in the chair opposite the sofa, as if her legs would no longer support her. She stared down at her hands for long seconds. Farrell knew better than to offer his analysis. This might be the only time Ivy would open up to him. If he inserted himself too much into her story, she would stop talking.

She seemed so small and fragile to him. He could only imagine what she had endured. A woman had to be very strong to come out of that situation and still be able to function.

"I've been so ashamed and embarrassed," she said, the words little more than a whisper.

He leaned forward, staring at her intently. "Why, Ivy? You're not to blame for anything."

Now she faced him bravely, her heart-shaped face, pointed chin and short haircut making her seem younger than her thirty-two years. "I didn't leave him," she said, her voice breaking. "I let three years go by. Then five, then six. He tracked my phone. He doled out my *allowance*. Because I wasn't allowed to get a job, I sneaked around and baked cakes and pies for the neighbors and squirreled away that money in a secret spot in the house."

"Because you knew you were going to leave eventually?"

"Maybe. Subconsciously. But first, I used it to see a counselor. With her help, I finally understood that the gratitude I felt he deserved for saving me after my parents died was a false equivalency. His original kindness was a means of subjugating me, so I didn't owe him anything."

"That must have been a bitter pill to swallow."

She nodded, her expression revealing relief. "I wasn't sure you would be able to understand. I felt so stupid and clueless. I'd let a borderline psychopath take over my life. During a year and a half of therapy I gradually saw the truth of what had happened to me. Harder still was learning to forgive myself."

"And then?"

"I told the therapist I wanted to leave him. She was concerned about my physical safety. I told her he had only hit me that one time. Still, he was clearly capable of violence."

Farrell knew there was worse to come. His stomach recoiled, but he kept his expression calm. "So did you leave or not?"

"He must have suspected. I did everything I could to act *normal*. But one night when he came home from a trip, he…" She stopped, swallowed hard and gave Farrell a look that hurt him to his core. "You don't need the details. But he sabotaged my birth control."

Eight

"Ivy…"

Farrell's look of compassion made her determined to show him she had survived. And thrived. "It was bad, but it convinced me the marriage was over."

"And then you left him?"

She shook her head, remembering the anguish she had felt. "I found out I was pregnant."

Before Farrell could respond to that, she glanced at the monitor in relief. "Dolly is awake," she said. "I should go get her."

She fled. There was no other word for it. In the study, she scooped up her perfect daughter and hugged her so tightly the baby protested.

"Sorry, love," Ivy said. Tears threatened, but no. She. Would. Not. Cry. Not now. The worst was over. Telling Farrell her story, or at least most of it, left her feeling like that awful dream where you're standing outside naked and you can't find your way home.

She was raw and exhausted but oddly calm.

Though it was cowardly, she sneaked out the side door of the house and made a beeline for the safety of her cabin. *Her* cabin. Already, it seemed like home. How long would Farrell want to work up here near the Canadian border? Two months? Three? What would Ivy do when he no longer needed her?

The baby's routine normalized the afternoon. Dolly had been crawling for some time now, but today, she was brave enough to reach for the edge of the sofa and pull up onto one knee.

"Careful, little munchkin. Don't get ahead of yourself." Would Dolly be walking by Christmas?

Thinking of the holidays was a mistake. Surely Farrell would go back to Portland for Christmas. Would he allow his housekeeper and her daughter to stay behind?

Ivy desperately wanted permanence for her child. Traditions. Continuity. The thought of staying here in the Maine woods during the winter was delightful. But without Farrell, everything would seem flat. Ivy had come to depend on his gentle good humor, his deep laugh, the sexy way his eyes crinkled when he smiled.

She cared about him.

While Dolly took her afternoon nap, Ivy made a batch of chocolate-chip cookies. She would take them to Farrell as a peace offering. Or a thank-you. Not many people wanted to hear what Ivy's life had been like. Fewer still offered to listen.

Farrell's presence as a quiet, compassionate sounding board had been cathartic. Though Ivy was desperately attracted to him, she wondered if the feeling was one-sided. There were moments when she thought *something* hovered between them. But that might be her overactive imagination.

It was mortifying to remember how she had shrunk away

from him when he tried to keep her from falling. Some atavistic instinct for survival had brought back old coping mechanisms.

She hadn't told Farrell the whole truth. Perhaps it wasn't important now.

Suddenly, she remembered the broken platter in the kitchen. She should have cleaned up that mess already. And now it was time to begin dinner.

After packaging the still-warm cookies, Ivy collected the baby and set out for the big house. When she entered the kitchen, it was spotless. Not a sign of broken pottery anywhere. The remaining platters sat out on the counter. Ivy paused long enough to text Katie the required information.

Then she set the cookies on the island and went in search of her boss. She wasn't a coward. She hadn't done anything wrong.

She found Farrell on the front porch replacing a section of the railing. He looked up when she stepped out of the house. Something pulsed between them. Awareness. Awkwardness. "I brought fresh cookies," she said, adjusting Dolly on her hip. "If you're hungry."

He stood and stretched. Ivy watched him, unable to look away. He was perfect. Tall. Strong. Intelligent. The muscles in his arms and shoulders were visible through his gray knit shirt.

The bottom fell out of her stomach, and her knees went shaky. She was more than attracted to him. She *wanted* him. The knowledge troubled her. Farrell Stone was the last man on earth she should set her sights on.

Farrell had lost so much, faced such devastating sadness. Ivy's emotional baggage was probably daunting for a man like him.

In the kitchen, they shared cookies and milk, their hands occasionally brushing as they passed a plate or reached for seconds. Ivy wondered if Farrell experienced the same sense of intimacy she did. Unfortunately, the vignette was *too* intimate, too perfect for Ivy's peace of mind.

To break the mood, she made herself open the pantry and peruse the choices for dinner.

Farrell spoke from behind her shoulder. "Forget fixing dinner," he said.

When she turned, puzzled, she caught him sneaking a fourth cookie, his expression guilt-ridden.

"A grown man can't live on sugar," she said as he licked chocolate from his fingertips. The way he was enjoying her baked offering pleased her.

"Not true," he said, grinning.

Her stomach quivered. Suddenly, she could see Farrell in bed with a woman, kissing his way from her belly to her—

Dear Lord... She slammed the pantry door and cleared her throat. "Well, I can't. What did you have in mind?"

"I ordered pizza," he said calmly.

"You're kidding me. Aren't we twenty miles from the nearest town with a pizza joint?"

"More like twenty-five. But it's amazing how the promise of a hundred-dollar tip motivates people."

"You didn't have to do that," she muttered, knowing he was thinking of her. "I could have fixed dinner."

He brushed the back of his hand over her hot cheek and took Dolly from her. "We could all use a junk-food night. It will be fun. And nothing to clean up. Am I right?"

His smile, though it wasn't at all suggestive, made her heart beat faster. "Pizza does sound good."

"I ordered three different kinds. Wasn't sure what you would like."

"Farrell..." She blurted out his name.

He glanced at her and froze. "What is it, Ivy?"

Her face must have revealed her agitation. "You don't

have to feel sorry for me," she said bluntly. "In fact, I don't want you to. I'm fine."

His narrow gaze made those green-and-gold irises burn bright. It was his turn to hesitate. But afterward, his jaw firmed as if he had decided that too much tiptoeing around the elephant in the room was a bad idea.

"Here's the thing, Ivy," he said. "Your emotionally fragile state is the only thing keeping me from kissing you, so I think it's best if I *do* feel sorry for you. At least for now. It's safer that way."

She gaped at him, her cheeks going hot. "You want to kiss me?"

"Yes," he said, tickling her daughter's tummy. "I do."

Farrell would have laughed at Ivy's startled expression had the situation been different. She stood frozen, trying to process what he had said. He could almost see the wheels turning in her head.

When she didn't come up with an answer, he leaned against the cabinet and put Dolly on his shoulders, letting her play with his hair. "Have I shocked you?" he asked.

"Um… I…" Still, Ivy stuttered.

"Why is that so hard to believe?"

"I'm not beautiful. Men like you and your brothers go out with beautiful women. It's a billionaire rule."

Her wry silliness amused him. "You *are* beautiful," he said. "Not in a runway-model way, perhaps. But you're something even better. You have an interesting face. A body that's so sexy it keeps me up at night, and a smile, although infrequent, that lights up a room. I find you utterly charming, Ivy Danby, and I'm not sure what to do about that."

The front doorbell rang, saving Ivy from having to respond. Farrell pulled a wad of cash out of his pocket. "Dolly and I will grab the pizza. Why don't you set the table?"

When he returned, balancing a squirmy baby and two very warm cardboard boxes, Ivy couldn't quite meet his eyes.

"Here," she said. "Let me take her."

In the handoff, Farrell's hand brushed the side of her chest. It wasn't deliberate. Even so, feeling the soft weight of her breast made him suck in a shocked breath.

Maybe he'd been attracted to her since that first day. Was it because she needed *saving*, and he liked being a hero? Or was the pull something more visceral?

They ate mostly in silence, except for Dolly, who jabbered constantly. The baby was a convenient third party, a place to center his attention. Ivy followed his example.

Why had he told Ivy he wanted to kiss her? Now that he'd said it, kissing her was all he could think about.

She was wearing her old clothes—soft faded jeans and a fleecy pullover in cinnamon. The color flattered her, made her skin glow. "Have another piece of pizza," he said. Ivy had eaten three to his six.

"No, thanks. I'm stuffed."

He combined the remaining slices into one box and put them in the fridge. Then he returned to the table, sat down and stared at her. "May I ask you something?"

Alarm flashed across her face. "Yes."

"Will you put the baby to sleep here? In the study? You and I didn't finish our conversation earlier. I'd like to hear the rest of your story."

"It's not important," she muttered. Her face had gone pale, her hazel-eyed gaze momentarily haunted.

If that had been the truth, perhaps he would have let it go. But he suspected Ivy needed to get the poison out of her system. Deprive her memories of their power.

He knew something about that process. Years ago, when he was finally able to let himself think of Sasha and not exert all his energy pretending those memories didn't exist, the healing had begun.

Ivy had suffered. She was still suffering. Maybe it wasn't his place to help her. But he was the only one around.

"Please," he said.

The silent standoff lasted for a minute or more as Ivy looked anywhere but at him. With a sigh, she stood and nodded. "I'll have to grab her pajamas and a couple other things."

"No problem. This little lady and I will entertain ourselves until you get back."

When Ivy left the kitchen, Farrell scooped the baby out of her high chair and carried her into his bedroom. "How would you like to play with a brand-new toothbrush?"

Ivy scurried around in the cabin, picking up everything she would need for Dolly's bedtime routine. Farrell didn't have a rocking chair, but Ivy could walk the floor and sing to her. That always worked.

She was only gone twenty-five minutes. When she returned, Farrell's kitchen was empty. She followed the sound of his voice and found her boss and her daughter on Farrell's giant king-size bed. Dolly was playing with a…toothbrush?

"Not to worry," Farrell said quickly. "It's fresh out of the wrapper."

The scene should have looked domestic. But it didn't, not entirely. Farrell *wasn't* the baby's daddy enjoying time at the end of the day with his offspring. Instead, he resembled a dangerous, lazy jungle cat sprawled on his side. A lock of hair tumbled across his forehead. Dolly had probably pulled on it. Hair torture was one of her favorite games.

Ivy stopped several paces from the bed. It was a huge four-poster. But not traditional. The wood was light, the design probably Amish or Shaker. The solid navy bedspread looked wildly expensive. She didn't get out much, but she had perused a lot of catalogs over the years. The only difference was, Farrell's bed didn't have a dozen fancy pillows. He wasn't the type to go for that kind of stuff.

Even without an allotment of extra shams and bolsters, everything in this master suite screamed wealth and sophistication. When she cleaned his bathroom each week, she was struck by the fact that it offered every possible luxurious amenity. From heated floors and heated towel racks to the hedonistic shower, this was a rich man's world.

She cleared her throat. "I'll take her now."

Farrell smiled. "If you must. She has a lot of personality for such a little person."

Ivy managed to snag Dolly without getting too close to the jungle cat. "She really does. Some days I wish she wouldn't grow up so fast."

"Why don't you meet me in the living room when you're done?"

It was phrased politely, but he had asked her to finish her life story, and Ivy had agreed. Why had she said yes?

As she changed Dolly into her pajamas and sang to her, Ivy found herself unsettled. This familiar nighttime routine was as much for mother as daughter. Tonight, there was no calm to be had.

When Dolly was asleep, Ivy tiptoed out of the study and stopped by the hall bathroom to freshen up. She could have changed into one of her new outfits, but those were for the house party. And besides, she didn't want Farrell to think she was primping for him.

She still didn't believe he wanted to kiss her. He'd probably said that to bolster her self-esteem. It was kind of him, but not very believable. She would bet a lot of money that he was still in love with his dead wife.

When she finally made her way into the living room, it was completely dark outside. A front had moved through in the last hour, bringing a drizzling rain and dropping temps into the low sixties. Farrell had built a fire that crackled and popped with warmth and cheer.

The overhead lights were off, but several lamps burned around the room. He had pulled two armchairs in front of the blaze. A bottle of wine and two glasses sat on the small table in between.

Farrell looked up when she entered the room. "Is she asleep?"

"Completely. I know how lucky I am that she's an easy baby."

"True. We have employees at Stone River Outdoors who come back from maternity leave or family leave looking haggard. No sleep for nights on end. It must be rough."

Ivy sat down in one of the plush, comfy armchairs and sighed. She kicked off her shoes and curled her legs beneath her. "I know. Particularly if you're the kind of person who needs a full eight hours."

Farrell laughed and joined her by the fire. "I'd say we all *need* it, but very few people I know manage to make it happen."

"May I ask you a personal question?" she said.

Something flickered across his face, but he nodded. "Sure."

"Why did you build such a big house for just you? I know you entertain, but was that the only reason?"

Farrell stared at the fire, his jaw carved in stone. She saw his shoulders lift and fall, and he scooted deeper into his chair. "Sasha wanted it," he said, the words barely audible. "We planned to have lots of kids. She was a good amateur artist. One day when she was sick, she drew this exact house. Then made a joke. Said if she didn't make it, I should build the house anyway."

"She wasn't serious?"

"No. It was only a way for her to entertain herself when days were bad. But it was always only the outside of the house she drew. She said a view of the ocean like this one deserved a worthy house on the cliff. After she died, I built it. Closure, I guess." He shrugged. "I like to think she knows."

Ivy's throat tightened, and tears stung her eyes. She couldn't imagine being loved like that. "I'm sorry if my question made you sad," she croaked. "I was curious."

"I'm fine. It was a long time ago."

Nine

The silence between them now was awkward. Farrell blamed himself. Why did he have to bring Sasha into the conversation? Ivy never would have known the difference. All Farrell had to say was that he wanted a large space for entertaining.

Maybe he was summoning Sasha's ghost to prevent himself from doing something stupid.

"Would you like wine?" He blurted it out, feeling alarmingly off-balance. With the chilly weather and the cozy setup he had created, this suddenly looked like more than it was.

"Yes," Ivy said.

He uncorked the bottle of Syrah and poured two glasses. "Cheers," he said, as he handed Ivy her drink.

With her nose scrunched up, she tasted it cautiously. "I'm not much of a red wine aficionado," she admitted. "Tell me about it. I'm guessing this one's expensive?"

"It comes from the Rhône Valley in France. I've seen

certain bottles go for upwards of four thousand dollars, but the vintage we're drinking is far more modest. What word would you use to describe it? Your first reaction..."

Ivy took another sip. "It's bold," she said. "Full-bodied. And I think I taste blueberries. Am I right?"

He lifted his glass. "Spot-on. But don't feel like you have to finish the glass. I won't be offended."

"It's very good," she said. "I seldom drink, though. I'll sip it, if you don't mind."

"Whatever you want. When our international guests are here, we'll have a wide variety of wines available. You can try them to your heart's content."

After that, the awkward silence came back.

Farrell drained his wine and poured himself another glass. "When Dolly woke up from her morning nap, you left me hanging," he said, keeping his tone light. "You wanted to leave your husband, but you found out you were pregnant. What happened next?"

Ivy shot him a sideways glance that could have meant anything. She set her half-empty glass on the table and rested her arms on the chair. But he noticed that her fingers clenched the upholstery.

"I know he did it on purpose," she said. "He thought if he got me pregnant, I wouldn't leave."

"Why would he believe that?"

"Because he knew how important family was to me. I missed my parents desperately after their deaths. Richard thought I would want my child to know his or her father."

"And did you?"

"Perhaps. But only for a moment. I became convinced that he would control our baby's life as he had mine, and that's when I knew I had to follow through with my original plan."

"So what did you do?"

Ivy stood abruptly and took a position in front of the fire, warming her hands. When she turned back to face him, her expression was tight with remembered struggle. "I hadn't counted on morning sickness. Brutal. Unrelenting. I lost eighteen pounds before I began to gain anything. I was so scared I would lose the baby. I threw up several times a day, and when I wasn't throwing up, I was so miserable all I could do was curl up in bed and sleep."

"And your husband?"

Her laugh was bleak. "He started traveling again. Two and three nights at a time. I barely had enough strength to force myself to eat. He knew there was no way I could summon enough energy to pack up and leave him. Unfortunately, he was right. And with every hour I stayed, I felt more like a failure. My daughter hadn't even been born yet, and already I was placing her in danger."

"You're too hard on yourself," he said. "You made it day to day. That's a lot."

"I suppose."

"Was childbirth as bad as the pregnancy?"

"Thankfully, no. Apparently I have good childbearing hips." She chuckled quietly. "I was happy in the hospital. Everyone was so kind. And I had Dolly. She was this perfect little miracle. I prayed every day that Richard's DNA wouldn't harm her."

"Or worse. How did he respond to becoming a father?"

"It was very odd. Almost as if he didn't care. *I* was the one he wanted to control. Dolly was a peripheral in his life. He ignored her mostly."

Farrell wanted to stop right there. Ivy was fine. The baby was fine. And the husband was uninterested. It was a good place to end the story. But that didn't explain how Ivy ended up back in Portland, broke and alone.

He could almost see the toll it was taking on her to tell this story. Had she ever shared it with anyone? Unlike Farrell, Ivy's dark days were relatively recent. Was he helping her or hurting her by asking for the whole sordid tale? He honestly didn't know.

"Was your husband at the house when you came home from the hospital?" Farrell asked. "Or did he pick you up?"

Ivy shook her head slowly. "Neither. He'd left an envelope in my hospital room with just enough taxi fare for me to get home. That was typical. He didn't let me have a job, and he never gave me more than what was needed for a particular purchase. He often checked the grocery receipts."

"Wait a minute," Farrell said. "Even I know that hospitals won't let you go home unless a car seat has already been installed."

"That was another indignity. They made me meet with a social worker. She asked all kinds of awkward questions. In retrospect, I might have been able to enlist her help in leaving Richard, but I had just given birth. I was exhausted and weak, and struggling to breastfeed. The timing wasn't right. Or at least that's what I told myself. I lied to the woman. Told her a friend was picking me up. With a car seat."

"But you actually went home in a taxi."

"Yes. I was lucky in one way. Over the years, I had been getting to know my neighbors on the sly. Because of that, some of them brought me meals and baby presents, including small amounts of cash. I was so touched. Richard did his best, always, to isolate me. But because he traveled, I had managed to make a few friends. Acquaintances really, but good people. I had to hide the gifts, of course. Richard came home when Dolly was one week old."

"Surely he bonded with her then. His own flesh and blood?"

"No. He complained if she cried. He insisted that I prepare his meals and do the usual chores. And then, I think, he realized that I was getting better every day. Recovering. Learning to handle the baby on my own."

"He felt threatened…"

"I think so. He must have sensed that my plans to leave—the ones he had destroyed almost a year before by getting me pregnant—were about to be resurrected. The atmosphere in the house was tense. I tried not to let Dolly know. When I was with her, I concentrated on being calm, focused."

Farrell held his breath. Ivy's story had slowed. It was as if every word had to be forced from her throat. He stood to join her by the fire. "You don't have to say anything else, Ivy. I never meant to cause you pain. I was arrogant enough to think you should bare your soul to me. Because it would help. But instead, it's tearing you apart. I can see it on your face."

Her small smile was curiously sweet. "Your instincts were good, Farrell. And I appreciate the fact that you understand grief and loss. This thing that happened to me is part of who I am. I can't forget it. Telling you is no worse than what I dream about at night." She paused. "I'm not the woman I was before I left him. I've learned to trust my instincts. Fear doesn't control my life anymore. Being here in Maine with you has brought me peace and healing. This is more than a job for me. It's a new beginning."

He brushed her cheek with the back of his hand, barely a touch at all. "I'm in awe of your resiliency. You actually walked away. With a brand-new baby."

"Not exactly."

"Oh?"

Her bottom lip trembled. "New mothers aren't supposed to have intimate relations until their six-week postpartum checkup. Richard forced himself on me. After that, I developed a terrible infection. Had to be hospitalized. My milk dried up, because I was too ill to pump."

Farrell couldn't bear it. He pulled her into his arms and held her. That was all. Simply held her. His body registered the fact that a desirable woman was pressed up against him. But he was in control.

"My God, Ivy. It's a miracle you're even standing here with me."

She rested her cheek against his chest. He felt the shudder that racked her. "I know. They told me I could have died. Dolly was the reason I pulled through and went home."

He stroked her hair, sifting his fingers through the short, fluffy strands. "Who cared for Dolly while you were in the hospital?"

"I don't know." Her voice cracked. "He wouldn't tell me. I have no idea if she was happy or sad or hungry or inconsolable. I left her with him, because I had no other choice. Knowing that has eaten away at me."

"Look at her, Ivy. She's perfect. Whatever happened or didn't happen hasn't had a lasting effect. I've never seen a happier baby."

She sniffed, swiping her wet cheeks with one hand. "Thank you for saying that."

He pulled the hem of his shirt from his pants and dabbed her face. "So when you were well, you left him."

Ivy pulled back and looked up at him. Her long eyelashes were wet and spiky, but her color had returned. "You keep trying," she said, with a tiny grin. "But you haven't gotten it right yet."

"What? What happened?"

She played with a button on his shirt. "Ten days after I got out of the hospital, Richard had a massive heart attack. The one they call the widow-maker. The EMTs said he was dead before he hit the ground."

"Jesus, Ivy…" He was incredulous and horrified. "So that was what? Five? Six months ago?" He'd done some quick math with the baby's age.

"Five and a half. I used the credit cards I found in his wallet. Paid for a private funeral. I had no idea who to notify, so it was just me and Dolly. When it was all over, I felt guilty, but overwhelmingly relieved. He couldn't do anything to hurt me ever again."

"Thank God."

"I began cleaning out the house so I could sell it. Nothing but bad memories lingered in that place. I didn't want to raise my baby there."

"How was the market?"

"The sale went through quickly. Dolly and I moved to a nice apartment near the university. I bought a stroller. We began going for walks in the afternoon. I knew I would have to get a job, but I wanted just a little more time with my baby first."

"Was there life insurance?"

"Yes, but not for me. As it turned out, Richard hadn't been traveling for work at all. Richard had been living under an assumed name in a town fifty miles away. He had another wife and two older children."

"Holy hell." This was a damn soap opera, and not a good one.

"The *other woman* knew nothing about me and vice versa. When her 'husband' disappeared, she hired a private investigator who eventually found the trail. And found me, of course."

"I don't know what to say."

"*Everything* ultimately went to her. Richard had a very basic will, with the other woman listed as beneficiary. They took all I had. Checking accounts, savings accounts, the credit cards, the proceeds from the sale of the house. Everything. The woman even demanded I pay back what I spent on the funeral and my living expenses in the meantime, but a judge intervened. He gave me five thousand dollars because he saw me as the innocent victim."

"Then how did you get back to Portland?"

"I mentioned to you that I had been subscribing to the

Portland newspaper online for a long time. It made me feel closer to home, closer to the happy days of my childhood. Katie's sister placed an ad for a roommate. I saw it, and that was that. I bought an airline ticket and headed north. With only that small pot of money, I knew I had to make it last."

"Is that all?"

A tiny frown drew her brows together. "Yes. Isn't that enough?"

The hint of indignation made him smile. He lifted her chin, stared deep into her eyes. So much heart, so much everything. "You are the most amazing woman I've ever met, Ivy Danby. Incredibly strong. Resourceful. You've been bent, but not broken."

What happened next was not something he chose consciously. But no force on earth could have kept him from expressing what he felt…what her story had done to him.

He kissed her gently, trying to convey his utter admiration.

But from the start, the kiss was never in that column.

When their lips met, Ivy gasped. Or maybe it was him. Didn't matter. Their souls connected for a moment. He'd told this woman things about Sasha that he'd never shared with another person. And by her own admission, Ivy hadn't had any confidants up until now.

Their shared tragedies had burned through several layers of social niceties and demolished a host of steps couples usually navigate in a relationship. Suddenly, they were deeply involved.

How had it happened? Farrell groaned her name and started to pull away, a knee-jerk reaction to his fear of intimacy. When Ivy leaned in and kept the kiss connected, her innocent pleasure seduced him. He was swept along by a dangerous current.

Like a calm ocean that conceals the treacherous undertow below, Ivy hadn't seemed a threat at all, until now. Abstinence wasn't the only explanation for Farrell's desperate hunger. He wanted *her*. Not just any woman. Her. Ivy had sneaked her way into his heart when he wasn't looking.

Damn it, he was lost. He cupped her face in shaking hands and tried to rein in his desire to gobble her whole. Her life story had made him angry and hurt on her behalf and utterly determined to show her how wonderful she was.

He took the kiss deeper, one heartbeat at a time. Always waiting to see if Ivy was with him. Her slender arms curled around his neck and clung. Her modest breasts pressed up against him, even as his hands settled on her hips and dragged her closer.

His erection was hard and urgent. He ached to fill her and please her and give them both what they so desperately needed. There was a sofa nearby. Hell, his bed was only a few steps down the hall.

"Ivy," he groaned. "I want you."

"I want you, too, Farrell," she whispered.

She kissed his chin, his nose, his eyebrows. Finally, she found his lips again. Her shy attempt at taking the lead twisted his heart and cracked it a little bit. When her tongue slid into his mouth and mimicked the kiss he had given her moments ago, his knees threatened to buckle.

"Wait," he said hoarsely, trying to regain control of the situation. "I never meant for this to happen."

Ivy jerked backward, almost stumbling. The stricken look in her eyes when he said those seven words made him hear how his protest might have sounded to her.

"I do want you," he said urgently. "But we have to be sure. And you have to understand the ground rules."

For the first time, she didn't look young and innocent. In her hazel eyes, he saw evidence of every time she had been struck down by life. He witnessed her resignation and her cynical acceptance of reality.

"No, Farrell," she said. "*You're* the one who has to understand. I gave up believing in fairy tales a long time ago. Farrell Stone is the prince in the castle, and I'm the girl down in the cinders trying to survive." She paused, her chest heaving. "Whatever *this* is…" She waved a dismissive hand. "I have no illusions. Am I interested in sleeping with you? Yes, damn skippy I am. But you don't have to worry. All I care about in this life is my daughter and her happiness. I don't need a man to coddle me or to protect me. My bogeyman is dead. So sleep with me or don't sleep with me. But do me the courtesy of understanding that I'm not a naive little kid. I know the score. I always have."

"That's quite a speech." Tension wrapped bands of pain around his head. Nothing about this was easy.

Ivy shrugged. "I believe in plain speaking."

"Then how's this?" he said, his jaw tight. "I want you, but I don't want to want you."

She flinched. Which made him feel like the worst kind of scum. Her chin lifted, and with careful dignity, she faced him down. "I know that, Farrell. You're still in love with your dead wife."

He wasn't. Not anymore. At least not in the way Ivy meant. But perhaps it was better for both of them if he let the lie stand.

While he struggled for a response, Ivy stared at him, gaze bleak. Then she turned and walked away. "It's time for me to take Dolly back to the cabin," she said over her shoulder. "Good night, Farrell. Thanks for the wine and the listening ear."

Ten

Ivy had never experienced such a wide range of emotions in such a short amount of time. Telling Farrell about Richard had been difficult. Extremely so. Because she still bore the shame and guilt about her part in losing a decade of her life.

But that was nothing compared to the exhilaration of being kissed wildly by Farrell Stone and then being condescended to as if she were some silly teenager begging for scraps of his affection.

She heard him on her heels and walked faster.

"Wait, Ivy. Wait, damn it."

She whirled to face him. "I don't need you fighting my battles or feeling responsible for me. The fight is over. I don't need you period." She glared at him. "Well, yes, for sex. But I can find anybody for that."

His eyes burned brightly. His lips pressed together in a menacing seam. "It's raining," he said. "I'll escort you and Dolly back to the cabin."

"Escort?" She gave him a derisive look. "What is this? 1840? I'm perfectly capable of getting wet in the rain."

Farrell took her wrist and pulled her close. The heat radiating from his body made her breathless. "I'm imagining it right now," he said, the words gravelly. Intense. "White skin. Raspberry nipples. Small, perfect breasts that fit in my hands."

The words mesmerized her. Heat pooled in her belly. Her knees pressed together involuntarily. "Stop it," she stuttered.

"Stop what?" He tangled his hands in her hair and brought his mouth down on hers. "Forget everything I said," he groaned. "This is all we need to talk about. And frankly, talking is overrated."

The kiss was deep and thorough. Ivy melted into him. Mortifyingly so. Where was her pride and her self-respect? She should slap his face.

But Farrell was so close and so perfectly masculine. And so gratifyingly hungry. His hands roved over her body, raising gooseflesh despite the warmth of the house. She wanted to jump into his arms and wrap her legs around his waist. Heat shot through her veins, dizzying and painful.

If he let her go, she would beg. She knew it.

But Farrell showed no signs of ending the kiss. He nipped the side of her neck with sharp teeth. Bit gently on her earlobe. Thrust one of his legs between hers.

They were both fully dressed. Her virtue was as safe as a nun's, at the moment. But holy hannah, she wanted him.

He was breathing hard when he finally released her. "I don't want to fight," he said, the words gruff.

She raised an eyebrow. "In other words, make love, not war?"

"It worked for an entire generation. Who are we to scoff?"

"Be honest," she said. "Did you ask me to sleep at your house during the retreat so we can have sex?"

"God, no." He stared at her, clearly outraged. "Why would I seduce you with a dozen people around?"

"Oh," she said, deflated. "I didn't think of it that way."

"I asked you for two reasons. I do need an official hostess, and I thought that you, as an outsider, could give me your perspective on how we present the company to our guests. I hoped the weekend would be fun for you, but that was a side benefit."

"Okay. I apologize."

"Go get the baby," he said. "We'll finish this at the cabin."

We'll finish this at the cabin.

Ivy parsed Farrell's enigmatic words as she gathered up the baby's belongings. Did he mean finish the conversation or finish this other thing they'd started?

Dolly was not happy about having her slumber interrupted. She was a warm lump in the port-a-crib. Ivy patted her back. "C'mon, love. I'll let you go back to sleep in just a minute." Ivy picked up her daughter and soothed her as she fussed. It was a bit late to realize that Ivy should have put on her own jacket first.

Oh, well. She wasn't going to freeze in such a short distance. But Dolly definitely needed to be wrapped up in a blanket.

Ivy met Farrell in the hall. "How hard is it raining?"

"Pretty hard. Let me carry her, so you can use an umbrella."

She clutched the baby. "You don't have to go with me."

His broad grin was unexpected. And it cut the sand from under her feet. "I'd like to, Ivy. If you don't object."

"It's your cabin."

He kissed her forehead. "But it's your home, and I won't intrude without an invitation."

Well, crud. Farrell was being a perfect gentleman. Ivy wasn't going to be able to call him out for pressuring her. "You're invited," she muttered.

His gaze heated, and a slash of red colored his cheekbones. "Thank you, Ivy. I accept."

In the mudroom, they donned rubber boots and rain slickers. The light rain from earlier had turned into a monsoon. "Watch your feet as we go," Farrell said. "Here. Let me have her."

When they opened the door, the wind blew in, bringing the scent of autumn rain and wet earth. The wild weather echoed the upheaval in Ivy's emotions. She stepped out into the black night...

Farrell was having fun. Traipsing through the driving rain with Dolly tucked up against his chest made him feel alive. Though he had long since recovered from losing Sasha, he realized in this moment that he seldom let himself do anything simply for *fun*.

Had he become a stuffy, nose-to-the-grindstone kind of guy? Did his brothers and his employees merely tolerate him? Did they roll their eyes behind his back and wish he would lighten up?

At the cabin, Ivy fumbled with the lock, opened the door and stripped out of her rain gear. "I'll put her to bed," she said. "You dry off. We should have both had umbrellas."

He handed over the baby. "I didn't trust myself to hold her one-handed. I'm not going to melt."

Ivy searched his face. For a moment, he thought she was about to say something. But she didn't. She simply left him standing in his wet clothes, feeling as if his world was tumbling around him.

When she was gone, he kicked off his shoes. Even his

socks were soaked. The rain slicker had kept him mostly dry, but the bottoms of his pants legs were damp. What sounded good right now was a hot drink.

He was still rummaging in the cabinets when Ivy showed up in the kitchen. "Do you have any of those tiny marshmallows?" he asked. "I've made some hot chocolate."

"You're in luck," Ivy said. She opened a cabinet he hadn't gotten to yet and tossed him a plastic bag. "This Mrs. Peterson person who stocked the kitchen must know you Stone brothers well."

"She knows Quin. I suppose she may have picked up a few things about the rest of us." He poured two mugs of frothy hot cocoa and dumped a handful of marshmallows in his. "You want some?"

"Cocoa, yes. But I'll pass on the marshmallows."

"You're missing out," he teased.

"Okay, fine. Give me five."

"Five? Not four? Not six?"

"Too much sugar is bad for you."

Farrell eyed her thin frame. "An occasional indulgence is a good thing," he said mildly. "Makes life worth living."

He carried the mugs to the table and waved at her to sit down. Cradling the drink in his hands, he leaned forward and took a sip. He jerked back, muttering a word that made Ivy give him a pointed stare.

"You burned your mouth, didn't you?" she said.

"Maybe." He looked her over from her tousled hair to her hazel eyes to her soft, unpainted lips. "Quin's the impulsive one in the family, but I can take chances, too."

Ivy blinked as her face flushed from her throat to her hairline. "Is that what I represent to you? Taking a chance? That's not very flattering."

Farrell had attended upscale parties where scantily-clad runway models mingled with the crowd. Never once had he felt for any of those women the need to persuade. To possess. To conquer.

Yet with Ivy, he knew all those urges. "I don't know what this is," he admitted. "Do we have to name it? Analyze it?"

She sipped her drink carefully, and when she set down her cup, she had a rim of marshmallow residue around her lips.

Before Farrell could think it through, he leaned forward and licked away the sweetness. "You're welcome," he said huskily.

Her eyes widened. "I didn't understand you at first. I thought you were a serious scientist devoted to his work. But you're really a renegade, aren't you? A hedonist. A rascal."

Farrell gave her a lazy smile. "Isn't it possible to be all those things? Can't I want to sleep with a fascinating woman in my spare time?"

She reached out and covered one of his hands with hers. Her smile was shy. "I hope there won't be *much* sleeping involved. Surely we can do better than that."

His heart rate jumped. He twined his fingers with hers. "Don't toy with me, woman. I need an unambiguous answer. Do you want to go to bed with me? Here? Tonight?"

"I do. Rainy nights always make my imagination run wild. But we'd better get a move on, because you-know-who wakes up early."

Farrell followed her into the bedroom. He was as hard as his surname already, and he wondered if he had it in him to be gentle with her. But he must. Ivy had known too much male aggression in her short life.

As they stood beside the bed, he saw her confidence falter.

"Don't be afraid of me, Ivy."

"I'm not." She gnawed her lower lip. "I'm afraid you'll

be disappointed in *me*. Richard messed up my head. I have a million hang-ups about my body. And I haven't ever…"

She trailed off, her expression anxious.

Farrell took her hand. "You haven't had sex with anyone other than your husband?"

"No." The single syllable encompassed misery and embarrassment.

"Then here are the ground rules," he said. "It's only the two of us in this room. No Sasha. No Richard. No painful past to bother us. Whatever happens between you and me is because we want each other. I plan to lose myself in making love to you, Ivy. I hope you'll do the same."

She searched his face, as if looking for evidence of his sincerity. At last, she smiled. "Okay."

Despite her whispered agreement, she flinched when he started pulling her top over her head. Though that tiny response bothered him, he kept his motions measured and careful as he undressed her. When she was completely naked, he threw back the covers.

"Get in and stay warm, Ivy."

"But shouldn't I…?"

He followed her train of thought easily. "I'll handle it this time."

When he made it down to his boxer briefs and stepped out of them, Ivy's eyes widened. She stared at his erect sex with a rapt expression that did wonders for his ego. Unlike many women, Ivy didn't try to be something she wasn't. She was like a baby swan, all small and fluffy and vulnerable to the dangers in the world.

"Scoot over," he said. "I promise to keep you warm."

Ivy curled up against his naked body immediately. He took that as a good sign. She sighed deeply. "This is nice."

He choked out a laugh, aching with arousal. But he was determined to back-burner his libido if it meant pleasing Ivy. "More than nice," he said gruffly. He ran his hands over her smooth ass. "You feel so good, Ivy. I've been fantasizing about this."

She rose up on one elbow and stared at him in shock. "You have?"

"Of course. Men do that, you know."

"Women, too." She wrinkled her nose. "But you never once let on. Why not?"

"I wasn't sure it was appropriate. You work for me. I didn't want to take advantage of you." He hesitated. "To be honest, I still feel guilty."

"Don't be absurd." She snuggled into his chest again, patting his collarbone. "This job you gave me is temporary. We both know that. When the time is right, you'll go back to headquarters at Stone River Outdoors, and I'll return to Portland to look for another position. It's all good, Farrell. Besides, didn't we agree to focus on this room, this bed, this night?"

He kissed the top of her head. "You're right. We did."

"May I ask you something?"

Because he couldn't see her face, he wasn't able to analyze the odd note in her voice. "Anything," he said.

"I'd like to explore your body." She touched his nipple as if to clarify. "I want to learn what you like. What you want. Is that okay?"

Farrell didn't know whether to laugh or cry. Ivy's guileless request sent hot arousal coursing through his veins, searing him from the inside out. Could he handle Ivy's fairly inexperienced experiment? Did she not understand the power she held?

"Absolutely," he lied. "I'm all yours."

She began by kneeling at his side. Her breasts were small but perfect. When he tried to touch her, Ivy protested. "None of that. Put your hands behind your neck."

Already, his arousal was at fever pitch. But he obeyed. "Be gentle with me," he begged, not entirely joking.

"I love your body," she said softly. "It's so different from mine." She traced the shell of his ear, tugging at the lobe. When she leaned over and put both hands on his collarbone, he trembled. Her breath was warm on his cheek.

The look of fierce concentration on her face charmed and seduced him. She was so damn cute, so damn precious.

He bit his lip to keep from groaning aloud when she ran a fingertip down his sternum. His hip bones were the next stop on her erotic route. Then she scooted over between his legs, spreading his thighs, getting comfortable. His body went on high alert.

At first, she only looked. No physical contact. The fact that his sex was fully erect and oozing fluid seemed to enthrall her. She collected the drop of liquid on her fingertip and touched his lips. "Do you know what you taste like?"

She was destroying him. "No," he croaked. "Do you?"

"I'm about to."

When she took him in her mouth, he shook as if he had a terrible jungle fever. Though she was ostensibly in control, her innocent delight in learning his physical attributes made him snap.

With a muffled cry, he came, embarrassing himself and surprising Ivy. She wiped her mouth and sat back, her eyes wide. "Are you okay?"

He could feel his face turn blood red. "Damn, Ivy. I'm sorry. You make me lose control."

A frown settled between her brows. "I don't believe you."

He reared up, weight on his elbows behind him, and glared. "I'm a grown-ass man of thirty-two. I haven't jumped the gun like that since I was a teenager. You arouse me, Ivy. Don't you understand?"

She moved off the bed and grabbed a robe. When she had tied the sash so tightly even Houdini couldn't get into it, she backed up against the dresser. "You should go clean up. There are spare towels in the bathroom cabinet."

Just to annoy her, Farrell climbed out of bed and faced her, buck naked. He would bet a hundred dollars she wanted to look away, but his Ivy was a brave woman.

He stalked her, grinning. "Do you like what you see?" Already, his erection was being reborn. When Ivy noticed, her eyes widened.

"You're a nice-looking man," she said primly. "I won't dispute that."

"But?"

"You're arrogant. And bossy. And I'm not sure I want to have sex with you anymore."

"Oh, really," he drawled. "I think you're lying."

Her affronted expression was priceless. "And I think you're an oversexed Neanderthal."

"Don't move," he said.

One quick trip to the bathroom, and he was ready to pick up where they'd left off.

When he returned to the bedroom, Ivy still huddled in her terry-cloth armor. She apparently had too much pride to let him think she was scared. Which suited Farrell just fine.

He pulled her into his arms and kissed her roughly. "Last chance, Ivy Danby. It's my turn now. Do you want me or not?"

Eleven

Ivy was still stunned. Had she really aroused Farrell Stone to the point he lost control? That was what he wanted her to believe. Still, it seemed improbable.

When he wrapped his arms around her and kissed her as if she were his last chance at life, her knees went weak. Hot male flesh, lightly dusted with hair, felt alien against her smooth skin. Alien and delicious.

Farrell's body was a wonder. As a man in his prime, he had serious muscles and a body that was honed by hard physical labor. Though he had the funds to hire a hundred laborers, she had often seen him tackling demanding jobs outside the house.

He tugged a lock of her hair. "I asked you a question, Ivy."

"Keeping on kissing me," she begged.

"Not until you admit you want me." He made her yelp when he slid a hand between her thighs and entered her with two fingers.

Farrell groaned. "You're wet and hot, my sweet. Your body doesn't lie. But I need the words."

It was Ivy's turn to hover on the brink of orgasm. She shivered and ached and yearned for him to take her. "Please make love to me, Farrell. I want you. I want you to—"

He put his hand over her mouth, his laugh more of a strangled wheeze. "I'll take it from here, sweetheart."

Tackling the knot on her robe took longer than it should. But at last he had her naked again. Scooping her up in his arms, he managed the two steps to the bed and tumbled them both onto the mattress.

Ivy's skin was chilled. He pulled the covers over them and nuzzled her neck. He could think of a million and one ways he wanted to pleasure her, but those would have to wait. Tonight, missionary style needed to be enough. He didn't want to overwhelm her. He sensed that sharing a bed with him was a huge step for Ivy. He would do nothing to make her regret it.

Beneath the sheets, he found the flat plane of her belly with his right hand. Dipping lower, he touched her center and lightly stroked her clitoris. Ivy's keening moan raised gooseflesh on his body.

Incredibly, he felt his body yanking at the reins, racing toward the finish line again. Suddenly, he remembered what he had forgotten. *Hell.*

He rested his forehead on her belly, his lungs gasping for air. "I'm sorry, Ivy. I forgot the condom. It's in my pants pocket."

She opened her eyes, her gaze hazy. "Hurry."

The single feminine demand galvanized him. Moments later, he was back, pausing only to take care of protecting her. Then he picked up where he had left off. Her sex was swollen, entirely ready for him.

Yet, oddly, he needed reassurance. He scooted up beside her and drew her closer for a desperate kiss. "Are you ready, Ivy? I want this to be good for you, for us."

She kissed him back, one arm curled around his neck. "If you make me wait one second longer, I swear I'll poison your pancakes."

Her humor in the midst of his own sexual desperation made him gape, then chuckle breathlessly. She was incredible.

Calling on all the control he could muster, he moved between her legs and positioned the head of his shaft at her entrance. Though she arched and scratched and pleaded, he took her slowly, inch by inch, increasing the torment for both of them. At last, he was all the way in, his sex wrapped tightly in her feminine heat.

He could feel her heartbeat when he kissed the side of her neck. Shuddering, he pressed his cheek to hers. "You have a beautiful, perfect body, Ivy. Made for my pleasure and yours. Don't ever forget that."

Perhaps he still saw doubt in her eyes. She didn't answer.

So it was up to him to prove it. He twisted her nipple gently. A rosy flush bathed her face. Her skin was damp and warm, her body limber and responsive in his embrace.

When he scraped the furled nub with his fingernail, her pupils dilated. Her chest rose and fell rapidly. "Farrell..."

The drowsy pleasure he heard in those two syllables squeezed his chest, filled him with elation.

He moved then, one strong thrust, then another. Ivy cried out his name and arched into him. Small hands clutched his shoulders. Sharp fingernails scored his skin. Her climax went on and on as he reached between them and gave her added stimulation.

When he was sure she had wrung every drop of pleasure from her release, he let himself pound into her, blind with hunger, lost to reason.

In the end, he lost a piece of himself into her keeping. It

terrified him, but there was no way to get it back. Ivy had stolen his obstinate refusal to live fully. Or maybe he had offered her his true self as a gift. Possibly the exchange had been unintentional on both their parts.

But the deed was done.

He closed his eyes and slept.

Ivy came awake in the dark, searching for what had awakened her. Automatically, she glanced at the baby monitor. But Dolly was sleeping peacefully. Then understanding dawned. The noise that had roused her was a gentle snore from the large man at her side.

She gulped and closed her eyes, trying to pretend she hadn't invited Farrell Stone into her bed. She might as well have coaxed a shark into the kiddie pool.

What had she done?

Lightly, she stroked his forehead, tucking aside the lock of hair that tumbled onto his brow. Moments later, the piece of hair was down again. In his sleep, he looked no less masculine, but far more approachable.

A heavy arm pinned her to the mattress, holding her just below her breasts. One of her legs was tucked between his. They were entwined like longtime lovers, not participants in a one-night stand.

Surely this was nothing more than that. Ivy had been lonely and hungry for physical contact. Farrell had needed to break his sexual fast.

She shouldn't make too much of this. But oh, how she loved having him to herself so intimately. His scent, a combination of warm male skin and something crisp and woodsy, marked her sheets.

Maybe she shouldn't wash them.

The clock read four thirty. She had at least another hour and a half before Dolly awoke. Carefully, she slipped from Farrell's embrace and made a quick trip to the bathroom.

When she returned, her lover was half-awake, frowning that she was gone.

"Come back to bed," he demanded, the words husky.

"I was planning on it." He was a bossy man, for sure. But since their plans aligned at the moment, she wouldn't complain.

She dropped her robe on the floor and lifted the covers. As she climbed in, Farrell made a noise that sounded suspiciously like a growl. He dragged her under him, bit the side of her neck and paused only to ask, "More, Ivy?"

"Yes," she sighed. "Oh, yes."

The next time Ivy roused, it really was Dolly who interrupted her sleep. The alarm hadn't gone off, but on the monitor, she could hear her daughter's little morning noises.

Ivy stretched, feeling groggy and sated. When she turned to the other side of the bed, she found the sheets cold and empty. But there was a note. Brief and impersonal, but a note.

Dear Ivy,
I need to get to the lab. Don't worry about breakfast.
I grabbed a banana from your kitchen.

Later, Farrell...

She frowned. *Later, Farrell?* What did that even mean? Her experience with "the morning after" was admittedly limited, but his blunt note wasn't exactly the stuff of romantic movies.

Then again, she and Farrell had been pretty clear about their expectations. He needed and wanted sex. Ivy had needed and wanted to feel normal again. Having sex with a man like Farrell meant she truly was healing.

Well, mission accomplished for both of them. No reason to feel sad or let down. Today was no different from yesterday. Life went on.

She would ignore the pain in the pit of her stomach that was evidence of bruised feelings. That wasn't an acceptable reaction to last night.

Because Dolly was still happy with her teddy bear at the moment, Ivy dressed quickly and prepared a bottle before going into the baby's room.

Farrell might have left without fanfare, but Dolly was gratifyingly happy to see her mother.

Ivy changed the baby's diaper, put her in one of the cute rompers Katie had gifted them with and then sat in the rocking chair to feed her. Dolly had begun eating mashed bananas and Cheerios and a few other simple foods, but Ivy still enjoyed giving her a morning and bedtime bottle.

When Dolly's tummy was full, Ivy knew she couldn't delay going up to the big house any longer.

Though Farrell had waved off breakfast, he might come back for lunch since he hadn't taken a sandwich. Ivy decided to make vegetable soup. It was still cool and misty today. Soup would hit the spot.

She was nervous. Might as well admit it. How was she supposed to act this morning? Maybe she could take her cues from Farrell. For one crazy second, she contemplated walking over to the lab.

But no. They didn't have that kind of relationship. Besides, even if Farrell and Ivy had been a real couple, he had said more than once that he focused with tunnel vision when he was working on a project. He certainly didn't need interruptions.

The lunch hour came and went. She kept the soup warming on the stove just in case. Ivy ate and fed the baby. Put Dolly down for a nap in the study. Still no Farrell.

At two o'clock, she heard her phone ding, signaling a text. Farrell's communiqué was as terse as his pillow note.

Ivy, something came up in Portland. I'm there now. Will return with Katie and Quin tomorrow morning. Farrell.

She stared at the phone, feeling her heart shrivel in her chest. Was there really an emergency, or had Farrell left because he wanted to be clear about last night? That it was no big deal. Did he think she had the wrong idea?

Even worse, maybe he was feeling guilty for betraying his wife. Sasha hadn't intruded in the bedroom last night. At least Ivy didn't think so. But what if Farrell had awakened this morning and found himself grieving for the only woman who'd ever captured his heart? The woman he still loved.

The empty house and Ivy's depressing thoughts combined to steal the joy from the day. She had been so happy here. A new job. A new friend. And yes, Farrell *was* her friend, despite everything that had happened.

Perhaps he didn't have the same regard for her.

Would she have to leave? If one night in Ivy's bed had spooked him this badly, it was possible they could no longer coexist.

The prospect of going back to Portland was heartbreaking. She loved everything about Farrell's enclave here in the northern woods. Some women might crave restaurants and nightlife and excitement. But Ivy had never really known that kind of lifestyle. To her, this private getaway was idyllic. If she had kept Farrell at arm's length, the situation would have remained stable.

Now, because she had let her feelings get out of control, she might lose her job and her home and have to start over yet again.

To distract herself from her dismal thoughts, she climbed to the second and third floors to do one last reconnaissance. Though she touched up a mirror here and straightened a rug there, everything was in order. Farrell's guest rooms were lovely. Each one had an individual theme or color palette.

Clearly, some had ocean views and some looked out over the forest, but she couldn't imagine any guest complaining about *anything*. Luxury stamped each square foot.

She was both nervous and excited about the upcoming house party. Katie would be there to lend a hand with names or any of the million and one details that were bound to crop up. That was a comfort.

But why had Farrell gone to Portland?

What did it mean?

Instantly, she made a decision. Farrell would have no cause to regret sharing her bed. Ivy would make it clear from the outset that she was not emotionally involved…that she intended to move forward with business as usual. If she let him know by her attitude that nothing had changed, perhaps they could go back to what they'd had before. A cautious friendship.

Wednesday dragged. Ivy would like to say she didn't know why, but the cause was obvious. Farrell wasn't here to lend his passion and energy to the house. She missed him.

That was a problem. But she would deal with it.

She and Dolly spent a pleasant afternoon and evening together. Ivy went to bed early. The next four days would be busy and challenging. She needed her rest. But her dreams were dark and disturbing. Farrell starred in all of them.

Thursday morning, she was at the big house early. Katie—not Farrell—had sent a text to say the three of them—Katie, Quin and Farrell—would arrive before lunch. Would Ivy mind preparing a light meal?

Of course Ivy wouldn't mind. It was her job, after all.

She jittered and watched the clock as she grilled chicken breasts and made a pasta salad. There were apples in the pantry that needed to be eaten, so she peeled and sliced them and threw together a fruit crisp.

Soon, the kitchen smelled delightful.

The sun had come out around ten, burning off the fog and drying out the surroundings. That was probably best when having foreign guests. Not everyone appreciated a rainy day the way Ivy did.

When she heard car doors slamming just before noon, she peeked out a window and saw the three adults climbing out of two cars. Her heart jumped and began to beat sluggishly.

Seldom did she have the opportunity to study Farrell unobserved. He looked even taller than she remembered. As she watched, he laughed at something one of the others had said. For a moment, he looked far younger than he was. This was the man Sasha would have known.

When the two Stone siblings and Katie entered the kitchen, Ivy was able to greet them with a smile. "Just in time," she said. "I hope you're hungry."

Quin dropped a briefcase in the hallway and stretched. "We got up too early. I'm starving."

Katie gave Ivy a quick hug. "Me, too. Everything smells delicious. May I help you?"

Farrell, noticeably, said nothing. He was flipping through a stack of mail in his hands. Perhaps that was his excuse for not acknowledging the woman he'd recently bedded.

Ivy nodded her head. "If you'll see what the men want to drink, the rest of lunch is ready." She took three plates and began doling out the meal.

Katie frowned. "Where is your plate?"

"I ate earlier," Ivy lied. "Dolly was up at the crack of dawn, so I was hungry already."

Katie seemed unconvinced, but she didn't press the issue.

Once Ivy put food on the table, she left the kitchen without fanfare and escaped to the study. Quietly, she opened the door and slipped inside. Dolly was still asleep, her little bottom up in the air.

Ivy sat down in a cozy armchair, leaned back and closed her eyes. She ached for Farrell, for the knowledge that he was giving her a wide berth. Had she ruined everything by sleeping with him, by giving in to the madness that had caught them up in a physical relationship that seemed inevitable?

Farrell had been so kind to her. So incredibly sexy. Was it any wonder that Ivy had a crush on him?

Being in bed with him, having him touch her and give her pleasure, had been an experience she hadn't known she needed.

With Farrell, she felt whole.

Twelve

Farrell handed Katie a sheet of paper. "Why don't you and Quin assign the rooms? I've penciled in a couple. I'll go find Ivy and see what else needs to be done."

As excuses went, it was clunky at best, but guilt burned a hole in his gut. How was he going to explain himself?

It took him several minutes to find Ivy. Only when he eased open the door to the study did he see the sleeping baby and her mother…also dead to the world. Or so it seemed.

Farrell slipped inside the room, closed the door silently and stood with his back to the wall. Watching the two females sleep made his chest ache.

Ivy hadn't heard him…yet. Either she was very tired, or the white noise of the fan had covered his quiet entry. Until a few minutes ago when he walked into the house with Quin and Katie, he hadn't seen Ivy since he climbed out of her bed yesterday morning. Thirty hours, give or take.

It seemed an eternity.

He'd been an ass in the kitchen just now. His first glance at Ivy had knocked the wind out of him. Pretending to read the damn mail was all he could manage, because he hadn't known how to act or what to say.

At the very least, Ivy deserved an apology.

On the other hand, if he wasn't planning to sleep with her again, it would be best to pretend everything was normal. Could he do it? Could he act as if sharing Ivy Danby's bed hadn't been the best thing to happen to him in the last seven years?

After several long minutes—when Ivy didn't stir—he decided Fate was giving him a nudge. *Leave well enough alone. Water under the bridge. Never look back.* Any number of clichés came to mind.

Though his conscience and his heart were unsettled, he made himself slide to the left, reach behind his back, turn the knob and exit the room.

Katie tapped her old-school yellow legal pad with the tip of her pencil. "I think that's it. The caterer will be here at eight in the morning. She's sent me all of the weekend menus for approval. We have one vegan. One peanut allergy, and two gluten-free. I think we're in good shape."

Quin kissed the top of his wife's head. "Isn't she amazing?"

Farrell chuckled. "She was my admin long before she was your wife. I'm fully aware of Katie's credentials."

"Not all of them." Quin waggled his eyebrows and kissed the side of Katie's neck.

"Eww, gross," she said, shoving him away. "This is a *business* meeting, Quin. Try to be an adult, please." Her bashful smile took some of the sting from the rebuke.

"Yes, ma'am." Quin's hangdog expression was patently false.

Farrell stood and stretched. "Well, if you two lovebirds

have everything under control, I think I'll hit the lab. Once the chaos starts, I'll be losing ground until Monday."

"How's the altitude-signaling device going?" Quin asked. "Any leaks?"

"None that I've heard of, which means there's a good chance the Portland lab really was vulnerable."

Quin sobered. "Zachary is trying to find an expert to analyze all the work computers."

Katie nodded. "But it sounds like a gargantuan task. If things are going well here, Farrell, I vote you continue working remotely until we know something for sure."

Farrell frowned. "What worries me is that we may *never* know."

Quin paced the kitchen restlessly. "If Stone River Outdoors has a corporate spy or a hacker or whatever they call it these days, we're *gonna* find out. End of story."

Farrell nodded. "I want to believe that. But the police don't have the manpower to pursue this. The suspect in your and Dad's car crash is dead. He was a drifter. A drug addict. And there's no evidence the crash was related to the theft of my designs, or that it was anything more than an accident."

"So we just drop it?" Quin's raw question held both anger and frustration.

"No," Farrell said. "As long as you and Zachary agree, I'd like to hire a private investigator."

"That will be damn expensive." Quin chewed his lip.

"But money well spent, right?"

"Yep. You have my vote."

Katie gathered her things. "I think an investigator is a great idea. But we have bigger fish to fry at the moment. Let's go to our house, Quin." She glanced at Farrell. "We'll be back at seven tomorrow morning. And what about Ivy?"

"What about Ivy?" Farrell tried to make the question casual, but Katie was eyeing him strangely.

She shrugged. "I wondered if you had filled her in on all the details, or if I need to do that?"

"I'm sure she'd appreciate anything you have to offer," Farrell said. "I think she's in the study with the baby. Dolly is usually awake by now. Feel free to check on them."

When Farrell strode out of the room, Katie glanced at her husband. "Was that weird?" she asked.

Quin rummaged in the cabinet for a new coffee filter. "Weird, how?"

"I don't know," Katie said, frowning. "They barely spoke to each other when the three of us arrived. I thought by now Farrell would feel comfortable with Ivy and vice versa."

"Katie," Quin warned. "It's not any of our business. You already made him hire Ivy. I think you've done enough."

"Hey," she said, hoping he was teasing. "It was the perfect solution."

"Maybe. But our Farrell is a certified hermit. Losing Sasha all those years ago changed him. He *likes* being alone. Having a live-in housekeeper and a little baby around may be wearing thin."

Ivy paused just outside the doorway, trying not to let on that she had overheard the entire conversation. Her face was hot and her stomach churned. Was it true? Had Farrell decided that peanut-butter sandwiches were preferable to having Ivy and Dolly underfoot?

Was he regretting the sex?

The hurt burrowed deep.

Half an hour ago, she'd been lightly dozing when Farrell sneaked into the study. She had snapped awake at the first tiny click of the doorknob. New mothers were trained that way. Any out-of-the-ordinary sound could be cause for alarm.

Holding her breath, she had waited for him to speak,

thinking she would open her eyes when he did. Instead, he'd simply stood there and watched her. What thoughts had gone through his brain?

Perhaps he had come to tell her that this weekend would be the last of her duties. That he had changed his mind about needing a housekeeper. If so, why hadn't he done it?

Surely he hadn't come to talk about their momentary indiscretion. Not that they'd been indiscreet, not really. Two grown adults. Single. Available. It wasn't as if the two of them had done anything scandalous.

They had each wanted and needed the other.

Dolly chortled loudly, meaning that Ivy could no longer hide her presence in the hall. Besides, this wasn't the time to analyze why Farrell Stone had made love to her like a movie hero and then shut her down cold.

Ivy cleared her throat, put a hand to her hot cheek and made herself walk into the kitchen. "Did I hear my name?" she asked cheerfully.

Katie looked stricken.

Quin smoothed the situation like a pro. "Katie was saying she needed to give you the update on our guests. Last-minute details. You know…"

"Oh, sure," Ivy said. "I need to know what you all want me to do this weekend."

Katie took Dolly and handed her off to Quin. "Grab her coat in the hall and walk her on the front porch for a few minutes, will you? Ivy and I need to put our heads together."

When Quin and Dolly exited, Ivy sat on a stool at the island. "Give me the rundown," she said.

Katie nodded and slid her notepad to Ivy. "Why don't you take a picture of this with your phone? It will help you keep the names straight. And the second page is all the dietary stuff. But the caterer has that under control."

Ivy frowned. "Your brother-in-law is paying me a generous salary. I feel like I should be the one cooking."

"Nonsense. He's been very clear. Farrell wants you as hostess."

"I've never done anything like that. My husband didn't even like to entertain on a small scale."

"That's the first time you've mentioned your husband to me," Katie said softly. "Are you handling things okay?"

Ivy nodded. "I'm fine. It wasn't a happy marriage, Katie."

"Oh." The other woman's eyes rounded. "I didn't know."

"No way you could have. I didn't even tell your sister when she advertised for a roommate. I was still processing Richard's death and what it meant for me and Dolly. Still am, I suppose."

Katie's gaze was filled with sympathy. "Would it make you feel better if I came to the cabin with you and we can choose outfits for the various parts of the weekend?"

Ivy exhaled. "Oh, gosh, yes. I've been agonizing over what to wear."

"Let me tell Quin where I'm going."

"Will he be okay with Dolly?"

"Of course. And if Dolly is her cute and charming self, perhaps she'll give my husband a few ideas."

Fifteen minutes later, Ivy unlocked the cabin with Katie right on her heels. Katie looked around with interest. "I like how you've settled in."

Ivy snorted. "If that's a polite way of saying we have toys everywhere, then yes. We're settled in."

Katie laughed. "It's organized chaos. I love it."

They made their way to Ivy's bedroom. Fortunately, Ivy had made her bed and tidied up that morning. "I've hung everything and pressed the wrinkles out of the few items that needed it. But there's so much."

Katie riffled through the hangers. "This for lunch tomorrow. First impressions and all that."

The outfit Katie indicated was a sophisticated black

pantsuit with a teal satin tank beneath and matching jewelry. Ivy had a hunch that the necklace and earrings probably cost as much as her first week's salary.

The black leather flats were designer-made. The fact that she now also owned a half-dozen new bras and undies still made her shake her head in disbelief. "And after lunch?"

"The Stone brothers have planned a three-mile hike, nothing too strenuous. They want to show off the property and in the process demonstrate a few of our most popular pieces of outdoor gear. You saw that I ordered you hiking boots and trail pants that dry easily. You've got several options for tops."

"No wonder Farrell wanted a caterer. If he's going to take the group on a forced march, they'll be hungry."

Katie grinned. "Indeed." She held up a hanger. "I love this. It will be perfect for tomorrow evening. The men have planned for cocktails overlooking the ocean and then a formal dinner."

The dress Katie had picked out from a catalog had three-quarter-length sleeves, a curved neckline and a hem that came down to just above the knee. But when Ivy tried it on several days ago, the deep red silk clung to her body in such a way that every one of her curves, modest though they were, presented a provocative image.

Ivy hesitated. "It's awfully...*red*," she said.

Katie laughed. "Of course it is. And it looks amazing with your skin tone. It's really very modest. You can pull it off."

"Maybe there's something else a little less fitted?"

"Red for tomorrow night," Katie said. "No question. Hold your head up and be fabulous."

"I don't think *be fabulous* is in my repertoire."

"It's in every woman's repertoire," Katie insisted. "But sometimes we let ourselves believe the negative messages.

From others and from ourselves. You're a lovely woman, Ivy. I'm sorry you had an unhappy marriage."

Ivy shrugged. "Maybe I'll tell you about it someday. Suffice it to say, Richard would never have let me out of the house in something like that. But *I'm* in charge of me now."

"All the more reason to shine. You're starting over, Ivy. Whatever the reason, crossroads in our lives are opportunities for growth."

Ivy smiled and sat on the edge of the bed, fingering the crimson fabric of the dress in question. "I'm beginning to see why you were the perfect person to bring Quin out of his funk. No wonder he fell in love with you."

"It wasn't me," Katie said. "I just gave him a nudge. Quin had to deal with the loss of competitive skiing on his own. Like any grief process, it took time. I'm really proud of him."

Ivy was envious of Katie. The other woman had clearly been confident *before* meeting Quin. From what Ivy had picked up, Katie had been running Farrell's R & D department back in Portland for several years. Now, though, Katie glowed with the certainty of a woman who knew she was well loved.

"Okay," Ivy said. "We've picked out Friday's wardrobe, but how about the rest? I never knew there would be so many opportunities to change."

Katie turned back to the closet. "This top and pants for Saturday morning. More outdoor stuff for the afternoon, and the deep blue dress for Saturday evening."

Soon, between the two of them, they had Ivy's closet organized in the order she would need things. Despite a certain level of apprehension, Ivy was looking forward to wearing such gorgeous clothes.

When the task was done, they went in search of Quin. They found him in the kitchen letting Dolly pull every pot and pan and lid out of the bottom cabinets. Both women gaped at the mess.

Katie put her hands on her hips. "Quinten Stone. Your brother has a houseful of important company on the way in the morning. What were you thinking?"

Quin's grin was sunny as he kept one hand on Dolly's waist to keep her from tumbling into the open cabinet. "She wanted to. What can I say? I'm putty in her hands."

Ivy was more amused than Quin's wife. "She has that effect on me, too. Don't worry about it. I'll clean it up later." Quin was quickly becoming one of her favorite people. His mischief and charming sense of humor made him a delight to be around. Unlike his solemn brother.

Katie squatted. "We'll do it now. Sorry, Dolly. This is a big weekend. We all have to be on our best behavior."

Ivy spotted the legal pad on the counter. Something on the housing list made her frown. "Why am I penciled in for the rose room? It's the nicest suite in the house. Ocean-front. King bed. That should go to one of our guests. I can sleep anywhere."

Katie and Quin exchanged a glance. Katie took the notepad from Ivy and glanced at it. "We're only using six of the eight upstairs bedrooms. Quin wanted you to be comfortable. He excluded the room with the twin beds at the back of the house and the bedroom with the smallest bathroom. The other guests are well taken care of, I promise."

Quin leaned against the fridge, letting Dolly play her favorite pull-the-hair game. "It's Farrell's house, Ivy. He calls the shots."

"But it doesn't make sense."

Again, the duo gave each other a look. It was Quin who spoke up. "My brother likes and appreciates you, Ivy. This is something he wanted to do. If I were you, I wouldn't make a big deal about it."

Ivy wasn't convinced. "Okay," she said slowly. She took

Dolly from him. "The two of you should go. I've kept you too long. What time will you be back for dinner?"

Katie leaned her head on Quin's shoulder. "Actually, my husband is cooking me a romantic dinner for two tonight. You and Farrell will be on your own."

Thirteen

Ivy took Dolly to the porch. They waved as Quin and Katie climbed into their car and disappeared down the road. Now Ivy's last line of defense was gone and wouldn't be back until tomorrow.

Her stomach fluttered as she debated her options. Surely she and Farrell needed to clear the air before the house party. But how?

Holding the baby on one hip, she extracted her cell phone from her pocket and sent a text to her boss.

What time would you like me to have dinner ready tonight?

There. That was simple and straightforward enough. No hidden agenda. Farrell didn't reply to her text for twenty minutes. When he did, the note was not reassuring.

I'll make myself a sandwich. Work is going well. I don't want to interrupt the flow. Why don't you and Dolly enjoy the evening?

Ivy frowned at the message, trying to read between the lines. The man was avoiding her. There was no other explanation.

This didn't bode well for the upcoming weekend, but short of dragging Farrell out of his lab and forcing a confrontation, she was out of options.

The impasse brought up something she had been thinking about recently. She and Dolly needed reliable transportation. Nothing fancy. If Katie and Quin would help her locate a used vehicle, Ivy had enough for a tiny down payment and regular payments.

Impulsively, she sent Katie a text to that effect. Then, because she felt guilty for interrupting their afternoon, she added a second note.

No rush on the car thing. We can talk about it later.

Katie sent a brief, cheerful response.

Afterward, Ivy was somewhat at a loss. The house was spotless. The boss didn't want dinner. Ivy might as well relax and play with Dolly…and later tonight, do her homework regarding the weekend guests.

Because she didn't want to risk the chance of running into Farrell again later—and because her stomach was growling—she popped Dolly into her high chair, pulled out a large wicker basket and began loading it with a few things. She would eat the leftovers from lunch as soon as she got back to the cabin. As for dinner, cheese and crackers and fruit would do.

When she had everything she needed, she managed to scoop up both the basket and her daughter. By the time she made it to the cabin, she was panting, not because it was a long way, but because a basket and a growing baby were an awkward handful.

She paused before unlocking the door to glance over into

the woods. It was possible to see the roof of Farrell's lab through the trees. What would he say if she simply showed up on his doorstep?

She didn't have the guts to find out.

Having a chunk of the afternoon and all of the evening to herself should have been a lovely surprise, and it was. Still, the remainder of the day dragged. Babies were wonderful miracles, but any conversation with Dolly was one-sided at best.

Because Dolly had only managed a single nap today and not two, Ivy was able to put her daughter down by seven thirty. The poor thing was half-asleep while Ivy dressed her in one-piece pajamas and read her a book.

When Dolly was completely out, Ivy showered and washed and dried her hair. The T-shirt and knit pants she put on dated back to college days. After watching a movie that failed to keep her attention, she was just about to head for bed when she heard a soft knock at her front door. Unless the nearest bear family had developed human skills, her visitor had to be Farrell.

Her heart pounded. She could ignore the knock. The front of the house was dark. He would think she was asleep.

Sadly, no force in the world could halt her footsteps. No matter the cost, she wanted to see him.

When she swung open the door, his face was in shadows.

"May I come in?" he asked.

She hesitated, still trying to be smart. "Of course."

He followed her inside and waited while she turned on a couple of lamps. The room glowed intimately. When she turned around to face him, he took her wrist, reeled her in and buried his face in her shoulder with a moan. "God, Ivy. I'm sorry."

She stroked his hair, her eyes stinging. His torment was palpable. "It's okay."

He reared back. "It's *not* okay. I slept with you and disappeared." His indignation might have made her smile at another time. Not now.

"And why was that?" she asked gently, already knowing the answer. So she said it for him. "You felt as if you had cheated on your wife. I'm guessing that's been the case every time you've been intimate with a woman for the last seven years."

He ran his hands through his hair and paced. "That was true at one time. Not anymore. Or if it is, it's subconscious." His jaw worked. "I didn't leave your bed Wednesday morning because of Sasha."

"Then why, Farrell? And why were you acting so weird today when you and Quin and Katie arrived?"

He dropped into a chair, then leaned forward to stare at the floor. When he finally looked up at her, the expression on his face told her that whatever tiny fantasies she had been weaving were dead in the water. Hopeless.

Shaking his head slowly, he drummed his fists on his knees. "I left because waking up beside you seemed natural. Good. But I can't do that, Ivy. I can't."

"Can't wake up with me?" She frowned. "I'm not sure I follow."

He rose to his feet again, shoved his hands in his pockets and stared at her, his posture rigid. "I can't care about you, Ivy. I won't. Not in that way. So for me to have sex with you is obscene."

She managed a smile though her heart was breaking. "It didn't *seem* obscene."

"This isn't funny." His tone was grim. "Losing Sasha nearly broke me. I swore I would never let myself care deeply about a woman again. I've lost my wife, my father and nearly Quin. I don't want to go through that kind of pain anymore. You and I have some kind of connection. I can't deny it, but I don't want it. And I certainly don't want to hurt you."

"But?"

"But I can't stop wanting you. It's eating me alive. What am I going to do about that?"

Did he really expect her to answer such a question? "It was just sex," she muttered.

He cocked his head, his gaze telling her he saw through the lie. "No. It wasn't. I'm guessing you wanted to know if you were still a sexually desirable woman. Or maybe you wanted to know if you had sexual feelings. I think we both found out the answer to that one."

"And you?" she whispered. Her hands gripped the back of a chair to keep from crumbling. "If it wasn't just sex, what was it for you?"

"I needed you," he said, the words flat. "Desperately, in fact. I hadn't been with a woman in almost a year. With my father's death and Quin's injuries, and then all the trouble at work, I had isolated myself emotionally. Told myself I could handle anything. But it wasn't true. You came along, and I began to want more. I wanted a connection."

"And yet you were deadly honest when you told me you didn't *want* to want me."

"I know." His gaze was bleak. "I'm screwed, aren't I? You should run far and fast."

Ivy shook all over. Her skin was icy. This moment mattered. Not only for Ivy, but for Farrell. How they went forward from here would send ripples into his future and hers.

"Here's the thing," she said, trying to sound reasonable and calm. "I've been through a bad time, but I'm good now. Or at least I'm headed in the right direction. Maybe one day I'll meet a guy who wants what I want, but clearly, that's not you. I need this job until I've saved enough money to move on somewhere else. You're so worried about using me or hurting me, but I know what I want. I'm capable of no-strings sex."

"I seriously doubt that."

He stared at her so long and so hard, she shifted positions restlessly.

"I am," she said. "I told you before. I'm no delicate, innocent flower. I've dealt with the good and the bad in my life, and I can tell you this—sex with Farrell Stone is good. But I respect your boundaries. You don't have to worry about me. I spent a decade married to a man who didn't love me. I have too much self-respect to repeat that pattern."

"You should have been a lawyer," he said, the grumbled words laced with resignation. "I'm not sure where I stand in this argument."

She held out her hand. "I forgive you for running away."

His lips twitched for real this time. "I did not run. It was more of a strategic relocation."

"Whatever helps you sleep at night." She withdrew her hand when he made no move to touch her. This sex-without-caring thing was going to be tough. "I can't compete with your sweet Sasha, Farrell. And I would never try. What is it that you want?"

He cursed, a tortured syllable echoing the corded muscles in his arms and the tension in his frame. "You know what I want."

"Yet you're still over there, and I'm over here. I don't need you to care about me, Farrell. I don't expect you to. All I'm asking for is a job and your sexy body. Fair enough?"

Slowly, he approached her. "When I first met you, I thought you were meek and mild. That's not true at all, is it?"

"I don't know. You tell me." She wet her finger with her tongue and traced his lips. "Does this feel mild?"

He scooped her up in his arms. "I don't know if I can handle a firecracker like you, Ivy Danby."

"Do your best, big guy."

* * *

Farrell had lost control of the situation the moment he knocked on Ivy's door. This little cabin had drawn him like a homing beacon. He'd been incapable of staying away. Though he had tried. God knew, he had tried. For the past two hours, he had dug through a box of Sasha's things, items he hadn't been able to get rid of for fear he might lose the last strand that bound him to his dead wife. Though her scent lingered in a treasured scarf, Farrell couldn't fully summon her image.

After seven years, Sasha was really gone.

Truthfully, Farrell had known and accepted that ages ago. What he hadn't come to terms with was being alone. As a deliberate choice. Because he didn't want to lose anyone else.

He carried Ivy carefully, set her on the bed gently. Inside, he was a raging mass of confusion and lust. A man in his condition shouldn't be allowed to make decisions.

The overhead light was off. A single lamp burned on the nightstand. Ivy's eyes were huge, rounded with a combination of apprehension and drowsy anticipation. The thin T-shirt she wore clung to her breasts, drew attention to her puckered nipples. The knit sleep pants outlined slender, toned thighs. A curvy ass. A narrow waist.

Maybe he should say something. The words wouldn't form. How did he explain something to Ivy that he hadn't come to terms with himself?

With jerky motions, he stripped off his clothes and rescued a strip of condoms from his pocket. He wasn't positive, but he thought Ivy blushed when she saw the condoms.

It was good that she was quiet. Earlier, that sexy, husky voice of hers had wrapped around him like warm molasses, making it hard to think.

"Scoot over, Ivy."

The bed was a queen, not a king. That was his fault. But

then again, he hadn't been planning to sleep here when he furnished the place.

Under the covers, Ivy put a hand on his thigh. "Farrell?"

Her fingertips were almost touching his sex. Was that intentional? Was she trying to drive him berserk? "Yeah?"

"Before we start, could I ask you a question?"

He closed his eyes and willed his heart rate to slow. It wasn't working. "Sure," he croaked.

Ivy curled on her side, facing him. "Katie said you wanted me to have the beautiful oceanfront room on the second floor. I appreciate the thought, but I'd rather take that small bedroom on the back side of the house and let one of your guests have the suite with the view."

"You'll be working hard this weekend, and I—"

She put a hand over his mouth, stilling the words. Her smile made him dizzy. "Pay attention, Farrell. I'm asking if I can sleep with you at night. If you're concerned about appearances, I'm happy to put my things in a guest room, but I was hoping you and I could…" She trailed off, perhaps because he hadn't said a word.

His brain froze, analyzing her request. Trying to subdue his strong reaction. His very positive reaction. "Sure," he said. "That would be fine."

Ivy blinked. Her gaze narrowed. "Fine? Well, never mind, then. It's too much trouble for *fine*." The pique in her voice was justified.

Farrell put his hand over hers. Over the small feminine hand resting on his thigh. "Touch me," he begged, pulling her arm to rest across his taut abdomen. "Hell, yes, I want you to stay in my room during the weekend. But right now, all I want is *you*."

The little gasp when he curled her fingers around his erection was Ivy's. Or his. Maybe both. He wasn't sure.

She must have finally recognized his utter desperation. Sliding down in the bed, she rested her cheek on his chest and sighed. "You have the most gorgeous body, Mr. Stone. I love how it's so different from mine."

And then she proceeded to touch every erogenous zone that sent his masculine libido into a frenzied state of high alert.

He wanted to complain when she abandoned his shaft, but having Ivy start at his ankles and stroke her way upward was its own kind of reward. After that, she skipped the high-dollar real estate and kissed his belly, his rib cage, his neck, his chin.

Then she settled on top of him, took his cheeks between her hands and kissed his mouth.

He shook like he had a fever. His hands grasped her butt, fingers digging into her soft, firm flesh. Ivy's tongue trespassed between his lips, stroking, turning him inside out.

Every inch of her touched every inch of him. She was draped over him like the perfect, sexy blanket.

But he wanted more. He needed more, or he might spontaneously combust. "Ivy," he whispered. "Can I have you now? Please?"

She pulled back and smiled, a cat-and-canary kind of smile that lit up her face and would have made him laugh if he hadn't been rigid with hunger. "Of course, Farrell," she said. "What are you waiting for?"

With graceless speed, he shoved her aside and reached for the protection. Moments later, he took about one-point-five seconds to decide. "On top," he grunted. "Hurry."

"Yes, sir."

It probably would have been less painful if Ivy hadn't helped. Her knee jabbed his hip; her foot nearly kicked his balls. At last, they were aligned as perfectly as planets in an orbital plane.

"Look at me," he said urgently.

Almost shyly, her gaze met his. "I'm looking."

His throat was tight. "I don't want you to have regrets," he muttered. It was the truest thing he had said. The words burst forth from some fount of wisdom deep inside him.

Her sweet Ivy-smile absolved him. "We're good, Farrell. Honestly."

Fourteen

Ivy knew she was headed for heartbreak. Knew it, and yet kept steering in the same direction. When Farrell entered her, she closed her eyes, concentrating on the exquisite feel of him. Inch by inch, he filled her, possessed her.

It was exhilarating and terrifying and, for her at least, earth-shattering. Richard had robbed her of so much. Now, at last, she had found her heart's desire. She loved Farrell Stone. More than she could possibly imagine loving any other man.

But he wasn't hers to keep. He never would be.

In this cozy bed, he made love to her with such passion and tenderness she wanted to cry. Feelings, so many feelings, rocked her, buffeted her.

Like a feather bounced on the winds of a storm, Ivy took a journey whose destination she couldn't see. On the other side, tragedy awaited. It was a certainty. She was smart enough to know that.

Still, nothing could make her give up these next days

of wonder and joy. Farrell rolled her beneath him without warning. Now he thrust forcefully, making her twist and groan as hot, sweet pleasure coursed from one part of her body to the next.

She wanted to make this moment last. Wanted to savor the time with him, this time when he was hers and hers alone, when she didn't have to share him with a ghost or even a houseful of guests.

But he was too good. Already he had learned her body. She felt her orgasm tingling in the wings. Farrell kissed the spot just beneath her ear, whispered hoarse words of praise. Ivy bowed up. Cried out. Tumbled over the edge of release and fell and fell and fell.

Until at last she rested in his arms.

They both slept.

Around two in the morning, Ivy roused. Farrell was sitting on the side of the bed, stretching. She put a hand on his warm back. "What's wrong?"

He leaned down to kiss her. "Nothing. Not a damn thing. But I just had an idea for the altitude beacon," he said. "I'm not running away, I swear."

She smiled, too sated and warm and lazy to be anything other than accommodating. "I believe you, Farrell. Go. This will be your last chance to work on it until Sunday afternoon or Monday—right?"

A tiny frown creased the space between his brows. He stroked her hair from her face. "You really don't mind?"

"Not at all. Do what you need to do. Seriously." She took his hand, held it to her cheek and then kissed his palm. "I'm going back to sleep. I'll see you in the morning."

Farrell was exhilarated. He'd spent four straight hours in his lab fleshing out details that would make absolutely certain his invention worked as it should. The ideas had come thick and fast, almost more than he could keep track of as he typed and sketched and tweaked.

Leaving Ivy's bed wouldn't have been his first choice, but he had learned long ago that inspiration often showed up at the most inconvenient moments. Tonight, the experience of creating had been transcendent. He'd been jazzed, pumped, buzzing with energy.

After a shower, fresh clothes and a forty-five-minute nap in one of the armchairs in the study, he now floated on the caffeine from three cups of coffee as he prepared to meet the day. Katie and Quin showed up right on time, both looking sleepy. With them was Delanna, Katie's sister, who had arrived late last night.

The younger woman greeted Farrell. "Where's Ms. Danby? And the baby? I'm ready to start ASAP. Sis tells me all the guests will be here soon."

Katie dumped her enormous tote on the kitchen island. "Quin and I will meet the caterer and help her get set up. Farrell, why don't you take Delanna over to the cabin?"

Farrell was accustomed to being "handled" by his efficient admin. He nodded. "Of course. Come on, Delanna. Follow me." It didn't hurt that Katie's suggestion took him to the one place Farrell wanted to go.

At the cabin, Delanna and Ivy got reacquainted. "Thank you for coming," Ivy said. "I still feel bad about leaving you in the lurch. Have you found another roommate?"

Delanna nodded. "I did, and she's great. Cooks, too. Don't worry about it, Ivy. Things work out the way they're supposed to."

Farrell winced inwardly at that careless bit of philosophy. In his experience, "things" often backfired in your face, but he didn't contradict Delanna. Katie's sister was a free spirit. Who was he to judge?

When Ivy finished going over Dolly's schedule and handed off the baby to her new sitter, Farrell pulled Ivy aside. "You look fantastic," he said, wanting to kiss her, but certain she would object in this situation. She wore slim-legged black pants with a matching jacket and a silky top whose color reminded him of the ocean at Martinique.

Her smile lacked conviction. "Thanks. I'm nervous," she confessed. "Katie had flats picked out for this outfit, but I went with the heels instead. Feeling taller gives me confidence."

He let his gaze drift from the silky wisps of hair that brushed her forehead to her flushed cheeks to the rise and fall of her chest. "Just be yourself, Ivy. All I need you to do is analyze the way we handle this get-together. Take note of anything you think should be altered or eliminated. Your insights will be important when we do an evaluation later."

"You make it sound so easy. This is my first billionaire house party. I won't know what to say."

He cocked his head, giving her a devilish smile. "*I'm* a billionaire," he said. "You seem to have plenty to say to me. Remember?" He mimicked her voice. "'Ooh, there, Farrell. Don't stop. More, harder, faster.'"

Ivy's face turned beet red as she glanced around frantically to see where Delanna had landed.

"Relax," Farrell said, chuckling. "She and Dolly went out the back door to look at the birds."

"Oh." Ivy put both hands on her hot cheeks. "That wasn't funny."

"Pretty funny from where I'm standing." He kissed her cheek, careful not to muss her hair. "You smell delicious. Do we need to take your suitcase?"

"I'll get it later when I change for the afternoon. I'm ready to head up to the house."

By the time they returned from the cabin, the caterer had taken over the kitchen. Katie and Quin had been banished to the front hallway. And the first of Zachary's caravan of limos had pulled up in the driveway.

The next half hour was organized bedlam. The introductions alone took forever. After everyone had met everyone, the three brothers—plus Katie and Ivy—began ushering couples to their various rooms.

Farrell kept an eye on Ivy, curious to see how she would react to the diverse group. But he needn't have worried. She plunged right in, chatting and listening, and offering help when it was needed.

The large dining room, a place Farrell seldom used except for weekends like this one, was already set up for the luncheon. When he checked on the caterer, the pleasant thirty-something woman gave him a thumbs-up.

By the time the crowd had raved about the view, freshened up and rested if necessary, Farrell already had a good feeling about his goals for the weekend. He and his brothers and Katie took one last look at the packets they would be passing out after the meal.

The navy folder with ecru lettering and the SRO logo—two mountains intertwined with a river—was filled with glossy, impressive images of the company's latest products, many of which would hopefully be adopted by the guests and their respective companies.

Everyone had been asked to convene in the dining room at eleven thirty. When Farrell walked in, he found Ivy chatting animatedly with the only "single" guest on the roster. Unashamedly, Farrell lingered behind the open door and listened.

Ivy laughed. "I'm serious," she said. "When Farrell told me a Swiss watchmaker was coming, I pictured a stooped old man with a long white beard and tiny gold spectacles. You're not at all who I pictured."

Luca Bain took her hand and kissed it with European flair. "I hope you are not disappointed, mademoiselle."

Farrell bristled unconsciously. The sophisticated, well-traveled bachelor was easily twice as wealthy as the Stone brothers. And he collected female hearts as a hobby—never in one piece. Until this exact moment, Farrell hadn't thought about the fact that Ivy might be vulnerable to Luca's suave charm.

Ivy blushed at having her hand kissed. Women loved that kind of thing. Farrell's misgivings grew.

She escorted Luca around the table. "I believe you and I are seated here by the window. And you speak French? Again, not what I expected. I would have guessed a German accent."

"My people are from western Switzerland," Luca said. "Our country has four national languages. Where I live, it is not uncommon to hear French."

The conversation continued, but Farrell was forced to abandon his spy post and greet his other guests. In addition to the Swiss playboy, the Italians had brought their twin nineteen-year-old daughters, whose presence evened out the numbers.

Farrell couldn't very well insist on sitting beside his lover. He and his brothers, along with Katie and Ivy, were spread around the table. Katie had found someone at the Portland office who was proficient in calligraphy, so the place cards were works of art. When everyone was seated, Farrell greeted the group on behalf of Stone River Outdoors and expressed his appreciation.

"We're delighted you're all here," he said. "Our hope is to show you a relaxed, enjoyable weekend…one where we can all get to know each other and hopefully make plans for our collaboration." He picked up his wineglass. "To future endeavors. May they bloom in each of our countries."

Ivy beamed at Farrell. She might be prejudiced, but she thought he was the most impressive male in the room. He had a natural air of command and, when he put his mind to it, a warm, welcoming attitude that made people feel at home in his gorgeous house.

Luca Bain, at her right hand, tried to monopolize her attention. He was handsome, probably *too* handsome. A little full of himself. At the appropriate moment, Ivy directed her attention to the gentleman on her left. The Namibians, native Africans, were an impressive couple. Tall and reserved, they spoke perfect English with a delightful accent.

Their safari company was one of the top three tourist businesses on the entire continent of Africa. Most of their clientele was European, so their impetus for traveling so far was to work with Stone River Outdoors and hopefully grow their client base in the US.

When lunch was done, the schedule allowed for an hour of free time before the afternoon's planned activity. Zachary pulled Ivy aside in the hallway. "Thank you for all you've done for my brother."

Ivy evaluated that statement and decided there was no way he could know about the sex. "Honestly, I should be thanking the Stone brothers. I was at a low point in my life. Needed a job. Katie vouched for me. Your company is paying me well to be helpful."

"Still," Zachary said. "Knowing you've been here to look after Farrell has given the rest of us peace of mind."

She frowned at him. "Your brother is a grown man. He hasn't needed a babysitter."

"I didn't mean it like that." Zachary lowered his voice. "He lost his wife some years back, as I suppose you know. It hasn't been easy. We love Farrell, but we worry about him disappearing into that damn lab and never coming out." He shrugged. "I've always looked up to my big brother. I want him to be happy again. But in the meantime, I'll settle for well-fed and not a vampire."

Katie interrupted. "Ivy, do you mind helping me with the snacks?"

Though the international visitors had some downtime, the rest of the group was busy constantly. Quin would be taking point on the hike. He and his siblings were providing brand-new backpacks and personal hydration systems for each guest.

After the fresh-squeezed orange juice and homemade granola bars were packed, Ivy rushed over to the cabin to change clothes and retrieve her suitcase. She had folded all of her new clothes carefully, and she wasn't going far. Delanna was reading a book while Dolly napped.

"I'll be here at eight to put her down for the night," Ivy said.

"Won't that be in the middle of your fancy dinner?"

"I'm sure they won't miss me."

By the time she made it back to the big house and climbed the stairs to the second floor, she was hot and flustered. Taking the smallest bedroom at the back of the house only made sense. And besides, it was only "less" desirable in comparison to the other rooms. The furnishings and decor were actually quite lovely.

She felt a little self-conscious in her new hiking gear. The price tag on the shirt alone made her gasp. Nothing but the best for the Stone family. And Ivy, it seemed.

Everyone had agreed to meet out front at two thirty. Ivy made it with three minutes to spare. Farrell frowned at her from across the porch. She wrinkled her nose at him and turned her back. He wasn't the one juggling two residences and a baby and a distinct lack of experience with social occasions.

The group set off through the woods with much chatter and enthusiasm. Each of the Stones' visitors was widely traveled and widely experienced in high-end physical challenges. The Italian couple, in their late fifties, had made their fortune in the wine business. Now their walking-tour company was more of a retirement hobby, or so they claimed. Katie had told Ivy they had a seven-figure income *solely* from Tuscany Travels.

It was the same for the expat Irish couple who did eco-tours in the British Virgin Islands.

Only Luca Bain was a bit of a puzzle. He'd been around the world, too. Had skied with Quin and raced Formula One cars with Zachary. He and Farrell climbed together in the Alps.

Even the Italian daughters were more cosmopolitan than Ivy. One had already begun an international modeling career, and the other was entering university in the spring, with plans to become a doctor.

Ivy was relieved to know she was able to keep up with the pace. Although this kind of trek was not something she normally did, she had exercised diligently after Dolly was born, and her body was fit. Because she had been so ill during her pregnancy, she'd not had as much baby weight to lose as some women.

The trail wound through the woods and up over a rise to a promontory overlooking the ocean. A breeze blew off the water, cooling heated skin. As everyone paused for a drink, Quin gathered the troops and gave them a quick, humorous summation of Stone family history.

They were standing on the northernmost point of their ancestor's land acquisition. He grinned. "I know you're all jet-lagged, but since you'll probably wake up early tomorrow, I recommend the sunrise. We're so far east in the continental United States, we catch the morning rays before any of our other countrymen. My great-grandfather always used to say that was why Stone River Outdoors prospered."

Katie joined Ivy at her elbow. They were standing at the back of the group, listening and watching. Katie sighed. "Isn't my husband wonderful?"

Ivy laughed softly. "He is, indeed. But Quin is the lucky one, because he found you. You're the perfect couple."

"I hope so." Katie sobered. "I worry that he'll get restless or bored with me. His life has been one adventure after another. As a single man with unlimited funds, the world is a smorgasbord of entertainment and experiences. Do you think he'll be able to settle down to domesticity?"

"Aren't you the one who told me to forget about the money? To jump right in and be fabulous? You're going to have a wonderful life together, Katie. The man adores you. He wants to be with you."

Unlike Farrell and Ivy. Farrell wanted sex with Ivy, but not a relationship. He couldn't have been clearer. Though her chest ached with poignant regret, she told herself to enjoy this time in Maine. It wouldn't last forever.

Amid the flurry of activity after Quin's speech, Ivy stepped closer to the edge of the small cliff, closer to the ocean. She'd spent half her childhood in Portland, the rest of her life near Charleston. Always, the sea had been a pull in her life.

Ivy was determined to make the next decade a memorable one. In her gut, she knew that leaving Farrell, losing him, would be a blow. But she was stronger now than when her parents died. Ivy would not be that vulnerable again.

She and her daughter were a family. Ivy wanted to give Dolly the kind of childhood here in Maine that she herself had experienced. The state was plenty big. She could stay out of Farrell's way.

She sneaked a peek at him. With the sun burnishing his hair and the breeze carrying his masculine laughter, he seemed like a star, a man far out of her reach. He was flesh and blood. That much was true. But billionaires didn't marry destitute widows with babies.

Maybe if she told herself that enough times, she would believe it.

Fifteen

Farrell nursed a cup of coffee while leaning against the front-porch railing of his house Saturday afternoon and brooded. Even the brilliant robin's-egg azure of a cloudless sky and the serene expanse of darker blue sea hadn't eased his mind. Parts of this weekend had skidded off track in the wrong direction. But that was personal, not business.

As far as Stone River Outdoors was concerned, the corporate retreat, or house party, or whatever you wanted to name it, was a success. He and his brothers had called an audible last night and changed up the plan with the caterer's permission. Instead of a formal dinner in the dining room, they had set up tables on the porch to take advantage of the near-idyllic weather.

Zachary had fired up two gas grills to cook bison burgers and chicken. The caterer then prepared all sorts of delicacies and served them alfresco. Katie suggested s'mores and made a not-so-quick dash for ingredients. Quin built an after-dinner bonfire. Farrell's sophisticated guests took to the distinctly American treat with enthusiasm.

But it had been a late night when all was said and done. Everyone was exhausted. Though Ivy had slipped away to put Dolly to bed, she returned as promised. Even then, she eluded Farrell's attempts to have a private conversation with her. Earlier, she had said she wanted to sleep in his room, but instead, she had excused herself when the Italian twins headed upstairs. She joined the two young women on the pretext of helping them find a TV program they wanted to watch. But she didn't return.

Perhaps Ivy was having second thoughts.

This morning, breakfast had been a riotous affair. The group was becoming more cohesive, which was part of the point of this exercise. During a two-hour brainstorming session before lunch, led by Zachary, Quin and Farrell, the guests had been enthusiastic and connected as everyone discussed ways to build reciprocity in their business relationships.

Ivy did not attend, which was fine.

But she had been there at the noon meal when Luca Bain snagged a seat beside her and wielded his European charm. Farrell couldn't tell if Ivy was affected by Bain's determined flirtation or not. But in this kind of situation, anything was possible.

During the afternoon's expedition—sea kayaking down at the tiny beach—Ivy had actually shared a kayak with Zachary, who professed himself more than happy to give the inexperienced Ivy a few lessons in how to paddle.

Farrell ended up with one of the gorgeous Italian twins in *his* kayak. The girl was funny and charming and game to try this new sport, but although Quin teased Farrell on the sly about his lovely companion, Farrell had no interest in a nineteen-year-old. The only woman he was focused on was Ivy. And she had clearly been enjoying herself with Zachary.

This was what happened when a man mixed business with pleasure.

Tonight's meal was formal. Farrell would be forced to shower and shave and don his best dark suit. But he made a decision on the spot. Ivy would sit beside him.

As he turned to go back into the house, something in his chest caught. Ivy was standing there. Watching him.

He cleared his throat, his grip tightening on his empty stoneware mug. "How long have you been out here?" he asked.

Her tiny smile was shy. "A bit. I like watching you," she said. "Especially outside. The sun catches the gold in your hair."

The innocent compliment made his face heat.

Before he could respond, Ivy joined him at the rail. "We've been so busy since you left the cabin Thursday night, I haven't had a chance to ask you about the device. Did you make progress? I know you were operating on very little sleep yesterday. I hope the lab time was worth it."

He inhaled her light, feminine scent, feeling his mood shift in a positive direction. Something about being with Ivy smoothed his rough edges. He knew it would embarrass her if he mentioned it, but her slow, sexy speech affected him strongly. Always had. Even that very first day.

Perhaps it was why he had hired her.

He set the mug on the rail, resisting the urge to pull her into his arms. They were surrounded by a dozen other people, even if none of them were close at the moment. Discretion was advisable no matter how badly Farrell wanted to hold her and kiss her.

"The weekend is going extremely well." He cleared his throat, fully aware that he wasn't saying what he wanted to say. "Thanks for everything you've done."

"Happy to help," she said. "They're a fun bunch of people."

The afternoon was unusually warm. Ivy was wearing another of the outfits Katie had picked out. The turquoise cotton dress with yellow polka dots bared Ivy's arms and emphasized her narrow waist. Yellow-and-gold sandals completed the look.

With her short haircut and delicate jawline, there was an innocence about her, a sweetness.

But in bed, alone together, Farrell had discovered another side of his prim Ivy. She was fire and heat when he made love to her. Her body was strong and sensual, drawing every bit of his hunger to the fore and then drowning him in blissful completion. Each time was better than the last…which gave him high hopes for tonight.

"Will you come to my room later?" he asked, the words barely audible, though he could just as easily have traced the shell of her ear with his tongue and whispered the invitation.

They were facing the ocean, shoulder to shoulder. Quickly, he touched her hand, tracing the bones in her wrist. Even that simple connection made his skin hum with need.

He needed privacy. "Will you, Ivy? You disappeared last night."

She shot him a glance, wrinkling her nose. "It was awkward. And late. And did I mention awkward?"

Her humor made him smile. "I understand. And to be clear, I could come to your room if that would make you more comfortable."

"No," she said quickly. "Downstairs is private. I'll come."

He bumped her hip with his. "Oh, yes, you will," he said quietly. "I'll make sure of it."

"Farrell!" Ivy looked behind them to make sure nobody had stepped outside.

"Relax," he said. "I wouldn't do anything to embarrass you, I swear." He squeezed her hand gently and then stepped away three paces, giving her a rueful grin that made him look like a sexy bad boy. "Once we're behind closed doors, though, all bets are off."

The heated certainty behind his teasing words made her stomach flip. Despite the fact that she had told Farrell she wanted to share his bed, she'd kept her distance from the "boss" since his guests arrived. She didn't need *anyone*, especially Farrell's family, to get ideas.

She yearned to be with him, but she was conflicted.

What Ivy and Farrell shared in private was theirs and theirs alone. It would go no further than this interlude in the Maine woods. No rosy future beckoned. But that didn't make her time with Farrell any less special.

Ivy felt the wind ruffle her hair. The new clothes were not so strange now. She no longer felt like a kid playing dress up. Katie had been right in that regard. When Ivy made the choice to relax and enjoy her flattering new wardrobe, the decision had given her self-confidence a boost.

The international guests had been a surprise in many respects. Ivy thought most of them would be high-maintenance. That they would demand and expect preferential treatment. A certain level of deference.

Instead, they had been—to a person—delightful.

It was possible Ivy had a chip on her shoulder about the wealthy. This weekend, her prejudices had come smack up against reality, and she'd had to make adjustments. Still, there were moments. Like when Farrell told her that Luca's company sold a couple of watches that retailed for two hundred grand apiece.

The zeros made her mind boggle.

"I should probably go change," she said. The words were wistful. These few moments with Farrell were precious. She ached for him. Avoiding a tryst last night had been nothing more than cowardice on her part. She wouldn't make that mistake again. "So dinner's at seven?"

The look he gave her threatened to melt the polar ice caps and turn her into a puddle. "I'd like to skip the stupid dinner and take you straight to bed. It's been almost forty-eight hours, Ivy. Why do you torture me?"

She started to make a flip comment until she saw that he was apparently in earnest. Not joking. At all.

"Umm…" What did a cautious woman say to that? "I want you, too," she whispered.

Farrell's face flushed. His eyes glittered. "Go inside, Ivy. Please. Before I do something reckless."

Farrell was ready for the weekend to be over. But he still had to make it through lunch on Sunday before he could say goodbye to his houseful of guests. After the days of peace and quiet with only Ivy and Dolly for company, his tolerance for strangers, amiable though they were, was waning.

It didn't matter that SRO business had gone spectacularly well. Or that his guests had been intelligent, charming and helpful. He was done. He wanted to be alone with Ivy.

As the crowd gathered for the evening meal, he watched the door for her. Already, champagne flowed like water. Tonight's mood was celebratory. The caterer, with a bit of help from Katie and Ivy, had dug out china and crystal and an enormous Irish linen tablecloth that was specially made for this table.

Katie had arranged for a florist to bring fresh flowers, pumpkins and gourds to mark the season. Large potted mums in yellow, bronze, magenta and white decorated the foyer, the hallway and corners of the dining room. As a centerpiece, the same florist had created a long, low arrangement of eucalyptus, baby pine cones, tiny white asters and several shades of moss interspersed with white votive candles.

Farrell was no particular judge of botanical creativity, but even he thought the table looked particularly beautiful tonight. It made him think of a mystical fairy forest. The whimsical thought ground to a halt when Ivy finally entered the room.

"Good God," he whispered reverently.

Katie was standing close enough to hear him. Her smile was smug. "I did well, didn't I?"

"I'm not sure," he muttered. Luca Bain was already making a beeline for Ivy. "We need to keep that Swiss lecher away from her."

Katie pooh-poohed him with a frown. "Luca is a lovely gentleman. Ivy is a grown woman. She can decide who she's interested in and who she's not."

"This is a *work* weekend," Farrell said, hearing his own truculence and unable to stop himself.

"Don't be absurd. The work is done. It wouldn't hurt Ivy to enjoy herself tonight. She's had a tough few months. If Luca wants to entertain her, what's the harm?"

Katie moved away to chat with one of the guests.

"Over my dead body," Farrell muttered. But he couldn't make his feet move. So he simply stared at her. At Ivy, that was. His Ivy. His sweet, unassuming, gorgeous Ivy, who looked beautiful to him no matter what she wore.

Unfortunately for Farrell's peace of mind, Ivy was dressed to kill tonight. Though the bodice and hemline of her fire-engine-red frock were modest, the cut of the dress left little to the imagination. It accentuated her small breasts and flattered her narrow waist and heart-shaped ass.

And those legs. Those legs.

He gulped his champagne, hoping to ease his parched throat. Only sheer force of will kept his erection at bay.

Honestly, there was nothing prurient about the red dress. But for a man who was ass-over-heels in lust with Ivy, it was the equivalent of waving a crimson flag in front of a raging bull.

Three hours, Farrell told himself. Three hours, and everyone would go upstairs to bed. Except for his Ivy.

The meal was exquisite, the guests complimentary. The caterer glowed. Interesting conversation rippled back and forth across the table.

If anybody had been keeping score, they would likely rank this as one of the best damn dinner parties in the history of dinner parties.

All Farrell could think about was how soon it would be over.

Dessert was generous slices of pecan pie slathered with recently whipped cream. Farrell was so far gone he debated asking the caterer to leave any leftover whipped cream in the fridge. So Farrell could use it later. To decorate his lover's body as he kissed her from head to toe.

In the midst of his lust, reservations lingered. He was getting in too deep with Ivy. He couldn't let himself get attached…or wish for more. To lose someone he cared about—again—would cripple him. No relationship was worth that kind of pain. He'd convinced himself he could handle a light, fun physical relationship. But what if he was wrong?

He loosened his tie and told himself no one ever died of sexual deprivation. Suddenly, he lurched to his feet, determined to move things along. Ivy was seated between the Irish husband and the Swiss watchmaker.

Farrell had not been able to rearrange the place cards at the last minute, so *again*, he wasn't seated with Ivy.

He extricated her suavely. "Could you help me with something in the study, Ivy?" He gave both men a genial smile. "We won't be long."

Ivy stood and followed him. In the hall, she gave him a puzzled look. "What was that for?"

Privacy, Farrell thought desperately. He needed privacy. Taking Ivy by the wrist, he pulled her along to the study. Once inside, he locked the door. Slowly, he backed her up against the wall.

"That dress," he grumbled.

She glanced down at herself. "I was supposed to wear this last night, but when you all decided on the more casual event outside, I went with the blue instead. What's wrong? Did I spill something on myself? I hope not. This silk is dry-clean only."

He placed his hands, palms flat, on either side of her head. "You didn't spill anything." His gaze settled on her full, rosy-red lips. The lip stain she wore must have been semipermanent, because the meal hadn't removed it.

His chest rose and fell with the force of his ragged breathing. "I'd like to kiss you," he said, the words ridiculously formal.

Ivy's eyes rounded. Perhaps only now did she understand the true nature of their errand. She licked her lips. "I thought we were waiting until later."

"Can't," he said gruffly. "That dress."

Slowly, he reached out and cupped one of her breasts. He gave her plenty of opportunity to say no…to shove him away.

Instead, she smiled. "Patience, Farrell. Good things come to those who wait."

"Says who?" He leaned his forehead against hers. "Let's go to your cabin," he muttered, only half kidding.

Ivy stroked his hair. "Dolly and Delanna are there… remember?"

He groaned. "Hell. I'm the only man I know who can build a fortress of solitude in the middle of northern Maine and still not find a quiet place to kiss a girl."

"I'm a woman, Farrell." She cupped his face in her hands and kissed him. Slow, sweet, hot as a firecracker.

The taste of her exploded on his tongue, sent urgent messages to his sex and all other stops along the way. He pulled her tightly against him, so tight he could feel her heart beating against his, or so it seemed.

Reaching around her, he shimmied the hem of her skirt up to her hips. The skin on her thighs was softer than the silk. When he found a lacy black pair of thong panties, he cursed. Undressing Ivy later was a treat he was going to savor. Though he yearned to strip her naked, he forced himself to find one last modicum of control.

His hands rested on her butt, although he kept them still.

His fingers itched to tangle in her hair and tilt her lips to his, but they both had to return to the dining room soon. She truly had blossomed since coming to Farrell's coastal hideaway. Any man would be lucky to have her, but that man wouldn't be Farrell. Soon, he would have some difficult decisions to make.

He kissed the side of her neck. "Do you know how special you are, Ivy? I've watched you this weekend. People love you. You're fun, and you get them to talk about themselves. You've made a huge contribution to Stone River Outdoors."

Ivy slipped her hands underneath his suit jacket and rubbed his back through his shirt. "Thank you for saying that. It's been great for me, too." She sighed. "We have to go back in there, Farrell. You know we do."

He squeezed her ass once, released her and stepped back. "I know. That's the hell of it."

Ivy smoothed her dress into place, checked her reflection in the mirror that hung over the fireplace and gave him the kind of smile women had been giving men for millennia. "Don't be so impatient, Farrell. We've got all night."

Sixteen

Ivy was not good at sneaking around. The one time she had tried ditching school for a day at the beach, her parents had found out and grounded her for a month. She was a *good* girl.

But look where it had gotten her. If she hadn't been such a people pleaser, she might have booted Richard to the curb long ago. Instead, she had tried to do the right thing. She had tried to make her marriage work.

In looking back, she realized it was never a marriage at all. Not in the truest sense of the word. She had been a prisoner of Richard's lies, her own grief and, ultimately, a deep-seated fear of being alone.

She wouldn't make those mistakes again. For one thing, Farrell had been completely clear about his inability to commit to a relationship. Ivy appreciated his honesty.

Going forward, she understood that she and Dolly were a family now. Whatever happened with Farrell was a pleasant blip in Ivy's life. Her job was to give her daughter a stable childhood, a happy home.

But tonight…

Ivy pinched her pale cheeks in the bathroom mirror. All she had to do was walk down the stairs nonchalantly. For all anyone knew, she might be getting a glass of milk.

The lovely, sophisticated nightwear Katie had picked out was the kind of thing Ivy had seen women wear in movies. The black satin gown slid over her skin like a caress, equally as comfortable as being nude, but even more provocative. Slit almost to her navel in front and to the base of her spine in back, it spelled out sex with every movement of her body.

The matching robe was also luxurious, but far more decorous, certainly modest enough to warrant a run-in with another guest without embarrassment for either party. She tightened the sash and knotted it firmly.

As it turned out, Ivy had worried for nothing. The house was still and quiet when she tiptoed down the main staircase and rounded the hall that led to Farrell's room. Not a soul stirred. Farrell's door was cracked, so she tapped lightly and entered.

A fire blazed in the hearth. The covers on the huge king bed were turned back. Farrell stood by the mantel, clad in nothing but a pair of low-slung navy knit sleep pants that left little to the imagination.

She sucked in a sharp breath and stopped, clinging to one of the bedposts when her knees wobbled and threatened to give out beneath her. "This looks cozy," she said, trying to sound like a woman of the world.

Farrell's grin warmed her cold toes. She had forgotten her slippers.

He crooked a finger. "Come by the fire, Ivy. Do you want a drink?"

"No, thanks." Alcohol at this hour would make her

woozy. She didn't want to miss the good parts of what came next.

It struck her suddenly with a sharp stab of grief that she had been dead wrong. She'd told herself that spending time with Farrell was something she wanted, something she deserved. That when the clock ran out and she and Dolly moved on, Ivy would be able to look back on this interlude and be glad she had known and loved Farrell Stone even for a little while.

The truth ate at her now, destroying her illusions. In an instant, she realized that leaving this place—walking away from this complicated, kind, generous, amazing man—was going to destroy her.

Farrell must have seen something on her face. His smile faded. "What's wrong, Ivy?"

She swallowed hard. "Nothing. I'm just nervous." It wasn't entirely a lie. Her heart was beating like a jackhammer, and her teeth were in danger of chattering. Even her breathing was shaky.

Farrell didn't wait. He came to her. "Relax, Ivy. This night is for us. No pressure. Just pleasure." He slid his arms around her from behind and rested his chin on top of her head. "Earlier tonight you looked amazing in that red dress. But now, even better. Like a package I want to unwrap." His nimble fingers unknotted the tie at her waist.

She slipped out of her robe and tossed it on a chair, shored up by his strength and caring. "I want that, too."

"So glad we're on the same page." He chuckled hoarsely.

There wasn't much talking after that. Both of them had done a lot of "adulting" this weekend. Playing host. Working hard to make sure the event went smoothly.

It was time for self-indulgence.

Farrell picked her up and carried her to the bed. His hair was overdue for a cut, but the slightly shaggy look suited him. He was his own man, not bound by all of society's strictures. Though he was stunning in dress clothes, Ivy preferred this less-civilized version.

She wanted to tell him she loved him. Would it matter? Would it make a difference?

Maybe he wouldn't believe her. Maybe he'd say it was too soon after her marriage...that a rebound relationship wasn't the answer.

And maybe he would be forced to let her down gently, to remind her that Sasha had claimed his heart and still held it, even now.

Because Ivy didn't know the answers to those hypothetical scenarios, she kept quiet. Better to juggle uncertainty than to face the humiliation of an outright rejection, no matter how kind.

Farrell was impatient. She liked that. His urgency made her feel special. Desired. Desirable.

Though he had expressed appreciation for her new nightwear, he wasted no time in removing the gown. His knit pants joined the discarded lingerie. When they were both naked in the center of the mattress, he pulled the covers over them and dragged her against his warm body. His very warm body. The way his strong arms held her was delightful.

She ran her hands over his back, feeling the muscles, the taut flesh. "I was jealous of the Italian girl in your kayak," she admitted, her nose buried in his shoulder.

His chest rumbled with laughter. "Then we're even. Because I wanted to punch my brother for offering you lessons."

Farrell regretted the words as soon as they left his mouth. That admission made him sound more emotionally invested in this thing with Ivy than he wanted to admit.

She pulled back to stare at him. The only light in the

room was a muted glow from the fireplace. "Are you serious?"

He shrugged. "Yeah. I thought we were all supposed to be taking one of the guests on board to show them the ropes. But then some of them wanted to go with their spouses, and suddenly Zachary ended up with you."

"Zachary is a wonderful man, but he's not Farrell Stone."

"What does that mean?"

"He's gorgeous and fun, but you're more like me, Farrell. You don't need a lot to be happy. Or that's how it seems to me. Am I wrong?"

Her assessment was startling. As if she really understood who he was. "He's always popular with women."

"You would be, too, if you didn't have this kind of grumpy, standoffish thing going on." She paused, her smile impish. "But I like you anyway, because you have other *qualities* I find interesting."

When her hand closed around his erection, stroking once…then twice, he inhaled sharply. "I see."

She handled him firmly, keeping him on the edge of madness. "You're hardworking even though you have a ridiculous amount of money. You're kind, though I suspect you'd rather not be described that way. And you've given me a chance to get my life back with this job."

"I don't want your gratitude," he snapped. He heard the bite in his own voice, but he couldn't help it. "What we are…here…in this bed…doesn't have a damn thing to do with kindness or gratitude or anything else. I want you, Ivy. I need you. Do you understand?"

"Yes," she said softly. "I do."

He reached for protection, took care of business and lifted her astride him. "I'm yours, Ivy. Show me what you want."

Though shadows draped the bed in intimacy, he was well able to see his lover's face. Her cute hair was mussed, her cheeks stained pink with heightened color. His Ivy was learning to be bold, to take and not simply give, but her innate shyness lingered. When she rose up on one knee and aligned their bodies, he literally couldn't breathe. Everything in his chest froze, waiting for the moment of joining. Waiting. Waiting.

Her body accepted his easily, though he was as hard as he had ever been. His fingers gripped her hips, held her still, while he entered her. *Holy God.* His eyes stung with moisture. It was good. So good.

He'd never thought to find such closeness with a woman again.

And it terrified him. Clear down to the marrow of his bones. He felt stripped raw. Vulnerable.

Ivy's small, capable hands rested, palms flat, on his collarbone. She bent to kiss him. The change in position made them both gasp. "I want you," she whispered, her lips feathering over his with tiny angel-wing kisses. "For as long as we have. And I won't ask for more. So make love to me again and again, Farrell. Hard. Fast. Everything in between. I've got a lot of empty years to make up for. I need you, too."

He lost control then. Rolled her beneath him. Pounded his way to release. Gasped for air in the aftermath.

His bedroom was silent.

Ivy's heartbeat was loud. So was his.

The moment seemed right for some kind of confession on his part. Surely she realized that his self-imposed ban on caring was flimsy at best. But fear kept him silent.

After yawning twice, he kissed her shoulder. "Are you sleepy, Ivy? It's been a heck of a day."

She nodded, echoing his yawn with one of her own. "Yes. I'm going back upstairs now."

He scowled. "Why would you do that? It's two in the morning. Stay, Ivy. Stay here."

She patted his cheek like he was a fractious toddler

demanding a treat. "I've decided I'd rather not take any chances with our guests. I'll be more comfortable in my own room."

When she rolled out of bed and bent to pick up her things, he was treated to a great view of her ass and her... He gave himself a metaphorical smack. "I could make you comfortable," he said, giving her a look that hopefully communicated his displeasure with this new plan.

Ivy donned the gown and robe and tied the sash. Her smile was weary and sweet. "I'll see you in the morning, Farrell. Get some sleep."

Ivy slept like the dead and awoke refreshed, even though she'd barely managed five hours. Last night had given her hope. Though perhaps it shouldn't have. Farrell had been so tender, so everything. Surely a man couldn't have sex like that without feeling *something*. Could he?

The morning passed quickly. After breakfast, guests returned upstairs to pack. The three Farrell men took turns transporting luggage to the front foyer. The limos were slated to arrive at two o'clock sharp to ferry everyone back to Portland. Zachary, Quin, Katie and Delanna would be heading that way, as well.

Soon, it would only be Farrell, Dolly and Ivy once again.

Ivy had missed her daughter, though Dolly had been having the time of her life with Delanna, who doted on her every move. Even though Ivy had been at the cabin for the baby's bedtime both nights, Dolly had clearly bonded with her weekend sitter.

While the Stone brothers and their guests were involved in one last short planning session after lunch, Katie and Ivy helped the caterer pack up her supplies. The woman had driven back and forth from Bar Harbor morning and night. Ivy hoped she was being paid well.

When the kitchen was spotless, Katie joined the meeting. Ivy ran upstairs to pack her own things. When she was done, she put the bag in the mudroom at the back of the house. Tonight she would return to her bed at the cabin. Farrell's plans were a mystery.

Not long afterward, everyone gathered on the porch for goodbyes. The group had bonded. Ivy liked them all. Delanna was there, too, carrying Dolly and getting in a few last snuggles.

Luca shocked Ivy by grabbing her up and giving her a more-than-friendly smack on the lips. His grin, when he released her, was unrepentant. "When you come to Switzerland, mademoiselle, you must find me and I will take you to dinner at the best restaurant in the world."

Ivy returned the smile, flattered in spite of the outrageous display. "I'll keep that in mind."

Quin and Katie joined her, laughing. "I think you made a new friend," Quin said, clearly joking.

Katie shushed him. "Don't tease." She squeezed Ivy's arm. "I know you wanted to save up money for a car, but Quin and I realized that my old sedan was sitting in the garage up here at his house gathering dust. Well, *our* house," she said, correcting herself. "You're welcome to it, if you like the way it drives. I put a lot of miles on it, but she's a good car."

Ivy stared at them. "You can't *give* me a car. I'll pay you."

Quin shook his head. "Your money is no good in Maine. I have more vehicles than I need, and I bought Katie a new Land Rover last month. You'd be doing us a favor by taking her old car off our hands." He reached in his pocket and handed Ivy a set of keys. "She's all yours. I'm sure Farrell can help you line up the title and tag transfer."

Farrell joined them, overhearing Quin's final words. He frowned. "Why does Ivy need a car?"

Katie's brows narrowed, telegraphing her displeasure

with the man who was both her boss *and* her brother-in-law. "A woman should be independent. Ivy and Dolly need safe, reliable transportation."

"I have plenty of cars," Farrell said. He turned to Ivy. "If you wanted to borrow a car, all you had to do was ask."

Now Ivy was caught. She moved closer to Katie. "I told them I wanted to *buy* a car. They're offering me Katie's old one."

"You can have one of mine," he said. "For free."

Ivy could tell that he was serious. "I appreciate the offer," she muttered. "But since I work for you, it's probably less messy if I deal with Katie and Quin."

"Messy?" His eyes glittered.

She stared at him, daring him to make a scene. No one knew that Ivy and Farrell were lovers. She wanted to keep it that way. "Let's change the subject," she said. "Your guests are ready to go."

Farrell strode to the far side of the porch, leaving Katie and Quin to stare after him in disbelief.

Quin turned to Ivy. "What was that all about? He was pissed, and I didn't even do anything." His aggrieved expression was comical.

Katie, on the other hand, stared at Ivy as if her brain was doing calculations and perhaps coming up with the right answers.

Ivy gave them a big smile, hoping to derail Katie's suspicions. "Who knows? That brother of yours can be a bit of a curmudgeon." She glanced around, searching for a way out. "If you'll both excuse me, I need to say a few more goodbyes."

She talked to the Namibian couple, then exchanged email addresses with the Italian mother and father and the two daughters. One of the daughters handed Ivy a small tissue-wrapped parcel. "For your baby," she said shyly. "It's a doll I made from a handkerchief. My stitching is not very good."

Ivy unwrapped the package and smiled. It was the perfect toy for an inquisitive toddler. "I love it," she said. "Dolly will, too. *Grazie.*"

The hired cars had pulled up adjacent to the base of the steps. Though the drivers exited and were standing by to receive their passengers, no one seemed in any particular hurry to go back to Portland.

Probably because the Stone brothers knew how to throw a party.

Zachary motioned for the drivers to collect the bags. Ivy moved in his direction and tried to pick up a carry-on or two. "I can help," she said.

"Not necessary, but thanks." He gave her a smile that was enough like his brother's to give her heart a squeeze.

The youngest of the drivers hefted three large suitcases, one in each hand and one under his arm, perhaps trying to impress the two Italian girls. When he swung around to descend the steps, the corner of a hard-sided bag bumped Ivy's hip. She stepped back instinctively to give the kid more room, but her foot found nothing but air.

She tried to regain her balance. It was too late.

The world turned upside down as she tumbled down the stairs.

Seventeen

Farrell was more than ready for everyone to be gone. He wanted his house to himself again. As he tried to usher people toward the transportation, he heard someone cry out. He spun on his heel, just in time to see Ivy fall down the steep front stairs.

His heart stopped. His feet refused to move. Fear paralyzed him. His vision narrowed, and for a moment, he felt as if he might pass out.

Dead. She could be dead.

Everyone surged en masse. Except Farrell. He tried to move, but his arms and legs felt uncoordinated, heavy. Zachary got to Ivy first. It wasn't until Farrell saw Ivy speaking to his brother that he was finally able to force himself down the steps.

Someone offered to call an ambulance. Farrell crouched beside his lover. "No point," he said gruffly. "It would be an hour until someone gets here."

Zachary touched the bleeding scrape on Ivy's cheek.

"He's right. My first-aid training is up-to-date. Let's evaluate her and make a decision."

Farrell nodded.

Ivy lifted an arm and waved her hand. "I'm right here. And I'm okay. It was my own clumsiness. I'll have bruises, but it's nothing serious."

"We'll be the judge of that." Farrell was curt.

Quin and Katie were having a whispered conference on the sidelines.

After Farrell and Zachary checked Ivy's arms and legs for broken bones, Farrell scooped her into his arms and moved carefully up the stairs, Zachary at his side. In the master suite, Farrell laid Ivy gently on his bed. The very same bed where he had lost himself in madness the night before.

Zachary checked her pulse. Examined her pupils. Barked out half a dozen questions. "Did you hit your head?" he asked urgently. "Tell us the truth."

"No," Ivy said forcefully. "I scraped my cheek on the corner of a step, but I don't even have a headache. My hip took the worst of it. Give me some ibuprofen, and I'll be fine. I need to get Dolly, so Delanna can leave."

Farrell stared at her, his heart still beating sluggishly. "Quin left with the group, because some of them had planes to catch. Katie stayed behind to look after the baby. Be still, damn it," he said when Ivy tried to get up.

She glared at him. "I know my own body. I'm not badly hurt."

Zachary shoved his hands in his pockets, his expression concerned. "Possibly. But we have to make sure you're not in shock. Farrell, you stay with her. I'll round up something for that wound."

Suddenly, silence descended. Ivy wouldn't look at him. Words he wanted to say hovered on his lips, but he choked them back. Sick to his stomach, he suddenly wanted to be anywhere but in this room.

Over and over in his head, he saw Ivy falling. Falling. Falling.

Zachary returned and cleaned Ivy's cheek. Then he added some antibiotic ointment and covered the deep scrape with a Band-Aid. "I don't think it will hurt to get it wet tonight. And you should sleep with it uncovered."

Ivy smiled. "Thanks, Zachary. I'm fine. Honest."

Farrell stared down at the bed. Why did Ivy look so impossibly small and defenseless? His heart turned over in his chest. What were these wild, tangled feelings that writhed inside him? He *didn't* love her. He was concerned. That was all.

"We'll let you rest," he said abruptly. He turned to his brother. "Let's find Katie and make a game plan."

In the kitchen, the three adults gathered. Katie grimaced. "Dolly is ready for her afternoon nap. What do you want me to do?"

Farrell paced, opened the fridge and extracted a beer. He downed half of it in two gulps. "Put the baby down in the study. Bring me the monitor. Then you and Zachary hit the road and see if you can catch up with the rest of the group. Quin will need help in Portland sorting everything out, because they're not all staying at the same hotel."

Zachary nodded. "Fair enough. And somebody—I can't remember who—is flying out tonight, not in the morning."

"I think it's Luca," Katie said. She held Dolly close, stroking her head. "Okay. I'll get this little one to sleep and say goodbye to Ivy. Zachary, let me know how soon you want to leave."

He glanced at his watch. "Fifteen minutes?"

"I'll meet you out front."

Farrell stared at Zachary. "Do you really think she's

okay? I don't want this to be one of those stories where a concussion goes unnoticed."

"She says it was only her cheek. I don't see any signs to worry about. I've banged my head a time or two in the day, so I know the drill. But watch her for the next several hours."

"You can bet on it."

Ivy opened her eyes when the bedroom door creaked. Seeing Katie gave her a sigh of relief. For some reason, Farrell was acting weird. She couldn't handle that right now. Her whole body ached.

Katie came to the bed and perched on the edge of the mattress. "I just put Dolly down for her nap. Farrell has the monitor. Zachary and I are headed back to Portland to help Quin at the other end."

"I'm sorry I disrupted your plans for nothing."

Katie cocked her head. "Falling down an entire flight of steps isn't exactly nothing. Are you sure you don't need a hospital?"

"One-hundred-percent sure. I'm sore from head to toe, but no serious injuries. I'm a single mom. I won't do anything to endanger my health—I swear. Dolly needs me."

Katie stood and blew a kiss. "If you're sure." She paused. "Farrell is acting odd in all of this. Are you and he—"

Ivy interrupted quickly. "Farrell and I are nothing, Katie. He's my boss. Besides, you know how he is. The man is an enigma wrapped in a puzzle. Don't try to figure him out. You'll only frustrate yourself."

"I suppose."

Zachary hollered down the hall, clearly forgetting the sleeping baby.

"Gotta go. We'll talk soon. Bye, Ivy."

When the house was silent, Ivy eased out of bed. Farrell would be outside saying goodbye. In the bathroom, she glanced in the mirror and winced. Her hair was a mess, and she was paler than normal, not to mention the damage to her cheek.

Five minutes later when she returned, Farrell was leaning against one of the bedposts, arms crossed over his chest. A dark scowl gave him a menacing air. "I told you to stay in bed."

"I had to pee," she said, daring him to chastise her further. "I don't need a nanny, Farrell, though I appreciate your concern."

He shoved away from the bed and went to poke the fire. "Rest," he said bluntly. "I'll watch the monitor for the moment."

"That's not necessary." Something was off with Farrell. He seemed angry. But why? She went to him and put a hand on his shoulder. "You need to go back to the lab. I know you're itching to get to work on your project. I'm fine. I found medicine in your bathroom cabinet. As soon as it kicks in, I'll be almost good as new." She rested her cheek on his shoulder. "This was a fun weekend, but I'm glad everyone is gone."

His big frame stiffened. Noticeably. He shrugged out of her light embrace and headed for the door. "You're right," he muttered, not looking at her. "I do need to work. But I want you to text me every thirty minutes and let me know how you're doing."

Suddenly, she knew she was losing him, though she couldn't explain it. "Okay," she said slowly. "Would you like to come to the cabin for dinner tonight? Nothing fancy. After Dolly goes to sleep, we could...relax." She couldn't bring herself to say the *actual* words to describe sex. Not when he was being all aloof and weird.

Farrell never even turned to look at her. "I'll probably work late," he said. "And there are leftovers in the fridge. I'll see you tomorrow. Don't forget the texts."

Stunned, Ivy watched him walk out the door.

Three hours later, she was no closer to understanding what had happened. Her body felt awful, every bruise making itself known. But that was nothing compared to the ache in her chest. Her silly, foolish heart was beginning to crack into a million pieces.

As promised, she texted Farrell every thirty minutes to let him know she wasn't dead. The dark humor suited her mood.

Last night, Farrell had made love to her as if he would never let her go. Today, he could barely look at her. His on-again, off-again mood swings made her furious. And they hurt, too, but she concentrated on the anger. She loved the infuriating man—quite desperately, in fact. If she found the courage to tell him so, and the feelings were one-sided, she would have to leave.

Farrell didn't even try to sleep. He paced the confines of his small lab and searched for a way out. He didn't love Ivy. He didn't. The sick fear he experienced when he saw her tumble down his stairs was nothing more than concern for a friend, an employee.

The prospect that he *might* let himself get too involved galvanized him. He *couldn't* lose someone he loved again. He wouldn't allow it. If there was any possibility he might fall in love with Ivy, he had to step away from the madness now.

Even in the midst of his panicked rationalizations, he knew he was lying to himself. And he was ashamed of his cowardice. With every day that passed, Ivy had become more and more dear to him. Of course he loved her. How could he not?

He'd done a damn good job of denying it, though.

Seeing her fall down the stairs had revealed the depth of his love and also the impossibility of telling her how he felt.

He wanted her delectable body. That much was true. But it wasn't too late to stop himself from making a terrible mistake.

Every moment he'd spent in Ivy's bed and vice versa had been exquisitely pleasurable. Still, he had lived without physical release before. Months on end, in fact. He could deny himself. He had no other choice.

He had to let her go…

Ivy slept fitfully. Monday morning dawned gray and cold and blustery. It was as if the weather had stayed perfect for their out-of-town guests, and now that the party was over, Mother Nature was having a hissy fit.

Delanna had done a wonderful job caring for Dolly, but the cabin was a bit of a mess. Ignoring the aches and pains from her accident, Ivy did two loads of laundry while cleaning the place from top to bottom, thankful that Dolly was happily occupied with her pots and pans on the floor.

At ten thirty, Ivy decided to go to Farrell's house and make a plan for dinner. She had no idea what food was left. But she would throw something together that was better than reheating leftovers.

"Come on, lovey," she said to Dolly. "Let's take a walk." It wasn't actually raining at the moment, but she and Dolly bundled up for the short trek.

It seemed odd to find the big house empty and quiet after all the commotion of the weekend. But having the serene space was peaceful, too. Plenty of time to think.

With Dolly on her hip, she wandered into the kitchen. There on the counter, propped up with a banana, was an envelope with her name on it. She recognized Farrell's bold handwriting.

Something told her she wasn't going to like the contents. Why hadn't Farrell simply sent a text if he wanted something special? Or maybe he needed her to clean all the guest rooms, because he hadn't found anyone else to tackle the task.

After tucking Dolly in her high chair and giving her a handful of dry cereal, Ivy opened the note with shaking hands.

Ivy:

Now that the house party is over and my project is wrapping up, I think it's best if you return to Portland. Because this change is somewhat sooner than you expected, I am including a severance check, as well as a letter of reference.

I plan to be at the house by two this afternoon. I'll help you pack up. We'll drive my SUV back to Portland, so the high chair and port-a-crib will fit. Feel free to text Katie if you need her to do anything on the other end.

F.

Ivy stared at the piece of paper, trying to decipher the words. *Sooner than you expected. Severance.*

And not even his whole name. Just "F."

She felt sick. Betrayed. Stunned. He had told her from the beginning that he wouldn't allow his feelings to be involved. It wasn't Farrell's fault that she hadn't believed him.

Anger would have helped. She tried to be angry. She *wanted* to be angry like she had been before. But her body was literally battered and bruised, and now her spirit was in equal pain.

Had Farrell somehow decided she was going to cling or make demands? Had he thought it best to end their short-lived affair before things got messy?

Tears stung her eyes, but she didn't let them fall.

Every paycheck she had earned sat in her purse down at the cabin. The severance amount in her hand was humiliating, but she didn't have the luxury of shredding it and leaving the pieces on the counter.

So she did what every survivor has always done. She picked up her child, and she walked out.

Farrell paced the confines of his Portland office, wanting to smash things. Both of his brothers and Katie sat nearby, watching him with sympathy in their eyes. That compassion ate at him, because those were the same expressions he had received from *everyone* when Sasha died.

He had hated it then, and he hated it now. Those looks meant that his life was screwed. Destroyed. Over.

For five solid weeks he had searched for Ivy and Dolly. But they had vanished from the face of the earth. Finally, in despair, he realized he needed help. So he had summoned his family and told them everything.

"When she had the accident on the stairs," he croaked, remembering that terrible day, "it was like having everything click into sharp focus. I understood that I was falling in love with her, and I was terrified."

Quin sighed. "So you decided to get rid of her."

Farrell winced. "I couldn't go through that again. Losing someone. Ivy could have died on those steps."

"But she didn't," Zachary said. "And now you've lost her anyway."

Farrell sucked in a breath, his chest heaving. Zachary was right. Farrell had made a terrible mistake, and he had to fix it. "You have to help me find her," Farrell said. "Please. She didn't even take all the baby's things."

Katie stood and went to the window, her face drawn with worry. "As a female, I can only imagine what she's going through. A woman like Ivy wouldn't offer her body easily. She must have cared for you, Farrell. But knowing

Ivy, she would have kept those feelings to herself, because she believes you still love Sasha."

"Why would she think that?" he bellowed, half-frantic with panic.

Quin put an arm around his shoulders. "Because we all thought that, Farrell. Until Ivy, you've not looked at a woman seriously in seven years. Ivy would have no way of knowing that you cared. Not without the words, especially since you sent her away."

Zachary's jaw firmed. "We'll find her, I swear. What ground have you covered so far?"

"I started in the Charleston area. Two weeks with a private investigator. All we managed to prove was that she hadn't been back since she came north and moved in with Delanna. So I returned here to Portland. I've combed every apartment complex in the city. Twice. I even had a buddy of mine at the DMV try to trace the registry on that car you gave her." He glared at Quin and Katie, though he knew who was really to blame for Ivy's flight.

Katie turned and gave all three men a look of disgust. "Think it through. Ivy would rather risk getting a ticket than having Farrell find her. She probably didn't register the car."

The truth of that struck Farrell like a death blow to the gut. What had he done? Good God, what had he done?

"So what next?" he groaned. "It's a big damn country."

"Bar Harbor," Katie said, her face beginning to reflect hope. "When I first drove Ivy and Dolly up to your house, we passed the turnoff for Bar Harbor. Ivy mentioned that she had always wanted to spend some time there. Her family visited Acadia briefly when she was a kid, and she was fascinated by the park."

Quin nodded. "It's no better or worse than any other idea."

Zachary drummed his fingers on the desk, his serious

expression far from the carefree facade he typically showed to the world. He sat in Farrell's chair making notes. "It's tricky, but I could get someone to trace her Social Security number."

"Won't work," Katie said. "If a woman wants to hide, she'll get a job that pays cash."

Farrell straightened his spine. "Then Bar Harbor it is. If necessary, I'll sell part of my shares in SRO to both of you to finance this search."

Quin rolled his eyes. "Don't be an asshole, big brother. And don't insult us. If Ivy is important to you, we're in on this. One hundred percent."

Eighteen

Ten days of searching the Bar Harbor area, and Farrell was so tired he was weaving on his feet. He'd barely managed three or four hours of sleep a night for weeks. Shame and regret and dread ate away at the lining of his stomach. It was torture to imagine Ivy laboring all alone to support herself and her child.

He loved that stubborn, precious woman, and he'd never told her. He'd let his fear drive her away. Among all the other reasons that kept him searching was the need to apologize. To tell her how he felt. And regardless of the outcome, to beg her forgiveness.

When she disappeared, she had left the baby bed. The high chair. Every last item of couture wardrobe Katie had helped pick out.

The woman who fled an abusive marriage and came north to Maine for a new start had left Farrell's home with little more than the clothes on her back.

Because he had hurt her. Badly.

Now, at last, he was about to confront his mistakes. At least he hoped so. True to their word, Zachary and Quin and Katie had committed all their time and effort to locating a woman who didn't want to be found.

Even in a relatively small community like Bar Harbor, those searches had taken time.

Now it was up to Farrell. He stared at the tiny, run-down motel from the anonymity of a rental car. The rental was to keep Ivy from spotting him and running again.

The Summer's Beauty Inn was anything but. Beautiful, that was. It was the kind of place that might have been a popular tourist haunt in the 1950s. Now it existed far off the beaten path, slowly decaying into the surrounding hillside.

Katie's familiar sedan, now Ivy's, sat in front of the unit marked 7E. The car was backed into the spot, so there was no way to tell if it had a license tag.

Farrell only knew that his quest was just beginning.

He wasn't a praying man, not particularly, but he muttered a few words of supplication in hopes that a benevolent deity might take pity on him. Or maybe Sasha might intervene on his behalf. Farrell would take any help he could get at this point.

When he glanced at his watch, he marked the hour. Six fifteen. Early enough that Dolly wouldn't be asleep. Late enough that the two females who held his heart might have eaten.

Farrell's appetite had been nonexistent for weeks.

He gathered his phone and his keys and climbed out of the car. The twenty steps toward the door with the peeling green paint felt like a marathon. What could he say to make things right?

Even worse, what if those words didn't exist?

Ivy flinched when someone knocked at her door. Old habit. She'd had a few drunken losers try to get in the wrong room since she had been here.

When she looked out the peephole, she moaned and put her back to the door, clutching Dolly to her chest. No. No. No.

She stayed perfectly still, heart pounding, mouth dry.

Farrell's deep voice accompanied a second round of knocking. "I know you're in there, Ivy. Open up."

He couldn't possibly know for sure. Of course, her car was out front. Katie's car, actually. Ivy was going to pay for it, just not yet. Living expenses were eating through her stash of money at an alarming rate.

Dolly, unaware that she was supposed to be quiet, started babbling. The little girl was becoming more vocal every day. Ivy was proud of her daughter, but now was not the time. "Ssh, sweetheart."

Silence reigned for one minute. Then two. Then three. Maybe Farrell had given up.

The fact that Ivy's first response to that possibility was disappointment meant she was in deep doo-doo.

If she peered out the peephole again, would he be able to see her eyeball? She'd never considered what it looked like from the other side of the door. But she was desperate to know if he was still there.

Sliding the drapes aside wasn't an option. The Farrell she knew would jump on that immediately.

If he hadn't walked away.

Before she could make up her mind, a small white business card slid under the door. It was Farrell's, of course. All of his various Stone River Outdoors info was on one side. But when she flipped the card over, there were only two words—*I'm sorry...*

Her eyes stung. It didn't really matter, did it? Not in the big scheme of things. But if he wasn't going to leave, she had to deal with him.

All she had to do was hold it together for fifteen or

twenty minutes. He would salve his conscience. She would absolve him. Then they would go their separate ways.

Could she bear it? She had missed him so badly, only sheer exhaustion allowed her to sleep. She dreamed about him. Every night.

She'd walked out of his cabin almost seven weeks ago and into the current, temporary arrangement. She was working toward a bigger plan. Once she had a decent nest egg for first and last months' rent and utility deposits, she hoped to rent a nice apartment in Portland. Jobs would be more plentiful there and not dependent on the vagaries of the tourist season.

She wasn't alone in the world. She had made friends with Katie and Delanna. Eventually, one or both of them could be the beginning of her new community, her circle of emotional support. But she hadn't contacted either of them yet. She hadn't wanted to chance having word of her whereabouts get back to Farrell. He couldn't have been too upset, though, if it had taken him this long to show up. Why was he here?

In her heart, she knew why. He was a decent man, and he knew he had hurt her feelings. That was all she would admit to… No reason for him to know how she really felt. No reason at all.

"I need you to be a cute distraction," she whispered to Dolly. The little girl slobbered and blew a bubble and tooted. Great. So much for backup.

The next knock sounded fiercer. "Open the door, Ivy."

Dear God, please don't let me make a fool of myself.

She looked down at her faded jeans and her long-sleeved navy Henley top. The casual clothes were a far cry from the beautiful wardrobe she had worn for the weekend retreat. Not to mention that she had a smear of mashed banana on her sleeve and a tiny hole at her elbow.

Cinderella was definitely back with the mice.

Before she could lose her nerve, she smoothed her hair with one hand and jerked open the door. "Hello, Farrell. What brings you here?"

Farrell had almost given up. If Ivy didn't want to see him, did he *have* to leave, or could he try to make amends? While he was still wrestling with that thorny question, there she was.

"Ivy…" His words dried up.

She stepped back. "Come in."

The motel room was dismal. That was the nicest description he could come up with. Ivy herself was everything he remembered and more. The hazel eyes with the wary gaze. Pointed chin. Unpainted pink lips that had kissed him and offered him joy again. He wanted to grab her and hold her and never let her go.

But even a blind man could sense the great chasm between them.

He cleared his throat. "I couldn't find you."

She frowned. "I'm only an hour from your house…give or take."

"Don't be coy. You hid in plain sight. I've been to Charleston for two weeks. And all over Portland. You didn't register the car, damn it." He was losing it, and Ivy's expression closed up.

She pursed her lips. "I'm sorry you've been inconvenienced, Farrell. But I'm not sure what that has to do with me."

He glanced behind him at the two beds. Both were covered with bilious green satin bedspreads that matched the door. "May we please sit down?"

She shrugged. "If you like."

Dolly was giving him the stink eye. Didn't the kid remember how many times he had played with her? Sung to her? Rubbed her back as she fell asleep?

An awkward silence fell. Where to start…

Ivy glanced at her watch.

Farrell decided to cut to the chase. "I'm not in love with Sasha anymore, I swear. She was my first love. And I will always honor her memory, but she's my past."

Ivy blinked. "Okay."

The stubborn woman wasn't going to make this easy on him.

He didn't really blame her. So he took a breath and kept going.

"I'm sorry I threw you out," he said. "That was cowardly. And wrong."

Another blink. "Got it. No worries."

"Please come back with me," he begged.

This time her eyes flashed fire, a fire he hadn't fully understood until this moment. "No, thank you," she said, her tone excruciatingly polite. "Dolly and I are fine."

"Do you even have a job?" he asked in desperation. "We tried tracing your Social Security number, but nothing pinged."

"We?" Her facade cracked. "Who's *we*?"

"Zachary and Katie and Quin, of course. I needed help finding you. So I told them everything."

Her eyes widened. "No."

He shrugged. "Yes. Not the intimate details, of course, but enough to give them a clear picture of the urgency I felt."

This time, she frowned. "What urgency?"

He took a deep breath. "I told them I loved you, but that I had treated you badly and made you run away."

Ivy went so white he thought she might pass out. The mostly-healed scrape on her cheek was visible still. She was far too thin. Had she not been eating well?

"Yes, you did," she said, her lips pale. "But I've pursued other employment."

"What do you do?" He didn't really care, but he sensed he needed to keep the conversation flowing or she would shut him down.

Ivy played with Dolly's hair. "I wait tables at a bar six nights a week. My shift starts at nine and ends at one in the morning. The lady next door comes here to my room and watches TV while Dolly sleeps. The bar tips are decent. I give her part of my paycheck for her trouble."

Good God. That meant Ivy was wandering the streets in the middle of the night, vulnerable to any number of dangers.

And all because of him. He hadn't thought his spirits could sink any lower. It wasn't so easy to speak casually this time, because his throat was tight with emotion. "When do *you* sleep?" he muttered.

Ivy stared at him. "From two until seven in the morning, when this little one wakes up. And again during her naps. It's not so bad. We're making it work."

Farrell looked around him at the awful orange-and-gold wallpaper and the threadbare carpet with the unidentifiable stains. He wanted to cry. And he would have if he thought Ivy would take pity on him.

Why should she ever forgive him for what he had done? At least her bastard of a husband had kept a roof over her head. Farrell had made her homeless. He swallowed hard.

"Did you hear what I said earlier?"

"About what?"

"I told Katie and Quin and Zachary that I loved you."

Her bottom lip trembled. "But you never told me." Huge tears welled in her eyes, rolled down her cheeks, wet the baby's head.

"Ah, God, Ivy." He went to her, his heart breaking, and knelt beside the bed. Taking her free hand in his, he kissed it, held it to his cheek. "I love you, Ivy Danby. You burst into my world, not like a blazing comet, but like a quiet, unremarkable moon on the back side of a planet. I barely knew you were there at first, and then I started looking for you. All the time."

The hint of a smile interrupted her tears. "That's a terrible metaphor, Farrell. Stick to inventing."

"I'm pretty sure it's a simile, but we can argue about that later." He looked up at her, letting her see the nights of agonized worry, the deep regret, the unquenchable hope. "I adore you, Ivy. I knew it when I made love to you that last night, but I thought I could keep my emotions out of it. Then you fell down those god-awful steps, and I realized how easily I could lose you. It terrified me. I didn't want to feel that pain again. So I shoved you away."

He laid his cheek on her thigh. "I am so sorry, my love. Sorrier than you will ever know. Forgive me for being such a complete and utter failure as a human being."

Slender fingers sifted through his hair. His heart stopped. Jerked. Beat again more rapidly.

Ivy exhaled, a broken, shaky sound that heaped more coals of fire on his head. "I forgive you, Farrell. I do. And I even understand. But I'm not the woman to replace your Sasha."

Farrell stood abruptly and lifted Dolly from Ivy's arms. He grabbed the baby's favorite stacking cups from the dresser and set her and the toy in the port-a-crib. A brand-new one. He patted the baby's head. "Give me ten minutes, Dolly. Please. And if we've got a deal, I'll buy you a pony on your fifth birthday."

Luckily for him, the little girl was in a mood to be entertained easily.

Farrell spun back toward the bed, took Ivy's cold hands in his and drew her to her feet. He squeezed her fingers, looking down into her glorious hazel eyes. "Listen to me, Ivy. You're *nobody's* replacement. Ever. You're not second-string. You're not the consolation prize. You're strong and brave and tough and vulnerable. I love everything about you. When you were in a bad situation, you fought your way through, and you made it. You kept yourself and your daughter afloat against all odds."

She shook her head slowly. Nothing in her expression told him she had heard or believed a word he said. "You don't have to rescue me, Farrell. I've rescued myself. I'm only here at the motel temporarily. I have several job interviews coming. I've made plans for the future, for Dolly and me. I enjoyed having sex with you. A lot. But I'm moving on."

"Don't lie to me, sweetheart. I was there. You gave me your precious body and you took mine as your right. We were *together* in every sense of the word. You're my future, Ivy. I can't live without you. I won't. If I have to, I'll book the room next door and wait up for you every night until you come home to me. You're mine, Ivy. I didn't know it would happen like this, and God knows, I don't deserve you, but if you'll give me another chance, you won't ever have reason to doubt me again."

He ran out of breath and out of words.

Only their hands touched.

Ivy's big-eyed gaze searched his face. He wasn't sure what she saw. He'd been torn apart and put back together so many times in these past weeks, he wasn't the same man. "Ivy?"

She reached up slowly, put her hands on his cheeks, tested the stubble on his chin, stroked his brow. "You mean it, don't you?"

He nodded, willing her to understand. "I've never felt like this before. I was a very young man when I was with Sasha. We were young together, and we were naive about what the world could throw at us. But you and I have been through hell and back, Ivy. We've been tested, tried. Neither of us knows what the future holds, but I will love you for as many days as we have on this earth, and I pray they'll be too many to count."

She sniffed and wiped her nose on his expensive Egyptian cotton shirt. "Engineers aren't supposed to be poets." She wrapped her arms around his neck and clung. "I love you, too. Almost since the beginning. And I won't let you go either."

Her admission sent a shudder through his body, a wave of pained relief. For the longest time, they stood there, wrapped in each other's arms, contemplating how close they had come to having nothing at all. At last, Farrell couldn't bear it anymore. He pulled back, found her lips with his and kissed her. Until they were both dizzy.

He ran his thumb over her soft cheek. "You're my world, Ivy. You and Dolly."

Her eyes sparkled. "And you're the best man I've ever known. I want to be your wife, please."

"Is that a proposal?" he asked, chuckling at her artless assurance.

The woman in his arms gave him a look that warmed all the cold places in his heart. "Take me home, Farrell, to your cabin in the woods. It's where all good fairy tales start. We'll live happily ever after."

"You can bet on it, my love. You can bet on it."

* * * * *

HOT NASHVILLE NIGHTS

SHERI WHITEFEATHER

One

Alice

I parked at the end of Spencer Riggs's long, narrow driveway and glanced out at the vine-covered arbor leading to his porch. Along the path, potted plants grew in colorful disarray, giving me a sense of elegant chaos.

I was trying not to panic about this meeting, but Spencer was different from my other Nashville clients. He was a former lover of mine, a dark shadow from my past.

Was it any wonder I was nervous?

I stayed in my car for a few more minutes, still gazing out the windshield. The music industry adored Spencer, and so did the women in this town. According to the social media buzz, he was quite the catch. An award-winning songwriter with a reputation for being a creative genius. A handsome twenty-eight-year-old who lived in a beautifully renovated old house and rescued abused and abandoned dogs. Talk about a new life. He didn't even have a gold-fish when I knew him. He'd been working as a bartender back then, struggling to sell his songs.

I'd heard rumors that he was considered unattainable now. Of course, that just made women want him all the more. But in spite of his female following, he kept his affairs private. No one was out there bragging about being with him. He wasn't dropping names, either.

I found that curious, considering my dirty-sex history with him. Our hookups only lasted a few months, but I'd never forgotten how wild he was in bed. Or how troubled he'd made me feel. During that time, I'd had all sorts of emotional problems, and my affair with him had only fueled the fire.

These days, I was a freelance fashion stylist, and I would be dressing him for an upcoming magazine photo shoot. The magazine was willing to provide Spencer with one of their stylists, but he wanted to hire me instead, footing the bill himself and paying me directly. I didn't relish the idea of working for him, but what could I do?

My career was still in its early stages, and I was in no position to turn down an A-lister. His name would look good on my resume. But even more importantly, a world-renowned photographer was booked for the shoot. If I impressed him, this could be a game changer for me. And the final kicker? I'd spent way too much money over the years, and the hefty sum I'd received from a legal settlement when I was just nineteen years old was dwindling. If I didn't take this job and use it to my best advantage, I might never get out of the hole I created.

I drew a breath, then exited my car and made my way to Spencer's door. It had rained heavily earlier, but it was just drizzling now.

I rang the bell, and he answered quickly enough.

Holy cow. It had been five years, and Spencer was hotter than ever. He stood tall and fit, with a naturally tanned complexion and straight, collar-length brown hair, parted on the side and swept across his forehead. His deep-set eyes were dark, almost black, and his jaw was peppered with beard stubble. He had strong features: prominent cheekbones and a wide, luscious mouth. He wore a plain beige T-shirt, threadbare jeans, torn at one knee, and leather sneakers. His left arm boasted a full-sleeve tattoo, but the ink was white, making it look like scarring against his dark skin.

"That's new," I said.

He blinked at me. "What?"

"The tattoo."

"Oh, yeah." He was staring at me as though he was having the same knee-jerk reaction that I was having to him. "How have you been, Alice?"

"Fine." When he shifted his stance, my long-lost libido clenched. I'd been celibate since I'd shared his bed, swearing off men until the right one came along—a decision that my reckless hookups with him had obviously factored into. I'd already been using sex to fill the void inside me and being passionately consumed with him had intensified the ache.

"Do you want to come in?" he asked.

I nodded, wondering what he would think if he knew how cautious I was now. Or how badly I wanted to fall in love, get married and have babies.

He stepped away from the door, and we both went inside.

He was no longer staring at me, but I suspected that he wanted to take another long, hard look. We'd had sex in every room of his old apartment. One of his favorite activities had been doing body shots off my navel or from in between my breasts. Everything we'd done together had been hard and fast, including midnight rides on his motorcycle.

He led me to the living room, where a shiny red piano made a bold statement. His house boasted vintage charm, but was rife with contemporary updates.

He wasn't born and bred in Nashville. He was originally from LA and never knew his father. He was raised by a single mother but somewhere along the way, she'd died and he'd moved in with an aunt and uncle. He'd only given me vague details. He knew far more about me than I did about him.

He gestured to an impressive wet bar and coffee station. "Can I get you anything?"

"That's all right. I'm okay." To keep my hands busy, I smoothed my top. I wore an oversize tunic, skinny jeans and thigh-high boots that served me in the rain. My bleached blond hair was short and choppy, left over from my cowpunk phase. It was the only wild side of myself that I'd held on to.

He sat across from me, illuminated by the cloudy light spilling in from the windows. My mind was whirring, working feverishly about how I was going to dress him. I envisioned a variety of looks, ranging from rebellious to refined. From what I recalled, he'd never really cared much about clothes, except when he was removing mine.

"You came highly recommended," he said, jarring me out of my thoughts. "Kirby suggested that I hire you."

I gaped at him. *"Kirby Talbot?"* The country superstar who'd destroyed my mother, who'd promised to buy her songs, but had merely slept with her instead. "Seriously, Spencer?" He knew damned well that I hated Kirby. Not only had Kirby ghosted my mother after their affair, he'd filed a restraining order against her when she'd tried to contact him again.

His heartless actions were a tragedy from which Mama had never recovered. I never got over it, either. Her depression had destroyed me when I was young. Now that I was grown up, Kirby kept trying to fix it. But I couldn't forget the pain he'd caused.

I frowned at my former lover. I was aware that he'd written some recent hits for Kirby, but beyond that I didn't know what their relationship entailed. "Just how chummy are you?"

"He's actually become a mentor to me." Spencer twisted one of the threads that looped across the hole in his jeans, then looked up, his gaze instantly riveted to mine. "I couldn't have gotten sober without him."

I blinked, then glanced at the bar, where bottles of liquor were clearly visible. "You're a recovering alcoholic?"

He continued looking at me. "I've had a problem with it for years. Don't you remember how drunk I used to get?"

"Yes, but I didn't know it was an addiction. I just thought you liked to party." I was feeling foolishly naïve. All those slurred, sexy nights, all those body shots. "Why do you have a fully stocked bar now?"

"I keep it around for guests." He ran his gaze over me. "I can resist the temptation."

I hoped he resisted his drink of choice far better than he was resisting his renewed attraction to me. The air between us had gone unbearably thick. *Temptation*, I thought. So much temptation.

And on top of that, I wasn't convinced that if push came to shove, he wouldn't fall off the wagon. He still seemed restless to me. "How long have you been sober?"

"Two years, three months, five days and—" He removed his phone from his pocket and checked the time "—six hours." He glanced up and laughed a little. "Give or take."

His jokey remark didn't ease my concern. "I'm glad

you're trying to turn your life around." I would at least give him credit for that. "But you know what sucks? That I used to tell you what a jerk Kirby was, but you still managed to bond with him. You'd never even met him when I was with you."

He scowled. "Well, I got to know him later. And what was I was supposed to do? Shun him because of you? He's been trying to make amends with you for years."

I tightened my spine, sitting ramrod straight. Spencer used to support my hatred of Kirby, but now he was siding with the enemy. "Did you hire me as a favor to Kirby? Is that what this is all about?"

"No." His scowl deepened.

"Then why did you hire me?"

He shrugged. "For old times' sake, I guess."

Meaning what, exactly? That he was curious to see me? That didn't make me feel any better. Our affair had started in the gutter. We'd hooked up on Tinder, strictly for the sex. I'd been all of twenty then. Young and promiscuous.

I gave him a pointed look. "You still shouldn't have blindsided me about Kirby."

He shook his head. "I don't understand your reluctance to forgive him. He apologized for what he did to your family, not just privately but in a press conference, too. He bought the rights to your mom's songs from you and your sister and made good on his promise to market them. You got a nice settlement from him."

"It wasn't enough to last forever. Going to college and starting a new business wasn't cheap." I'd definitely spent a huge chunk on those things. But I'd blown tons of it, too. Not that I was going to admit that to Spencer. But in my defense, I was still running wild when I first got the money.

"Yeah, well, it's just crazy that you won't give Kirby

a chance." He shook his head again. "Your sister is even married to his oldest son."

"That doesn't mean I have to accept Kirby the way she has. Besides, Mary has a softer heart than I do." She was also blissfully happy with Brandon and their children. I was still waiting around for my dream man.

We sat quietly, until he said, "When Kirby first recommended you as my stylist, he didn't know that I was acquainted with you. He knows now, though. I told him that we used to date."

"Why in the hell did you do that?" I could have strangled Spencer, murdered him for real.

"Because it was too weird for me to pretend that we were strangers."

"And now he thinks that we went out, way back when?"

He stared me down. "Would you have preferred that I told him the truth?"

"Of course not." I didn't want Kirby knowing my personal business. "I would have preferred that you kept your trap shut."

"At least I made it sound respectable."

"Whatever." I didn't want to talk about it anymore.

"Well, you know what?" he snapped. "Maybe you and I shouldn't work together."

Screw him, I thought. "You're going to fire me already?"

He jerked his head. "I might."

"Whatever," I said again. I was too damned mad to care.

In the tense silence that followed, I studied the pale ink on Spencer's arm. His tattoo was a predominantly Native American design. Kirby had a half-Cherokee son named Matt with one of his former mistresses, and Spencer was of mixed origins, too. He'd never told me what tribe he was from, though. When I'd asked, he'd claimed it didn't matter. But now he was covered in artwork that seemed to prove otherwise.

I brazenly said, "It's interesting that Kirby has a son with a similar heritage to yours. If I didn't know better, I'd think that you could be one of his kids, too."

He rolled his eyes. "Yeah, right."

"Maybe you actually are his son," I taunted him. Not because I believed he was Kirby's heir, but just because I wanted to get back at him for not keeping quiet about us. "You might be his kid, and you don't even know it. With the way Kirby messed around, he could have dozens of illegitimate children out there."

He sighed. "Go ahead and make up whatever stories you want. But biologically, him being my father is impossible. Kirby is white, and so was my mom."

For some unknown reason, I'd always assumed that his mother had been Native American, but Spencer's brown skin had obviously come from the father he'd never met. I swallowed my pride and apologized. "I'm sorry. I shouldn't have said any of that." I had no right to bring his family into my foolishness. I made a sheepish expression and said, "Truce?"

He lifted his eyebrows, making me wait for his reply. Was he going to tell me to get lost? Had I blown this job? Had my stupidity gotten in the way?

"You're something else," he said a few heartbeats later. He didn't sound amused. But he didn't sound angry anymore, either. He expelled a breath and added, "But you always were feisty."

I used to be a full-on brat, but I wasn't going to cop to it now. I flashed a hopeful smile. "You're not firing me?"

"I guess not." He glanced at my lips, as if he was remembering the taste of them.

He stood and walked over to the bar. Seconds ticked

by, or maybe it was minutes. I wanted to break the silence, but I couldn't think of an intelligent thing to say. I was remembering the taste of his lips, too.

"Are you sure I can't get you anything?" he asked.

I blinked at him. "Anything?"

"To drink. I'm going to have a ginger ale."

Actually, I was getting thirsty. Or maybe my mouth had gone dry as a reaction to him. The air between us had gone thick again. "I'll have what you're having."

"Do you want yours on ice?"

"Yes, please."

He turned, opened the mini fridge and poured my drink.

"Here you go." He came toward me with my ginger ale, and I reached out to take it.

He returned to the mini fridge, retrieved a soda for himself and took a swig directly from the can. I sipped my drink, the ice clinking in my glass. He leaned against the bar, facing me now. So tall, so dark, so damned handsome.

I steadied my voice and asked, "Is the photo shoot going to be here at your house?"

"Yes, it'll be here, showcasing how I live."

He kept drinking his ginger ale, with the off-limits bottles of hard liquor behind him. The wine rack on the bar was full, too. He was surrounded by the forbidden.

I was, too. Not the alcohol. That wasn't a problem for me. My forbidden was Spencer himself. Crazy as it was, I was about to invite myself to his bedroom.

"Do you mind if I look in your closet to get a feel for your wardrobe?" I asked.

"No, I don't mind." He gestured to his attire. "Expect lots of jeans. Fancy clothes aren't really my forte."

He waited until I stood, then headed for a set of etched-glass doors that led to another part of the house. As I followed him, he glanced back and said, "I like your boots, by the way. They're really…"

He didn't finish his statement. I suspected he was going to say "sexy" or "hot" or something of that nature. But he let it drift instead.

I let it go, too. He guided me down a hallway riddled with artfully framed movie posters. I spotted a black-and-white still from *The Wild One*, featuring a young and defiant Marlon Brando, and my interest was piqued. The actor sat on a Triumph motorcycle, sporting 1950s biker gear. I knew the history behind his clothes. I'd taken a class about fashion in film.

Spencer opened the door to the master suite. "This is it, where my closet is."

The first thing I saw was his king-size bed. It sat on a platform frame constructed from natural wood. The covers were tan and gold. Masculine. Overall, his room was warm and inviting, with an adjoining bathroom and French doors leading to the backyard. The curtains were open, with a view of his pool. Beyond it was acres of grass.

"Your home is beautiful," I said. "I should have told you that when I first got here." I wandered over to the doors and peered out.

He joined me, pointing to a flagstone path that cut through the grass. "My guesthouse is out that way. I turned it into a dog rescue. I have a slew of people who help me with it. Some are paid employees and some are volunteers."

"I don't have any pets." I wondered if that made me lacking. "Mary and Brandon have a husky named Cline. My niece and nephew adore him. He was Brandon's dog before he met my sister, and now Cline is the family dog."

"I have two dogs."

"You do? Where are they?"

He mock-whispered, "Hiding under the bed." He smiled and said in a normal tone, "They're just checking you out, deciding if you can be trusted. They were my first rescues, and I couldn't bear to let them go, so they became mine."

Curious about his companions, I glanced at the foot of the bed. Sure enough, there were two little white faces poking out from under it.

"They're adorable," I said. "They look like dust mops with eyeballs. What are they, actually?"

"Maltese. Normally they're a fearless breed, but Cookie and Candy came from a traumatic situation. Once they get used to you, you'll see whole new sides of them."

"How long will it take for them to get used to me?"

"I don't know. Sometimes they come around quickly and sometimes they don't. If they're agreeable on the day of the shoot, we might use them in some of the pictures. They already met the photographer and liked him."

"That's good." The shoot was a little over a month away, so there was plenty of time for his dogs to cozy up to me. "Has the photographer discussed his vision with you and what sort of image he wants you to project?"

Spencer winced a little. "He said they want to go with a reformed bad-boy thing."

I cocked my head. "You don't like that idea?"

"It's okay, I guess. We all have a brand these days, and that's how mine is unfolding."

"I can certainly build your style around it." I knew just how bad he used to be. "I should check out your clothes now."

"We can go into my closet together. It's big enough for both of us."

That was true. His walk-in was more like a room. Still, once we were inside, I imagined turning out the light and pressing my mouth against his. The first time I'd ever kissed a boy was in a closet. But not the urgent way I used to kiss Spencer.

To keep myself sane, I inhaled the fabric-cluttered air. His clothes smelled clean and fresh. He was right. There were a lot of blue jeans.

"I have a few suits," he said, and showed me the garment bags.

As I unzipped them to check the labels, I almost felt as if I were undressing him. I shivered at the memory.

He stood back and his gaze roamed over me, and I hastily said, "You have great taste for someone who doesn't place much importance on fancy clothes." His Italian-cut suits were impeccably tailored. He'd certainly spent some money on them.

Spencer shrugged, but not in a casual way. He seemed as if he had a lot on his mind. I knew the feeling.

Finally, he said, "When I was a kid, my aunt and uncle used to make me dress up for their dinner parties and whatnot, so I guess some of it stuck. I know that I never told you this before, but they were rich as sin."

I widened my eyes. He'd been raised with wealth and privilege? I hadn't seen that coming. But as vague as he'd always been, how would I have known? "How old were you when you went to live with them?"

He frowned. "Ten. That's when my mom died."

I understood his pain, the ache I heard in his voice. I knew what being motherless was like. My poor mama had succumbed to heart failure when I was eighteen, and I missed her every day. I preferred to think of her before she got so depressed, but it wasn't easy. I was eleven when Kirby had damaged her, when her struggles had begun. For me, those memories ran deep, and so did my rebellious behavior. By the time I was in high school, boys were writing my name on bathroom walls.

"No child should have to lose a parent," I said.

Spencer stepped a little closer. "My mom was an aspiring actress, but she didn't live to see her dream fulfilled. Mostly she worked at department stores, walking around spritzing perfume." He paused to clear his throat. "My aunt and uncle are in commercial real estate, with properties all over the world. When my mother passed, they carted me off to their big, stiff mansion in Hidden Hills. It's a gated community in LA."

Were they as controlling as they were rich? Based on his description, I assumed that they were. I'd grown up in a low-income area in Oklahoma City, where Mama struggled to pay our bills. "They sound pretty uppity."

"I learned all sorts of proper things from them." He gestured to the suit in my hand. "I know at least twenty different ways to tie a tie."

"Well, I've got you beat." Had he rebelled because of them? Were they part of his cause and effect? "I've perfected thirty. Knots are one of my specialties. Ties, scarves. I can do it all."

"Too bad we never discussed this before." He teasingly added, "We could've had some bondage fun back in the day."

"That's not funny." But I laughed anyway, sensing that he needed to lighten the mood and quit talking about his family.

I closed the garment bags and continued looking through his things. He had a couple of high-quality motorcycle jackets. I reached for one of them and ran my hand along the leather.

Before I stroked it too much, I turned my attention to the bottom shelf, where his shoes were perched. I noticed a pair of wonderfully scuffed biker boots with a vintage vibe, similar to the ones Brando had worn in *The Wild One*.

"Is it safe to assume that you still ride?" I asked.

"Yeah, Harleys are still my thing."

I checked out more of his shoes. He had a nice selection of cowboy boots. "Horses, too?"

He nodded. "I have a barn just beyond the rescue with two really pretty palominos." He looked directly at me. "But you already know I'm partial to blondes."

I forced myself to breathe, with his all-too-hungry gaze practically devouring me.

We exited the closet, and I felt my skin flush. I was horribly warm, overheated, in fact.

After an awkward beat of silence, I headed for the French doors and said, "It's raining again." I wished I could open them, go outside and let the water drench every anxious inch of me.

He came over to where I was. "It's not supposed to let up until tomorrow."

We stood side by side, body heat mounting between us. Even the dogs under the bed had crept closer to the edge, waiting to see what we might do.

"So, what happens now?" he asked.

I assumed he meant in relation to me being his stylist. But my mind was spinning in all sorts of directions. "Once we work out a budget, I'll shop for you. Then I'll bring everything here for you to try on. We can incorporate some of your belongings into the designs, too." I wanted to see him in those motorcycle boots. I loved how battered they were.

"I'll also need to take your measurements before I leave here today. That'll give me an accurate handle on your sizes. I can't just rely on the labels from your clothes."

"That's fine." He shifted his feet, and one of the dogs pawed at his shoe.

He reached down to pick her up, and she cuddled in his arms. I didn't try to pet her. Touching her would bring me too close to him. I was already stressing about taking his measurements.

I'd promised myself that I wouldn't get intimately involved with anyone unless it promised to develop into a meaningful relationship. But now I was fantasizing about hooking up with my old lover and having hot and dangerous sex with him again. Did Spencer have the power to turn me back into the reckless girl I used to be?

God, I hoped not.

But a shameful part of me wanted to find out.

Two

Spencer

Damn, I thought. Alice McKenzie was doing a number on me all over again, just like the first time I'd met her. We'd both swiped right on Tinder, and after one flirtatious chat, I'd invited her to the trendy club where I used to work. Later that night, she'd followed me to my apartment, and I had the best sex of my life.

But things were different now.

So much different.

I hadn't even kissed anyone since I quit drinking. For now, I was abstinent.

Painfully abstinent.

Funny, but I hadn't actually thought of it as painful until today, and that was because of Alice. Pretty Alice, with her sultry brown eyes, spiky blond hair and killer boots. As much as I hated to admit it, I'd never really gotten her out of my head. I'd thought about her a lot over the years. The abrupt way she'd ended our affair had always bothered me. At the time, we'd still been going hot and heavy, and she'd left me wondering what I'd done wrong. Even now, I was trying to figure out what Alice really thought of me. Was that the reason I'd hired her to work for me? Was I looking for some sort of closure?

While my thoughts scattered, Cookie whined to be free. I set her down, and she scampered back to Candy. The two of them stared up at Alice as if she was a spaceship that had just landed. I was probably looking at her that way, too. I used to call her Alice in Spencerland when she was in my bed. I didn't know what to call her now.

"Do they sleep here?" she asked.

My brain fogged. "I'm sorry. What?"

"The dogs. Do they sleep in your room?"

I shook my head. "They have their own beds in another room. But they like hanging out in here. They spend a lot time at the rescue, too, playing with the other dogs."

"That's nice that they have other company." She hesitated before she said, "I should probably take your measurements now."

I'd been measured by tailors before. When I was a kid, it seemed like a regular occurrence, given how fast I was growing and with all of the dress-up occasions I'd been forced to attend. But knowing that Alice was going to put her hands on me was a whole other matter.

She reached into her bag and removed a tape measure. She got out an iPad, too. "I'm going to do your chest first. Don't flex or anything. Just stand normally."

I did as she asked, and she wrapped the tape measure under my armpits and around the fullest part of my chest. She recorded my size on her iPad.

She did my neck and sleeve length and recorded those

sizes, too. When she got to my waist, my stomach muscles jumped. But she kept going. She put a finger between my body and the tape measure, giving me room to breathe. My inseam was next, a measurement that was going to require her get on her knees in front of me. She instructed me to remove my shoes, which I did.

When she dropped down and ran the tape measure from the lowest part of my crotch to my foot, I watched her, remembering the erotic things she used to do to me while she was on her knees.

I could've kicked myself for letting my mind go there. Were her thoughts straying in the same direction? I did my damnedest not to get aroused, and she seemed to be doing her damnedest to be quick and efficient.

She said, "I need to measure your feet, too."

"Sure. Okay." I couldn't protest, even if it meant that she had to stay on her knees.

She had one of those devices in her bag that they used in shoe stores. She placed it in front of me, and I stepped onto it.

Afterward, she stood and fussed with her bag. I put my sneakers back on. There was awkward energy between us. She was the first woman I wanted since I got sober, and I wasn't sure how to deal with it. There was no denying that she was as attracted to me as I was to her. That much, I could feel. But feeling it and acting on it were two different things.

She said, "I should probably get going."

I searched my brain for an excuse to keep her. Regardless of the effect she was having on me, I didn't want her to leave. "Why don't you stick around and let me show you the rescue?"

She bit down on her bottom lip. "I am curious to see it."

I'd always been fascinated by the shape of her mouth.

Her cranberry-colored lipstick intrigued me, too. It made her look dangerously kissable.

I broke my stare. "Let's grab our jackets and go."

She glanced out the glass doors, where the rain was pounding even harder now. "I left my hoodie in the car. I'll have to go back and—"

"I can loan you something." She'd already measured my body and handled some of my clothes. Her borrowing a jacket from me was the least of my concerns. I gestured to the closet. "You can choose what you want. Pick one out for me, too. Doesn't matter which one." I had plenty to go around.

"Okay." She returned to my closet.

Once again, my thoughts drifted to the past and the things Alice and I used to do. We'd always had sex at my place. I don't know why she'd never invited me to hers. At the time, I hadn't bothered to ask. I hadn't been big on conversation then. But now it made me curious to see how she lived. Was she neat and tidy? Or did she keep things strewn about? I envisioned her being beautifully messy. I'd been taught to be orderly, even when I was torn up inside.

She came back with two basic hoodies, gray for her and black for me. We slipped them on. The one she was wearing was big on her. She was only five-four, five-five at the most, with a slim build. I was six-two with plenty of muscle. Somehow, though, our hip-thrusting always seemed to work, even when we were standing in the shower, getting soaking wet.

"Ready to see the rescue?" I asked. "It's about a five-minute walk." Just long enough for us to get wet, I thought.

She gazed out the French doors, assessing the weather. "Sure. Let's do it." She lifted her hood.

We ventured outside, and I led the way, past the pool and onto the flagstone path, with the rain beating down on us.

I glanced over at Alice and noticed how troubled she suddenly looked, her expression as dark as the clouds. Was she thinking about me? About us? Or did she have Kirby on her mind?

Her opinion of him disturbed me, especially with how much I'd come to care for him. I trusted him with my inner feelings, something I'd never done with anyone else before. He understood my tortured psyche. I could confide in him about anything. Yet I'd lied to him about Alice, pretending that she and I used to go on casual dates. Not that Kirby was naïve. He knew that I was a drunk back then and that Alice used to party. But I'd played down my relationship with her, making it seem light and easy. In spite of her hatred for him, he was fiercely protective of her, so I figured the truth wouldn't have sat well with him, anyway. Granted, what he'd done to Alice's mother was wrong. But he was sorry for the pain he'd caused and truly wanted to ease Alice's suffering. I admired him for that.

I said to her, "Kirby told me that you helped choose the artist who recorded your mother's songs. That Tracy Burton was your top pick."

She snuggled deeper into my jacket, tucking her hands into the pockets. "At the time, I wanted someone who was new to the business, but who understood the importance of Mama's music, too. Tracy and I have become really close since then. I guess you could say that she's my BFF now."

"Then it sounds like things worked out." I'd never met Tracy or worked with her, so I wasn't about to comment on how fleeting her fame had been. She'd had a great run with her debut and the songs Alice's mother had written, but as far as I knew, things had gone downhill from there.

I felt fortunate for my skyrocketing career. I'd come to Nashville with nothing, and now I was a Grammy Award-winning, highly sought-after songwriter. My aunt and uncle had refused to help me along the way, and I hadn't heard from them since. Not one measly phone call, congratulating me on my success.

Alice and I continued walking, with the rain still falling between us. The path narrowed, and I stepped onto the grass, giving her more room.

When we arrived at the rescue, we both wiped our feet and removed our damp jackets, hanging them on hooks in the entryway.

I introduced Alice to the staff and showed her around. The guesthouse had been remodeled to my specifications. We had kennels for when we needed them, but we also had canine-friendly rooms where the dogs could nap and play and socialize. There were tons of outdoor activities, too, on nicer days.

"This is a wonderful setup," Alice said, as we stood near the kitchen.

"We do our best." At the moment, a volunteer was preparing a meal for one of our newest residents, a poor little pup with a digestive disorder. "We have quite a few special-needs dogs."

"Are they difficult to place?"

"Yes." It was an unfortunate reality and one we faced daily. "Finding the right homes for them can be challenging."

Alice went quiet. The she asked, "What makes you do all of this, Spencer?"

I automatically replied, "I just want to make a difference in the world." That was my standard response, what I'd gotten used to saying. But it went deeper than that, so much deeper. I'd felt like a stray dog when I'd first landed on my aunt and uncle's doorstep. They'd fed me and clothed me and taught me to sit up and beg, rewarding me when I behaved and punishing me when I didn't. But I knew that no matter what I did, I would always be the mongrel they never really wanted.

During my darkest days, I used to fantasize about searching for my father, a man who didn't even know I existed. Sometimes I still thought about it.

"You have made a difference," Alice said.

For a second, I didn't know what she meant. Then I realized that she was referring to the rescue.

"Do you want to meet our mascot?" I asked. "He's a three-year-old English bulldog who runs the show around here. We're not going to adopt him out. He loves greeting people in the office, so that's where he is most of the time. He's Candy and Cookie's best buddy, too."

She smiled. "I'd love to meet him. What's his name?"

"We call him Peterbilt. Pete for short. We chose that name because he'll come at you like an eighteen-wheeler, pestering you to pet him."

An amused expression brightened up her face, making her even prettier than she already was. "I'm going to be delighted to make his acquaintance, I'm sure."

I took her to the office, a woodsy room that overlooked one of the fenced yards. For now, the office was vacant. No one was manning the desk. Pete lounged in his doggie bed, but when he caught sight of us, he roused himself quickly and ran toward us. He gave me a sloppy grin and made a beeline for Alice, barreling right into her.

She nearly tripped, and I grabbed her arm before she fell. She burst into a hearty laugh. Pete was a comical dude, with droopy eyes, a massive jaw and crooked teeth. Short and stout, with thick white wrinkles, he weighed about fifty pounds, moved with a crablike gait and drooled excessively.

Alice dropped to the floor to pet him, and he climbed onto her lap. I sat across from them and reached over to scratch his ears.

"Did you find yourself a new girlfriend there, buddy?" I asked him.

He grinned at me again. He was in canine heaven, but I could hardly blame him. I knew how it felt to be physically close to her. She wrapped her arms around him, soaking up his affection, and I envied him for charming her so easily. Of course, I'd done that, too, way back when.

"Can I bring him a toy next time I come by?" she asked. "Would that be okay?"

"Sure. You can bring him whatever you want." I wasn't going to deny Pete. Or her. She seemed to need to connect with him. "He's good about sharing his toys with the other dogs, too. He isn't territorial."

She lifted her eyebrows. "Not even with his girl-friends?"

"No, not even with them."

"I guess he has a lot of female companions, then."

"He has enough to keep him busy. But he's neutered, so it's not the real deal. He still likes the ladies, though." Nonetheless, I didn't think it was the dog's girlfriends who interested her. I suspected that she was fishing to see who I slept with these days. I furrowed my brow and asked, "Will you tell me something?"

She squinted. "What?"

"Did I hurt you? In the past, I mean."

Her breath rushed out. "What makes you think that?"

"Because you're the one who ended it, who just texted me one day and said that you wouldn't be back. I know we weren't committed to each other or anything, but it didn't seem like you were getting tired of me, at least not when we were together. But I must have done something to upset you."

She frowned. "It doesn't matter. It's over."

"Come on. Tell me what I did." I wasn't letting up, not until I understood it better.

"Just drop it, Spencer."

"Tell me." I prodded her again.

"Fine." Her gaze slammed into mine. "I stopped seeing you because I needed to be someone new. To change my ways. To quit sleeping with men who didn't care about me."

Her remark stung. But it was true. I hadn't cared about myself then, let alone been capable of caring for someone else. Now I was wondering if I should've left well enough alone, instead of bugging her for a response.

Then she said, "I probably shouldn't tell you this. But I've actually done a good job of cleaning up my act. I've been celibate since I was with you."

Hell's fire. I merely stared at her. She hadn't had sex in five years? I couldn't have been more shocked.

After giving myself a second to comprehend her news, I said, "That's crazy, I mean, it's just so…" Before she misunderstood my reaction, I anxiously added, "I haven't been with anyone since I got sober."

Now it was her turn to stare at me. "I hadn't expected that you…" She shook her head. "It's weird that we both…"

Yeah, weird. I didn't even know what to say next.

She paused before she asked, "Do the women who follow you online know? Is that why they've been calling you unattainable?"

"No. They only say that about me because I haven't shown any interest in them." It wasn't because they knew that I gave up sex. "I prefer not to advertise what I do. Or don't do," I clarified.

She shifted the dog in her lap. He was falling asleep, his eyes drifting closed. "Me, neither."

It made me feel strange that I was the last guy she'd been with. The last man to be inside her. To make her come. It almost seemed romantic. But I knew that it wasn't.

"I really was the wrong guy for you," I said.

She sighed. "You were wrong for everybody back then."

"I still am." I shrugged off my discomfort. I wouldn't know how to do a relationship if it smacked me over the head. "Just call me Mr. Wrong."

"Well, that's funny," she replied solemnly. "Because after I ended it with you, I decided that I was going to wait for Mr. Right. That I wouldn't sleep with anyone until he came along. I'm hoping he'll be the man that I marry someday."

"The white picket fence thing." I'd never pictured her in that role. But I'd never pictured her anywhere, except naked in my bed.

She lobbed a curious look at me. "While we're on the subject, why did you stop having sex?"

Lucky for me, I had a solid answer. "Abstinence is part of my sobriety program."

"Through what? AA?"

"No, but it's something similar at a private rehab center. Kirby introduced me to it. We both attend meetings there." I explained without going into too much detail. "It's an outpatient program. Not one of those places where you check yourself in."

"And they advocate abstinence for two whole years? That seems like a long time for a program like that."

"Typically, it's no dating and no sex for a year. But after my first year was up, I just wasn't ready to jump back in."

She sent me another curious look, snaring me with her next question. "When will you be ready?"

"I don't have a guideline to follow." As badly as I wanted her, I was already losing ground. "I guess I'll just know. But for now, I'm still trying to figure myself out. What about you? Have you at least been on some dates?"

"Yes, but it never amounts to anything." Her shoulders drooped. "The chemistry just hasn't been there."

My chemistry with her was a bitch. I could feel it tightening its noose around me. "I haven't even kissed anyone."

She squeezed her eyes shut. "Me, neither."

I cleared my throat. "Not even on any of those dates?"

She opened her eyes. "I don't kiss on first dates anymore, and none of them ever got past that point." She glanced at the sleeping bulldog. "I'll bet Pete would kiss me if he could."

I watched her with anticipation. "Sloppy dog kisses don't count." But my mouth on hers would. I wanted to do it in the worst way.

When Alice lifted her head, our gazes locked. The rain was slashing against the office windows, intensifying the moment. Neither of us spoke, not one word, not one syllable.

I finally said, "I feel like I'm in junior high again."

She blinked at me. "Is that when you had your first kiss?"

"With tongues, yeah. How about you?"

She winced. "I was in elementary school. Fifth grade, at someone's birthday party. I went into a closet with a boy I liked."

"Damn, girl. You really were a wilding." I tried for a bit of humor. "Do you want to go back into my closet with me?"

She broke down and laughed. "You wish."

Darned right, I did. My heart jumped when I said, "I can only imagine how good a kiss would feel after all this time."

"Really good," she said, her voice turning soft.

We stared longingly at each other. But we didn't lean forward or put our mouths together. It seemed too risky, too wrong. We were former lovers, in the midst of celibacy, and this wasn't a path either of us was supposed to be taking.

No matter how hot and satisfying it would be.

Three

Alice

I wanted to kiss Spencer, so help me I did. He was arousing me from the inside out, just the way he used to.

He ran a hand through his hair, and I went warm all over. I imagined running my hands through it, too. It fell across his forehead, the thick dark strands messy from the rain. God, he was tempting: so familiar, so gorgeous.

So celibate.

Somehow that should have made him seem safer, but it didn't. He was making me feel like a sex-starved mess. Spencer had changed, but he wasn't any better for me now than he was before. I needed someone who was ready to settle down and raise a family. I needed security, not a recovering alcoholic, trying to find himself.

To keep myself from staring at him any more than I already had, I glanced down at the dog. Pete was still out like a light.

"At least he isn't snoring," I said, trying to make regular conversation. We couldn't keep talking about how good a kiss would feel or how long it had been since we'd had sex.

Spencer seemed relieved that I changed the topic. He quickly replied, "Pete used to snore. He had breathing problems when we took him in. We had his palate surgically corrected. He had a few other health issues that we dealt with, too. As you can see, he's totally fine now."

"Where did he come from? What's his background?"

"He was left at a kill shelter, and his time was almost up when we heard about him." Spencer blew out a tight breath. "I guess his owner didn't think he was worth it. It makes me sick, the way some people treat their pets, as if they're just so damned disposable."

"I think the work you're doing here is wonderful." I was impressed by how nurturing he seemed and how much he obviously cared. Would he be a gentle lover now? There'd never been any sweetness during our affair, no snuggly warmth. As much as I'd wanted him to hold me afterward, he just hadn't been the type.

I shook away the memory. But somehow, the longing remained. "What about Candy and Cookie? Were they left at a shelter, too?"

"They were orphaned. They'd been alone in the house with their owner when she accidentally fell down the stairs. She died on impact, from a spinal cord injury." He frowned and continued with, "The dogs were so traumatized, they dug their way out of the yard and started living on the streets. People tried to catch them, but they just kept running away. Then I found them hiding under my front porch."

"Really? You found them yourself?"

He nodded. "They were dirty and matted and covered in burrs. Candy's legs were scraped up, and one of Cookie's ears was torn. I called a mobile vet, and he came out to the house and tended to them. Since there wasn't anyone associated with their owner who was able to take them, I offered to let them stay with me until I found another home for them." He drew his knees up. "But I got attached and kept them instead. After that, I decided to start a rescue. There's a lot of work that's involved in running a place like this. It didn't happen overnight."

I pondered the story he'd told me. It was certainly better than mulling over our past. "I never really thought about what happens to pets when their owners die."

"My mother died in a similar way. From a fall."

"Oh, my goodness. I'm so sorry." He'd mentioned his mom earlier, and now he was talking about the manner in which she'd left this earth. It didn't get more painful than that. I shuddered and asked, "Were you with her when it happened?"

"No." He glanced at his shoes, at the bits of mud and grass on them. "I was at school, and she was home, painting the beams in our apartment. The ladder tipped over, and she suffered a head injury." He kept studying his shoes. "She thought she was okay at first, but then she started feeling dizzy and confused and called a friend to take her to urgent care. But by then, her brain was already starting to swell."

He finally lifted his gaze. He'd done more talking today than he had in the entire time I'd known him.

Before he slipped back into his old silent ways, I said, "It must have been awful for you, going to live with your aunt and uncle after something so traumatic."

"Yeah. It pretty much sucked."

"Which one of them is your blood relative?"

"My aunt. She's my mother's older sister. They came

from a dysfunctional family." He paused slightly. "Their dad was an alcoholic."

I gauged the discomfort in his eyes. Those dark, brooding eyes. "I heard it can be hereditary. The alcoholism," I added, making my meaning clear.

He shrugged it off. "My grandfather was a mean old cuss who died from liver disease. I hardly remember him."

"At least you weren't a mean drunk."

He snared my gaze. "I was rough with you in bed."

Was it necessary for him to remind me of that? "We were both rough with each other." I used to rake my nails all over him, clawing and scratching. "It's just what we did."

"I know, but I should have been gentler."

"It doesn't matter," I said, even if it did. I'd always left his apartment feeling lonely and confused.

He replied, "I'm sorry if I wasn't more romantic with you."

His apology went straight to my heart, making it skitter. "Is this part of your sobriety? Saying sorry to all of the women you never cuddled?"

No." He spoke lower, raspier. "I'm only saying it to you."

I tried to act normal, to not let my emotions show. "I appreciate your concern, but it isn't necessary."

He watched me, a bit too closely. "I just don't want you feeling bad about the past."

Or letting it affect the present? It was too late for that. I wasn't just struggling with my memories, I was troubled by his current association with Kirby, too.

"How well do you know my sister and Brandon?" I asked. I'd never told Mary about my affair with Spencer, and she'd never mentioned his name to me, either. But that didn't mean they weren't acquainted.

"I've never met Mary. Or Brandon. My friendship with Kirby doesn't extend to his kids. Not that I have anything against them. It's just easier for me to keep my relationship with him private."

"That makes sense, I suppose." It was easier for me, too, to keep my sister out of the loop. She knew that I used to sleep around and that I was waiting for the right man now. But we didn't have major conversations about it. Mary had been through enough with me when I was a kid, always worrying about my wild side. Before those reckless feelings came flooding back, I said, "I better get going."

Spencer frowned. "You don't have to run off."

"I'm not." Thankfully, I had a reason for leaving. "I'm having lunch with Tracy today, and it's all the way across town." I had plenty of time, but it was still a good excuse. Besides, I was eager to see her. Unlike Mary, I used Tracy as my confidante. I'd already told her about Spencer, talking about him on and off throughout the years, and now I would be telling her even more. "It was nice seeing the rescue and meeting Pete, but I really have to go."

He was still frowning. "Then I'll walk you to your car."

"All right. But how do I…?" I was concerned about startling the sleeping bulldog.

He bent over to help me. "Just roll him off you. He probably won't even wake up."

We moved Pete together, and he landed belly side up, with his feet in the air and his tongue lolling to one side.

"Told ya," Spencer said, and we both smiled.

I climbed up off the floor. He stood, too. At least the tension was gone. But I knew how quickly it could return.

We retrieved the jackets we'd worn, put them back on and left the rescue, heading back into the rain. We didn't chat along the way. But we'd said plenty already.

He took me through a side gate that led to his driveway, where I was parked.

I started to unzip his hoodie to return it to him, but he said, "You can keep it until next time."

"I have my own in the car."

"If you take it off now, you'll get soaked."

That was true. The rain was coming down hard. If only it would knock some sense into me. I was losing my mind, fantasizing about giving up my celibacy for him. Would he stop being abstinent for me, too?

Struggling to keep my wits about me, I deactivated the alarm on my Prius. Spencer looked as if he wanted to eat me alive. Or at least nibble me to death.

I imagined feasting on him, using my mouth in ways I knew he would enjoy. I glanced away, trying to keep my cool. Working for him wasn't going to be easy, but I couldn't bail out, not with how badly I needed this job.

"I'll be in touch," I said, forcing a professional air.

He nodded, and I ducked into my car and started the engine. He stood in the rain, looking tall and dark and shadowy. I put the shifter in reverse and backed out of his driveway.

Desperate to escape.

I wore Spencer's jacket to lunch. I could have switched to mine, but I was already wearing his. Or that's the excuse I used. Truth was, I just wanted to keep something of his next to me. My hunger for him was crushing my common sense.

I sat in the cramped entrance of the mom-and-pop diner and waited for Tracy to arrive. She wasn't late; I was actually a little early. But it gave me time to catch my breath. Or try to. There wasn't a table available yet, anyway.

When Tracy showed up, she breezed in like the rough-

and-tumble country girl that she was. She'd been raised
on a dusty old horse farm by her rodeo cowboy dad. Her
mom died when she was in middle school. All these lost
mamas, I thought. Hers, mine, Spencer's.

I stood to greet her, and we hugged. After we separated,
I stood back and said, "Wow. Check you out."

Beneath her straw Stetson, her long brown hair tumbled over her shoulders, as pretty as could be. Her jeans fit
her to a T, but she had one of those sensually curvy bodies that filled out every seam. Without makeup, she had
wholesome features. But she knew how to doll herself up.
Today, her eyes were as smoky as mine, only they were
blue, like the sky on a brighter day.

"I'm trying to fool people into thinking I'm still a celebrity," she replied.

"You'll always be a star to me." She certainly looked the
part, even if her success had been short-lived. She'd spent
most of the money she'd earned fixing up her dad's property. She'd bought herself a place, too. But everything had
faltered so quickly, she was fighting to keep her mortgage
afloat. She'd been through hard times before. One of the
things we had in common was growing up poor.

The hostess escorted us to a vinyl booth near a window.
When it came time to order, we both chose the special:
baked macaroni and cheese and collard greens. Comfort
food was another thing we had in common. So was sweet
tea with lots of ice.

After they brought our tea, Tracy asked me, "How did
your meeting with Spencer go?"

"Terrible." I didn't hold back. I was used to sharing my
screwed-up feelings with her. "It was like going back in
time, with how badly I want him again."

She reached for her glass. "Maybe you're just getting
cabin fever. Or celibate fever, or whatever."

"He's celibate, too."

She gaped at me. "No way."

"Yes, way." He was as inactive as I was.

"Dang, really? A guy like him? Why is he keeping all that manliness to himself?"

I repeated what he told me, about him being a recovering alcoholic and abstinence being part of his program, even if he'd carried it out for longer than the usual year.

"Is he struggling with his sobriety?" she asked.

"He said that he can handle the temptation of drinking, but I think it's more difficult for him than he's willing to admit. Of course, that's just my opinion. I'm not an authority on addiction." Not unless my attraction to him fell into that category.

"It's tough to know what another person is going through. But we've all got some sort of problems, don't we?"

"Yes, we do." And mine were escalating now that I'd seen Spencer again. "You know what makes it harder? Spencer is super close to Kirby. Kirby even helped him with his sobriety."

"Yikes." Tracy screwed up her face. "That's major. You can't mess with that kind of bond."

"Don't I know it." Kirby had been clean and sober for a long time. But when he was drinking and using, he'd hurt a lot of people. He'd even published a bestselling biography about his wrongdoings. He'd left Mama out of the book, though. He didn't acknowledge her until after she died, for all the good that had done. "I hate how Kirby expects to be absolved for all of the terrible things he did."

She took a long, cool sip of her tea. "You're the only person out there who hasn't forgiven him."

And rightly so, I thought. "Speaking of apologies… Spencer said he was sorry for not being more romantic when we were together."

She watched me with empathy in her eyes. "I'll bet that made seeing him even harder for you."

"I'm just glad I have you to talk to." Without her, I'd really be lost.

Our conversation halted when the waitress appeared with our specials. After she left, we dug into our meals.

A few minutes later, Tracy looked up from her plate and asked, "Did Spencer happen to mention that he's going to be working with Dash on his next album?"

"No, he didn't say anything about that." Dash Smith was Tracy's former fiancé. They'd gotten engaged years ago, when both of them were still trying to make it. But nowadays, Tracy was struggling again, and Dash was a big star. At the moment, he was off on a world tour. "How do you know Spencer is going to be working with Dash?"

"I read about it."

"You need to stop reading about Dash and following his career."

"I know." Beneath the brim of her hat, her expression turned tortured. "I'm a glutton for punishment."

I was, too, apparently, judging how badly Spencer was affecting me. But my hang-up was based on lust. Somewhere in the pit of her broken heart, Tracy was still in love with her ex. "It's not healthy for you to obsess about him."

"I only do that because he's so famous now." She glanced toward the rainy window, then back at me. "I don't begrudge him his success. I know how hard he worked for it. Dash was poorer than you and I ever were. He barely had food on the table when he was growing up. But it's just so painful to see him out there, living the high life, while I can't even get another record deal." She blew out a sigh. "Even my indie career sucks."

"I hate that you're going through this." These days, Tracy was putting her music out there herself, without a label to back her. But nothing was really happening. She was barely getting any downloads, even though her songs were really good. "Just don't lose hope. You know how things can turn around in this business."

"They certainly turned around for Dash. He has the number one country album in the world. He's even crossing over into the pop charts."

"I'll bet he's lonely on the road." Or I hoped that he was, for her sake.

She rolled her eyes. "Oh, sure. With all those groupies out there, he's probably suffering something awful."

"Maybe you should reconsider his offer to help you." She'd told me before that Dash had been reaching out to her. He'd even suggested them doing a duet.

"Are you kidding? I don't need his charity. When I top the charts again, it'll be because I earned it, not because I'm riding my ex's coattails."

"As much as I admire your principles, maybe you're being stubborn about this, Trace."

"Oh, yeah?" She shot me a silly grin. "At least I've gotten laid in the past five years."

"Okay, smart-ass." I laughed in spite of myself. "Punish me for being a good girl now."

She leaned forward, pressing against the table. "Do you think Spencer wants you as badly as you want him?"

"Yes, I do." I wasn't going to pretend otherwise. I'd seen it on his face; I'd felt it from his reactions to me.

She sat back in her seat. "I understand that you're waiting for the right guy, and I want nothing more than for you to find him and live happily ever after. But if something does happen between you and Spencer, it won't be the end of the world, will it? I mean, at least it'll be with someone who's being cautious about his sex life, too."

I swallowed the last of my mac and cheese. "That's your answer to my problems?"

"No, of course not." She gentled her voice. "But it seems pretty obvious that your attraction to him isn't going to go away anytime soon."

"Maybe not. But just thinking about being with him scares me." The man who'd triggered my celibacy, who'd made me long for a husband and children and everything else I was missing.

She gestured to our near-empty plates. "Do you want to share a piece of pie since we're almost done eating?" She pushed the free-standing dessert menu toward me. "It might make you feel better."

I could definitely use something sweet today. "Maybe I should get my own slice instead of us sharing."

I flipped through the laminated pages, even if my hunger for Spencer wasn't something a warm gooey pie was going to satisfy. But it was safer than Tracy's other suggestion.

I knew better than to slip back into bed with my old lover. I just needed to stay focused on working for him.

And nothing else.

Four

Spencer

I got up early, gulped down a ridiculously strong cup of black coffee and took a long, hot, stare-at-the-walls shower. After that, I spent the next few hours working on some new songs. Or trying to, anyway. I was distracted with thoughts of Alice.

When I'd first hooked up with her, I'd sympathized with her position that Kirby was a rich, spoiled, womanizing superstar who only cared about himself. But when I met him a few years later, I saw a strong and stable man sorry for his sins. He'd hurt lots of people. By no means was he perfect. Sometimes he could still be brash and arrogant. But overall, he had a damned fine heart.

I wasn't going to let Alice taint my opinion of him. But that wasn't my only problem with her. I wanted to strip her bare, all over again. I wanted to hold her in my arms afterward, too, and remove some of the stigma of what we'd done before.

Was that a foolish fantasy on my part? Me, trying to play the gentleman? In all honestly, I had no idea what kind of lover I would be now. What if I sucked at being romantic? Drunk or sober, what if that wasn't who I was?

Dragging Alice back into my mess wouldn't be fair. Beautiful, temperamental Alice, searching for Mr. Right. We didn't belong together, and I had no business wanting her.

I glanced at the bar, with its shiny glass bottles lined up in pretty rows. If I sat here long enough, steeped in a woman from my past, would I get the familiar urge to drink?

Fighting my fears, I rose from my piano seat and moved about the room, telling myself that I could handle any hardship that came my way. But because she had me tied up in knots, I decided this would be a good day for a meeting. I knew the next one was at two o'clock. I had the schedule memorized.

I texted Kirby, asking if he would be there. We were part of a group that included a number of celebrities. In this town, it was mostly music industry folk. Our counselor was a heavily tattooed dude named Sam who'd seen and done it all. There was nothing you could say that would surprise Sam.

My phone signaled a text. It was Kirby, telling me that he planned to go. I replied, letting him know that I would see him at the clinic.

I wasn't going to discuss my attraction to Alice with the group. I couldn't tell my story without revealing the edgy stuff I used to do with her, and I couldn't do that in front of Kirby, not without putting my sordid history with her on display. It was better left unsaid, not just for Kirby's peace of mind, but for mine and Alice's, too.

The meeting brought a bit of calm to my storm, and once it ended, Kirby invited me to his house. He lived in a plantation-style mansion, with a big sweeping staircase in the entryway and a sparkling stream running through the backyard. The property also included a recording studio and a menagerie of luxurious guesthouses. The entire compound had become known as "Kirbyville."

We shared a picnic bench near the stream, eating barbecued beef sandwiches and crispy fries his chef had prepared. The weather was nice, but already I was missing the rain.

I glanced across the table at Kirby. At sixty-six, he was a rough-looking guy, handsome in a country outlaw way, with hard lines in his face, graying hair and a salt-and-pepper beard. As a self-taught musician who'd worked his way up the ranks, he'd been around Nashville a long time. He had three sons, six grandkids, one supermodel ex-wife and countless everyday women who'd become his former mistresses.

What I'd told Alice was true: I'd never met anyone from Kirby's family. He kept trying to make it happen, though. He invited me to all of their gatherings—birthdays, holidays, the whole bit—hoping I'd warm up to the idea. But I always declined. After my mom died and my aunt and uncle took over, I'd lost my zest for being part of a family. Just being in those types of settings gave me a cold sweat.

"Did you ever contact Alice about that magazine thing?" Kirby asked, interrupting my thoughts.

"Yep. I sure did." I tossed out an easy vibe. The last thing I wanted was for him to notice how she affected me.

"She came by my place yesterday. We'll be working together on the shoot."

"That's great. She's a little spitfire, isn't she? But I guess you already know that since you used to date." He paused. "How long did that last, anyway? You never really said much about it, other than how casual it was."

"I can't remember how long it was. A few months, maybe, here and there." In reality, it was every time we needed each other, day or night, which was pretty damned often. "Mostly we just hung out at clubs." At least that part wasn't a complete lie. On the night we'd arranged to meet, she'd sidled up to the bar where I'd worked, eager to check me out. She'd even dared me to spike her mojito mocktail with an illegal shot of rum. Serving alcohol to a hot little twenty-year-old could have cost me my job, but I was so taken with her, I almost did it. Later, when we were in the shower, having our second round of sex, I played a stupid game and poured Bacardi all over both of us.

Kirby dipped a fry in the glob of ketchup on his plate. "Did she tell you what a jerk she thinks I am?"

"Yes, but she told me that when I knew her before. She's always been testy about you."

"She talked to you about me before you and I ever met?" His voice turned tight. "Why are you just telling me this now?"

"Because it didn't seem relevant until now." I braced myself, waiting to see if he would accept my response without further scolding. Sometimes Kirby had the same fiery temper as Alice.

"You're right." He backed down. "It doesn't matter what she used to say about me. It's what she's still saying that counts. I love that I'm so close with her sister. Mary has completely forgiven me. But Alice…"

"She made a crack about you maybe being my dad. She didn't mean it, though. She was just messing with me."

"That's an odd thing for her to come up with." He gave his head a quick shake. "What made her say it?"

"Because of my heritage and your affair with Matt's mom. I hadn't really told her much about family before. She didn't know that my mom was white."

He met my gaze. "I'd be proud if you were my son. You're a good man, Spencer."

"Thank you." His words warmed my heart. "I'd be proud to have you as my dad, too." Unlike my aunt and uncle, he cared about my well-being.

He studied me, gently, kindly. "Are you still thinking of searching for your dad? You haven't mentioned him in a while."

"Yes, I still think about it." Only I had other things on my mind now that I'd seen Alice again. "But there's no rush."

"You definitely need to be ready to tackle something like that. But I think paternity matters. I'm still ashamed of what an awful parent I was to my boys when they were growing up."

"You've made up for that now." He'd done everything in his power to redeem himself. He loved his sons with every fiber of his being. He adored his grandchildren, too. His family was everything to him. "You're not the same guy you used to be."

"I wish Alice saw me the way you do."

"I wish she did, too. But with all of the pain it's causing both of you, maybe you should let it be for a while."

"And quit trying to win her affection? I can't do that. I need to keep trying."

I understood that he felt guilty about hurting her mom, but now I was worried that he might be taking it too far.

With a bit of goofy sarcasm, I said, "Be careful, or some-one might mistake you for being her dad."

I expected him to scoff at my remark, but that wasn't what happened. Instead, he flinched like I'd never seen him flinch before, squeezing the sandwich in his hand so hard some of the filling came out.

He replied, "You don't actually think…"

"Come on, Kirby, I was kidding. You being her dad is as impossible as you being mine." But seeing how panicked he was, my stomach dropped, like an elevator speeding to a bottom floor. "Isn't it?"

"Yes, of course." He eased his grip on his sandwich, even if he'd already done considerable damage to it. "Alice was eleven years old when I got involved with her mom."

I watched him stuff the mangled roll into his mouth and take a big messy bite.

"You didn't know her mom before then?"

He shook his head. He was still chewing his food.

"For real?" I pressed him. "Alice isn't your daughter?"

"No." He shifted in his seat. "Her old man was a truck driver named Joel McKenzie."

I remembered Alice telling me that her father had died when she was a baby. But that was all she'd ever said about him. "Did you have some sort of connection to Joel? Some-thing Alice doesn't know about?" Was there more to this than Kirby was letting on?

He sent me an annoyed look. "I never even met the man." He put his sandwich down and pushed his plate away. "There's nothing nefarious going on. You're bark-ing up the wrong tree."

"Then why are you acting so strange?"

"Because your joke about me being Alice's dad wasn't funny. You shouldn't have said something like that."

"You're right. I'm sorry." He'd never lied to me before,

so why would he start now? In spite of his sullied past, I trusted him more than anyone. But here I was, lying to him about my affair with Alice. Should I admit that my relationship with her was more difficult than I'd let on? Or should I continue to keep it private? I chose the latter. This wasn't the time to open Pandora's box. "You deserve better than that from me, and so does Alice." I tried for a smile, hiding my feelings. "But we should probably change the subject now."

I didn't want to keep talking about Alice. Or thinking about her. Or wanting her. I was already anxious about seeing her again.

Two days later, Alice was back at my house with some clothes for me to try on. As she draped the garment bag over the back of my sofa, I caught sight of her profile. Her makeup was especially dramatic this afternoon. She'd even drawn those little lines in the corners of her eyes, for a catlike effect. It seemed fitting, considering what a hellcat she used to be in bed.

Would she still scratch and claw? Or would she be tamer now? I still had the foolhardy fantasy of being romantic with her. But I had feral urges, too, with how hot my blood ran every time she got near me. Not that it mattered. I wasn't planning on starting another affair. The issue wasn't how gentle or rough the sex would be. It wasn't her celibacy or my abstinence, either. Our problem was another man. The guy Alice had been waiting for. The Mr. Right who wasn't me.

"I brought a toy for Pete," she said.

I redirected my attention. I'd been too busy analyzing the affair we weren't going to have to notice the shopping bag at her feet. She reached into it and removed a squeaky toy shaped like a truck.

I let down my guard and smiled. It was damned cute. "He's going to love it."

She delved into the bag again. "I brought these for Candy and Cookie." Two more squeaky toys. "The cupcake is for Candy, because it has candy sprinkles on it. And the cookie is obviously for Cookie." She waved it around. "It looks like it already has a bite taken out of it."

Kill me now, but I wanted to take a lusty bite out of her. Being Mr. Wrong wasn't making my libido behave.

I shifted my stance and said, "Thank you for thinking of them. That was sweet of you."

"I hope the noise doesn't drive you crazy." She squeezed the cookie. "They're pretty loud."

"No worries. I'm used to it. They have lots of those types of toys. Sometimes I accidentally step on them. They always seem to leave them in my path."

"Then I better put these out of the way." She placed them on the coffee table. "Do you want to check out the stuff I brought for you?"

"Sure." As long we were on the subject of clothes, I took an appreciative gander at her outfit. She wore a flouncy little mini dress and ankle boots. Her legs were sleek and bare. Touchable, I thought. Or untouchable, depending how I looked at it.

She reached for the garment bag. "I still have a lot more shopping to do for you. But I wanted you to try on these shirts for now."

I would try on whatever she gave me. I'd hired her to be my stylist. That was the point of her being here, even if it had become an exercise in restraint.

She continued talking. "I have this idea to put you in a formal shirt, hanging loose over a pair of holey jeans, like the ones you had on the last time I was here. We can even use those, if you want, rather than me getting you a new pair and tearing them up." She ran her gaze along the length of me. "You wear your jeans well."

I sported a different pair today that were less trashed. But the way she was looking at me was giving me goose bumps. Should I give up the fight and seduce her? For all I knew, she was already seducing me. My mind was too boggled to know who was doing what.

She unzipped the garment bag. "I got you three different shirts: a white, a black and a red one." She handed me the white shirt. "Let's try this first. Oh, and do you mind putting on your holey jeans, too?"

"No problem. What sort of shoes am I supposed to wear with this look?"

"I'm going to get you some leather oxfords. Dress shoes with a dress shirt. But I also want to try your biker boots and one of your motorcycle jackets with it, too. We'll just mix everything up and see what we get."

I went into my room to get dressed. I didn't invite her to come with me, but I wanted to. If this kept up, I was going to need a cold shower. Damn Alice, anyway.

I returned wearing the outfit she'd designed, down to the boots and jacket. I left the shirttails loose, as she'd suggested. Her eyes lit up when she saw me.

"Oh, my God," she said. "That's so badass. Now let me see it without the jacket."

I ditched it and tossed it aside.

"We could do it both ways. You look rebellious, but handsomely refined, too."

Like the reformed bad boy that I was supposed to be? She admired me from every angle. I wanted to tell her to knock it off.

She handed me the black shirt. "Try this."

Instead of going back to my room, I changed where I was, and she watched as I bared my chest. She even bit down on her bottom lip. A nervous habit of hers. Well, it served her right, torturing me the way she was.

While I buttoned the black shirt, she came forward to help. "You missed some," she said.

She finished closing the rest of the buttons, and I inhaled her soft, floral scent. It wasn't the same fragrance that she used to wear, but it was just as enticing. I wanted her so badly, I imagined kissing her right here and now.

As she stepped back, her breath rushed out. "I like it, but the white was better, I think."

"Should I try the red now?" I was doing my best to concentrate on anything except sweeping her into my arms.

She nodded, and I switched shirts. This time she didn't help me button it. She seemed to recognize her mistake.

"That's definitely a possibility," she said, wringing her hands and twisting her fingers together.

Was she doing that to stop herself from touching me? My body was on fire, the embers burning hot and slow.

After a moment of heart-thundering silence, she said, "I think we should consider using a tie to create some contradiction."

"Torn jeans and a tie." I tried to sound as if I was mulling it over it. But mostly I was just battling the heat.

"I'll bring a selection with me next time. Or I'll go through yours and see if any of them will work. Your hair should be a little more tousled, too."

I tunneled my hands through it, pushing it away from my face. "Like this?"

"Yes, just like that." She breathed heavily again. "Also, will you roll up your shirtsleeves so part of your tattoo is visible?"

I followed her instructions. "Is this good?"

"It's perfect." She just stared at me.

I stared back at her, too, awkward as could be.

Then she said, "It's such a big tattoo. You must have put a lot of time and thought into getting that."

I broke eye contact and responded, "It was my gift to myself after I got sober." Getting inked was part of my growth, of my reawakening, of trying to create a new identity. But now it just felt like another facet of my uncertainty, of struggling to know who I was inside. Being around Alice wasn't helping those feelings, either, not with how hungry I was for her. "I wanted something that seemed primal, that connected me to my heritage."

"You used to say it didn't matter. You wouldn't even tell me what tribe you were from."

"That's because I don't know what my tribal affiliation is. My mom met my dad in Arizona when she was on a road trip with some friends. I don't know if that's where he was from or if he was just passing through, too."

Alice leaned against the side of the sofa. "Was it a one-night stand?"

"That's what I gathered, yeah. I was pretty young when she first told me about him, so I pieced most of it together later. His name was Edward. No last name. I guess they never got around to sharing specifics. If she'd known that she was going to get pregnant by him, then maybe she would've taken notes."

"I wish you would have told me all of this before. You were always such a mystery."

I shrugged. Sometimes I still was, even to myself. My sobriety hadn't changed that. But at least I had my work to express myself. "Creative people are supposed to be mysterious."

She picked up the toy she'd gotten for Pete and glanced at it. "Did I ever tell you that my dad was a trucker?"

"No, but Kirby did. He also said that your dad's name was Joel."

She scowled. "Well, that figures, doesn't it? Kirby yapping to you about my personal business."

"He didn't say all that much. Just your dad's name and profession." I wasn't about to admit that I'd accused Kirby of being her father. I wasn't in the mood to get my head chewed off. I'd already caught enough hell from him.

Her frown waned, making me relax a little. But I was still sort of jittery, too, always trapped in the middle with her.

She expelled a sigh. "Here's a tidbit that Kirby might not know about me, unless Mary told him. My parents named me Alice because my dad's favorite band was Alice in Chains. He wasn't into country, not like Mama. He preferred glam and grunge and rock."

Alice in Chains. Alice in Spencerland. Now I wasn't sure which nickname fit her better. I thought they both sounded disturbingly sexy.

She placed the squeaky truck back on the table. "I've never met my dad's family. He was originally from a small town in Washington. His parents are gone, but his brothers and sisters are still there. Just this year, I started reaching out to them on social media. It's been nice having an online rapport with them."

Immersed in what felt like an emotional moment, I said, "Someday I might try to find my dad."

"Really?" Her gaze locked onto mine. "How would you go about doing something like that?"

"I could submit my DNA on the ancestry sites that help you search for biological family members."

"I think that's a great idea."

"You do?"

"Absolutely." She stepped closer to me. "You have a right to know who your dad is."

"Yeah, but I probably won't get any hits, anyway.

How likely is it that my father or someone from his family would've submitted their DNA? And even if by some miracle I do locate him, he might not want anything to do with me." I'd already been cast aside by my aunt and uncle. I didn't want to pin my hopes on a stranger, too. "When I was a kid, I spent a lot of time imagining what he would be like, but that doesn't mean he's going to live up to my expectations."

"I have expectations about who my future husband is supposed to be. And I'm not going to give up on finding him."

"We could both end up being disillusioned."

"I hope not." She moved away from me.

"Yeah, me, too." I kept opening myself up to her, sharing my insecurities, saying things I never intended to say. "Are we done? Can I change out of this shirt now?"

"Certainly."

"I left my T-shirt in the bedroom. You can come along, if you want to. To give Cookie and Candy their toys," I clarified. I wasn't inviting her for any other reason.

"Are they hiding under the bed again?"

"Yes. But I think they'll come out to snag their toys and sneak another peek at you."

Alice joined me in my bedroom. I removed the red shirt and yanked my T-shirt back over my head.

"Should I put the toys on the floor?" she asked.

"Sure, just set them down."

She placed them near her feet. The bait worked. The dogs came creeping out. They looked at me to get my approval. I nodded and said, "Have at it, girls."

They each grabbed a toy and started chewing the rubber. The squeaking noise was deafening.

Alice laughed in sheer delight, and I smiled, too.

"They're so cute," she said, bouncing on her heels. "Did they pick the right ones?"

"No. But they'll swap at some point."

"I can barely tell them apart. They look like twins."

"Cookie's ear is a little tweaked from her injury, and Candy is a little fluffier."

She studied the dogs. "Oh, yes, I see that now. My niece and nephew are twins, but it's easy to tell them apart."

I stated the obvious. "Because of their gender differences?"

She laughed again. "Yes, but their personalities are different, too. My nephew is wonderfully behaved."

"And your niece is a hellion?" I lifted my eyebrows. "Like her auntie?"

"Who me?" She made an innocent expression, putting her hands beneath her chin and batting her lashes. "I had nothing to do with it."

"Yeah, I can see how sweet you are." Little vixen that she was. "The twins are cute kids. I've never met them, but Kirby shows me pictures of them all the time. He's an adoring grandpa."

"It's nice that you think the twins are cute. But I'd rather that you left Kirby out of it." She grabbed the shirt I discarded. "I know he dotes on the kids. I hear about it from Mary all the time. I don't need you singing his praises, too."

"At least Kirby is a real person. It's better than you talking about a fictional husband you might never even meet," I snapped.

She glared at me. "That's a low blow."

Okay, so she was right. It wasn't fair for me to squelch her dreams. But her attitude annoyed me. "You can't get mad every time I say something decent about Kirby."

She huffed out a breath. There was no reasoning with

her when it came to Kirby. We could argue about this until we were blue in the face, and never get anywhere.

I tried to make nice by asking, "Do you have your wedding all planned out? You know, the details women sometimes think about?"

She jerked her head. "No."

I didn't believe her. I inched forward, showing as much interest as I could. "Not even a little?"

"Maybe," she conceded.

"Come on. Tell me what parts you've thought about."

She hesitated, as if she didn't quite trust me with the information. But she gave in and said, "I want a black diamond for my engagement ring."

"Really?" I was surprised by her choice. It seemed a little gloomy to me. "Why?"

"I like how unconventional they are. Besides, black diamonds represent strength and power."

Now that I had time to reconsider her jewelry preference, I was intrigued by it. "That is kind of cool."

She fussed with the shirt in her hand. "I haven't picked out the type of dress I want. I don't want to go overboard when I don't even have a groom yet."

"You've got plenty of time for that." I glanced at the dogs and realized that they'd stopped squeaking their toys. Did they sense that Alice and I were discussing something important to her? Something that was totally foreign to me?

I knew nothing about weddings. Or phantom husbands. Or wannabe wives. I couldn't fathom spending eternity with someone. I was just trying to get through each day.

"How many more fittings do you think we're going to have?" I asked, changing the subject.

"It depends on my next shopping excursion." She

seemed to be studying me now. "Would you rather I make fewer trips over here?"

"No, it's fine. You can come by however often you need to. But maybe we could do one of the fittings at your place."

She gave me a weird look. "Why do you want to do that?"

"Because you never asked me to come over before, and that always made me feel a little slighted. But you can make up for it now." I chanced a half-cocked grin, using what little charm I had left. "You can cook me dinner or something."

She rolled her eyes. "Are you seriously trying to beg a home-cooked meal off of me?"

"I seem to recall you telling me that you liked to cook."

"I do," she said, making me wonder if she just might do it.

I never really knew with Alice. She was a hard nut to crack. This woman from my past, invading my mind and disorganizing my life. I was suffering just by being in her company. But that didn't stop me from wanting to spend more time with her—in whatever troubling ways I could.

Five

Alice

I invited Spencer to my home for the final fitting. For the past few weeks, I'd been going to his house and working out the wardrobe with him. But now, at the very end, he was coming to me. He wanted to see my place, so I caved in. I was cooking dinner for him, too.

To keep the evening from seeming romantic, I asked him to bring the dogs. By now, Candy and Cookie had become accustomed to me, so I figured they would be comfortable here. Spencer was also bringing Pete, per my request. The more company, the better.

Much to my dismay, I thought about Spencer day and night. I touched myself in the shower and imagined his hands on me. I rolled around in bed and fantasized that he was deep inside me. I did all of the breathless things that women did when they were consumed with a man.

I shook away those feelings and focused on the Mexican-style coleslaw on the counter in front of me. I made it look festive, with red and green cabbage, fresh corn directly from the cob, black beans and diced peppers. For the main course, a tamale casserole was bubbling in the oven. A pan of Spanish rice simmered on the stove, too.

Spencer was due any minute. I'd changed my clothes twice already, finally settling on a lace-trimmed camisole, a lightweight printed shrug, skinny white jeans and pink cowboy boots.

When the doorbell rang, my heart leaped to my throat, and I rushed to answer it. All three dogs were on leashes. Candy and Cookie took ladylike steps into my condo. The bulldog was his usual self, engine revved and ready to go.

Spencer held a bouquet of pink carnations in his other hand. He smiled at me. "These are from Pete."

"Thank you. They're lovely." I took the flowers. The dog was already slobbering at my feet.

"I guess we chose the right color," Spencer said.

I assumed he meant the carnations and how they matched my boots. "Yes, you did." It was cute how he'd said "we" as if the dog had actually had been involved. But it was weird, too, because it was the first time Spencer had given me flowers. I wasn't sure how to feel about that.

"You look pretty, Alice."

"You look great, too." He was as handsome as ever, in a slim black T-shirt, fitted jeans and black roper boots, scuffed at the toes. "I'll put these in water."

He let the dogs off their leashes, and man and animals followed me into the kitchen.

"Dinner will be ready soon." I filled a vase and arranged the flowers. I petted the dogs and put a water bowl on the floor for them. "I thought we could eat on the patio since the weather is so nice tonight."

"It smells wonderful." Spencer stood near the stove. He

lifted the lid on the rice. "It looks good, too." He glanced up at me. "Remember when I used to live on frozen pizza?"

Now I had visions of his old apartment and eating those pizzas in bed with him. "Yes, I remember." Every memory that pertained to him involved sex, or post sex, or something I would be smart to forget. I wished he hadn't brought it up. But what else were we supposed to reminiscence about?

"I still keep my favorite brand around for when I need a junk food fix."

I agonized over the deliberate way he was looking at me. "The messy kind with the cheese-stuffed crust?"

"Yeah." He broke eye contact. "I cook a little now." He checked out the slaw I'd left on the counter. "Not like this, though."

I redirected the conversation. "Do you want to see the rest of my place?" My condo consisted of an ultramodern living room, a cozy den, two spacious bedrooms and two full baths.

He nodded, and I gave him a tour, with the dogs following along, their little paws tapping on the hardwood floors.

Spencer seemed intrigued by my bedroom. He glanced around, taking it all in. I'd decorated in jewel tones, with lots of shiny knickknacks. The bed was crisply made, showing no signs of my restless nights. I'd made sure of it.

"As you can see, I set up your wardrobe in here." The clothes I'd purchased for him hung on a rolling rack, and his shoes and accessories were stacked in clear plastic boxes. "I figured you can use my bathroom to change."

"Whatever works." He glanced around again. "I expected your room to be messier."

"You thought I'd be a slob?"

"No, just that things would be scattered about."

I pulled a guilty face. "Actually, I cleaned up today since you were coming over. Normally I am on the messier side."

"Then I had you pegged right."

"Yes, I guess you did." I sometimes left my bras and panties on the floor, but I wasn't going to tell him that. "Did you bring the rest of your stuff for the fitting?" I asked. "Your jeans, boots and jacket that we'll be using?" He was responsible for providing those items.

"They're in my truck. I'll get them later, after dinner."

"Then let's eat." By now, I knew the food would be ready.

We returned to the kitchen, and I removed the casserole from the oven. I filled our plates, and he helped me carry them outside, along with a pitcher of sweet tea.

We sat at a glass-topped table. My patio offered brick pavers, a built-in barbecue and a fire ring, set amid leafy plants and a fragrant herb garden. The dogs made themselves at home, lolling on the pavement and enjoying the chew sticks Spencer had brought for them.

"You have a nice yard," he said.

"Thank you. I rented this condo when I first got my share of the money from Mama's songs."

He motioned to the windchimes hanging from a wooden post. "Those are a great touch. They're beautifully tuned," he added, as a light breeze stirred them.

Curious to know more about his creative side, I asked, "What made you want to be become a songwriter?" I'd never questioned him about his goals and dreams in the past. But he was always so reluctant to talk about himself then, he probably wouldn't have told me, anyway.

He swigged his tea. Was he gathering his thoughts?

Finally, he put down his glass and said, "I've always been good at writing, at putting words together. It was one of my outlets when I was growing up. I used to write short stories and poems. My writing got pretty dark after my mom died. Sometimes it still is."

I nodded. He'd become known for penning the lyrics to some very famous, very tragic songs. "Do you sing fairly well? My mother used to say that it helped if songwriters could sing their own songs."

"I wouldn't be able to make my living as a vocalist, but I sing well enough to make my own demos."

"What about the actual music part?" People in the industry praised him for being a brilliant composer. "How did that come about?"

"My aunt and uncle forced me to take piano lessons." He scooped up some of the casserole. "I hated it in the beginning. My teacher was brutal, and my aunt and uncle made it feel like punishment."

"Were you being classically trained? Chopin and Bach and all of that?"

He ate the food on his fork, then replied, "Yes, but classically trained doesn't just mean the type of music you're taught to play, it's technique, too. And I was good at it, really, really good. So good, my teacher was trying to prepare me for a music conservatory. She told my aunt and uncle that I could have a career as a concert pianist, if I put my heart and mind to it."

I tried to envision him, young and troubled, being forced to do something he didn't want to do. "How old were you when you first started to play? When the lessons began?"

"Eleven. I appreciate the classics now. But back then, they were torture."

"When did you change your style?"

"When I was fourteen, I saw a movie about Jerry Lee Lewis. And that was it for me. I started playing old rockabilly tunes. I loved the sound, but I was also doing it to piss off my aunt and uncle." He laughed a little. "I'd pound out those songs first thing in the morning, giving them a whole lotta shakin' going on."

I laughed, too. "And hence your days of being a bad boy began."

"Yeah, but it wasn't just about being bad. I was trying to soothe my soul, too."

I gently asked, "When did the drinking start?"

"It was around the same time. But even before that, I used to watch my aunt and uncle mix their favorite nightcaps. When I finally got the urge to try it, it became easy for me to raid their liquor cabinet. I only did it a little at first, though." He paused. "Then a lot later on."

"I guess it makes sense that you became a bartender, since you grew up in a house where cocktails were being served."

"I suppose so. When I turned eighteen and moved here to Nashville, I got a job as a barback in a restaurant. Then later, I started tending bar at the club where I met you in person for the first time."

I didn't respond. I didn't want to talk about that night or how sinful it was. I ached in all the wrong places just thinking about it.

As Spencer fell silent, I watched him eat. He mixed up everything on his plate, whereas I was keeping each dish separate. Was I trying to control my urges, even with my food? Normally I did what he was doing, letting the flavors seep together.

Before things turned too quiet, I said, "I got ice cream for dessert. I'm not a baker. My sister is a pastry chef, but I'm no good at it."

"Ice cream works for me. What flavor did you get?"

"I got two. Banana chocolate chip and cookies and cream."

He smiled. "Then I'll take some of each."

"That's what I plan to do, too." His laid-back, sexy smile was making me weak. Everything about him was dragging me under his spell, just like last time.

We finished dinner and cleared the dishes, taking them inside. The dogs didn't follow us. They stayed on the patio, but I left the sliding glass door open for them.

I served the ice cream in the living room, placing our bowls on the coffee table and offering Spencer a seat on the sofa. Before I sat down, I streamed some music, and he grinned when "Great Balls of Fire" started to play. It was the title song for the Jerry Lee Lewis movie he'd mentioned earlier.

"Great choice," he said.

I joined him on the sofa. "I aim to please." But not too much, I thought. I wasn't supposed to be thinking about pleasing him in other ways.

"Will we be listening to any of Kirby's songs tonight?" he asked.

"Not a chance," I replied.

"Not even the songs I wrote for him?"

"Nope. I'm afraid not." I dipped into my bowl. In some way or another, he always managed to bring Kirby into it.

"I wonder if they'll ever make a movie about his life."

I heaved a sigh. "They probably will when he's dead and gone. Or maybe they'll do it before. As arrogant as he is, he's probably shopping his book for movie deals as we speak."

"He stayed with me when I was going through withdrawals. He took care of me the entire time."

I tried to picture Kirby as Spencer's nursemaid, but it was tough for me to see him in that role. "Was it really bad?" I'd heard that alcohol withdrawal could be serious.

"It sure as hell felt bad to me. I had the shakes something awful." He held out his hand as if to check his steadiness now. "I was sweating and sick, you know, the whole shebang. It comes in stages, and it seemed like it was never going to end."

"How long did it last?"

"About a week."

"You mentioned before that you're involved in an outpatient program, but couldn't you have checked into a treatment center, instead of having Kirby stay with you?"

"Going to a place like that would have made me feel trapped. And I like that Kirby took care of me. He made me feel valued. He still does."

"It's weird that the man who helped you is the same man who destroyed my childhood. Don't you think there's a warped sort of irony in that?"

"I don't know. I guess." He shifted beside me. "Maybe I should get my stuff out of the truck now so we can do the fitting."

"That's probably a good idea." We were both done with our ice cream, and I didn't want to keep talking about Kirby.

He got up and left, and I shut off the music. The dogs came inside. Cookie looked around for Spencer and started to whine.

"It's okay," I said to her. "He's coming right back."

She kept whining, so I picked her up, hoping to comfort her. But then Candy and Pete pawed at me, wanting affection, too. I sat on the floor and let all of them climb onto my lap.

Spencer returned and marveled at the sight. "Look at you."

"What can I say? I'm the new dog whisperer." Cookie remained with me, even though her beloved owner was back. Candy and Pete stayed put, too, determined to keep me close.

"More like the new dog spoiler. I should have hired you to be their stylist, too. You could put them in ribbons and bows. Or leather jackets or whatever."

I got up off the floor. "I think I better stick to getting you ready for your shoot."

He nodded. "Yes, ma'am."

We went to my room so he could try everything on. The dogs came with us, finding cozy spots to relax.

The fitting went well, with Spencer standing in front of my closet door mirror while I checked each outfit. But when we took a break, he sat on the edge of my bed, and the moment turned painfully intimate. He looked so big and broad, wrinkling a delicate corner of my bedspread.

"There's supposed to be a makeup and hair person on the shoot," he said.

I tugged at the edge of my camisole. "I assumed there would be. I was going to talk to them about tousling your hair for the rebel looks I created."

"I'd rather do it myself." He stood and moved away from my bed. "Or let you do it."

"I guess we'll see how it goes." For now, I was just trying to keep my perspective. "You need to change for me one more time." I gestured to the final outfit.

He grabbed everything and went into my bathroom.

I glanced at the dogs while I waited. Pete was leaning against a decorative pillow that was propped in a corner, using it as a cushion. The girls were curled up next to him. All three were fast asleep.

Spencer returned. The last ensemble was sporty: a plaid shirt, cargo pants and brown chukka boots. It was perfect on him. But everything was. I came up beside him, so that both of us were reflected in the mirror.

"Do you need to make any modifications?" he asked.

I gazed at him in the glass. "I got a beanie to go with it, but it's up to you if you want to wear it."

"Can I see it?"

I removed the knit cap from its labeled box and gave it to him.

He tried it on. "If they do any pictures outdoors, I could wear it for that."

I adjusted the cap a little lower on his head. "I like it this way better."

"Yeah, but don't pull it down over my eyes. Or I won't be able to see how sexy you are."

"You shouldn't be looking at me that way, anyway." But it was too late. He already was.

He reached out to skim his thumb across my cheek, and I leaned into him, my mind spinning like a pinwheel. He moved closer, making me even dizzier.

We nearly kissed, until I came to my senses and pulled back. My hand slipped, knocking the beanie off his head.

"Sorry," we both said at the same time. A mutual apology, for a shared mistake of getting too close.

He crammed his hands in his pockets, as if he didn't know what else to do with them. I didn't know what to do, either. If we'd kissed for real, what would have happened afterwards? More kisses? A desperate night of forbidden sex?

He frowned. "I wish I wasn't so damned attracted to you."

"I'm feeling the same. It's torture." My pulse pounded, between my legs, where I wanted him most. I even pressed my thighs together.

A muscle flexed in his jaw. "I'm not going to sleep for shit tonight."

"I've barely slept since we've gotten to know each other again." I picked up the beanie off the floor, returning it to its box. "But what do two celibate people know? We're probably making more out of it than it is."

"I hope so." He shifted his stance. "But I should go now."

He headed to the bathroom to change into his regular clothes, and I leaned against my dresser, struggling to breathe.

While I was still dragging air into my lungs, he emerged and handed me the outfit he'd removed. I hung everything on the rack, and he woke up the dogs.

We went into the living room, and he gathered the leashes. Once the animals were secure, we all stood at the front door.

The shoot was a few days away. Then this job would be over, and I wouldn't have to see Spencer again. But how was I supposed to cope with my feelings until then?

He thanked me for dinner, and we said an awkward goodbye. He left, the dogs falling into step with him.

After I shut and locked the door, I returned to my bedroom to reorganize his wardrobe. But handling his clothes only intensified my unfulfilled ache. As I smoothed the pants he'd just worn, running my hands along the fabric, I closed my eyes.

And imagined that I was touching him instead.

Six

Alice

On the day of the photo shoot, I did whatever I could to impress Derek Jordon, the world-renowned photographer I'd been so eager to work with. Thankfully, he loved all of the looks I'd created. But I didn't want to get overly confident.

Derek was a perfectionist, with his own unique sense of style. He sported a shaved head and a nose ring. The hair and makeup person, a chipper brunette named Nellie, was his college-aged daughter.

Spencer asked her if I could style his hair for the rebel pics. Even after our close encounter at my condo the other night, he still wanted me to do that. Nellie was agreeable. She backed away, letting me handle it alone.

Spencer settled into a director's-style chair in the dining room, which was where Nellie had set up her kits and portable mirror. I intended to work from behind him, looking into the mirror, but he invited me to stand between his legs. He made room for me, and I moved into place, facing him, with my heart thumping in my chest.

I used a dollop of gel and ran my hands through his thick dark locks, tousling each strand just so.

"Are you enjoying this?" I asked.

"*This?*" he replied, his gaze roaming over me.

"The shoot," I clarified. I wasn't referring to me doing his hair.

"Yeah, it's been fun so far." He was still looking too closely at me.

I sucked in my breath. "Candy and Cookie did well." The dogs had already been in a couple of pictures with him. They were at the rescue now, to keep them from getting underfoot. But they were the least of my worries.

I finished his hair, but I didn't want to stop touching him. I glanced toward the living room, reminding myself of the importance of this job. "You should go. Derek has the next shot lined up."

"Are my clothes okay?"

"You look great." I loosened his tie a bit more. "But you really should go."

"You need to *let* me go, Alice."

I didn't understand what he meant. Then I realized that I was still standing between his legs. I mumbled an apology and stepped out of his way.

Mercy me.

Spencer rose from his chair, and I watched him pose for the next round of pictures. With the shadows playing across his face, he was a sight to behold. I could've drooled all over myself, especially when Derek had him straddling his piano bench.

Spencer's shirtsleeves were rolled up, exposing part of his tattoo. I could tell that Derek was fascinated with it.

Soon, he asked Spencer to change into a tank top so he could photograph the tattoo in its entirety. Spencer made the switch, and his body art became a focal point. Derek used diffuser boxes to light it, making the details more pronounced.

Following the tattoo pics, we broke for lunch. While we ate, Derek and I talked shop, Nellie texted her boyfriend and Spencer listened to music with headphones on.

After lunch and a wardrobe change, we moved to the garage. In this setting, Derek shot Spencer in his biker gear, using his Harley as a prop. Spencer caught my gaze from across the garage, leaving me in a rush of unwelcome heat. He looked damn fine, perched on his shiny new bike. All that chrome, all that male muscle.

Trying to distract myself, I shifted my gaze to Nellie. But that didn't help. She smiled and winked, letting me know that she was wise to what was going on. Apparently, she could tell that Spencer and I were hot for each other. By now, I figured that Derek knew, too, and had been channeling Spencer's desire for me into the shoot. I could only imagine how sexy the pictures were going to be.

Derek took the final ones outdoors on the lawn. Spencer wore the plaid shirt and cargo pants for those. Rain was in the forecast, and Derek was hoping for a downpour. He wanted to catch Spencer in it.

I provided disposable rain slickers for Derek, Nellie and me, in case we needed them. Spencer didn't get one.

When it started sprinkling, he crammed the beanie on his head, and Derek caught some candid poses.

The rain intensified, and the photographer got the shots he'd been hoping for. I adjusted the hood on my slicker and stared lustfully at Spencer. He was getting drenched, his shirt clinging to his skin.

A short time later, it was over. While Spencer changed

into dry clothes, Derek and Nellie packed up their gear. I exchanged business cards with them, and Derek and I agreed to stay in touch. Apparently, I'd made a positive impression and now had the important industry contact I'd hoped for.

After father and daughter were gone, I stayed to wrap things up with Spencer, helping him put away the wardrobe.

"I can wash your wet clothes," I said, still acting as his stylist. "Or take them to a service, if you prefer."

"That's okay. I'll wash them later. For now, I just threw them on top of the dryer."

"Well, you certainly nailed every shot." I was genuinely impressed with his modeling skills.

"I couldn't have done it without you. It really helped having you here."

"I'm glad you think so." Should I head home now? Or keep finding things to talk about? Clearly, I was struggling to leave. I glanced down at the floor. Now I wished that we would've kissed at my condo. At least then, if I never saw him again, I would have a memory of a recent kiss.

"Do you want some hot chocolate?" he asked.

I lifted my gaze. "That sounds nice." I was glad that he'd offered me a legitimate reason to stay. But the urge to kiss him hadn't gone away, and that was dangerous.

I followed him to the kitchen, and he poured the instant packets into our cups and heated the water in the microwave.

Neither of us spoke. It was still raining outside and I could hear it beating against the roof.

When the hot chocolate was ready, we drank it where we were, standing at the counter.

"Are you hungry?" he asked.

For food, no. For him, yes. I waited an anxious beat before I replied, "I'm still full from lunch. But if you want to eat, go ahead."

He shook his head. "I'm full, too. I was just checking on you."

Suddenly I couldn't take it anymore. I said what was on my mind. "We should have kissed when we had the chance."

His gaze locked onto mine. "We still can."

I moistened my lips, eager, excited, but painfully cautious, too. "Just one kiss, just to see what it feels like again."

"Whatever you want, Alice. Whatever you think is best." He set his cup down. "But let's try to make it count, okay?"

I put down my drink and took a step in his direction. A part of me wanted to turn tail and run, afraid that one kiss would never be enough. He watched me, anticipation in his eyes.

Once I was upon him, I lifted my face to his. I reached for him, getting ready. He leaned forward, and I pressed my lips to his. He tasted like chocolate and marshmallows, but I probably did, too. The two of us, warm and sweet.

He wrapped me in his arms, and our tongues met and mated.

Were we making it count? Was this the kiss we'd both been waiting for? Not by a long shot, I thought.

"More," I whispered, against his mouth. "More."

He cupped my ass and dragged me against his fly. I relished his hardness. My softness. The godawful hunger.

I wanted him beyond reason. Beyond logic. Beyond everything that was keeping me on the sexual straight and narrow. Forget Mr. Right. I would find him later. For now, there was only Spencer.

He deepened the kiss, and I made up my mind, dangerous as it was. I was going to sleep with him, here and now.

I pulled back and asked, "Do you have protection?"

He stared at me, as if my words didn't quite register. Or maybe he was just trying to remember if he had condoms. I searched his gaze, antsy for his reply. I needed to get him out of my system, out of my blood, but I couldn't forgo the protection.

He said, "They're in the bottom of my dresser, with some old clothes I never wear. But I hope they're still good."

I reached for his hand and shivered from the feeling. "Let's go find out."

He threaded his fingers through mine and led me to his bedroom. I stood off to the side while he retrieved the condoms. He checked the expiration date on the box.

My heart pounded. "Are they okay?"

He nodded. "We'll be safe."

I sighed in relief, and he pulled off his T-shirt. He was already barefoot. All that was left were his pants. I was wearing a lot more clothes than he was.

He gestured for me to remove something of mine, and I slipped out of my boots and peeled off my socks. But I didn't go any further. I couldn't seem to manage it, not with how shaky I was beginning to feel.

"What's wrong?" he asked.

"I'm actually a little scared." The five years I'd been alone seemed like an eternity now.

"We don't have to do this if it's too much for you." He spoke gently, reminding me that I was in charge, that this was my choice.

"But I want to be with you." The need was too great to walk away, even if I was nervous.

"Maybe I can help you relax."

"I'd like that." I wanted him to make it easier somehow. He approached me, and I looked up at him, captivated by the handsome angles of his face. He kissed me, and the kiss was much softer than the one in the kitchen. I rocked forward. No one had ever been protective of me before, and especially not him.

He whispered in my ear, "Can I undress you?"

I gave him permission, and he divested me of my blouse and bra. As he thumbed my nipples, I swayed on my feet.

"You're perfect," he said. "But you always were."

I had small, perky breasts and pointy pink nipples. He leaned down to take one of them into his mouth, and I cupped the back of his head.

Back and forth he went, from one of my breasts to the other, licking and sucking. He undid my jeans and slid his hand down the front of my panties. He applied silky pressure, working his fingers in tiny circles.

I gripped his shoulders. Nothing had ever felt so good. Yet I knew it was only going to get better. He continued to tease me, to arouse me, to make my head spin.

I came, slick and warm, with him touching me that way.

After it was over, he helped me out of my jeans, peeling my panties off with them. I stood naked before him, and he scooped me up and carried me to bed.

He leaned over me, and I tugged him down. I opened his jeans and put my hand inside his boxers. I felt him up, just as he'd done to me.

He groaned in satisfaction, and all too soon, he was naked and fully aroused. He put on a condom and braced himself above me. Eager for his penetration, I parted my thighs.

He entered me, and we moved in unison, in a rhythm that came naturally. No words were exchanged, only moans and murmurs and rough sounds of pleasure. He lifted my legs and pulled them higher and tighter around his body.

Good thing I was bendy like that. He was agile, too, and with muscles to die for. I skimmed a hand down his abs, feeling them ripple.

We kissed, tongues tangling, teeth clashing. Together we were lethal, fast and furious, wild and desperate.

I dug my nails into his shoulders, and he thrust even harder and deeper, pushing both of us toward completion.

I didn't need any extra stimulation. Just having him inside me, moving like a maniac was enough. I came in convulsive waves, drowning in my own sticky wetness.

He arched like an animal, rearing up during his orgasm. I watched him, thinking how magnificently primal he was.

He collapsed on top of me, and neither of us moved. Finally, he lifted his head and peeked at me through one eye. The other eye was covered by his free-falling hair.

He rolled off of me, but he stayed close, holding me, making me sigh. Feeling the almighty afterglow, I curled up against him, letting the sensation engulf me. I wanted it to last, but before I got too accustomed to it, I eased away from him.

Silence hovered in the air. He seemed confused that I ended it so soon. But as comforting as it felt, as much as I liked it, I feared that I might get attached to him.

My old lover. My new lover. Were we back to having an affair? The thought both scared and excited me.

Spencer frowned, almost as if he was trying to read my mind.

"Is the offer to eat still good?" I asked, creating a diversion. I didn't want him to figure me out.

"You worked up an appetite?" Now he seemed amused.

I fluttered my mascara-spiked lashes, playing the femme fatale, keeping him distracted. "Sex can be hard work."

"The hardest." He glanced down at himself. He was

still wearing the condom. "I better go get rid of this. Meet me in the kitchen?"

"Okay." I got out of bed. He did, too, but before he headed for the bathroom, he kissed me, making me long for the afterglow again.

We separated, and I got haphazardly dressed, wearing only my blouse and panties.

I entered the kitchen and opened Spencer's fridge. I spotted an assortment of deli meats, along with eggs and cheese and other basics. I checked the freezer and uncovered a stack of the frozen pizzas he favored. Then, as I stood there, staring into the freezer's chilly abyss, I heard his footsteps behind me.

I spun around. He was attired in his underwear, looking rough and messy, like the bad boy he used to be. Was sleeping with him a mistake? Had I acted too impulsively?

"What do you want to make?" he asked.

I removed one of the pizzas. "How about your old standby?"

"That works for me." He preheated the oven, setting the digital dial. "I'm going to have a ginger ale now. They've become my go-to since I got sober. Do you want one?"

I nodded. Anything to keep myself busy.

He went to the mini fridge in the bar where he kept the sodas. He returned with two chilled cans. He handed me mine, and I opened the tab and took a hasty drink.

"Are you having second thoughts?" he asked.

"About what?" I responded inanely. I knew what he meant, but I didn't want to seem too obvious, even if he'd managed to figure me out.

"About us." He studied me. "Are you having buyer's remorse?"

I looked past him, landing my sights on the kitchen window. The glass was fogged, misty and gray. "I didn't buy anything," I replied, returning my gaze to his.

"You gave up your celibacy. That's a big buy-in after five years." He pulled a hand through his already messy hair. "I'm sorry if I'm not the right guy for you."

"You have nothing to be sorry for." It was just sex, I reminded myself, but with some sweetness tossed in. "It was nice being back in your bed. It's what I wanted, what I needed."

He swigged his soda with a noisy swallow. "Then do you want to keep doing it?"

I should have said no. That this was the only time we would be together. But I couldn't bear to let him go this soon. "Maybe for a little while."

"A little while is all I have to give, Alice."

"I know." And that was all I needed from him, I decided. No more. No less. I couldn't keep worrying about getting attached, either. I had to release that fear.

He came forward and wrapped me in his arms. He was getting adept at cuddling. He nuzzled the top of my head and said, "I think you're going to become my muse."

I stepped back, needing to look at him, to see the usual darkness in his eyes. "Have you ever had a muse before?"

"No, but I like the idea. Don't you?"

"It could be interesting." Some of the most beautiful songs in the world were inspired by real live muses. But some of the most troubling were, too. It went both ways.

The oven beeped, reaching the desired temperature. I'd almost forgotten about the pizza. But now I was grateful for the reprieve. I didn't want to think too deeply about being Spencer's muse.

Thirty minutes later, Spencer piled the pizza onto paper plates, giving us each three ginormous pieces.

"Let's pig out in bed," he said. "Like we used to."

I didn't protest. Eating in bed with him was a naughty memory I didn't mind repeating. Besides, I was trying to relax and not keep stressing about everything. For now, there was nothing wrong with being his lover, or his muse.

We retreated to his room, sat cross-legged amid the rumpled covers and feasted on our meal, with a stack of napkins nearby.

"It's hard to imagine you growing up so rich," I said. "Especially while you're gnawing your way through frozen pizza."

He chewed and swallowed. "It's not frozen anymore."

"You know what I mean." He was already on his second slice.

He shrugged. "When I lived with my aunt and uncle, we had a personal chef who made all of our meals. I wasn't allowed to have junk like this."

"Then it stands to reason why you enjoy it so much."

He tore at the cheese-stuffed crust, pulling it apart and making the mozzarella seep out. "Robert and Roberta wouldn't be pleased."

"Those are your aunt's and uncle's names?" I burst into a laugh. "Seriously?"

He laughed, as well. "He goes by Rob and she goes by Bobbie. But it's still annoying how alike they are, right down to their names."

I popped a piece of pepperoni into my mouth. The pizza was loaded with them. "Did you have a nanny?"

"Yes, but she wasn't very nice. Bobbie hired someone who ruled with an iron fist, and Rob thoroughly approved. Eventually I got too old for a nanny, so she went off to discipline some other poor kid, I guess."

"Your aunt and uncle sound wretched." That was the only way I could think to describe them. "They could have at least hired Nanny McPhee or Mary Poppins or someone who could've protected you."

"Yeah, don't I wish. It's weird, the relationship my mom had with my aunt. They didn't get along worth a damn, but they still saw each other all the time. Bobbie was always pressuring Mom to give up her acting dreams. The fact that Mom used to borrow money from Bobbie didn't help. My aunt liked to throw that in my face. How irresponsible she thought my mom was. How our rent would've never gotten paid if it hadn't been for her."

"That's a terrible thing to say to a child." The way they'd treated him was deplorable.

"I think my mom would've been a successful actress, if she'd lived to see it through. She never did any TV or movies, but she was studying her craft and working toward the future." He ate the gooey crust he'd pulled apart. "She did mostly corporate stuff, like job-training videos. Her favorite one was for a bank, where she got to play a teller who was being robbed. When she rehearsed it at home, she let me pretend to be the robber."

I couldn't help but smile. I envisioned him with a bandit mask over his eyes. "What about the department store work? Wasn't that enough to pay the rent?"

"The perfume gigs? That was freelance. She tried to keep her schedule open for auditions. When she didn't have a babysitter for me, she would take me along."

I liked the way he spoke of her, the loving tone in his voice. "What was her name?"

"Lynnette." He reached for a napkin and handed me one, too. "I know that your mom's name was Cathy Birch. I saw her songwriting credits. Was Birch her maiden name?"

"Yes. She and my dad were never married. They just lived together and had us kids. That always bothered me."

"Them not being married? Why? It was still a committed relationship, wasn't it?"

"Yes, but Mama wanted him to marry her. She used to say how it made her sad that he didn't believe in marriage."

"Maybe that's why marriage is so important to you now."

"Maybe." To stop him from delving deeper into how badly I wanted a husband, I said, "Wait until your aunt and uncle see the photo spread of you, looking all badass and beautiful. You should send them a signed copy."

"Badass and beautiful?" He laughed. "I hope that isn't how the magazine describes me." He leaned closer to me. "Now you…you're the beautiful one."

Fueled by his compliment, I kissed him. He pulled me onto his lap, rubbed against me and made both of us moan.

All over again.

Seven

Spencer

Alice and I rolled over the bed, knocking our plates and leftover food onto the floor.

I tore open her blouse, the buttons popping. Immediately realizing what I'd done, I cursed to myself and said, "Sorry. I'll get you another one." I would buy her anything she wanted.

"It doesn't matter." She ran her nails down the front of my body, leaving scratch marks on my chest and stomach.

I went after her panties, practically tearing them off, too. Then I gripped both of her wrists, held her hands above her head and kissed her soft and slow, bringing the frenzy to a halt. She stopped thrashing and sighed against my lips.

After the kiss, I looked down at her. She was looking up at me, too, waiting to see what came next. I was still holding her hands above her head.

I released my hold on her and said, "I need your permission."

"For what?" she asked, blinking at me.

"To go down on you." I wanted to hear her tell me to do it. I leaned forward and whispered, "Will you let me?"

"Yes," she replied. "Do it." She was already arching her hips in anticipation. "You were always so good at it."

"I still am." Or I sure as hell intended to be. I worked my way down, breathing against her skin. I paused purposely at her navel, teasing her, making her wait.

She pushed her hands into my hair. "You're probably going to haunt my dreams."

"Just the erotic ones, I hope."

"Definitely." She arched her hips again, her hands still tunneled into my hair.

I put my face between her legs. She was smooth, fully waxed, and I parted her with my thumbs. I used my tongue, swirling, licking, making her half-mad.

I could feel her excitement, her honey-slick moisture, her sensual shivers. She kept moving closer to my mouth, making me aroused, too.

When she came, her entire body quavered, and I continued my foray, absorbing every last shudder.

I raised my head and kissed her, slipping my tongue past her lips. She pressed against me, and I got even harder.

She was already naked, and I was nearly there. I removed my boxers, tore open a condom and put it on as quickly as I could.

I positioned her on top, and she arched her glorious body. Cloudy light spilled in from the French doors, bathing her in a hazy glow.

I circled her waist with my hands, and she impaled herself, riding me into the kingdom of heaven—or the depths of hell—in furious pursuit of whatever this hungry sensation was. She moved slowly, taking me inch by inch. I groaned my approval, watching her hips rise and fall. She increased the tempo, taking us both to new heights.

Was her heart beating at a runaway pace? Mine was, in every pulse point of my body. I missed this feeling. I missed having sex. And she was making it so damned good. She adjusted herself on my lap, creating deeper friction.

My vision blurred; my muscles tensed; my mind slipped into caveman mode. I wanted to hang on, to let the thrill last. But I was too far gone. I gave up the fight and let myself fall, coming strong and fast.

I went into the bathroom, came back, put my boxers on and cleaned up the pizza off the floor. Alice offered to help, but I told to her stay put. I liked how cozy she looked in my bed.

I rejoined her, getting under the covers. I took her in my arms, doing the romantic thing, or trying to. It was still new to me.

She made a dreamy sound and put her head against my chest, so I figured I must be doing it right.

I wasn't sure what to expect from this affair. Was it going to be sex-only again? Or would we go on some actual dates? I was scheduled for a business trip next week, and now I was thinking of asking her to join me. But this didn't seem like the time to broach the subject, so I just held her instead.

To keep myself occupied, I played with the spiky tips of her hair. I'd seen it brushed flat before, but mostly it was stiff and pointy.

"What color is it for real?" I asked.

She stirred in my arms. "What?"

"Your hair."

"It's blond, but I bleach it to make it whiter."

"I'm glad you're still wearing it this way. I always liked how retro it seemed, like Billy Idol or something."

She moved onto her side. "Didn't I ever tell you that 'Rebel Yell' was my karaoke song?"

I chuckled at her expression; she was shooting me an Idol-type snarl. "No, I don't recall you ever saying that. But I remember that you used to listen to early punk."

"It was the fashions that first caught my attention, pictures of people in the seventies and eighties, with their tough and trashed clothes. I was especially interested in cowpunk. Mama raised us on country, and I thought the combination of country and punk was cool."

"And you had the right attitude to pull it off, with how rebellious you were." I thought about the troubled kid I used to be. "In the beginning, I did everything my aunt and uncle told me to do. But later, I copped plenty of attitude, too."

"Yes, of course, you pounding away on the piano."

"I still play that way when I'm all alone, letting my frustrations out."

She softly asked, "Did you cry when your mom died?"

"I bawled like a baby. But that's the last time I cried. What about you?"

"I cried when my mama passed. But I've cried a lot since then. Not just when I'm sad, but when I'm mad, too."

"You never cried around me." I'd never seen that side of her. "But we barely knew each other."

"We're making up for that now."

That was for damned sure. I'd never shared my feelings with a woman before. But maybe it was part of being sober, of learning how to be someone's lover without being wasted. I was different now. Alice was, too, with her thirst for a husband.

I popped off with a smile, teasing her, poking at her

hair again. "I'm surprised 'White Wedding' isn't your karaoke song."

She kicked me under the sheet. "That's not funny. Have you seen how goth that old video is? The nails in the coffin and all that."

"Says the girl who already knows what kind of engagement ring she wants. A black diamond. That actually sounds kind of goth."

She snorted. "Maybe you should write a song about it."

"Maybe I will." I'd already decided that she could be my muse. "Alice in Spencerland. Who wouldn't want to write about you?"

"It'd better be a good song."

"It'll be my best." Or I hoped it would. But I couldn't just rush something out. It had to come naturally. "Do you want to watch TV?" I asked. "As long as we're lying around, we might as well stream something."

"That sounds nice. But I'm going to put my bra and panties back on first."

"That's fine." I'd already climbed into my boxers earlier. I watched her get out of bed and slip into her underwear.

"What should we watch?" she asked, returning to my side and propping up a pillow for herself.

"I don't know. Let's look and see what our choices are."

After scrolling through tons of movies and shows, we picked *Sons of Anarchy*, even though we'd both seen the entire series before.

"This is one of my favorite shows," she said.

"Mine, too. It's pretty twisted, though."

"That's why I like it."

"Same here." Which made us twisted people, I supposed. But that was part of why we'd hooked up to begin with. Alice and I weren't normal. We'd had problems from the start.

Turning silent, we binged on the show.

We watched the first three episodes of the first season, before she decided it was time to go. By now, it was long past dusk. We'd spent the entire day together.

I offered her a sweatshirt to cover her torn blouse. She accepted it, and I got the feeling she liked wearing my clothes. I wondered when I was going to see her again. Last time, we just texted each other when we wanted sex. But this time, we hadn't discussed the specifics.

We hadn't talked about working together again, either. Maybe I would benefit from having her as my regular stylist. Then again, did I even need a regular stylist? It wasn't as if I was attending fancy events or doing photo shoots every day. Mostly, I was just a songwriter, working from home.

While she finished getting dressed, I mentioned my upcoming trip. "Did I tell you that I was going to Los Angeles next week?"

"No, you didn't. Is it for business?"

I nodded. "I'll be meeting with the music director of a film who wants me to compose the score."

She cocked her head. "How long will you be gone?"

"About three days. I reserved a bungalow at the Chateau Marmont." I shrugged, smiled a little. "I chartered a private plane, too." I forged ahead with the invitation. "You should come with me."

"Really?" She sounded surprised. "Are you sure I won't be in the way?"

"I'm positive." It would solve the issue of when I was going to see her again. "It would be nice to have the company and since we agreed to keep hanging out for a while, I figured why not travel together."

She furrowed her brow. "We didn't agree to hang out, Spencer. We agreed to keep sleeping together."

"I know." I hesitated, hoping I wasn't biting off more than I could chew by whisking her off on a trip. "But it's just for fun." I wasn't suggesting anything more. "Besides, have you ever been to LA?"

"Yes, but I spent all of my time in the fashion district. I've never really seen the sights." She paused, as if she was debating the fun we were supposed to have. "If I go with you, will you give me a tour?" she asked.

"Absolutely." I moved closer to where she stood. "I'll rent a fast car and take you wherever you want to go."

"Now how can I say no to that?" She smiled, the idea of traveling with me obviously growing on her. "I like fast cars."

"What about fast men?" As quick as could be, I kissed her, cementing our deal. But I didn't tell her that this would be the first time that I would be returning to LA since I'd left home. I would tackle that anxiety later. For now, I just wanted to kiss her a few more times.

After Alice left, I got the dogs from the rescue and brought them home. They crawled straight into their beds and slept. My cell phone rang, and I checked the screen. It was Kirby.

"Hey," I answered. "What's up?"

"I was wondering if I could come by and talk to you," he replied.

"Today?" I glanced at my piano. I planned on working for the rest of the evening, keeping myself from obsessing about the LA trip. I was glad that Alice would be joining me, but I was still nervous about returning to the place where I'd been immersed in so much pain.

"Is this a bad time for you?" He sounded upset.

"No, it's fine." I couldn't turn him away, not after everything he'd done for me. "Are you okay?"

"I'll explain when I get there. I'm in my car, so it won't be long."

"All right. I'll see you soon." I hoped he wasn't having the urge to drink or use. He'd been clean and sober for a lot longer than me. He was my rock, the person I relied on. If he faltered, was I strong enough to get him through it?

He arrived looking like he was headed to a funeral, shrouded in black, but without his usual silver jewelry or Western bling. We went into my living room, and he plopped onto a chair. His leg was jittery.

"Did somebody die?" I asked.

"Yeah, me," he said.

I asked the next question, dreading his response. "What happened? Did you get high? Did you drink?"

He scowled at me. "No."

I sighed in relief. But he was still scowling. I watched him run his hand across his beard. I'd never seen him so agitated.

"Did you have a fight with one of your kids?" I was playing twenty questions, trying to drag it out of him. He'd come over to tell me his problem, but now he seemed reluctant to say it.

He blew out a windy breath. "Everything is fine with my sons."

"Your lady then?" Kirby was dating a woman who worked for the Country Music Hall of Fame. In the past, he hadn't been faithful to anyone. But as far as I knew, he was loyal to her.

"Debra is fine, too." He snared my gaze. "This is about Alice."

My heart knocked against my rib cage. Did he suspect that I was involved with her? Had he figured it out?

Did it matter if he did? I asked myself. She and I were

both consenting adults. It wasn't Kirby's place to repri-
mand me. I could sleep with whoever I wanted.

"I lied to you," he said.

My pulse jumped. "About Alice?"

"And her mom." He scooted forward in the leather chair
he was occupying. "I knew Cathy before Alice was ever
born. About nine months before," he added.

Holy crap, I thought.

He got up and went over to the bar, pouring himself a
soda. I watched him, making sure that he didn't spike it.

"Is Alice your daughter?" I asked, point-blank.

He winced. "I can't say for sure, but there's a darned
good possibility."

"Why in the hell didn't you tell me this before?"

"Because you caught me off guard last time, and I panicked. I haven't told anyone else, but no one has suspected
it except for you."

I considered how this news was going to impact Alice.
Would she explode in a devastating rage? Would she sink
to the floor and cry? Would she come after Kirby with a
knife? I imagined all sorts of horrible reactions.

I tried to clear those awful things from my mind but
I couldn't shake them completely. "How long have you
known that she might be yours?"

He returned to his chair. "I suspected it when I met
Alice for the first time."

I gaped at him. "She was only nineteen then." They'd
met for the first time in his son's law office, when they'd
negotiated the terms of the settlement related to her mom's
songs and signed the papers. "I can't believe you suspected
it all this time."

"I wasn't sure. I mean, it was just a feeling I had. But
I couldn't remember exactly when I was with Cathy. As
stoned as I used to be, I wasn't keeping track of who and

when." He gulped his soda. "But then, a few months ago, I was going through some old stuff I had in storage, and I came across a letter that Cathy had written to me during our first affair. When I saw the date on it, I realized that the timeline could absolutely make me Alice's dad."

I studied him from where I stood. "So, let me get this straight. You had two affairs with Cathy? The first one when Alice might've been conceived, and then another one years later?"

"Yes, but Cathy approached me the second time with the sole purpose of trying to sell her songs. She was struggling to raise her daughters and was hoping to make a better life for them. She hadn't intended to sleep with me again, but I lured her back into bed without buying the songs."

"And she never told you that Alice might be yours?"

"No. She didn't say a word about that. She kept contacting me about the songs. But she didn't mention Alice."

"Don't you find that odd? If she was struggling to raise her kids, then why didn't she request a paternity test and try to get child support from you? You're a rich man. The payout could have been substantial."

"I know, but maybe she didn't want to stir up something that would make her look bad in her children's eyes. Maybe she couldn't bear to admit that she'd cheated on Joel when she was with me the first time or that her daughters might have two different fathers."

"That could be it. But are you sure the timeline of that letter is accurate? You could be confused about being Alice's dad."

"I'm not confused. I even told Alice during our first meeting that if I ever had a daughter, I'd want it to be someone like her. There was just something about her that made me feel as if she could be mine, and now I know that I wasn't so far off the mark."

I wasn't going to dispute his emotions or the paternal feelings he had for her. I appreciated that his heart was in the right place, but there was still going to be hell to pay with Alice. "When are you going to tell her? As difficult as it's going to be, she has a right to know."

"I was hoping that you could help me get closer to her before I say anything."

"Me?" I flinched. "That's not a good idea."

He shot me a chastising look. "Why? Because you used to get drunk and sleep with her? I'm not an idiot, Spencer. There's no way that you and Alice had a respectful thing going. With as wild as both of you used to be, that's just not feasible."

"You suspected all along that I was lying?"

"Yes, I did. But I lied to you, too, so I think that makes us even."

"I'm seeing her again." As long as we were clearing the air, I laid that out there, too. "But Alice and I agreed that it's only a temporary thing. She wants a husband some-day, and I couldn't even begin to contemplate a relation-ship." My only goal was to stay sober, but I figured that went without saying, especially to Kirby.

"I understand. But promise me that you'll be good to her while you're together."

"I will." The last thing I wanted was to hurt her. "She's going to LA with me next week. I have some business deal-ings there, and I invited her to come along."

His gaze sought mine. "Will you help me get closer to her?"

As desperate as he was, how could I refuse him? He'd never turned me down for anything before. "I'll certainly try. But I have no idea how I'm supposed to accomplish it."

"Just say nice things about me."

"She gets mad when I do that. But I'll keep doing it and

try to bring her around." It was obvious how much Kirby wanted to be her father. That in his heart, he already loved her. "I don't want her to keep hating you."

He rewarded me with a smile. "I think you'll be a positive influence on her. If anyone can make her see the good in me, it's you."

I hoped he wasn't giving me more credit than I deserved. "I'll do my best. But how long are we going to keep this a secret?"

"I'll tell her as soon as you think she's ready."

"Then we'll just take it day by day." I didn't expect overnight results, if I got them at all. But I wanted to make a difference. No one had ever needed me for something so important.

And regardless of how it turned out, the possibility of Kirby being Alice's father was about as important as it got.

Eight

Alice

I sat on Tracy's sofa, surrounded by her woodsy décor, clutching an embroidered pillow to my chest—one of those old-fashioned "Home Sweet Home" things. The scented candle she'd burned earlier had gone out, smoldering down to its wick, as I told her about sleeping with Spencer.

"The sex was amazing. And so was the time we spent together afterward." I couldn't deny how attentive Spencer had become.

She set her chair in motion, an old bentwood rocker she'd gotten at a flea market. "Then why do you still seem scared?"

"It's my fear of getting too close. While I was with him, I kept warning myself not to get attached, but what if I do?"

"You're bound to feel that way after so many years of being alone. But the idea is to have some fun, right? Isn't that why he invited you to go to LA with him?"

"Yes, but our affair isn't going to last. He already told me that he can't be my Mr. Right."

"Is that what you want him to be?"

"I don't know. I'm just confused, I guess."

"Then maybe you shouldn't go to LA with him."

"But I want to see him again." I wanted to crawl back into his big strong arms.

She watched me squeeze the pillow. "Then you have to decide what's best for you."

"Truthfully, I just want to have some fun and quit worrying about it. But my past keeps coming back to haunt me. The wild girl who'd made all of the wrong decisions."

"You're not that girl anymore, Al. You've grown up since then. And in my opinion, you're allowed to have some adult fun, to be with a sexy guy, even if he's not Mr. Right."

I nodded, grateful that she was encouraging me to live a little. "After five years of celibacy, I deserve to have a good time." To quit beating myself up about the past, I thought, and to quit panicking about getting attached. "I'll just have a great affair with Spencer. Then later, I'll find the man I'm meant to be with." Somehow, someway, I would meet the guy of my dreams—when all of this was over with Spencer.

She smiled. "There you go. Your decision is made."

But would it be that easy? I asked myself. God, I hoped so. Nothing about my life had been easy this far.

Tracy went silent, and I got the sneaking suspicion that she was thinking about her ex. I watched her, waiting to see if she would mention him.

Then she said, "Not that it should matter, but I wonder how well Spencer knows Dash. If they're friends or just new acquaintances."

Bingo, I thought. She couldn't go a week without Dash's

name coming up. Deep down, she was as troubled as I was. "I don't know. But I can ask him, if you want."

"Sure, okay." She seemed reflective, as always, when it came to her ex. "Do you think Spencer knows that Dash and I used to be engaged?"

"I have no idea. But I can ask him that, too."

"A lot of people in this town know. But a lot don't. I guess it depends on how gossipy they are."

"Spencer doesn't seem particularly gossipy. But he has been talking about himself and his family, telling me about his past. He never used to do that before."

"It's good that he's opening up. That he trusts you with his past."

"It's been nice having real conversations with him. I think there are still some subjects that make him uncomfortable, though."

"Dash had trouble sharing his feelings with me. And when he did share them, they weren't very comforting."

Because Dash didn't believe in love, I thought, and Tracy did. "They say love hurts."

She touched a hand to her stomach. Was she thinking about the baby she'd miscarried? The child she should've had with Dash?

She looked up at me. "It only hurts when it doesn't work the way it's supposed to. But it's going to be perfect when it happens to you. You're going to marry someone who's going to love you to the ends of the earth."

"Someone who isn't Spencer," I said, confirming that no matter how wonderful my affair with him was, it had absolutely nothing to do with love. I couldn't risk my heart on a man who wasn't interested in marriage.

On the night before Spencer and I were scheduled to leave for Los Angeles, my sister asked me for an emergency favor. Her nanny was sick, and she needed someone to babysit the twins. Naturally, I agreed to watch them. I adored Hudson and Hailey.

I was in the master bedroom with Mary, and so were the kids. They loved watching their mommy get fixed up. She and Brandon were attending a black-tie event, something they often did. Brandon was downstairs, attired in his tux and waiting for his wife. He'd greeted me earlier, when I'd first come to the door. He was a wonderful husband and father, even if he was Kirby's son.

I turned my attention to the kids. They sat on their parents' bed, dressed in their pajamas. At four years old, they were smart and spry, with their dark auburn hair and bright blue eyes. Hailey was being a pistol, as usual. Since I'd arrived, she'd already spilled some of Mommy's perfume on the floor. Hudson hadn't done anything, except smile at me like the pint-sized gentleman that he was.

"What do you think?" Mary asked, as she spun around in her emerald-green gown.

"Mommy pretty," Hudson said.

"Very pretty," I agreed. I was Mary's stylist, so I'd picked out the dress for her. Her closet was filled with choices I'd made. "Your hair looks amazing, too." She'd styled her long red locks in a chic updo. When we were younger, she'd always looked like the girl-next-door type. These days, she was far more glamorous.

"What about you?" Mary asked her daughter. "Do you think I need some earrings? Maybe a necklace?"

"Yes!" Hailey bounded off the bed.

She always chose the jewelry her mother wore on formal occasions. But the kid had a great eye. She'd inherited her style from me. Her rebellion, too, I supposed. Even Spencer had teased me about that, and he didn't even know Hailey.

I watched my niece sort through her mother's jewels.

She examined each piece carefully. Of course, Mary didn't leave it around for Hailey to get into on her own. She kept it locked in a safe. Otherwise the little girl might be tempted to wear it herself or put it on her dolls or bury it in the yard like a hidden treasure.

Hailey chose a diamond ensemble with ruby accents that complemented the shiny red soles on Mary's heels.

"Now Mommy perfect," she said.

"Yes, she is." My sister had everything I hoped for: a kind and loving husband, two beautiful children, a successful career.

"Will you tell Daddy that I'm almost ready?" Mary said to the kids.

"Yup!" Hailey pulled her brother down off the bed, and they dashed off, excited to deliver the message.

"What's going on?" Mary asked me after the twins were gone. "You seem preoccupied."

Rather than hide my feelings completely, I said, "I'm seeing someone. In fact, I'm taking a trip with him. We're leaving tomorrow afternoon. He has business in LA, and he asked me to accompany him."

"Really? Who is he?"

"His name is Spencer Riggs."

"The songwriter?" She angled her head. "He's friends with Kirby, isn't he?"

"Yes. Kirby recommended me to him. But I knew Spencer from a long time ago, too."

"Is it serious?"

"No." I wasn't about to admit that he was the last guy I'd slept with before I became celibate. Mary didn't know about my sordid history with Spencer, and I wasn't keen on telling her, either. "He's just someone I'm seeing for now."

"Are you still hoping to meet the right man someday?"

"Yes, I am. I just have to be patient enough to find him."

She glanced at her wedding ring. "I hope falling in love is easier for you than it was for me. The way I lied to Brandon in the beginning, hiding my identity from him."

"I still feel awful for being such a big part of that." I'd orchestrated her deception, encouraging her to hurt Brandon. I'd believed at the time that he'd been involved in destroying Mama, which wasn't true, and Mary had gotten close to him under false pretenses to find out the truth.

"It's over now." She gazed at her ring again. "Everything turned out the way it should."

I swallowed the lump in my throat, envious of her life, but glad for her, too. "You better get going or you'll be late." I picked up her gold clutch and handed it to her.

She took the purse, checking her belongings inside of it. "Brandon must be keeping the kids busy. Otherwise they would be back to see what's taking me so long."

We went downstairs together. Me in my comfy babysitting outfit, and Mary in her gown.

Brandon was in his home office, sitting at the computer desk with the twins on his lap. He was letting them type on his laptop. Brandon was an entertainment lawyer, a high-society guy who loved art and music and fine wine. He had smooth black hair, regal features and stunning blue eyes, like the kids.

"I'm ready," Mary said from behind them.

Brandon spun around on his chair, taking Hailey and Hudson for a spin, too. He let out a low whistle and said, "There's my gorgeous wife."

She smiled. "And there's my handsome husband."

The twins jumped off his lap and ran over to me. They seemed to know that their daddy was going to stand up and kiss their mommy. Sure enough, he did. It was just a chaste kiss, but it made my heart jump, reminding me of the future I longed to have.

But in the interim, I had Spencer to keep me entertained. And tomorrow, I would be headed to California
with him, immersed in lust and passion.

Spencer picked me up at my condo and loaded my bags
into his truck. I'd overpacked, but I was a clotheshorse, so
that was normal for me.

As he pulled out of the parking lot, I said, "You look
like a California boy today." He wore his usual torn jeans,
a plain T-shirt and slip-on sneakers with a checkerboard
pattern.

"I just wanted to be comfortable." He frowned. "I probably should have mentioned this before, but I haven't been
back since I left."

"This is your first time going home?" I considered the
circumstances. "I haven't been back to Oklahoma since
I left, either." I was settled in Nashville now, and there
didn't seem to be any reason to return to where I'd been
raised.

He drove toward the interstate that would take us to the
airport. "I have good and bad memories of living in LA.
But the bad ones always seem to take over."

"What's your favorite part about LA?" I asked, trying
to cheer him up. I knew the pitfalls of being consumed
with the bad stuff.

"The beaches," he replied, his mood brightening already. "I used to surf a little."

"I can see you doing that." Tall and tan, with his skin
tasting like saltwater. I touched a finger to my lips, almost
as if I could taste it on him, too. It made me want to kiss
him, everywhere, all over his body.

"Venice Beach was one of my teenage hangouts. I liked
the artsy vibe, the weirdness, I guess. The surfing was
good, too."

I was getting more excited about this trip, anxious to spend time with him. "Can we go there?"

"Sure. I think you'd enjoy it."

"I wonder if three days will be enough to fit everything in." Suddenly, it seemed too short, too rushed.

He changed lanes, then glanced over at me. "Do you want to stay for a few extra days?"

"Do you think we could?" I'd already made up my mind to have a good time and try not to stress about the future. But somehow, I still had butterflies in my stomach over it.

"I don't see why not. I can check with the hotel about extending the reservation."

"Then let's do it." The longer we stayed, the more fun we could have—in and out of bed.

Or at least until my butterflies subsided. Or our affair ended. Whichever came first.

This was the life, I thought, as we boarded the plane. We checked in easily, with comfort and style, using a different part of the airport from where the commercial flights took off and landed. Both the pilot and our flight attendant greeted us, introducing themselves and giving us special treatment.

Once we were settled into our seats, I said to Spencer, "I've never flown this way before."

He studied me, his dark eyes locking onto mine. "You've never been on a private plane?"

"No, never." Aside from my association with Mary and Brandon, I wasn't part of an elite crowd.

"My aunt and uncle used to charter planes. It spoiled me, I suppose. As much I hated living with them, I appreciated some of the luxuries."

"Who wouldn't?" This jet had a glitzy black-and-tan décor with a dining table, two sets of sofas and a big-screen TV. "I used to rent party boats on the river. I burned through a lot of my settlement money, trying to live the high life and show off to my friends. But it caught up with me. I only took the job with you because I wanted to work with Derek and I was worried about my finances."

"I figured it was something like that." He nudged my arm, his elbow purposely bumping mine. "I guess it's a good thing I didn't fire you."

"Smart aleck." I adjusted my seat belt to fit more securely.

He watched me. "You're not a nervous flyer, are you?"

"Maybe a little." Soon we would be taxiing down the runway. "I've never really flown that much."

"You can have a glass of wine, if that will help. Or a cocktail or whatever you prefer. I don't expect people to avoid drinking around me."

"That's okay. I don't need anything." I wasn't comfortable putting alcohol under his nose, in spite of his claim not to care. I chanced to ask, "Is it tough staying sober?"

He sat perfectly still, almost as if he didn't want to react. Then he said, "I already told you that I can resist the temptation. Otherwise, I wouldn't have a bar at my house."

"Sometimes you still seem restless, like you used to be."

As the plane started to move, he replied, "You seem that way, too."

"Yes, but I'm not a recovering alcoholic." To me, that made my restlessness less dangerous than his.

"Don't worry about it, okay? Kirby will always be there to help if I need it." He watched me again, deeply, closely. "One way or another, I'm going to make you see him for the decent guy that he is."

"That's never going to happen," I shot back.

"You're always so damned stubborn." His voice turned

rough, sexy, commanding. "Maybe I'll just have to kiss you to keep you in line."

My body went unbearably warm. The plane was gaining speed, making my breath catch in my throat. "Right now?"

"Hell, yes." He leaned over and slanted his mouth over mine, using his tongue to tempt me.

I closed my eyes and returned his kiss, needing him, wanting him. In the background, I could hear the rumble of the engine. I jolted as the plane bounded into the air.

But mostly, it was my lover jarring my emotions and lifting me straight off the ground.

Nine

Spencer

The Chateau Marmont had been inspired by a Gothic French chateau, and the bungalow I'd rented was artfully crafted, offering a breezy sitting area, an elegant bedroom and bath, a private patio and a fully stocked kitchen. I'd requested groceries ahead of time, giving us the option of dining in or going out, depending on our mood.

Alice seemed impressed. She wandered in and out of the rooms, with a girlish light in her eyes.

After we entered the bedroom, she removed her sandals and flopped back on the ornately carved bed, her sundress billowing around her. I wanted to free my mind and simply enjoy looking at her, but my thoughts were too damned scattered.

Was Kirby her father? I wondered.

There was no way to know for sure, not without a paternity test. Kirby seemed certain of it, making me inclined to believe it, as well. Yet, if Alice was his daughter, I was still baffled about why Cathy had kept quiet about it. I hadn't considered this before, but maybe Kirby himself had been the problem. Maybe Cathy had concerns about his addictions back then and didn't want him participating in Alice's life. Whatever her reasons, things were different now. Alice was a grown woman, and Kirby was clean and sober. If Cathy were alive today, she wouldn't have anything to worry about.

"What made you choose this hotel?" Alice asked, pulling me back into our surroundings.

"The music director I'll be meeting with lives nearby, so I figured it would be a convenient location." I glanced toward the window. Sunshine slashed through the blinds, creating a mysterious pattern on the floor. "I was fascinated by the things I'd heard about it, too. In the old Hollywood days, they used to say that this was the place to go to get into trouble. It has a history of celebrities behaving badly here."

"Really?" She sat up and leaned against the headboard. "Oh, how fun."

"Yes, but the really wild stuff was kept secret. All of the rooms, bungalows and cottages are soundproof, and the staff has always been discreet, particularly during that era. The Chateau was considered a luxurious hideout back then." I almost felt as if Alice and I were hiding out. Former lovers renewing their affair. That, in itself, seemed sort of scandalous.

"Can't you just imagine what old Hollywood must have been like?" She struck a glamorous pose, as if she was tossing a long, sleek scarf over her shoulder.

"Yeah, I can imagine it." I could actually see her dressed like a movie star. "But tragic things occurred here, too, later on. John Belushi overdosed in one of the bungalows."

I figured she would know who he was, given her interest in the '70s and '80s.

"Do you know which bungalow it was?" she asked.

"I think it's over that way." I'd already looked it up on the net. "I'm sure they've remodeled it since then, but there have been reports of him haunting it over the years. I don't know if that's true or just people making up stories."

Her gaze sought mine. "Do you believe in ghosts?"

"I'd like to think that they're real. When I was a teen-ager, I used to go to our old apartment and park in front of the building, wishing my mom would appear. She never did, though."

She gave me a sympathetic look. "Was it hard for you when you left LA? Did you feel as if you were leaving her behind?"

I nodded, my heart clenching at the memory. "She loved this town. But it changed for me after she died."

"Will you take me to see your old apartment? We can park out front the way you used to do."

"Maybe we can do that tonight." She understood my loss. Her mother was gone, too. But how was she going to feel when she learned that Kirby might be her dad?

She got to her feet and came over to me. I put my arms around her, stroking a hand down her back and inhaling the citrusy scent of her perfume.

Now that her paternity was on the line, should I work toward discovering mine, too?

We separated, and I said, "I'm going to look for my dad. Once we get back to Nashville, I'll submit my DNA to the ancestry websites and see where it leads. There are two main sites I'm going to use."

"That's wonderful. I think it's important for you to know where you came from and who your father is."

"It's worth a try." Was my old man out there somewhere? Would I find him? "But I'm not going to idealize him like I did when I was a kid."

"Are you still concerned that he might reject you?"

"Yes." In her case, Kirby wanted to be her dad. She was lucky in that way, even if she didn't know it yet.

She comforted me, skimming her fingers along my jaw. "Just try to be positive."

I embraced her again. "You're right. I need to believe it's possible." Because who could say what would happen for sure? Maybe I would get lucky and my father would be as interested in me as Kirby was in her.

In the evening, after Alice and I dined at a new steak house in Studio City, I drove the Porsche Cayman I'd rented to my old apartment. It wasn't the best neighborhood, but it wasn't the worst, either. Mostly it catered to striving actors, models and musicians. Some regular folks, too. Not everyone had stars in their eyes. Some of the surrounding areas were laced with drug activity, but I'd always steered clear of those parts. I'd never been a druggie, not like Kirby and some of the other addicts I knew. For that much, I was grateful. I didn't need any more demons.

I parallel parked, wedging the car into a tight space, with a streetlamp overhead giving us a bit of light.

Alice sat in the passenger seat in a slim black outfit and designer heels. She'd changed out of the sundress and into something sexier.

And now here we were, where I used to live. It looked the same to me. The Spanish-style accents: the tile roof, the stucco exterior, the arches. There wasn't a lot of foliage, just a few low hedges on either side.

"Which unit was yours?" she asked.

I pointed to a second-story window. "That was my bedroom. I used to keep some of my toy soldiers on the windowsill, lined up and ready for war."

"I wonder who lives there now."

"I have no idea." The blinds were closed. "When it was my room, it had blackout curtains. I thought those were cool. Mom decorated her room with a seashell motif. She was even buried at sea."

Alice turned to face me. "Did you sprinkle the ashes?"

"My aunt didn't think it was appropriate for a child my age. She had the captain of the boat do it."

Sorrow edged her voice. "That wasn't fair to you."

"Nothing ever really was. But later when I started surfing, I felt at peace in the ocean. Sometimes I would run my hands through the water and imagine that Mom was there, all around me."

"I know what you mean. My mother was cremated, too. Mary and I sprinkled her ashes at a park she used to take us to when we were kids, and that's where I'll always think of her."

"I wish I could have met your mom." I didn't know much about her, other than what Alice or Kirby had told me. But I was beginning to feel a kinship toward her. "We could've shared our experiences about songwriting."

"I think she would have liked that." She glanced out the windshield. "But now I'm getting emotional, sitting here on your childhood street, talking about life and death."

I felt it, too. But I didn't want to admit how deeply this moment was affecting me. "You suggested coming here."

"I know. But normally the only other person I ever have these types of conversations with is Tracy." She hesitated, squinting at me. "Did you know that she used to be engaged to Dash Smith?"

I frowned a little. "No, but is there a reason I should be aware of that?"

"Not necessarily. Except that you're going to be working with Dash on his next album, aren't you?"

"We haven't collaborated on any songs yet. But we plan to once he gets off tour."

"How well do you know him?"

"Not well. We've only met a couple of times."

"He's been asking Tracy to do a duet, but she isn't interested in making a record with him."

That was news to me, but all of this was. "If she changes her mind, then maybe I'll be working with her, too."

"I don't think she's going to change her mind."

I didn't ask what the problem was or why their engagement ended, but I did say, "Just so you know, Kirby figured us out."

She flinched. "What?"

"He could tell that I was lying about my past with you."

She set her mouth in a grim line. "Did you tell him that we were together now?"

"Yes, but I explained that it was only temporary."

"And what was his reaction?"

"He made me promise to be good to you."

She scoffed. "As if he cares."

"He does care." I couldn't tell her how much. She wasn't anywhere near being ready to hear the truth. But at least I was planting whatever seeds were possible.

She huffed, headstrong as ever. "It's none of Kirby's business what we do."

"Yeah, but it's still nice of him to be looking out for your best interests. Speaking of which, do you think we should just be open with everyone else, too?"

"I already told Tracy that I slept with you again."

I should have suspected as much. "Does your sister know?"

"She knows I took this trip with you."

"Then it doesn't matter if people see us together in Nashville, does it?"

She scrutinized me, looking me up and down. "I guess we could be open about it. That's probably better than keeping it a secret, like we did in the past."

"Gee, thanks for the enthusiasm." I leaned over and gave her a rough kiss, refusing to let her get the best of me.

I almost expected her to push me away, but she climbed over the console and onto my lap. Was she trying to prove that she was the boss?

She straddled me in my seat, rocking back and forth, a triumphant expression on her face. I wanted to reach around to fondle her ass, but I kept my arms at my sides, refusing to let her win. She rubbed me some more, bumping my fly, causing friction.

Electricity. Human sparks.

Was she proposing a quickie in the car? Was that her intention? I groaned and said, "We can't do this here. If we get caught, we'll get busted for indecent exposure."

She shrugged. "I'm not exposing anything, are you?"

I glanced down the front of her blouse and spied her bra, the push-up kind that created extra cleavage. "You're torturing me."

"That's the idea." She returned to her own seat, leaving me with a raging hard-on. She knew how to make me suffer.

But I knew how to seduce her, too.

"This isn't over," I said, letting her know that I was going to do unspeakable things to her.

As soon as we got back to the hotel.

After a night of rowdy sex, I awakened before Alice. I leaned on my elbow and watched her sleep. She looked innocent, with no makeup and wispy hair. Her spiky do was flat this morning.

What was going to happen when our affair was over? Would I become abstinent again? Or would I take another lover? Replacing her was going to be difficult. I hated to even think about it.

I crept out of bed and climbed into my jeans. Alice stirred, turning sideways in her sleep. We'd left the windows open, and now a breeze was dancing around the room.

I stood back and leaned against a wall, wondering if she was dreaming. If she was, I hoped her dreams were soft and safe.

I used to have recurring nightmares of monsters clawing at me, chasing me inside my aunt and uncle's mansion. Sometimes I still had them, except the monsters attacked my sobriety now, taunting me to fail, to take another drink, to destroy the man I was working so hard to become.

Alice stirred again, coming awake. She reached over to my side of the bed and found it empty. Had she been hoping to cuddle?

She sat up, and the sheet fell to her waist, giving me a delicious view of her breasts. She glanced toward the wall, where I was, and gasped.

"Oh, my God, Spencer. You scared me."

"Sorry."

"What an image to wake up to." She blinked as if I was a tall, dark mirage, coming to life from the desert air. "My heart is still pounding."

"I'm going to make a pot of coffee."

She adjusted the sheet, pulling it back up and over her breasts. "Should I meet you in the kitchen?"

"Why don't you stay here, and I'll bring you a cup."

She ran her hand through her hair, letting it flutter

through her fingers. "Are you going to make breakfast, too?"

"I can whip up some eggs." I quirked a deliberate smile. "Unless you want frozen pizza."

She grinned. "Nice try. But I'll take the eggs."

I left her alone and went into the kitchen. I'd never actually cooked for anyone before, at least not from scratch. But I could handle breakfast.

I brewed the coffee, fried four strips of bacon and scrambled three eggs. I made toast, too, and buttered it. I looked around for a spot of color and went onto the patio, plucking a purple-and-yellow bloom from one of the pots.

I prepared a tray, placing the flower beside her plate. I included milk and sugar for her coffee. I preferred mine black.

I returned to the bedroom, set the tray in front of her and removed my cup.

She glanced up at me. She was dressed now. While I was in the kitchen, she'd borrowed one of my T-shirts. For all I knew, she was wearing a pair of my boxers, too. I couldn't see her lower half, but I rather hoped that she was. Her interest in wearing my clothes turned me on.

"Thank you. This looks great," she said. "But why aren't you eating?"

"I'm not hungry. Besides, I've got my business meeting today, and it's supposed to be a brunch."

She added a dollop of milk and two packets of sugar to her coffee. "I'll probably take an Uber to Rodeo Drive while you're gone. It's on my list of places to see."

I sat at a nearby desk and pushed the hotel stationery out of my way. "There's some nice stores on Sunset, too." I made a deadpan expression. "You could check out Hustler Hollywood."

She rolled her eyes. "The erotica boutique? I think I'll

pass." She hesitated, seeming a bit more serious. "Unless you want me to go there."

"It's totally up to you, but I was only kidding around."

A few breathless beats later, she said, "I think I better stick to regular stores."

I sipped my coffee, amused by her newfound sense of propriety. "Yeah, after all of the raunchy stuff we did last night, who needs sex toys, anyway."

She threw the flower at me. But it flopped onto the floor, missing me by a mile.

I came up with a legitimate plan. "You know what we should do? Take some vacation selfies together and post them online."

"I guess that would be all right. But let's not go overboard with kissing pictures or anything like that. I don't want to seem unprofessional."

"Actually, I think it'll boost your profile to be romantically linked to me. Not to brag, but I have lots of followers."

"I know how popular you are." She gazed at me from beneath her lashes. "And I suppose you're right. Your followers will probably take an interest in me. A positive one, I hope." She bit into her toast. After she ate half of it, she added, "We didn't take selfies with each other before."

"No, but remember how we used to sext?" My cup clanked when I put it down. "And the nude pictures you sent me?"

Her cheeks went pink, an uncharacteristic blush for such a naughty girl. I didn't call her on it. I kept the visual to myself, wanting to remember it later.

"You sent some to me, too," she said.

"Mine were dick pics. Any idiot can do those. The stuff you did was beautiful." Alluring, sensual, sweetly wicked.

I wished I'd saved them, tucked them away in a secret file. "Will you send me one later today?"

Her jaw dropped. "While you're at your meeting? I wouldn't dare."

I challenged her, flirting, playing a lover's game. "Then at least come over here and kiss me."

She set the tray aside, baiting me right back. "I think you should come over here."

She didn't have to ask me twice. I leaped onto the bed and tackled her, making her laugh and squeal. I lowered the sheet. She wasn't wearing my boxers. She didn't have any bottoms on at all.

I grabbed my phone off the nightstand and snapped a picture of her butt. She tried to wrestle the device away from me, and I took another one. I knew she would make me delete them, but for now, I was having fun.

I liked the feeling, the freedom. At times like this, I wanted to pretend that my life was easy. But there was nothing easy about what I'd been through. Alice's past wasn't easy, either. But at the moment, we were together— and enjoying every playful second of it.

Ten

Alice

Spencer and I sat side by side on a bench, sipping blueberry slushies. As we looked out at the ocean, dusk dimmed the sky.

We'd spent the entire day here at Venice Beach, soaking up the sun, gathering seashells, swimming in the ocean and eating junk food. Spencer had also bought me some trinkets, including a temporary tattoo, but I hadn't applied it yet.

"It's probably raining again in Nashville," I said. "I can't believe how nice it is here." Even now, with the sun setting over the water, it was comfortably warm.

"We got lucky with the weather. Sometimes it's chilly in the spring. But I like the beach when it's cold, too."

I glanced around. There were still people everywhere, treating it like a summer day. Or evening, now that daylight was waning. "I'll bet it has a completely different energy when it's cold."

He nodded. "It's calmer, quieter. A good place to be alone and reflect."

"Did you used to do that a lot? Come here to be alone?"

"Yeah." He turned to look at me. "I'm glad I'm not alone right now."

"So am I." My heart skipped a beat. "I could get used to this. To the beach," I clarified. I could get used to being with him, too. A part of me never wanted our time together to end. But that wasn't something I should be imagining, not when I knew that our affair wasn't meant to last.

He set his drink down. "Let's put your new tattoo on."

"We'll need a damp cloth. It won't stick without water."

"We can use a corner of a towel." He removed one from our beach bag. "I'll be right back."

I watched him walk over to a drinking fountain across the boardwalk. While he was gone, I dug through my shopping bag for the tattoo, a design with black roses and a swirly pink butterfly. Spencer had picked it out for me.

He returned with the damp towel and resumed his seat. He looked natural in the setting, tall and tan in a ribbed tank top and colorful board shorts. Me? I'd slathered on a high SPF lotion to keep from getting burned.

"Where should we put it?" he asked. "Where do you want it?"

"Where do you think it should go?" He knew my body well, and I trusted him to make the decision.

"How about at your bikini line? Then I can see it every time I touch you there."

Please, yes. I got up and removed my sarong, standing before him in my bathing suit, tingling with anticipation.

No one paid us any mind, not even when he tugged my bikini bottoms down a little. Immersed in his task, he saturated the tattoo with moisture from the corner of the towel, holding it against my skin.

Sixty second later, he peeled off the paper and exposed my new body art. In the silence that followed, he dabbed off the excess water and rubbed a tiny bit of sunscreen on it.

He righted my bikini bottoms. "The lotion will help make it last longer."

I glanced down at the design. It was partially concealed beneath my bathing suit, but still beautiful. It would look even better when I was naked in his arms.

I reached for my sarong, covering myself up. He watched me with unfettered desire in his eyes.

We went back to drinking our slushies. I needed to cool off. He obviously did, too.

After we finished them, he said, "Your lips are blue."

"So are yours."

We laughed and took a selfie. We'd taken tons of them today, posting them on Instagram. Our affair was definitely out in the open.

"Do you think we'll remain friends after we stop seeing each other?" I asked, battling a sudden burst of emotion.

"I don't know. What do you think?"

"I don't know, either." I glanced at a trio of teenage girls who passed by. They acted brash and bratty, mirroring what I used to do, flaunting themselves to a group of boys watching them. It made me worry for the girls and distrust the boys. "Have you stayed friends with any of your other lovers?"

"No." He frowned. "Have you?"

I shook my head. "It doesn't sound like the odds are in our favor."

"Yeah, probably not."

It wasn't feasible, anyway, I decided, since we were both supposed to move on with our lives and not look back. Me, in particular, I realized, with my wifely pangs to settle down.

He turned toward the ocean again. I did, too. Someone was playing music now. A live performer, banging a drum. It was getting dark, and people were getting rowdy.

"Do you remember when I wanted to pierce your eyebrow?" Spencer asked, still watching the sea.

It was a strange conversation for him to start, but I went with it. "Yes, I remember." It had been toward the beginning of our Tinder hookup, maybe just a few days in.

"Why did you want to do it?"

"It was just one of those rebellious things, I guess. Piercing someone else."

We faced each other, the drumming getting louder, like heartbeats on the shore, rising with the waves.

"Why did you refuse?" he asked.

"Honestly? I've always been scared of needles."

He smiled a little. "I wouldn't have hurt you, not if I could've helped it."

I returned his smile, enchanted by how he was looking at me. His eyes were black against the backdrop of the sky. But they were always dark, always compelling. "Don't even think of trying to talk me into it now."

"Which one was I trying to convince you to pierce?"

I pointed to the left. "It's a little less arched than the other side."

He kissed the brow in question, making my pulse flutter. He was good at being gentle. He excelled at being sensual, too. Whatever he did pleased and excited me. And for now, I was going keep him as close as I could.

Until I couldn't keep him anymore.

We ordered breakfast from room service, and the dining room table in our bungalow was laden with food. Neither of us wanted to cook, and by now most of our groceries had run out, anyway. We would be flying home tomorrow, our trip coming to a close.

While we ate, I thought about all of the touristy things Spencer and I had done. One of my favorite places was Griffith Observatory. Not only was the hilltop view specular, portions of *Rebel Without a Cause* had been filmed there. Yep, the location where James Dean had worn his iconic red jacket. Fashion was everything to me, especially with how hard I'd worked to become a stylist. If I lived in LA, I would probably be dressing movie-industry people instead of country music personalities, like in Nashville.

"What do you want to do today?" Spencer asked. "Any ideas of where you'd like to go?"

I opted for something personal. "You can take me to your old high school." I explained my interest in it by saying, "I'm curious to see where you misspent your youth."

He cocked his head. "As opposed to where you misspent yours?"

"I went to a public school with overcrowded classes and overworked teachers. And besides earning a slutty reputation and having my name written on various walls and desks, I was always in detention with the other misfits."

"Spending your Saturdays in the library?"

"Not quite." I crinkled my nose. "Our punishment was picking up trash in the yard, like some sort of prison road crew."

He lifted his brows. "What was the nature of your crimes?"

"Mostly I got into trouble for mouthing off to my teachers." I'd always had an aversion to authority.

An amused look appeared on his face. "Now, why am I not surprised?" The amusement faded when he said, "I attended a private academy. Rigid, disciplined. The kind that's supposed to keep its students in line."

I watched him cut into his pancakes. "I'll bet you found plenty of ways to break the rules."

"I got suspended a few times. But they never expelled me. I was a bit of an enigma back then. A troubled kid who always made the honor roll. As messed up as I was, I was still a good student."

"Not me. I was lucky that I graduated and finally buckled down in college." I tasted my eggs Florentine. We'd gotten separate entrees, but we were sharing a fresh fruit platter and a basket of muffins. "Can we go to your old school? I just want to see the outside of it." I didn't expect to wander the halls with him.

"If you insist. But it's just a big stuffy campus with rich kids in preppy uniforms."

"I still want to see it."

"All right, but please don't ask me to drive by my aunt and uncle's place."

"I would never do that." I knew better than to subject him to revisiting the home he'd hated. "Besides, it's a gated community, isn't it?"

"I still know people in that area, and I could get in if I wanted to. But I prefer being locked out." He blew out a noisy breath. "I keep hearing that you're supposed to forgive the people who hurt you. Not for them, but for yourself. But it's not easy, letting the pain go."

"That's how I feel about Kirby."

"Yes, but Kirby wants to repair the damage he caused." He softened his voice. "You're like family to him, Alice. You should give him a chance."

I tensed, my spine going stiff. "He's not my family."

"He could be if you'd let him."

"Why? Because he's related to my sister's husband? Your aunt is family and look how awful she was to you."

"My aunt doesn't give a crap about me. But Kirby cares about you, more than you realize."

"I'm so sick of you taking his side." I got up to leave the table, stomping over to the living room.

Spencer followed me. "I'm sorry if I upset you."

I glared at him, standing my ground. "Why can't you take my side for once?"

"And why can't you accept that Kirby cares about you?"

I scoffed, and he reached for me, ever so gently, ever so warm. He had a knack for doing that. I tried to wriggle away from him, but he wouldn't let me go. I shivered, hating the effect he had on me.

Hating it. Loving it. Feeling confused by it.

"You can't be all nice now," I said. "It isn't fair."

"I'm just trying to do the right thing."

"And making me want you." In spite of how angry I was, I caressed his face, skimming the back of my hand along his beard stubble. It was impossible not to touch him.

He leaned forward. "Now who's making who want who?"

I pulled him closer, rubbing my body against his. I played with his hair, wondering how it would look if he grew it long.

We stripped each other bare and stumbled into bed, almost as if as we were drunk on each other. It wasn't a reference I should've used, but it was the only one that came to mind. As I moaned and sighed, he traced my temporary tattoo, peppering my skin with warm, wet kisses.

He used his tongue between my legs, and I gripped the sheet, tugging on the material, eager to come. I knew it wouldn't take long. I was already losing my sense of reason. I closed my eyes, going hot and damp.

Suddenly I couldn't remember anyone else ever making me this aroused. Only him. I climaxed, making throaty sounds, bucking against his face.

I opened my eyes and saw that strong, handsome face. I reached out to trace the sharp edges of his cheekbones.

We switched places, and I used my mouth on him, giving him the same intimate pleasure that he'd just given me. He stopped me before I went too far, even if his muscles were quavering, even if I could've taken him all the way.

I took charge of the condom, rolling it over every big, hard inch. He groaned and entered me, pushing deep inside. I clasped my legs around him, squeezing tight.

I didn't want to go home tomorrow. Or maybe I just didn't want to go back to living alone. I liked sharing this space with him, sleeping beside him each night and waking up with him each morning.

But I had to stop thinking about things like that. Once we were back in Nashville, I couldn't let him matter so much.

My plan didn't work. We'd been back in Nashville for a month now, and the more time I spent with Spencer, the more important he became. I was knee-deep in our affair and protecting my heart, too. By now, I was beginning to want more. But his feelings hadn't changed, not as far as I could tell.

On this sunny afternoon, I arrived at his house, with a stack of copies of the magazine he was featured in. I'd gone downtown to get them, to an old brick-and-mortar bookstore. I had a digital copy on my iPad, but I wanted hard copies, too.

I rang the bell, but he didn't answer. I tried the door and found it unlocked. He'd obviously left it that way for me.

I set down the magazines and called his name. He didn't

respond, so I searched for him. Finally, I spotted him in the backyard with Cookie and Candy, playing fetch with them. It made me wonder if he would be good with kids, too.

Not that I should care, I told myself. Spencer wasn't going to be the father of my children. At some point, our affair would be over.

I went outside to greet him, and the dogs dashed over to me. They wagged their tails, rolling over at my feet. I scooped both of them up and nuzzled their furry heads.

Spencer watched me, and I leaned over and embraced him, with the dogs between us. He laughed when one of them pawed at his shirt. They were his babies. For now, they were mine, too. But someday, I still wanted the human variety.

I released the dogs and said, "I got the magazine. I bought all of the copies they had."

"I don't understand why you want so many of them."

"Because I have a crush on you." I fanned my face, pretending to swoon, even if the feeling was real. "Let's go look at it together."

He ducked his head, embarrassed by my enthusiasm. "I've already seen it, Alice."

"You saw the digital version. You haven't seen the glossy pages. You look even sexier that way."

He cringed, but it only endeared him to me that much more. He seemed boyish today, chuffing like a kid.

"That's all I need," he said. "To ogle myself."

"Come on." I tugged him inside, leading him into the living room, where I'd left the magazines on the coffee table.

The dogs accompanied us, jumping onto the sofa to see what the fuss was about.

"Check this out, girls." I opened one of the copies to Spencer's layout. "The new heartthrob in town." I turned to a photo of him perched on his motorcycle, where he'd been looking off camera at me. "This is my favorite."

Cookie sniffed the picture, and Spencer groaned. He could deny his sex-symbol status all he wanted, but his Instagram had blown up since the magazine came out. He already had tons of female followers, but as of yesterday, his fan base had practically doubled. I'd also picked up new followers, simply from being associated with him. He'd definitely been right about that. Having a hot lover was making me popular. Luckily, I'd gotten work out of everything, too. Derek had referred me to some important jobs. The work I'd done for Spencer was changing my life.

"He's a reformed bad boy," I said to the dogs. "See, it says so right here."

Cookie sniffed the magazine again, and I bumped Spencer's shoulder, teasing him. But deep down, I couldn't bear to think about the next woman who was going to share his bed.

Why couldn't he be the right man? Why couldn't he be my future? I ached that I wasn't allowed to love him, that I had to fight my feelings.

"Kirby called me this morning," he said.

I closed the magazine with a frustrated snap. Kirby was the last person I wanted to discuss.

Spencer continued by saying, "He's planning a get-together at his house, and he invited us. It's going to be a family party, with his kids and grandkids and whatnot."

I frowned. "Mary didn't say anything about it."

"He hasn't spoken to anyone else about it yet. He wanted to check with me first."

"Why? What's going on?"

"Nothing, except he's hoping I'll finally give in and meet his family." He met my squinting gaze. "I said that I'd go if you did."

I debated my options. On one hand, I worried that I was being railroaded into this. But on the other, I thought that Spencer needed more family-type ties. Why? I asked myself. Because I wanted him to become a family man himself? Either way, at least I would get a chance to see how well he got along with children. For all I knew, fatherhood might actually be in his future someday.

I could hope…couldn't I? That maybe he could morph into my Mr. Right. That eventually he might start having the same types of feelings for me that I was having for him.

I said, "We should accept the invitation."

"Really?" He pushed his hair away from his forehead. "I expected you to put up more of an argument or refuse to go at all."

"I think it'll be nice for you to bond with Kirby's family. They're the best part of him." Especially my niece and nephew, I thought. My sister and Brandon, too.

He cleared his throat. "There are other things about him that are admirable."

"If you say so." Which he did, over and over, like a broken record, annoying me to no end. "When is this party, anyway?"

"He hasn't set a date yet. But I'll let him know that we're on board."

"Are you nervous about it?" I couldn't tell by his expression.

"A little, I guess." He leaned in my direction. "But it should be easier having you there."

"I'm only going to support you. I'm not doing this for Kirby." I leaned toward him, too. "But for now, why don't you take me out to the garage and ravish me on your Harley, like the hot guy in the magazine would do?"

"Come on, Alice, that guy isn't real."

"He is to me." I put my hand on his thigh, creeping toward his fly, letting him know that I was serious about what I'd said.

"Damn." His eyes glazed over, and his body went taut.

I sucked my bottom lip between my teeth. I was opening his zipper now. "I thought you might see it my way."

"You're very persuasive. But let's do this right." He scooped me up, carrying me in his arms. A man on a passionate mission.

He stopped to get a condom out of the bedroom, tossing me onto the bed while he secured it in his pocket. He picked me up again, and I clung to his embrace.

He balanced me, shifting me in his arms, and headed down the hall. He went through the laundry room and pushed open the garage door. With everything we'd done in the past, we'd never messed around on his Harley.

"This might not be very comfortable," he said. "For either of us."

"I don't care."

"Neither do I." He set me down and peeled off my panties, draping them from one of the handlebar grips.

I wore a loose dress, making it easy to straddle the machine. He climbed in front of me, and we kissed, wet and rough, slick and hard.

A moment later I said, "When I started having fantasies about being with you again, I was worried that you were going to make me reckless, like I used to be."

"That's not what I'm doing. You're still going to marry Mr. Right and have a respectable life."

I was having a tough time picturing that now, not unless he turned out to be that man.

I felt Spencer's hand moving under my dress. I gasped and lifted my bottom off the seat.

"Just a bit of foreplay," he whispered.

I glanced down and saw that his jeans were still undone. "Can I touch you, too?"

"Not yet." He continued his sexual foray. "I want you to come first."

I leaned back, giving myself over to him in every way I could. Except for loving him, I thought.

I was still too afraid to do that.

Eleven

Spencer

I sat on a padded stool in Kirby's studio, my booted heels pressed against the footrail, and thought about Alice. We'd gotten down and dirty in my garage less than twenty-four hours ago, and now she was on my mind again. I couldn't go a day without craving her. But it wasn't just the sex. It was other things, too: the warmth, the friendship, the closeness we'd come to share. I was starting to have feelings for her that scared me.

Bonding-type stuff.

Maybe even love-type stuff.

Kirby sought my gaze, and I did my damnedest to relax. He'd invited me over to listen to some new tracks, but we hadn't done that yet. We were talking about the party instead.

"Alice agreed to be there for sure?" he asked, seeking to confirm what I'd already told him in a text.

"Yes." I made another attempt to relax. I was just a guy in recovery, trying to keep his head on straight. What did I know about love?

Nothing, I thought. But it was okay; I didn't need to freak out. Sooner or later, I would stop seeing Alice, and then these scary feelings would go away.

Kirby blew out his breath. "I really hope this gathering will make her feel more comfortable around me."

I understood his reasoning. He wanted to create a sense of home and hearth, drawing her into the fold. "I know how important this is to you, but maybe you better not get your hopes up too high."

"At least it gives me a chance to see her. The only other times I'm able to do that is at the twins' birthday parties, and she ignores me at those functions."

"She might ignore you at this one, too." I wasn't trying to be negative, but I hadn't seen any signs of Alice softening toward him.

"Maybe it'll be all right if you're there, guiding her through it. I can't tell you how glad I am that you're going to meet my family. I know how you long you've been avoiding these kinds of situations."

I'd gotten used to being a lone wolf. And now I was putting myself in a position of being part of a pack. I was also waiting for the results of the DNA test I'd submitted on the ancestry sites to find my own father and see if there was a familial match. My world was spinning. But so was Kirby's. We both had a zillion things on our minds.

"Maybe you should do it soon after the party," I said.

"You mean tell Alice that I might be her dad?"

I nodded, and he rubbed a hand across his beard. He looked old and tired. Worried, it seemed, about how she was going to react when the time came. Would she learn to love him, to accept him? Or would she hate him even more? I prayed it wasn't the latter.

After a bout of anxiety-ridden silence, I said, "Maybe she'll be ready to hear it by then. And even if she isn't, we can't drag this out forever."

"Has it been hard on you, keeping my secret?"

"Everything just seems like it's getting more difficult." Sleeping with her. Lying to her. Getting close to her. "I never expected to have this kind of affair with her."

Kirby squinted, making the lines around his eyes more pronounced. "Are you falling in love with her, son?"

Damn, I thought. Did he have to go and say that? I glanced around, looking for an escape. The walls were closing in.

"Spencer?" He prodded me.

I gripped the undersides of my chair, my knuckles going as white as the ink on my tattoo. "I don't know." I stared at him, needing his guidance, his wisdom. "What does it feel like to fall in love?"

He came closer to where I was, grabbing a stool for himself and placing it next to mine. "I think it's a little different for everyone, depending on their situation. When I first fell in love with my ex-wife, I thought I'd be with her forever, considering how open our marriage seemed. But it got tense later, and I hurt her by having a child with another woman."

"Did you love any of your mistresses?"

"I loved Matt's mom, but that relationship went awry, too. I'm not a good example of how a man in love should behave. I was too selfish to give someone else what they needed."

"What about now?" I asked. "Are you better at it with your girlfriend?"

"Yes, but I'm not consumed with being in a relationship and neither is she. It's a different dynamic. Calmer, more mature."

I was consumed with Alice, but did that mean that I loved her? "I'm confused about how I feel."

"I understand that you're struggling to come to terms with your feelings. But you're a good man with a good heart, and I'd be thrilled for you and Alice to stay together."

"Thanks for your confidence. But I'm not right for her." I wasn't Alice's dream man. Was I? At this point, everything seemed chaotic.

"Maybe you should ask her how she feels. She might be confused, too."

It was sound advice, but could I do it? Not now, I decided, not this soon. "It might be too much to throw at her, with everything else that's going on. I think it would be smarter to wait."

"All right. I'll call my boys and set a date for the family gathering, and you just try to breathe easy. Okay?"

"You, too." He still looked worried about how Alice was going to react to his news.

We were both stressed over the same woman, but for different reasons. And I feared it was only going to get worse before it got better. If it got better at all.

Two days later, Alice asked me to spend the night at her place. But I probably should've stayed home. I was in a lousy mood. Just that morning, I'd learned that there were no matches for my DNA. No hits whatsoever. It made me feel more alone than ever.

I waited to tell her until bedtime, and she reacted with empathy in her eyes.

"Did you get the results from both websites today?"

I nodded. "Neither of them panned out. No distant cousins. Nothing."

"I'm sorry."

"It's okay." I gazed at the TV mounted on her wall. We were streaming *Sons of Anarchy*, the way we'd done at my house on the day of the photo shoot.

She muted the sound. "No, it isn't. I can tell how disappointed you are."

"I didn't really expect it to be that easy. To just submit my DNA and magically find my dad or someone from his family."

"I know. But you still had hope that maybe it would work."

I shrugged. I was all screwed up. Not just about whoever my dad was, but about how Alice was making me feel, too.

Was I falling in love with her? Was that happening to me?

She rolled over, skimming her hand along my tattooed arm. The temporary one from LA was long gone. I missed seeing it on her skin, knowing that I'd put it there.

"I can help you," she said.

I glanced up. "What?"

"To find your dad."

"How?" I asked, becoming suddenly aware of her silky white nightgown. She rarely wore those sorts of garments to bed. It made her look like a bride. Or my vision of one.

I frowned at my own idiocy. Weddings were the last thing that should be crowding my already cluttered mind.

"We could contact a private investigator and give them whatever information you have."

"I hardly have any info. And I don't want to get a PI involved." It just felt too personal to me, handing my family history over to someone else.

"Then we can do it ourselves. We can talk to your mother's old friends, the ones she was traveling with when she met your dad. They might remember something useful."

"I have no idea who took that trip with her. Besides, I haven't seen any of her friends since she died."

"Do you know any of their last names?"

"I remember Joanie Pierce. She was an aspiring actress back then. She's the one Mom called to take her to the hospital, who was with her when she passed." When my life had been blown apart, I thought.

Alice touched my arm again, softly, comfortingly. "Then we can start there. We can do this together."

I reached for her, more confused than ever. She was offering to help me find my father, and I was withholding information about hers and panicking about falling in love with her.

"Maybe we should wait a while," I said. "I don't think I'm ready to continue my search just yet." I couldn't go on a daddy quest, not now, not like this.

"Just let me know when you're ready." She nuzzled against me. "I'll be here for you, Spencer."

Overwrought with anxiety, I held her. But in the pit of my screwed-up soul, I wanted to run and hide. To bow out of Kirby's get-together. To not search for my father. And most of all, to stop seeing Alice. Yet as overwhelmed as I was, I couldn't seem to let her go.

She said, "I hope that when you're ready, we're able to find your dad or someone from his family. Ever since I reached out to my dad's family and connected with them online, it's brought me some comfort."

Her attachment to Joel's family wasn't going to help matters, not with the likelihood of Kirby being her father. But for now, I needed a reprieve, not just from our dads, but from my jumbled feelings for her.

I moved away from her and gestured to the TV, where crimes were being committed. "Do you want to finish watching the show?"

"Okay." She reached for the remote.

She unmuted the volume, and I let the noise engulf me.

I appreciated the diversion, until the scene changed, showcasing a painfully tender moment between star-crossed lovers.

I suffered through it for a while, but when it dragged on longer than I could bear, I said, "Maybe we should turn it off now."

"But we just started watching it again."

I made a face. The couple on the screen were locked in an emotional embrace. "It's getting late, and I think we should get some sleep."

She checked the time on her phone. "It's not even eleven."

I defended myself. "I've been up since really early, and it's been a long day."

She conceded. "You're right. I'm sorry." She pressed the off button on the remote. "We can finish it another time."

I motioned for her to extinguish the light. The lamp was on her side of the bed.

She darkened the room, and we closed our eyes and spooned. But sleep didn't come easy for me. I stayed awake, pressed against her. And as I listened to her breathe, as I kept her unbearably close, my angst intensified.

Right along with my fear of love.

I woke up the next day, feeling exactly the same way. Alice wasn't beside me anymore. She'd gotten up and left me alone.

I searched for my phone and checked the time. I'd slept until noon. I dragged my ass into the shower and soaped down.

Afterward, I got dressed and found Alice in the living room, curled up on the couch, with her nose buried in her laptop. Was she shopping for one of her new clients? I should be working, too, composing at my piano. But I was here instead, staring longingly at her.

She glanced up and spotted me. "Hey, sleepyhead."

"Afternoon," I replied, hiding my emotions.

"Are you hungry? You missed breakfast, but I made pasta salad for lunch. There's a bowl of fresh melon, too. I already ate, but it's in the fridge if you want some."

"I wouldn't mind a few bites." Some fuel to restore my brainpower. I went into the kitchen and got the food.

I came back and sat next to Alice, watching her out of the corner of my eye.

She closed her laptop and said, "You had a tough night."

At least I hadn't been plagued with one of my nightmares. That would have left me in a sickening sweat. "Did I wake you with my tossing and turning?"

"Yes. But I fell back asleep. Were you stressing about what we talked about? About finding your father?"

"I guess so." I couldn't admit that I was frazzled about my feelings for her. Or that I was keeping a secret about her family.

"Too bad people weren't doing selfies back then. If they were, your mom probably would have snapped one with your dad."

I put my plate down. "Do you have pictures of your parents you can show me?" I was especially curious to see her mother—the woman Kirby had swept into two troubling affairs.

"I have some separate ones of them in here." Alice re-opened her laptop. "I just need to find them."

She had tons of current photos. I peered over her shoulder, watching as she scrolled through them. Her sister and the kids were in a lot of them. Her BFF Tracy, too.

"Oh. Here's my dad." She opened it to full view.

I analyzed Joel. He had a lanky build, sandy blond hair and a casual demeanor, the exact opposite of Kirby's rugged appearance and outlaw persona. Alice didn't resemble Joel. She didn't look like Kirby, either. I couldn't begin to guess which of the two men was her father.

"He seems like he would have been a nice guy." I felt bad that her mother had cheated on him, but he was gone now. Kirby was still alive, worrying that Alice might be his daughter.

"His family says great things about him." She clicked to the next picture. "This is Mama, before she got so depressed."

Cathy had refined features, framed by dark red hair tumbling past her shoulders. She posed playfully for the camera, radiating innocence, sprinkled with a dash of sex appeal. Were those the qualities she'd conveyed when Kirby had first come upon her?

"She's so pretty." So intriguing, I thought. "You favor her." Except Alice looked much wilder.

"Do you have any pictures of your mom I can see?"

I nodded. "Most of them are in boxes in my attic, but I scanned a few onto my phone." I removed it from my pocket and opened the file. Up until now, I'd kept the album private. Alice would be the first person to view it. Rather than narrate, I handed her my phone.

She studied the first image, a headshot from my mother's portfolio, showcasing her long, wavy brown hair, expressive eyes and glittering smile.

"Oh, Spencer. I can see her being an actress. She probably could've modeled, too. She was a natural beauty." Alice lifted her gaze. "You don't look like her, though. Even with as handsome as you are, you don't have any features in common with hers."

Clearly, I favored my unknown dad. "My aunt used to

say that I inherited my mom's spirit." Of course, coming from her, it hadn't been a compliment. But to me, it was.

Alice continued going through the album. "Is this you?" She grinned at the screen.

I leaned over to see what it was. "Yep. Yours truly." I was about five, dressed in a fireman's costume, the red plastic hat practically wobbling on my head. "I wanted to be a firefighter back then."

"You were adorable."

"I was shy."

"And now you're all grown up." She roamed her gaze over me. "Big and strong and sexy. You can put out my fire anytime."

I stared back at her, admiring the way her stretchy little top clung to her breasts. "I think I'd rather ignite it."

The sound of a text interrupted our flirtation.

She returned my phone to me, without glancing down at it. I appreciated her respecting my privacy.

I checked the notification. "It's from Kirby. He said that he can do the party this Saturday. I guess everyone else is available then. Is that too soon for you?"

She sighed. "It's fine."

"It's okay with me, too." I wanted to get it over with, the sooner the better. "I'll let him know."

"I'm excited about you meeting the twins." She scooted closer to me. "You like kids, don't you?"

"I haven't been around that many. But yeah, I like them. Children and animals make the world go around." When she smiled, I skimmed her cheek. But before I touched her too much, I said, "I should go. I have to work."

"Me, too, actually. But we'll see each other on Saturday."

I got up and carried my barely touched food into the kitchen. I'd gotten too sidetracked to eat.

She walked me to the front door and kissed me good-bye, her lips tenderly fusing to mine. I slipped my arms around her waist and examined my feelings for her once again. Yet I left without getting anything resolved.

I was still as confused as ever.

Twelve

Alice

I rode with Spencer to Kirby's party. I wasn't thrilled about socializing with Kirby, but I was determined to get through it. I wanted Spencer to get comfortable in family settings, and that was worth having to cross paths with Kirby.

We stopped at the security gate, and the guard let us in. Kirby's house was an elaborate Southern mansion, renovated to fit his needs.

We parked in the circular driveway. We weren't the first to arrive. In fact, it looked as if everyone else was already there.

Sure enough, they were. The family were gathered outside on the patio, a huge entertainment area flanked by grass and a playground for the grandkids.

I spotted Hailey and Hudson on the swing set with their cousin, Zoe, who was Tommy's six-year-old daugh-

ter. Tommy was the middle Talbot son and a country superstar like his dad. He used to have a playboy reputation;
groupies went wild for his messy-haired, hazel-eyed, dare-
devil charm. He was happily married now, and Sophie, his
lovely brunette wife, was pregnant with their second child.
I'd heard it was a girl, due sometime next month.

They were the first to greet us and make Spencer's acquaintance. When Sophie waddled over and initiated a
hug, her big beautiful belly bumped against me. It gave
me a warm feeling, and I imagined the babies I hoped to
have one day.

The men shook hands, and Spencer congratulated
Tommy on his new reality show. The first one Tommy
had done was so successful, the network had created another one exclusively for him. He liked working in televi-
sion because it kept him home with his family instead of
out on the road touring.

I looked around for Kirby, but I didn't see our host
anywhere. I spotted Mary organizing the dessert table
with pastries she'd baked. She never showed up anywhere
empty-handed. Brandon was by her side, helping her. Kirby's chef and his staff stocked the main buffet, getting it
ready, too.

Soon Mary and Brandon made their way over to us,
and I introduced them to Spencer. I'd told Mary that my
romance with him wasn't serious, but I wasn't sure if she
believed it now that she'd had the opportunity to see us
together. Maybe she could tell that I was fighting my feelings for him. Or maybe I was just so consumed with it myself, it felt obvious to me.

The final Talbot brother, Matt, and his wife, Libby,
approached us. They lived on a recreational ranch in the
Texas Hill Country with their three sons. Their oldest boy,
a thirteen-year-old named Chance, was Libby's son from

a previous marriage. Sadly, her first husband had died. She'd gotten to know Matt while she was researching the biography Kirby had hired her to write.

I watched Matt and Spencer converse. It was interesting to see them together, these two mixed-blood men. As far as I knew, Spencer didn't socialize with any other Native Americans. He didn't attend tribal gatherings; no pow-wows or drum circles. Maybe that would change if he ever met his father or got to know that side of his family.

I decided to inquire about Kirby. It seemed odd that he was absent. "Where's your dad?" I asked Matt.

He replied, "In the barn with my boys."

"Chance wanted to take his little brothers to see the horses," Libby interjected. "And Kirby went with them."

"That's nice," I said. I meant about the kids seeing the horses. But I let Libby draw her own conclusions.

She nodded and smiled. She was a perky blonde with peekaboo dimples. I had no idea what she saw in Kirby, but she adored him, along with the other women who'd married his sons—my sister included.

Kirby finally showed up, strolling back from the barn in his custom cowboy gear. Matt and Libby's sons dashed ahead of him and joined the rest of the kids in the play area. Chance carried his youngest brother piggyback style, the little boy clinging happily to his neck. At Chance's age, I was already running wild and getting into trouble.

Kirby acknowledged Spencer, and they embraced.

Kirby turned to hug me, and I went stiff. He embraced me, anyway. "I'm so happy you accepted my invitation," he said. "Thank you for coming."

"I'm here for Spencer," I replied.

"I know." Kirby smiled. "He's a great guy. It's nice that you two…" He fumbled a little, then said, "You get prettier every time I see you, Alice."

I could feel Spencer watching us, and it made me feel even more awkward around Kirby. Normally I did whatever I could to avoid him. Admittedly, though, we'd worked well together on Tracy's album when Kirby had used me as consultant on my mother's music. But there had been plenty of tension, too, with me snapping at Kirby whenever things didn't go my way.

Was I being too hard on him after all of these years? Should I try harder to forgive him?

I glanced over at Matt, thinking about what he'd overcome. He'd forgiven Kirby for abandoning him when he was young. He'd found the strength to let his pain and anger go. From my understanding, he'd done it for his wife and children, not wanting to raise his family from a place of resentment and hate.

If I had a family of my own, would this be easier for me? I moved closer to Spencer, realizing full well that he was the man I wanted to marry.

The man I loved.

As difficult as it was, it was foolish to keep fighting it. Yet there was no turning back now that I'd admitted it. I had no choice but to accept my feelings. Nonetheless, my heart knocked against my rib cage.

"I'm going to check on the kids," I said. I needed an excuse to be alone, to calm the palpitations.

I walked away, forcing my legs to carry me. Spencer remained with Kirby. I could tell that as two recovering addicts, they really understood each other.

Did I understand Spencer? Would I make him a good wife? I shook my head, realizing how foolish my inner dialogue was. Spencer and I weren't headed down the aisle.

But if we did get married, in my fantasies, anyway, I might consider getting closer to Kirby. Not for myself, but for Spencer. I couldn't go around hating his mentor.

I plunked down on the grass, released the air in my lungs and observed the kids. In addition to the swings, their playground consisted of a bouncy castle, a slide and a roundabout. I used to love those when I was little. I would hold the handles and run as fast as I could, then jump back on and spin. I didn't need to do that now. I was already dizzy from my thoughts.

I stayed by myself for a while, immersed in the activity around me. By now, parents were calling their children, gathering them for lunch.

Spencer came over to me, and I gazed up at him, my breath catching at the familiar sight of him. If only I could tell him that I loved him.

"Are you okay?" he asked.

"I'm fine." I shined the spotlight on him. "How about you? Are you having a good time? Are you connecting with Kirby's sons?"

He nodded and crouched beside me. "I really like Matt. He's so down to earth, so real. I like Brandon and Tommy, too. I'm glad I'm getting to know everyone."

"I think you fit right in." He already seemed as if he was part of this group. "I'm glad we came."

"You are? For sure?"

"Yes. I might even try to say a few words to Kirby." Maybe it wouldn't hurt to make a teeny bit of effort, just in case Spencer and I actually became a bona fide couple someday.

"Oh, Alice, that would be great. He was hoping that we would sit at his table." He motioned to the buffet. "Should we get our food?"

I agreed, and we filled our plates with picnic-style entrees and colorful side dishes. I loaded up on fried chicken and potato salad. Spencer took extra helpings of the barbecued ribs, messy as they were.

Kirby's girlfriend, Debra, arrived, running late from work. Tall and trim with graying blond hair and a professional sense of style, she certainly seemed nice enough. But Kirby always surrounded himself with goodhearted women.

I chatted with her about inconsequential things. I made small talk with Kirby, too, even if it pained me to do so. Whenever he looked at me, I thought about the anguish he'd caused my mother: the nightly tears, the daily despair.

My teeny bit of effort wasn't the least bit effective. I was angry at him all over again.

After we ate, I asked Spencer to sit on the lawn with me. I needed to get away from Kirby and try to relax.

Hailey and Hudson wandered over to us, and I smiled, eager for Spencer to engage with them. Except that the kids were quiet for now. Hudson was being his usual reserved self, and Hailey kept glancing over her shoulder, probably waiting for her cousin Zoe to join us. The last I saw, Zoe had spilled a cherry-filled, chocolate-covered dessert on her blouse and was getting cleaned up.

Matt's boys had gone back to the barn. Hudson could've hung out with them, but he stayed with his sister instead. He'd always been fiercely loyal to her, even before they could walk or talk. I assumed it was a twin thing and the time they'd spent together in the womb, just the two of them, preparing to enter this big, bad, crazy world.

Zoe came running up with a damp spot on her top, and soon she and Hailey were holding hands and swinging their arms back and forth. Rather than be left out, Hudson crawled onto my lap. I nuzzled the top of his silky head. The girls, however, stared blatantly at Spencer.

"Hey, ladies," he said, and made them giggle.

Zoe sized him up, her long, brown ponytail swishing

as she bobbed her head. Then she looked at me and asked, "Is he your boyfriend?"

Her question made my heart jump. I sucked in my breath and debated how I should respond. I glanced at Spencer, but he didn't give me any indication of what to say.

"Yes, he is," I finally replied. Maybe it was the dreamer in me, but calling him that made me feel deliriously good.

Zoe shifted her attention back to Spencer. "Are you her boyfriend because you kiss her?" She nudged Hailey, and my mischievous niece puckered her lips and made smooching sounds.

I struggled not to laugh. I envisioned the two of them creating all sorts of chaos when they got older. They'd certainly poked some childish fun at me and my "boyfriend."

He furrowed his brow. "I don't think we should be talking about this."

"Why not?" Zoe was an outspoken first-grader, determined to get a straight answer out of him. And on top of that, Hailey was still making kissy noises.

"Because we just shouldn't." When both girls frowned at him, he seemed to be searching for something to say that would distract them. He settled on, "Did you know that I have lots of dogs?"

"How many?" Zoe asked, taking the bait.

He told the kids about his rescue, and Hudson chimed in and babbled about Cline, the husky his dad had named after country crooner Patsy Cline. Only Hudson referred to her as "Patty." Spencer grinned, amused by the boy's mistake.

The boyfriend topic was forgotten. But not by me. It gave me hope, feeding my dream of having a future with the man I loved.

The party ended, and Spencer and I returned to my house. But when he entered my condo, he fell silent.

I removed my shoes and sat on the sofa, looking up at him. "Is something wrong?" He was acting strange.

"I don't know. There's just a lot…" He hesitated. "I just…"

"You just what?" My heart sank. Was he concerned about me calling him my boyfriend? Was it bothering him now? Was he getting ready to break things off? Would this be our last night together? I waited for him to say what was on his mind.

He finally responded, "I have feelings for you that confuse me. You and I weren't supposed to be getting this close." He remained standing, watching me through troubled eyes. "I'm not the guy you're meant to be with, but I…"

I released the breath I'd been holding, hope spiraling inside me. "Do you want to be with me?"

"Sort of. I think so. I don't know." He sat beside me, with the late-day sun streaming through the blinds and creating a sudden glare. I squinted, and he shifted his body to shield me from the light. After a moment of us just staring at each other, he said, "I don't want to mess up your plans. Or disappoint you."

"You could never disappoint me. Not unless you stopped seeing me. Not unless you went away." I wanted to tell him that I loved him, but I was afraid to say it this quickly.

He reached for my hand. "Does that mean you want us to try to make a go of this?"

"Yes." I wanted everything with him.

"Are you sure? Because we both know that I'm still coming to grips with who I am. I don't ever want to drink again, but what if I screw up? Resisting the temptation isn't as easy as I keep saying it was."

"I already knew you were exaggerating that. Or I assumed you were. I didn't think it could be that easy."

"Sometimes it keeps me up at night. I have hideous nightmares about it."

I squeezed his hand. "I read a study about dreams once, and it said that nightmares were a normal reaction to stress and can even help people work through their fears."

"Yeah, but what if I can't handle the pressure?"

"Of your nightmares?"

"Of me and you."

I tried not to panic. "Of being my boyfriend?"

"Of loving you, Alice." His voice turned shaky. "I think I might be falling in love with you."

To be sure I'd heard him correctly, I repeated it. "You think you *might* love me?" It wasn't exactly a vow of forever, but, by heavens, it was a start. "That's what you said, right?"

"Yes, but what do I know? I've never been in love before."

Nether had I, not until I'd fallen for him. "I don't blame you for being scared. It's all so new and different." I'd already struggled with it myself.

"I'm not freaking you out?"

"No." Hearing him say that he "might" love me gave me comfort. I looked into his eyes. "I tried to fight it. But I love you, Spencer. I absolutely do."

He blinked at me. "You trust that I'm the guy you want?"

I nodded. I had no reason to distrust my feelings. "I know how important your recovery is, and how hard you work at it. I think that you'll stay sober." I needed to believe in him, to support him, to help him overcome his fears. "But if you ever slip up, you'll have me to catch you when you fall."

"That's a huge commitment."

"It's what people in love do."

He frowned. "I hope you don't change your mind later."

I stuck to my guns, clinging to my belief in him, the way a caring partner was supposed to do. "I won't."

"You could." He spoke gently. "I want to protect you. I want to keep you safe."

"I already feel safe with you." I couldn't imagine not having him in my life. Alice in Spencerland. I smiled at the thought. It was a place I never wanted to leave.

"I wasn't prepared to be having this conversation with you, to be talking about love. Not with everything else that's going on."

"What do you mean?"

"I can't get into the details right now. I wish I could, but I can't."

Was he keeping a secret about himself? Was there more to his past than I knew about? I tried not to worry. "Is it something bad?"

"It might seem that way at first, but it doesn't have to be. It can actually be something good, if you let it." He trailed a finger across my cheek. "I just want you to be happy and accept whatever is meant to be."

I leaned into his touch. Now he was being mysterious. But if he thought his news bordered on good, then I would wait to hear what it was. I didn't want to destroy the moment. I needed this closeness with him.

He kissed me, lightly on the lips. Then he said, "I swear, I'm only trying to do what's right. But I hope you understand that I need to talk to Kirby about it first."

I fought the urge to flinch. I hadn't expected Kirby to be part of Spencer's secret. Or whatever this was. But given how tight they were, I shouldn't have been surprised that he'd involved his mentor. "If that's what you need to do, I'm not going to stand in your way."

"Thank you for trusting me."

I refused to let Kirby spoil my belief in Spencer. "I'm

supposed to trust you, especially now that you're my boy-friend."

He laughed a little nervously. "The kids sure teased us on that one. But I think I can do this without being so afraid."

"You'll have to write a song about it, asking yourself 'Do I love her? Am I in love?'"

"Is that how the answer will come?" He fixed his gaze on me. "Is that how I'll know for sure?"

"Maybe," I said, hoping he found a way to unscramble his feelings. In spite of him saying that he was less afraid, he still seemed scared.

On Monday afternoon, Spencer called and told me he wanted to disclose the secret he'd been keeping. I still couldn't fathom what it could be, but I was glad he wasn't dragging it out. Nonetheless, he'd warned me that Kirby was going to be there, too. I wasn't happy about that, but it seemed important to Spencer to have his mentor in the mix.

Anxious, I got ready to go. I did my hair and makeup and slipped on a trendy jumpsuit, fitted with a high neck and long sleeves. The weather was on the cooler side.

I arrived at Spencer's place and spotted Kirby's luxury SUV in the driveway. I dreaded seeing Kirby, but at least I was supporting Spencer. My lover was waiting for me on the porch. He smiled and greeted me.

"You look nice," he said, reaching for my hand.

"Thank you." We went inside, and as we entered the living room, I glanced past him and spotted Kirby on the sofa. He jumped up as soon as he saw me.

Suddenly, I sensed that this wasn't going to go in my favor. I was beginning to feel like an outsider, particularly with the looks the men were exchanging.

"What's going on?" I asked.

"Kirby's needs to talk to you," Spencer replied.

I frowned. "About what?"

His breath hitched. "The secret I've been keeping for him."

Spencer's secret was Kirby's secret? I didn't like the sound of that.

"Maybe you should sit down," Kirby replied. "Because we… I have a lot to tell you."

"I'd prefer to stand." They were both standing, too, with Spencer's shiny red piano in the background.

He gently asked me, "Can I get you anything?"

"No." I didn't want a soft drink or whatever he was offering. I just wanted to hear what his mentor had to say. I clutched the chain strap on my purse, pulling it tighter against my shoulder.

"Try to keep an open mind," Spencer said. "And please, give Kirby a chance."

I zeroed in on the older man. He shifted his weight, moving from one foot to the other.

"A chance at what?" I asked him.

He replied, "To be your father. I think I might be your dad, honey."

I stared at him, unblinking, unmoving. Was I going into shock? Nothing made any sense. "That's impossible. I was eleven years old when you met my mom."

"I knew her before then. I had an affair with her about nine months before you were born. But I never told anyone about that affair, and neither did she." He reached into his pocket and removed a crumpled envelope. "I have a letter that your mom wrote to me during that time."

My blood roiled in my body, in my heart. My breath stuck in my throat. I was too livid to look at Spencer. I kept my focus on Kirby, on the enemy. "Did she tell you that I might be yours? Is that what's in the letter?"

"No. The only reason I wanted to show it to you is because of when it's dated."

"A date that proves you might be my dad?" That he'd slept with her nine months before I came along? I felt queasy now, dizzy and sick. I didn't want Kirby to be my father. I wanted Joel to be my daddy. The man my mother was supposed to have loved.

"I suspected that you might be mine on the day I first met you. I took one look at you and felt an overwhelming connection. But I couldn't be sure, so I kept my feelings to myself. Then, earlier this year, I came across the letter and all of the pieces seemed to fit."

I locked my knees to keep them from buckling. "How long has Spencer known about this?" I still couldn't bring myself to look at him.

"I told him right after you two started seeing each other again."

"I'm sorry," Spencer interjected. "But I couldn't tell you about it, Alice, not without betraying Kirby's confidence. It needed to come from him."

I didn't care what his excuse was. He'd known the whole time we were lovers, and that wasn't fair. I'd never felt so betrayed. I ached so badly, I wanted to scream.

Kirby said, "I'm hoping that you'll agree to take a paternity test. In my heart, I believe that you're mine. But I want for both of us to know for sure."

Was he kidding? There was no frigging way I was submitting my DNA for him. "You're not my father."

"I think I am," he countered softly.

I shook my head. I couldn't let him be my dad. I just couldn't. "If you were, my mother would have told me."

"Maybe she didn't know for certain herself. Or maybe

she knew and just couldn't face it. With the way I seduced her, she hardly stood a chance. She was a sweet lady, and she deserved better."

"You're despicable." I hated him more now than I ever did.

"I know, and I'm sorry for hurting your mama the way I did. But I've been trying to right my wrongs." He clutched the letter that was still in his hand. "I really want us to be family."

"Family?" I shot back. "Give me a break." I hated him, but now I hated my mother, too, for her part in the lie. Was there anyone I could trust? Anyone who'd been truthful? I finally looked at Spencer, with his dark eyes and strong-boned features, with his tall, tanned body and white tattoo. "As for you, *my boyfriend*, *my lover*." I mocked those words. "I never want to see you again." Before I collapsed into tears, I turned on my heel and headed for the door.

I rushed outside and accidentally dropped my purse, the contents spilling out of it and littering Spencer's porch.

"Alice." I heard his voice from behind me. He'd followed me out.

I was already on the ground, trying to gather my belongings. He knelt to help me.

"Don't," I said, firing my pain at him. "Just don't."

He didn't listen. He stayed there, insisting on helping me. My things were everywhere. I grabbed my lipstick before it rolled off the porch and into the dirt.

"I'm so sorry." He handed me my wallet, his voice turning raw. "I never meant to cause you harm."

I started to reject his apology, but he kept talking.

"Kirby didn't tell you right away because he was concerned about what your reaction would be. He asked me to help him get closer to you, and he left it up to me, as to when I thought you'd be ready to hear it. I didn't know what to do. But after I started having deeper feelings for you, I thought the time was right. I wanted to make everything better, to get it out in the open. I swear, I only had your best interest at heart." He paused, with his voice still raw. "When I was doing the DNA search for my dad, I kept thinking how strange it was. Me looking for my father, when Kirby could possibly be yours. I know how hard this is for you, but I think it would benefit you to know the truth, to take the test to see if he's your dad."

My pain and anger intensified, his explanation falling on deaf ears. I tersely said, "You conspired with him the entire time you were with me." I shoved my wallet back into my bag. "I should have known better than to trust you."

"I was just trying to bring the two of you together. And then later, I was trying to figure things out with you and me, too." He rocked forward on his knees. "Please, don't leave. Don't go."

I pushed his hand away when he tried to reach for my compact. "Why? Because you *might* love me? Sort of like Kirby *might* be my dad." I scoffed at both scenarios.

He watched me, his face shadowed, his eyes hooded. "I can't help how confused I've been. But don't give up on us."

"Us? There is no us anymore." I couldn't bear to be needed by him or wanted by him or anything that involved his disjointed feelings for me. "I can't be with you."

I crammed the rest of my belongings into my purse. I didn't know if I was Kirby's daughter. I didn't know anything, except that deep in my battered heart, where it hurt the most, I still loved Spencer.

And for me, that was the most devastating part of all.

Thirteen

Spencer

I watched Alice leave, hating what I'd done to her. I hated myself, too. These past two years of self-exploration had just turned to self-loathing. I'd hurt the woman I loved.

The minute she was gone, I recognized my feelings, understanding them fully. I was desperately, hopelessly in love with Alice McKenzie. But I couldn't jump on my Harley and chase after her. How hypocritical would that be? I couldn't return to the house and write a song about love and redemption, either. This wasn't one of my bullshit compositions, garnering praise and winning awards. This was my reality, my failure, and even my music seemed like a farce now.

I'd kept a secret from her that I shouldn't have kept. Mr. Right wouldn't have made a mistake like that. He would've known the difference.

Kirby came outside and approached me. There was a moment of silent reflection between us.

I spoke first. "I lost her. She's gone."

"I'm so sorry," he replied quietly, shamefully. "This is my fault."

"No. It's mine." I wasn't going to let him take responsibility for my actions. "I could've refused to keep your secret."

"And I should've left you out of it altogether. I involved you in something that put you in a difficult situation. I created a hardship for you and Alice." He leaned against the porch rail. "It's obvious that you love her."

"It doesn't matter."

"That isn't true. She needs you."

"What? You're the authority on love now?" I gave him a frustrated look. "The last time we talked about love, you said you weren't the best person to give advice."

"I'm not. But I know love when I see it."

"That doesn't mean I can make it work. What she needs is the man she's been dreaming about. And I'm not him."

"I think you are."

I wasn't going to listen to him. His judgment about me was clouded. Alice had seen the true me: the jerk who'd hurt her. "She deserves better than what I can give her."

"She deserves to know how you feel."

"No, she doesn't." By now, I was craving a drink. God help me, but I wanted to belt down a quick, hard shot.

I turned away from him, afraid that he would read the craving in my eyes. Intent on keeping my expression steady, I stared out at the arbor embellishing the walkway.

But instead of falling silent, I said, "Did I tell you that she offered to help me search for my dad?" I barked out a cynical laugh. "While I was withholding information about who her father might be, she wanted to unite me with mine."

"You were only trying to protect her. To keep my secret until the time was right to tell her."

"Yeah, and look how that turned out. Not just for Alice and me, but for you, too." I released a rattling breath. "I'm sorry she refused to take the DNA test."

"She has a lot to deal with."

"More than enough." She'd chosen to end it with me, and I could hardly blame her. All I could think about was the bar in my living room, beckoning me, offering to numb the pain.

I kept staring at the arbor, focusing on the vines creeping up and around the woodwork. I sensed Kirby studying my profile. Was he analyzing me?

"Maybe you should come home with me, son."

No way, I thought. No effing way. I didn't want him being my watchdog. I turned toward him again, as if I had nothing to hide.

"Thanks for caring," I said, trying to sound grateful, the way I'd always been in the past. "But I really need some time alone."

He squinted suspiciously at me. "You're not going to do anything stupid, are you?"

"Of course not." I wasn't going to admit that I was on the edge of destruction. I had to make Kirby believe that I had myself under control. After what had just happened with Alice, I didn't want to involve him any deeper than he was already was. Or maybe I just wanted an excuse to fall off the wagon. Either way, I couldn't handle being around him right now.

He grabbed my shoulders, almost as if he meant to shake my disease out of me. "Are you sure I can trust you?"

"Absolutely," I lied through my teeth. "I just need some

space." I turned the tables on him. "What about you? Are you going to be all right?"

"I'll be fine." He squeezed my shoulders. "I really wish you'd come home with me."

"I understand your concern." I preyed on his kindness, telling him what he needed to hear. "I'm not naïve. I know how something like this could affect my sobriety. That I could freak out once I'm alone." I looked him straight in the eye, determined to seem strong and true, as honest as a broken man could be. "But I swear, I'll call you if I get even the slightest urge to drink."

He released his hold on me. "Promise?"

"Yes," I lied again, anxious for him to leave me alone with my pain. Because, really, what difference did it make? Whether I got drunk or strayed sober, Alice would still be gone.

And I would still be missing her.

As soon as Kirby got in his SUV and drove away, I paced my living room with my eye on the bar. I hunted it like a vulture, getting closer to the drink I craved.

On the night Alice and I first hooked up, I'd poured rum over us in the shower, dousing our naked bodies with it. Was that the liquor I should have now?

Hell, yes, I thought.

I uncapped a bottle of Bacardi and inhaled it, remembering how intoxicating it had smelled on Alice's skin— like oak and molasses, heady and sweet.

Maybe I could guzzle half of it and take a sloppy bath with the rest. I could keep my clothes on if I wanted to, drenching them, too. I could do whatever absurd thing I felt like doing. There was no one here to stop me. No prying eyes. Not even the dogs. I'd taken them to the rescue earlier.

Squeezing my eyes shut, I took another desperate whiff, my hands quaking, my breathing coming in short, addictive bursts. I couldn't help but think how good the rum was going to taste, how buzzed I would get, how much I wanted it.

I sank to the floor, clutching the bottle, debating, with a sickening feeling in my gut, whether or not to take a drink.

I opened my eyes, shame coiling inside me. Was this what I'd reduced myself to? A liar? A cheat? A coward? A pitiful drunk, feeling sorry for himself?

I caught my reflection in the glass panels on the bottom of the bar, and my shame deepened.

I didn't do it. I didn't let the alcohol pass my lips. I didn't bathe in it, either. I got up off the floor and recapped the bottle, returning it to the bar. But I was still shaking, still trying to catch my breath.

Now what? I asked myself. What was my next brilliant move?

The answer knocked against the walls inside my brain. I knew exactly what to do. I got my phone and called Kirby.

He answered on the second ring. "Spencer?"

"Yeah, it's me." He already knew who it was, obviously. My name would've appeared on his screen. "I lied to you earlier. I was having terrible urges when you left here. But I managed to get through it."

"Oh, thank God." His breath rushed out. "Do you want to come to my house now?"

"I'd rather stay here." In the place I called home, I thought. "But I need to attend a meeting." To share my feelings with the group, to admit that I'd almost relapsed, using the woman I loved as an excuse to crack open a bottle.

"The next meeting isn't for a few hours."

"I know." We both had the schedule memorized. "But if you want to hang out with me until then, that'll be okay."

"I'll be right over." Relief sounded in his voice. "I'm so glad you called me. Should we dismantle your bar when I get there? Pour all of that temptation down the sink?"

"No." I stated my case. "It's imperative for me resist it on my own, not remove it from the equation. Besides, I can't pretend that it doesn't exist."

"That's not what I'm asking you to do."

"Yeah, but that's what getting rid of it would feel like to me."

"All right. We'll do it your way. I'll see you soon."

"Okay."

As I waited for Kirby, my house seemed eerily quiet. I decided to bring the dogs home. I had time before Kirby arrived to get them. I grabbed a jacket and left through the back door, taking in the crisp Tennessee air.

It felt good to walk, but I was still overcome with emotion. I needed to write a song for Alice, telling her how sorry I was, telling her that I loved her. I was wrong about my music being bullshit. My work was an extension of myself, the good and the bad, the light, the dark, the man, the musician, the recovering alcoholic.

I didn't know if she would ever forgive me. But I wanted her to know how I felt about her. She was my heart, my soul. As clichéd as that sounded, it was true.

I couldn't erase the affair Kirby had had with her mother or take away the possibility that he might be her dad. I wasn't a miracle worker. I was just a guy who loved her.

I had no idea how long it would take for me to create a song like that. A few days? A few weeks? The rest of my life? I couldn't attest to anything anymore, except how much she meant to me.

I made it to the rescue and found Cookie and Candy in one of the fenced yards, playing with Pete. The three of them ran over to me, and I knelt to greet them. Pete nudged me, and the girls danced in happy circles, looking like dust mops. I smiled at the memory of Alice calling them that. I missed her so much, I could barely breathe.

I didn't want it to be over, but the choice didn't belong to me. Once I offered her my heart, she would have to decide what to do with it. For now, all I could do was pray that I hadn't lost her for good.

I didn't go straight home after the meeting. I headed to a neighborhood rife with specialty shops. I had a compulsion to buy a loose black diamond, a stone to remind me of Alice. A talisman, I thought, something to bring me luck.

There was only one jewelry store, a quaint little place near a music shop I frequented. I liked the vibe of this part of town.

I entered the jewelry store and approached the front counter. An older man glanced up from beneath his glasses. He resembled Albert Einstein, with his electric white hair. I imagined him having the perfect stone, just waiting for me.

I told him what I wanted, and he furrowed his bushy white eyebrows. My hope waned. His reaction didn't strike me as positive.

"I only have one black diamond," he said. "And I just set it in a piece this morning."

"If I buy it, can you remove it from the setting?" I was determined to make this work in my favor. I didn't want to leave empty-handed. Or empty-hearted, I thought.

"Sure, I could do that. But maybe you better take a look at it. It's over five carats and is a rare stone. I'm not trying to lose a sale, but it's a pricey piece of jewelry."

"I'm not concerned about that." I would spend whatever was necessary to have a stone and have it today. I'd already talked myself into thinking I needed it.

He looked me over, probably thinking I was crazy. Maybe I was. But I didn't care. I was hell-bent on leaving here with my talisman.

"It's over this way." He came out from behind the counter and led me to a small glass case.

I spotted the diamond before he pointed it out, and my heart slammed to the back of my throat. It was set in a woman's ring. A solitaire. Just the stone and a shiny gold band.

"It's an emerald cut," he said.

I didn't know one style from another, but the diamond was a rectangular shape. The color was opaque, denser than I would've expected. Yet it still seemed magical. I leaned over the case, staring at it through the glass.

"Most black diamonds on the market are man-made," he said.

"But this isn't?"

"No. It's completely natural and untreated."

I was mesmerized. Not only by the diamond, but by the ring itself. Now I wanted to buy it for Alice, which made no sense. There was no guarantee that I would win her back. Or that the song I was going to write would even reach her ears. She might refuse to listen to anything I had to say.

But I still had to try. I wasn't going to mention how close I'd come to relapsing in the song. That needed to be said in person, face to face, eye to eye, if I ever got the opportunity to talk to her again.

"Is it an engagement ring?" I asked.

"That's what I designed it to be." He unlocked the case and removed it, turning the price tag in my direction.

The cost didn't deter me. I held the ring in my hand, feeling its energy. "I heard that black diamonds represent strength and power."

"That's true. They do. But they also represent relationships that are destined to prevail, no matter what the odds."

Now I knew, absolutely knew, I was making the right decision. I loved Alice enough to devote myself to her, to try to be the man she needed. So why not ask her to marry me, if it was possible? A humble proposal, I thought, fraught with hope.

"I want it," I said. "But don't remove the stone from the setting. Keep the ring intact."

"That's a wise choice." He studied me. "Wise, indeed."

Did he suspect that I was lost and trying to find my way? Could he tell that I was aching over an estranged lover? Or how desperate I was to win her back?

We returned to the front counter, and I gave him a credit card for the purchase.

He put the ring in a velvet box and said, "This is some of my finest work. Natural black diamonds can be difficult to cut. That's part of why they command a higher price. I could've easily fractured it."

"But you didn't." And now the ring was in my possession. A symbol of strength and power and defying the odds.

But would Alice give me a chance? Or did I have too many strikes against me to repair the damage I'd done?

Fourteen

Alice

I spent several distraught hours alone in my condo, trying to escape the pain. I wanted to crawl into a deep, dark cavernous hole and never come out. But when the solitude became too much to bear, I called Tracy and my sister, asking them to come over.

After they settled in, the three of us gathered at my dining room table. I sipped the chamomile tea Mary had brewed and relayed my story.

"Oh, no," was all Tracy could seem to manage. She looked stunned beyond words.

Mary, however, slipped into repair mode. I recognized the fix-it need in her eyes. It was her nature to try to hold everything and everyone together. She hadn't been able to cure Mama's depression, though. Our mother should have gotten professional help for that.

"Would it be so bad to have Kirby as your father?"

Mary asked. "It's obvious how much he cares about you. Plus, you'd have Brandon, Tommy and Matt as your big brothers, and their kids would be your nieces and nephews. You'd have a whole new family." She paused. "You should agree to take the DNA test. You should try to embrace this, no matter how it turns out."

I gaped at her. "Don't you even care that Mama cheated on Daddy? That she lied to us and told us she only had one affair with Kirby?"

"It concerns me, yes. Absolutely. But what's the point of being angry about it now? Mama is gone. We can't be mad at her over it. That'll only make things worse."

Easy for her to say, I thought, with her perfect life. "You're not the one whose paternity is in question." She hadn't been betrayed by the man she loved, either. I still couldn't believe that Spencer had kept Kirby's secret the entire time we were lovers. "If Kirby is my dad, then what? Am I just supposed to forget about Joel and his family?"

"Of course not. This isn't a case of you shunning Joel's family or not keeping him close to your heart. He's my dad, too."

"He's your dad for certain," I reminded her.

Mary sighed. "I get that you're hurting. And I know you're devastated about Spencer's involvement in it, too. But I think he really was trying to protect you."

"I don't want to be in love with him anymore." I glanced at Tracy, drawing empathy from her. She knew what it was like to be left in shambles by someone she loved.

"I'm sorry this is happening to you," Mary said, interrupting my sad exchange of looks with Tracy. "After everything you went through when we were kids, you deserve to be happy." She heaved another sigh. "I can't do much about Spencer. But do you want me to kick Kirby's ass for you?"

I knew she was joking, but I appreciated her saying it, anyway. "Thanks, but you care about him too much to do that." He'd even walked her down the aisle at her wedding. "He should be your dad, not mine."

"Oh, sure." She cringed. "And how creepy would that be? Me married to his son?"

"That might be a bit of problem." I found the will to laugh. But mostly I was just trying to keep from crying. Kirby was the last person on earth I wanted as a parent.

I finished my tea, and Mary popped up to refill it. She probably would've baked my favorite raspberry cookies if the ingredients were available.

"What are you going to do?" she asked.

"About the DNA test?" I shredded the cover of a fashion magazine I'd left on the table, tearing it bit by bit. "I can't even think about that right now. I can't deal with any of this, least of all what Spencer did to me. I was so careful when I first started sleeping with him, doing whatever I could not to get attached."

Mary put the teapot down. "You can't help who you love."

"And he doesn't even love me back."

My sister frowned. "How do you know he doesn't?"

"He never said that he did, not even when I called him out on it."

Tracy caught my gaze. "Would you get back together with him if he said it?"

"I don't know if there's anything he could say or do that would make a difference now." I piled up the shorn paper. "He didn't just keep an important secret from me. He broke my trust, my heart."

Ripping me clean apart.

* * *

I cried myself to sleep that night, and the next morning I got up, needing to get away from Nashville. I texted Mary and Tracy and told them I was leaving town for a few days and not to worry about me.

But where should I go? I considered flying to LA and staying at the Chateau, but that would only remind me of Spencer.

I opted for Oklahoma City, returning to the place where I grew up and where my youthful rebellion had begun. I wasn't sure what, if anything, that was going to accomplish. But it was where my fractured heart was taking me.

I got myself together and packed a bag, preparing for a long drive. On a good day, it would take about ten hours.

And this wasn't a good day.

I took breaks along the way, stopping to eat and use public restrooms. By the time I made it, it was pitch dark, and I was exhausted. I checked into a motel with an old-fashioned neon sign, a gimmicky illusion of simpler times.

My room was adequate: a full-size bed, a standard nightstand, a faux wood table and a generic TV. I could've gone to a luxury hotel, but I liked the privacy this offbeat motel provided.

I showered, using the mini soap, and went to bed in wrinkled pajamas. I was far from the fashionista I normally was.

I slept fitfully, pushing the covers away, then pulling them back up. Nonetheless, I awakened early and decided on fast food for breakfast.

The mopey teenager behind the counter kept stealing glances at the world outside her job, and I was tempted to tell her to appreciate her youth and not throw it away like I'd done. But I doubted that she was interested in hearing what a lonely twenty-five-year-old had to say.

I sat by a window, with a dismal view of the parking lot, and picked at a ham-and-egg sandwich.

Two cups of coffee later, I drove to the park where Mary and I had sprinkled Mama's ashes. It pained me to hate my mother, especially with how vehemently I'd loved her in the past.

I exited my car and walked down a bumpy path, heading for the enormous oak we'd chosen as Mama's unofficial marker.

I found it, tall and strong, amid a grouping of smaller trees. Thankfully, there was no one in this section of the park except for me. I stood at the base of the tree, its branches spiraling above my head.

Was Mama's spirit here?

"Why did you keep so many secrets?" I asked her in a soft and shaky voice.

I waited for her to defend herself. But there was no answer. Not even a leaf blowing at my feet.

"And what about Kirby?" I went on to say. "Is he my father? He seems to think that he is."

Once again, there was nothing, no insight into Mama's side of the story. Clearly, this was getting me nowhere. But I kept waiting for a sign. A hope, a glimmer. Something that proved she was listening.

I dropped down in the dirt and drew flowery pictures with a stick. I even glanced up at the sky and looked for heavenly shapes in the clouds. But no ghostly stirrings materialized, no mother-daughter comfort.

I should've called it quits and left the park. Instead, I told her about Spencer. I talked and talked, revealing how deeply he affected me. I'd never shared these sorts of feelings with her before. But there'd never been a boy worth mentioning until now. Of course, Spencer wasn't a boy. He was the man I'd mistakenly fallen in love with.

I paused, then said, "Spencer and Kirby are really close. They're extremely loyal to each other. But it's so confusing, with how hurt and angry I am." I glanced up at the sky again, frustrated that I couldn't feel her presence.

Still, I prattled on. "Kirby said that he's sorry for everything he did. He even took responsibility for seducing you. And get this—he wants to be my dad. He seems to want it more than anything." I sighed to myself. "Maybe I need to take that DNA test. Maybe knowing the truth will make it easier."

But could I do it without Spencer? I put my hand in my pocket and clutched my phone. Should I call him? Should I confide in him? Or would that be too painful?

"Tell me what to do, Mama," I said, still talking to my dead mother and getting no answers.

Was I wrong, the way I'd left Spencer, with no concern for his feelings or well-being? I'd told him that I loved him, but what kind of love was that?

Did I owe him an apology for getting so angry, for blaming him for everything that went wrong? I hadn't given him time to come to terms with his feelings. I'd chastised him for his fear and confusion, instead of letting him work through it. Maybe if I'd stayed there with him, if we'd…

Just as I prepared to call him, my phone vibrated against my hand. I checked the notifications and discovered a text from Spencer with a video attached.

Oh, my God.

I watched the video, my heart quaking, my pulse skittering. He'd written a song for me, a haunting ballad, and taped himself singing it at his piano.

I played it, over and over. The music was soft and compelling, the lyrics honest and tender. I found it beautifully romantic, but laced with angst, too. A man struggling to find his way back to the woman he loved and asking for her forgiveness.

He'd titled it "Spencer in Love."

I was wrong when I'd told Tracy that I didn't know if Spencer could say or do anything that would make a difference to me now. His song was a reflection of who he was, of how he felt, of how much he loved and needed me.

Just as I loved and needed him.

I peered up at the sky one last time. Maybe Mama was here after all, guiding me toward my future.

I called Spencer, and we raced through an emotional conversation, our hearts beating much too fast. We needed to talk calmly in person. He offered to come to me, saying that he would book the first available flight, whether it be a private jet or commercial airline. Then tomorrow, we could drive back to Nashville together.

We ended the call, and I heard from him again a short time later. He couldn't get a flight as soon as he'd hoped. He wouldn't be here until tonight.

I headed to the mall and shopped for a new outfit to wear, then spent the rest of the day cooped up in my motel, thinking about how it was going to feel to see him.

Evening finally rolled around, and I sat on the edge of the bed, awaiting his arrival. He was due any moment. He'd texted me from his Lyft.

A knock sounded, and I jumped up.

I opened the door, and there he was, all six feet two inches of him, dressed in a leather jacket and his usual torn jeans. Yet in spite of his familiarity, he seemed different. When I searched his gaze, I noticed a nervous flicker in his eyes. But I ignored it. I was anxious, too.

"Alice." He said my name, and I practically fell into his arms.

He wrapped me in his warmth, in the strength of his body, and we stood in the doorway, locked in a desperate embrace. His mouth found mine, and we kissed. I stood on my toes to reach him. He was wearing boots, and I was in ballet-style flats.

We separated, and I led him into the room. Neither of us spoke for a minute. We simply breathed each other in.

Then he said, "You look so pretty. But you always do."

"Thank you." I gestured to my ensemble. "I bought this today." A feminine blouse and a short black miniskirt. "We can go to a nicer place. A hotel, if you prefer."

"I'd rather be here, where you chose to stay." He glanced around, as if he was picturing me alone the night before. "I'm sorry that I put you through so much misery."

"I'm sorry, too, for not giving you time to figure yourself out." I paused to consider the look in his eyes. He still seemed nervous. Maybe too nervous? It made me wonder if something was wrong.

He removed his jacket and hung it on the back of a dining chair. "I made so many mistakes."

"We both did." I couldn't fault him for his, not when I'd created problems of my own. "I love the song you wrote for me." I'd told him over the phone how incredible it was, but I thought it was important to repeat it. I'd also told him that I'd made peace with my mother at the park, and I was willing to take the DNA test to unmask my paternity.

He released an audible breath. "You were always meant to be my muse, but I never expected to need you so badly."

"I feel the same way about you."

We stared silently at each other, and in spite of the depth of emotion between us, our reunion turned awkward. Something definitely wasn't right.

Unsure of what else to do, I inquired about his mentor.

"Does Kirby know you're here? Did you tell him I was in Oklahoma and that you were coming to see me?"

"Yes, I'm keeping him informed." He hesitated. "Are you going to be able to handle it if he's your dad?"

"I'll do the best I can." I didn't want to hold grudges anymore, to keep hating Kirby. I'd spent too many years mired in anger. I didn't know how easy it was going to be, letting go of all that hurt, but I was willing to try. For myself, for Spencer. I was even doing it for my mom. "It's going to be scary taking the test, though."

He nodded. "Waiting for the results will probably be the hardest part."

"I'll definitely be on pins and needles." I studied his solemn expression. "I still want to help you find your dad when you're ready."

"Thank you. That means a lot to me." He tugged a hand through his hair, pushing it away from his forehead. "I need to tell you something that I didn't include in my song."

"Go ahead." At least now I would know what was troubling him.

He frowned. "I almost drank again. When I was alone and missing you, I opened up a bottle of rum, the same brand I played around with on the night we first hooked up."

My heart skipped a worried beat. "But you didn't drink it?"

"No. But I came horribly close."

"Are you still craving a drink?"

"I'm not craving anything except to be with you. But are you sure you want to be with me? Even if I stay on the straight and narrow, even if my nightmares go away, I'll always be a recovering alcoholic. That'll always be in my blood."

I moved closer to him. "I love you, Spencer. All of you. The sober man and the one who almost messed up."

He looked into my eyes, as if he were memorizing me for all time. "I love you, too. So damned much. But I fell apart when I shouldn't have."

"But you're here now, opening up to me about it." Trusting me with the hardship he'd endured.

"I'm going to do everything in my power not to relapse or let anything like that ever happen again. I want to stay sober for you, for the life I want us to have together. But mostly I have to do it for myself."

"As well you should. But I want to support you." I sat on the corner of the bed and gazed up at him. "Do they have meetings for friends and family members at your recovery center?"

"Yes, and I would love for you to attend them."

I made an earnest vow. "Then I will."

"It feels amazing to love you, to be loved by you. To make promises to each other. But I want to do this right."

"Do what?"

"I'll show you." He walked over to where his jacket was and reached into the pocket, removing a small jewelry box.

My heart nearly stopped. Was it a ring? Was he going to propose? Here, on this very night? It seemed so unexpected, so fast, so exciting. He was making me feel reckless, like he always did. Reckless in love, I thought.

He came over to me and opened the box. It was definitely an engagement ring, a gorgeous emerald-cut black diamond in a yellow gold setting. I gasped like the future bride I was about to become.

He said, "There's a story behind it." He proceeded to tell me how he'd searched for a talisman and had uncovered the ring. "As soon as I saw it, I wanted to buy it for you.

But I didn't know if you were going to take me back or if I would ever have the opportunity to give it to you." His dark gaze latched on to mine. "The jeweler who designed it told me that black diamonds mean more than strength and power. They also represent relationships that are destined to prevail against the odds."

"I've never heard that before." But it seemed so right. We were prevailing at this very moment.

He shifted his stance. "I know I'm not the man you dreamed of. I'm not the stuff fairy tales are made of. But I'm going to try to be the best husband possible." He got down on bended knee. "Will you marry me? Will you be my friend and lover for the rest of our lives?"

"Yes." My answer sprang from the deepest part of me, from how much I loved and wanted him.

I leaned forward, and he slipped the ring onto my finger. It was a little big. We smiled knowingly at each other. We were already off to a sweet and candid start.

He sat beside me. "We'll have it sized. But for now, maybe this will work." He yanked some threads from his jeans with a thin piece of denim still attached.

I returned the ring to him, and he wrapped it, as if he was using yarn. I held out my hand, and the diamond went back onto my finger.

He reached for me, and we kissed. It was deep and true, and I felt wonderfully close to this man. I couldn't imagine loving anyone more.

Fifteen

Alice

I gripped Spencer's shoulders, feeling his muscles bunch beneath his shirt. I tugged him down, and we sank onto the bed.

We kissed and kissed, and he asked, "How many babies do you want?"

"As many as we're meant to have," I replied. "But not until after we're married."

"I wasn't suggesting that we start a family now." He smiled. "But someday."

Yes, someday, I thought. I wanted to be the mother of his children. I imagined how perfect they would be, with a combination of our features. "Did you bring anything with you so we can—"

"Make love?" He lifted his wallet from his back pocket, produced a shiny packet, and tossed the leather billfold onto the nightstand.

I pressed against him. "We don't have to take our clothes all the way off." I liked the forbidden feeling of being half-dressed on the night I'd gotten engaged.

I opened my blouse, then removed my panties and rolled my short tight skirt up around my waist. Following my lead, he pulled his T-shirt over his head and shoved down his jeans and boxers.

Sheathed in a condom, he slid between my legs, filling me in one fell swoop. I unhooked my bra, and the garment went slack. He lowered his head to lick my nipples, moving from one side to the other, making me ache.

Pressure built upon need, upon lust, upon love. He breathed in the fragrance of my skin, and I watched him with intensity, welcoming every powerfully driven thrust.

I roamed my hands down the front of his body, heading toward his navel. I accidentally scratched him with my ring, but he didn't seem to mind. I was still getting used to the glorious weight of it.

Soon he withdrew, and we switched positions. I climbed onto his lap and looked down at him—my sexy fiancé, his jeans pushed past his hips, his stomach muscles flexing.

I impaled myself, riding him, slow and slick and wet.

"Do it again," he said. "With the diamond."

I gazed breathlessly at him. He wanted me to scratch him purposely? "Are you sure?"

"Yes." He took my hand and showed me, making the shape of a heart.

I did what he asked. I marked his chest with the stone, not deep enough to scar, but enough to make an impact. A wicked smile appeared on his face, and he lunged forward, stealing a passionate kiss and encouraging me to move faster, increasing the tempo to a mind-dizzying speed.

I don't remember exactly what happened next. Maybe I

was too aroused to think straight. But somewhere between the heat and hunger, we both climaxed.

I collapsed on top of him, and he nuzzled the side of my cheek, holding me protectively in his arms.

My lover. My dearest friend. My Spencer.

Upon our return to Nashville, I found a lab that would provide the results of a paternity test within a matter of days. And now that day had come. They were due to arrive by special delivery this afternoon.

I hadn't seen Kirby yet, but Spencer had been communicating with him, acting on my behalf. At the moment, the older man was on his way to my condo. He'd asked if he could be here when I opened the envelope. A copy was being delivered to his house, too, but he wanted us to get the news together. Apparently, he was too anxious to do it alone. I was anxious, too, so I agreed to do it this way and get it over with.

I glanced over at Spencer. He was here for moral support. Later this week, I would be packing up my belongings and moving in with him. He'd already informed Kirby that we were engaged. I'd told my sister and Tracy, too. Everyone within our circle knew. We'd set the date for six months from now. We were young and eager, and it seemed foolish to wait.

"How are you holding up?" he asked.

"Truthfully? I'm a bit of a wreck." Regardless of the DNA outcome, I'd vowed to forgive Kirby. But what if I couldn't do it? What if all of those angry feelings came flooding back?

"It'll be okay." Spencer came over to me, sitting next to me on the sofa.

He stroked a hand down my back, helping me relax.

I turned toward him, and we kissed, the exchange warm and tender, his lips gentle against mine.

Afterward, we looked into each other's eyes, a stream of silence between us. Until the doorbell rang.

"Do you want me to get it?" he asked.

I nodded, my heart picking up speed.

Spencer went to the door, and I could hear him in the entryway, greeting Kirby. I suspected that they were embracing, as they often did.

They came around the corner, to the living room, where I was. Kirby looked fraught with anxiety.

"Hi," I said, rising from the couch.

"Hi," he parroted. "How are you?"

"I'm all right. Just waiting, you know."

"Yeah." He crammed his hands into his pants pockets.

He sported slim black jeans and a black gaberdine shirt with silver piping. His snakeskin boots had Cuban heels and a kerchief tied around one of them. I'd always liked Kirby's over-the-top style, even if I never wanted to admit it.

"Can I get you anything?" I asked.

He shook his head. "No. But I'd love to see your ring."

I approached him and held out my hand.

He let out a low whistle and grinned. "A black diamond? Now that's my kind of jewelry. You're a girl after my own heart."

"I always wanted a black diamond." I smiled at Spencer. "And he gave me one." Five carats and counting. It made quite a statement.

"I'm so happy for the two of you." Kirby sounded like a proud parent.

Was he my father? Was that what the test was going to reveal? I took a moment to analyze my feelings. My hatred hadn't returned. I wasn't consumed with resentment or malice. But did that mean that I'd forgiven him? Or was there still some hurt buried deep inside?

While we waited, I put on some music. The three of us sat, making minor chitchat. It seemed easier than saying anything too personal.

A short time later, the doorbell chimed. I nearly leapt out of my skin. Kirby looked just as antsy.

"I need to answer it," I said. The envelope would be addressed to me, and I would have to sign for it.

As I made my way to the door, I hoped it wasn't a false alarm, with my neighbor's kid selling cookies or something.

Thankfully, it was a delivery person from the post office. I accepted the envelope from her and returned to the living room.

My palms turned sweaty. "Will you do it?" I asked Spencer. I couldn't seem to manage it.

"Of course." He took the envelope from me.

I turned the music down and glanced at Kirby. He scooted to the edge of his seat.

Spencer opened the results and read them quickly to himself. A second later, he said, "It's not a match. You're not related. Kirby isn't your father." He shifted his gaze to his mentor. "I'm sorry, but she's not your daughter."

Kirby seemed stunned. He barely moved, scarcely breathed. He'd obviously expected a different outcome. I hadn't known what to expect, and now I had mixed emotions.

Joel McKenzie was my father, leaving me with the same DNA I'd always had. But Joel was gone, and Kirby was here, looking sad and dejected.

Oddly enough, I started to cry. For him. For me. For my mother. For all the pain and betrayal over the years.

Spencer came toward me, but I shook my head. I went

over to Kirby and cried in his arms instead. He held me, like a father would do, and rocked me back and forth.

I glanced up and saw my fiancé watching us. He understood how badly I needed this. Kirby needed it, too. I was forgiving him, completely, wholly. It didn't matter that he wasn't my father. He was treating me as if I belonged to him.

When I stopped bawling, he handed me the kerchief from around his boot and let me blow my nose on it. I looked up at him, and we both laughed.

A long silence followed, and I thought about Mama and wondered what she would think of all of this. "Will you tell me about when you first met my mother?" I asked Kirby. "I'd like to connect the dots, to try to understand who she was back then."

He winced a little. "It's not a pleasant story."

"I know. But I need to hear it, to make peace with it."

"I understand." He cleared his throat. "I met her at the record store where she worked in Oklahoma. I was there for a promotion, signing CDs and doing a radio interview. She told me that she was working on some songs, but she didn't think they were very good. I encouraged her to keep at it. I even said that someday when she was ready, she could show her songs to me." He made a shamed expression. "She agreed to have dinner with me that night in my hotel room, and one thing led to another. I think she got swept up in my celebrity, in having such a famous man show an interest in her."

"Where was my father all this time?"

"He was out of town on a trucking job. He didn't know anything about where she'd spent the weekend. I remember her telling me that she was in a relationship, and that they had a child together. Your sister would have been around five then, I think."

"Did my mom say anything about my dad?"

"Just that he didn't want to get married. That he didn't believe in it or something. She seemed hurt by that."

"Did she know that you were married at the time and that you had children?"

"Yes, but I told her that I had permission from my wife to sleep with other women, which was true. The only rule was that I wasn't supposed to have kids with anyone else." He shook his head. "But I didn't honor that agreement. I already had Matt by then."

"I have one last question." One more thing I wanted to know about my mother. "What was in the letter Mama wrote to you?" The note with the postmark that made him think he might've been my father. "What did it say?"

"She was thanking me for encouraging her to believe in her music." He blew out a sigh. "But I took advantage of her when she came back to me, nearly twelve years later, eager for me to hear her songs and hoping that I would buy them. I wasn't her beacon of hope. I was just a self-serving prick who used her, making promises I didn't keep. The worst part was the restraining order I filed, just to get rid of her."

I merely nodded. I couldn't deny that being labeled a stalker had been Mama's biggest downfall.

"I'm not making excuses," he went on to say. "But I was a terrible person then. My substance abuse was out of control, and I was going through women like water. Your mom was just one of many. I blocked her from my mind as time went on, until I pretended that I'd forgotten all about her. But I never really did."

"It's over now," I assured him. "And we both have to stop hurting over it."

"I know, but I'm always going to wish that you were my daughter. I can't help but feel that way."

"We can still learn to be close, spending time to get to know each other. Weekends, holidays, whatever it takes." I offered him a smile. "We can be friends who seem like family."

He smiled, too, his eyes going misty. "I would love that."

This was a milestone for him. And for me, as well. I'd just given Kirby, my old archenemy, a piece of my heart.

I glanced at Spencer. His expression was filled with joy. Clearly, he loved the idea of me bonding with his mentor.

I went over to Spencer and sat beside him. He took my hand and held it. I breathed softly, almost dreamily, just having him near me. A burden had been lifted from my shoulders.

I was finally free of the turmoil that had dictated my life. Free to move forward with the man I loved.

And become his wife.

Epilogue

Spencer

Today was my wedding day, and the ceremony would be taking place at my house, outdoors on the lawn. Alice hadn't allowed me to see her gown yet. I would be viewing it for the first time during her bridal march.

For now, I was in one of my guest rooms, where I'd just put on the designer tux Alice had chosen for me. I stood alone in front of a mirror, thinking about who I was and how far I'd come.

We hadn't located my father yet. I still didn't even know his last name. I might never meet him, and I was okay with that. But we would keep searching, in case he was meant to be found.

As for the wedding, Alice had asked Kirby to walk her down the aisle, which thrilled him to no end. It made me extremely happy, too. I loved seeing them together.

I'd chosen Sam, my alcohol counselor, as my best man, and Tracy, of course, was the maid of honor.

We'd also gotten Kirby's family involved. His sons were my other groomsmen, and his daughters-in-law, including Alice's sister, were the other bridesmaids. The Talbot grandchildren were our flower girls, ring bearer and pages. The youngest granddaughter would be wheeled along in a festively decorated stroller.

Our reception was going to be banging, with Kirby, Tommy and Tracy as the entertainment. The three of them had agreed to perform, each taking the stage at different times. Per Alice's request, Tracy would be singing the songs Alice's mother had written.

I'd included my mom, as well, by wearing a small framed picture of her attached to my boutonniere. Alice had ordered it for me, and it was a beautiful charm and tender keepsake. I know that my mother would've adored Alice.

I took an eager breath and prepared to go to the make-shift altar. Right on time, I made my way to the ceremony, where our guests were already seated.

When the procession started, the bridesmaids and groomsmen walked together, paired in couples.

The kids were next. A couple of the boys walked my dogs. Yep, Candy and Cookie were part of it, wearing rhinestone collars and cute little veils. The doggie duds were Alice's idea. Pete tromped along, too, in a bow tie. The oldest grandson held his leash. The last boy to appear was Hudson, clutching the ring pillow. The flower girls followed him. Zoe pushed the floral-draped baby stroller, and Hailey scattered glittered rose petals.

Then it happened…

The music changed, and I saw my bride. I watched as she held Kirby's arm and smiled at me. Her long white gown boasted a pearled neckline and a slim black sash, tied elegantly at her waist. Her white-blond hair was spiked, as usual, but the very tips were dyed black. I loved how wild and unconventional it was.

I wanted to break tradition and kiss her as soon as she reached me, but I waited.

Kirby handed her over to me, and I told her how beautiful she looked. She reached up to skim my jaw, and we gazed romantically at each other.

The vows were clean and simple and true. Within no time, we were married. We kissed, and our guests erupted into cheers and claps. Even the dogs barked their approval.

Alice laughed, and I swept her into a playful hug and swung her around. I'd found my lifelong partner, my shining muse, and I was never letting her go.

* * * * *

COMING SOON!

We really hope you enjoyed reading this book.
If you're looking for more romance, be sure to
head to the shops when new books are
available on

Thursday 11th June

To see which titles are coming soon, please visit
millsandboon.co.uk/nextmonth

MILLS & BOON

MODERN

Power and Passion

Prepare to be swept off your feet by sophisticated, sexy and seductive heroes, in some of the world's most glamourous and romantic locations, where power and passion collide.

MILLS & BOON
HISTORICAL

Awaken the romance of the past

Escape with historical heroes from time
gone by. Whether your passion is for
wicked Regency Rakes, muscled Viking
warriors or rugged Highlanders, indulge
your fantasies and awaken the
romance of the past.

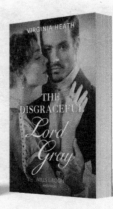

MILLS & BOON

HEROES

At Your Service

Experience all the excitement of a gripping thriller, with an intense romance at its heart. Resourceful, true-to-life women and strong, fearless men face danger and desire - a killer combination!

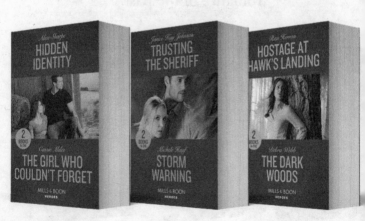

JOIN US ON SOCIAL MEDIA!

Stay up to date with our latest releases, author news and gossip, special offers and discounts, and all the behind-the-scenes action from Mills & Boon...

 millsandboon

 millsandboonuk

 millsandboon

It might just be true love...